The Lost Diaries of

FRANS HALS

A NOVEL

Michael Kernan

ST. MARTIN'S GRIFFIN 🐾 NEW YORK

To Margot Starr
always

THE LOST DIARIES OF FRANS HALS. Copyright © 1994 by Michael Kernan. All
rights reserved. Printed in the United States of America. No part of this book
may be used or reproduced in any manner whatsoever without written
permission except in the case of brief quotations embodied in critical articles
or reviews. For information, address St. Martin's Press, 175 Fifth Avenue,
New York, N.Y. 10010.

"A Thomas Dunne Book"

Design by Sara Stemen

Library of Congress Cataloging-in-Publication Data

Kernan, Michael
    The lost diaries of Frans Hals / Michael Kernan.
        p.   cm.
    ISBN 0-312-13117-8
    1. Manuscripts—Collectors and collecting—New York (N.Y.)—
Fiction.   2. Hals, Frans, 1584–1666—Diaries—Fiction.   3. Painters—
Netherlands—Haarlem—Fiction.   4. Haarlem (Netherlands)—
Fiction.   I. Title.
[PS3561.E587L67   1995]
813'.54—dc20   95-843
                                                                                        CIP

First published in the United States by St. Martin's Press

First St. Martin's Griffin Edition: May 1995
10   9   8   7   6   5   4   3   2   1

Author's Note

Most of the names and all of the public incidents in this book are actual. Many are taken from the sections of the Haarlem town archives that concern Frans Hals, conveniently printed in the National Gallery of Art catalog for its 1989 Hals show. There is also a map of 17th century Haarlem pinpointing the artist's various street addresses. The personalities and the details of most domestic incidents in this book are imaginary.

For their permission to reproduce various Hals paintings, I am indebted to: the Frans Halsmuseum of Haarlem where resides the great portrait of the almshouse directors, the Carnegie Museum of Art in Pittsburgh, the Mauritshuis Museum in The Hague, the Bildarchiv Preußischer Kulturbesitz in Berlin, the Statens Museum for Kunst in Copenhagen, and the Art Gallery of Ontario in Toronto.

To Simon Schama, for his scholarly yet wonderfully readable *The Embarrassment of Riches; an Interpretation of Dutch Culture in the Golden Age*, goes nearly all the credit for the authenticity of my depiction of ordinary life in 17th century Haarlem. And most of all, there was Reagan Arthur, my editor at St. Martin's Press, who saw from the very first.

"A brilliant entertainment in the antiquarian sleuthing tradition of Julian Barnes and Peter Ackroyd."
—John Ashbery

"The reader is introduced to one of the most wonderful characters ever to breathe life into ink on a page. . . . *The Lost Diaries of Frans Hals* is entertaining, compassionate, and full of life."
—*Tulsa World*

A "smart, funny first novel. . . . a loopy tale that manages to be both intellectual and fun."
—*Kirkus Reviews*

"Charming. . . . lively and convincing, displaying the same lack of self-consciousness, the willingness to appear shrewd and foolish in a single paragraph, that Samuel Pepys forever made the genre's standard. . . . Contains lovely lines and vivid scenes."
—*The Washington Post Book World*

"Kernan succeeds on many levels, for many reasons. He brings the artist plausibly to life through windows to his temper and times. No biographer could have done better."
—*Austin American-Statesman*

"Kernan has an eye for telling detail and an astounding ability to use words that the artist of a painting might have used in describing his work. . . . He draws readers into the novel, blurring the lines between story and history, casting the spell of art."
—*The Baltimore Sun*

1

On April 29, 1992, Christopher Barnett, the twelve-year-old son of Don Barnett, a successful Honda automobile dealer who had just bought a farm near the eastern tip of Long Island, found a large packing case buried under a thick mat of stale hay in the barn loft.

The crate, measuring 36 by 46 by 30 inches, bore the barely legible name S. Kitterman & Sons and an address in lower Manhattan. The senior Barnett discovered that an art dealership under the name of Kitterman had existed in New York in the last decade of the nineteenth century but had long since disappeared, leaving no clue as to possible surviving successors. At this point, on the advice of his attorneys, Barnett claimed the crate and opened it.

The box, secured with heavy twine, was lined with heavily waxed cloth, sealed airtight. When he first cut into it, Barnett reported, he noted a strong odor of oil paint.

The crate contained three oil paintings in massive plaster-and-gold-leaf frames, one a forest scene by the fairly obscure German artist Johann G. Meyer von Bremen, the other two genre works portraying, apparently, eighteenth-century Dutch interiors, and signed with the name van Opps. The latter two were of indifferent quality, and intensive scholarly investigation has so far revealed no mention of a Dutch artist by the name of van Opps.

At the bottom of the crate, Barnett found a heavily wrapped package 14 by 9 by 7 inches, bound in thick twine. The name Hals had been penciled across the face of the wrapping paper, but it was otherwise unidentified.

Inside, Barnett discovered four volumes of what appeared to be a journal. The volumes, bound in heavy black buckram, were in various states of repair. One had been badly damaged, possibly by rodents—and most likely before being wrapped, as it was found in the middle of the pile. One had sections torn out, whether by the author or later persons is not known. Barnett speculated that the volumes had lain unattended for many years before being rediscovered and wrapped some time in the late 1800s.

The writing, in an antique script, covered both sides of the pages, as far as could be determined from the parts not washed out by water damage.

Dates were written into the narrative only casually. One volume contained entries for several years; another appeared to be mostly undated. The last few pages were more accurately dated than the other parts. The lack of consistency indicated that the journal had been put aside and resumed many times during the writer's life.

Don Barnett was by nature a secretive man. The first thing he did was to warn his son against telling anyone, even his school friends, about the discovery. Then he scoured the local library for books on Hals. There were none, but the name Frans Hals turned up in several histories of art and encyclopedias, and after further research Barnett learned the basic facts about the artist, who to his surprise turned out to be one of the more prominent so-called Dutch masters. Finally, after an evening of careful thought, Barnett disclosed his find to the art-appraisal house and gallery of Silverstein and Silverstein in New York. He had gone to school in Brooklyn with Henry Silverstein and had kept up in a casual way over the years. Silverstein was cautious but mildly encouraging. He wanted to see the journal right away, of course.

Barnett, a compact, ruddy man, took the journals into town one June morning. He took a cab from Grand Central Station to the Silverstein gallery on Madison Avenue. The gallery was in the East Eighties, set amidst an entire row of galleries and antique shops. Brittle old women with parchment faces fantastically wrinkled by decades of smoking and sunning tottered past, dressed elaborately in the very latest couturier designs, though everybody else in sight wore light cottons and shorts, for the yellow sky threatened another muggy summer day. He tapped on the glass door with a key, as he had been directed to, and was let inside by an assistant. It was a Monday and the place was closed. He was taken to the director's private office. Silverstein, tall and balding, with a graying short, pointed beard, greeted him cheerfully and took the journals from him.

"This is it, huh?"

"That's it. I don't know what we got, but . . . "

Silverstein set the big package on his broad desk after carefully clearing away the papers on it. He opened the wrappings and stood, arms akimbo, staring at the worn old volumes. In his business one does not show much, either enthusiasm or disdain.

"If this is real . . . " Barnett muttered.

Silverstein glanced sidelong at him, his mouth curling up in a gentle smile. "I will be very surprised," he said. "But someone did a lot of work here."

Gingerly, he lifted the top cover and sniffed at the musty pages. He turned past the first page to where the writing started and studied the edge of the paper, looking through it from the back. The faded scrawlings on the other side did not show through to interfere with the similar scrawlings on this side. There was no visible watermark. He turned a few more pages, set aside the top volume, then looked into the next, and the next. He hefted the lot of them, examined the covers and binding of each one and squinted down the spine.

"Hmmm," he said. "I don't know a word of Dutch. You've been through them, huh?"

"I flipped the pages. It's all the same handwriting."

"The paper's old, that's for sure. Couldn't say how old."

"Well," said Barnett, "should we have someone check it out?"

"Of course. It should go to a lab. It should be looked at by the conservators. Costs money."

"I'm sure."

Silverstein chuckled. "What we need right now is somebody who knows some Dutch. All I know about Hals is that he lived forever and he was poor."

He rubbed the roots of his beard along his jaw. "Why don't you leave them with me? I know some people."

For a long moment the two men gazed at the stack of books, which smelled faintly of ancient dust. Finally Silverstein turned to his friend.

"I still don't believe it. It's just too neat. Anyone else but you, I would have thought it was a gag." He gave Barnett a quizzical smile.

Barnett nodded. "Well, it still might be, for all I know. When I first saw it, I thought maybe my kid's art teacher at the school could have done it. A bit of a nut, you know. Met him at a PTA meeting and he followed me around all evening. Wanted to talk about cars." He waved both hands airily to indicate a bit of a nut. "But then I stopped and thought, and I realized it had to be there for at least five or six years. I mean, that hay was rotten. It was undisturbed—till my kid got into it, and he had to dig at it with a pitchfork."

"Oh yes, it can happen. It does happen. Once in a lifetime maybe, if that." Silverstein snorted. "Did you know Sotheby's has a cattle call every now and then for people to bring in their family heirlooms? They have a squad of bright young art history graduates look over the stuff. I talked to one of them once. She said it was depressing. People bring in a cheap Botticelli print and think they actually own a Botticelli. Maybe once a year someone shows up with something worth selling. She said in four years the only thing that jumped out at her was a Bruguière photograph, one of those cut-paper studies."

They stared at the books some more. The books lay there adamant, vaguely defiant. One moment they seemed touched by the aura of fame, incandescent with portent. The next they looked like a pile of old and tatty journals. Then Silverman roused himself and glanced at his watch.

"So. First thing, let's find out what we have here, huh?"

Barnett nodded.

"If I can persuade you to leave it here, okay? I'll give you a receipt. I think I've got someone who should see it."

Barnett agreed, took a one-page receipt for the books, and left. He trusted Henry Silverstein as much as he trusted anybody, which was not all that much, but it passed quickly through his head that if anything happened, he could sue, after all.

That same afternoon, Silverstein phoned Dr. David Smith, an art historian who at Columbia University specialized in Netherlandish painting. Smith laughed.

"A diary by Frans Hals?" he said. "Give me a break. That guy has been gone over with a fine-tooth comb."

"What you mean? I thought—"

"Why Henry, scholars have pulled out every mention of him in the Haarlem town archives, every lawsuit and christening. They have all the records. They know so much, they even know when the records are wrong."

5

"Oh yeah?"

"Yeah, they found where he was arrested as a drunk. But it turned out to be another Frans Hals. There were two unrelated Hals families in town, which caused everybody a lot of problems, you can imagine."

"I thought there was very little about him. I thought we knew almost nothing about Hals."

Smith chuckled. "That's what they said about Shakespeare. But in fact, we have an enormous amount of historical data on the man's life."

"But no diary."

"No." Smith laughed. "No diary. If you have a diary by Frans Hals there, I will eat it for breakfast. Don't you think it would have surfaced hundreds of years ago? Or at least been mentioned somewhere by some Dutch historian?"

"David, maybe I'm a sucker. If I had the slightest inkling it was some kind of hoax . . . " He cleared his throat. "All I know is the kid was digging in the hay barn and turned it up, and for sure he wasn't in on it. All I know is I have this thing, this object here. I have these books written on very old paper in very old ink, and it says Hals on it, so what am I gonna do?"

Dr. Smith hesitated. "You say you have no idea what it says."

"Except it's got dates—seventeenth-century dates. And I found the name of Leyster. Wouldn't that be Judith Leyster? Didn't she have something to do with Hals?"

Smith didn't answer for several moments. The silence hummed. As it happened, Smith's closest friend, now dead, had been one of the journalists involved a few years before in the scandal of the Hitler diary hoax, which had ruined reputations on two continents. That purported diary, too, had been found in a hayloft, incidentally—a hayloft in East Germany. The friend, a magazine editor named Fox, had been fired on the spot, merely for passing the thing up the line with his tacit endorsement. He had, in fact, privately consulted Smith about the possibility that a Hitler diary could exist and the chances that it might be authentic, and from the close description he gave, Smith had allowed, offhandedly, as how it could well be real, though he had not actually seen it. The man had never spoken to Smith again. Smith cleared his throat.

"Yes, Leyster was a student of his in Haarlem. I think she sued him at one point. But I don't know, here. Hals? I don't know."

"Well hell, what's the harm of translating a little of it? Let's just see what we got."

"Henry, just so long as you don't expect me to get up on the stand and testify for you."

"Hey, come on. Come on, David."

For the next several minutes they chatted about anything but Hals.

"Tell you what," Smith said at last. "I have a guy I might be able to talk to. He's Dutch. Been working on his doctorate for years. He's also a goof-off. He's supposed to be doing his paper on de Hooch, but I'm beginning to wonder if he ever will. But he's all right. You'll pay him something decent?"

"Of course."

"He can use the money, I'm sure. He's intelligent. Get him interested and he'll do well. You want me to call him?"

"I can call him. What's his name?"

"Peter Van Overloop. He'd get a kick out of it. Bit of a flake, but bright."

"Flake, huh?"

"Well, perhaps that's a bit strong. Just never got it together is what I would say. I would call him a doctoral dropout, but he does keep touching base with us every six months or so."

"Will he work?"

7

"Oh yes. Get him interested, he'll do the work."

So it was that Peter Van Overloop showed up at the offices of Silverstein and Silverstein two mornings later, a self-contained, nimble young man, lean but not very tall, with a head slightly too large for his body. He wore his blond hair in a long British-style shock that fell boyishly over his right eye. His face was broad, with strong cheekbones that gave him an almost Indian look.

The showroom was nearly bare, New York chic. A large Nevelson hung from one wall, with a Warhol Marilyn painting across from it. A sculpture, a Roman portrait bust, was exhibited on a chest-high stand in the center of the bare bleached hardwood floor. A white door almost invisible in the white wall led to the back office, which contained a large desk, curvy modern chairs done in nubbly fabric, and a bookcase. Peter was reassured by Henry Silverstein's diffident manner; the man didn't seem quite sure what he wanted. He had called Peter the night before and had taken twenty minutes to explain the project.

"I can tell you, Dr. Smith is extremely skeptical," he was saying now, peering over his half glasses, "and I'm not at all sure how far we need to take this." Peter found half glasses irritating in most middle-aged men—why couldn't they face it and get bifocals? who cares?—but somehow they gentled Silverstein's angular face and balanced the pointed beard. Joseph Conrad with glasses, hmm, what a thought. "What I'd like to have you do is start off, get into a few pages to see how it reads, if it makes sense, whatever. Then maybe skip about a bit."

"Skip about." Peter smiled encouragingly. He sat at a chair to the side of Silverstein's littered desk. He had heard that a lot of important businessmen made their visitors sit in a lower chair facing them, like subjects for court-martial. He was glad to see it wasn't so. Dr. Smith had made Silverstein sound really threatening, like Bernard Berenson for Christ sake. He set an elbow on the desk and relaxed a little.

"Yes. Uh, for instance, we know that Hals painted Descartes sometime around 1649. He would certainly have something to say about that. I'm giving you a really fine catalog of the big show in '89 and '90, the big Hals retrospective. Here, I have it right here."

Silverstein brought up from a lower drawer a massive paperbound volume with a portrait head on the front. "Here. This has a very good rundown on Hals's life and dates, all the known references in the Haarlem records, names of people, the provenance of the paintings. It's even got a map of old Haarlem. Now what I want you to do is try some spot translations in the diary, where he gives the dates, and see if they check out."

"Okay."

"I mean, no point in translating the whole damn thing if it's a fake."

"So I should keep going—"

"Yes. Basically. Keep going until you find definite evidence of something wrong."

"Okay," Peter said dubiously. Silverstein glanced sharply at him.

"Of course, I'm not putting the burden on you. I don't expect you to judge the manuscript for us. I do want the translation. I do want it into English, modern English where possible. Let's see what we get with the first book."

He studied the younger man, who seemed slightly bemused by the instructions. "All I'm saying is that if you run into some obvious clinker right off the bat, just let me know and we'll rethink it. Don't worry, you'll get paid anyway."

Peter nodded. Silverstein slid a small worn, volume across the desk. "Here's another one you might want to look at. This contains a monograph on Hals by a guy named Houbraken.

9

Full of errors. Said Hals was a drunk and beat his wife. All kinds of things that we know were not true—because there was another Frans Hals in the town at the time. You might check the diary against this. Only in this case"—Silverstein laughed his curious indrawn laugh—"you know it's a phony if it does agree with the source."

"Okay," Peter said again. He watched as the man added two or three more monographs and art history books to the pile in front of him as he continued talking. Peter sometimes tuned out of conversations without really meaning to. It was something he meant to work on.

"That's, uh, four weeks to the day. Okay?"

"For the first book?" Peter asked.

"Yes!"

Silverstein sounded slightly testy. He must have just said that. "We'll pay you five hundred then and five hundred for the next book. And then we'll see where we are."

"Okay," Peter said.

"And needless to say"—Silverstein froze, one hand holding a paperback history still poised above the desk, while he gave Peter a severe stare—"this is totally confidential. We are not talking to anyone. *Anyone*. Is that clear?"

"Yessir."

"That's what the five hundred is for. That's a lot of money."

"Right," Peter replied in his most sincere, manly tone.

"So. Here we are." Ceremoniously, Silverstein brought from a drawer a time-blackened book, thin as a volume of poetry, encased in a glassine envelope. Gingerly, he teased it out. Respectfully, he shoved it slowly across the desk toward Peter.

Who just as carefully lifted the cover and opened the pages. An odor of antique dust wafted up. The paper was stiff with age. Bending closer, Peter studied a page at random near the beginning. The writing was faded but clear. He was too self-conscious to take in any more details, but the words in Dutch leapt out at him:

———————————◄○►———————————

. . . face marred only by the interior look of the self-regarding eyes. The potato nose. The stubby cork nose. The arrow-straight nose, breathtaking, and the arrow-straight nose with a bulb on the end, such a disappointment. The Roman nose that planes straight down from the forehead (not a very intelligent look). The staircase nose. The long thin aristocratic nose with beautifully carved nostrils. The nose that is a chunk of putty stuck on any old way. And brows: the ones that go straight across, the circumflex ones that do their little dance of irony upon the face. The bristling . . .

———————————◄○►———————————

Already pulled into the narrative, Peter started to turn the page but then became aware that the older man was watching him with impatience.

"Seems to be a list of faces."

Silverstein shrugged. "Wonderful. Whatever. It's in your hands. Wait a minute."

Deftly, he picked up the volume and folded it into a sheet of bubble wrap that he pulled from his top drawer, then sealed the package with masking tape. He handed it over with a little bow of his head, smiling. "Now it looks professional," he muttered. Peter placed the book in his backpack along with the other books.

"I have to get back before four because I'm house-sitting in Tribeca and I have to meet . . ."

Silverstein waved dismissively. He seemed to be at home with people who left sentences unfinished.

"Oh, uh, Peter," he said abruptly, surprising him with the sudden force of his voice. "Remember. Do remember. I

11

shouldn't have to remind you about this, but it's important. This is an extremely valuable property."

Peter nodded and looked responsible. Silverstein studied him carefully.

"Yes, I know you are an archivist. You know about handling delicate things. And these things seem to be in amazingly good shape, good bindings. But the pages are really brittle. You understand. Handle it with extreme care. If it's real, it would be worth—" Silverstein shrugged. "Well, you understand."

Peter wondered where the man had gotten the notion about being an archivist. It must have been Professor Smith. Must have found it on his vita. A summer intern at the Library of Congress would hardly be an archivist. Oh well. He smiled to himself.

———————

Peter stood in front of the grim, dilapidated warehouse on Franklin Street, one of a row of grim, dilapidated textile warehouses, some of them yuppified, a few converted to mysterious, chic business offices, in a neighborhood close to Chinatown. He announced himself on the intercom, and when the buzzer rang he pushed open an unpromising steel door cut crudely out of a larger corrugated steel entrance, which itself had been forced upon the age-blackened, massively scaled, noble facade like a pie slapped into a face. He dragged his large suitcase through the opening, lifting it over the six-inch-high lintel, and struggled up three flights of bare, sagging, loudly complaining stairs, pausing at the landings.

Laura was waiting when he reached the top. She looked concerned as he puffed and hauled his way up the last steps.

"My God, let me help you," she said. He shook his head and swung the load up to the open doorway.

12

They shook hands. Laura was a friend of Amy and used to work at the Museum of Modern Art's store. Amy said Laura was a kick, but that was all he knew about her. She and her friend George were off to the south of France for a month.

"Boy, am I glad to see you. I was getting worried," she was saying as she ushered him into the apartment. "We have to be at Kennedy by six, and you know how traffic is all the way out there this time of day, I'm meeting George at the airport, but he has to come from his office, so I'm nervous. One time I had to get to La Guardia and it took over three hours. My God, I was just limp." She watched him as he set down his load. So far, he hadn't said a word since she had buzzed him in. "I told him he should take off early, he should be leaving his office right now, and I was gonna call him just then when you got here. I think it's okay now that you're here, but I should be outta here in five minutes. Here."

She handed him four typewritten pages of instructions. Laura was slender, almost as tall as he, with sleek black hair cut off above the shoulders. Like Louise Brooks, whom he had just seen in *Pandora's Box*. So sexy, that straight shiny black hair. She was still talking. She had large brown eyes, very bright, and a big aquiline Virginia Woolf nose. Very thin face. Probably anorexic, he thought. So skinny—flat—in her cotton blouse and jeans.

"And this is Dave, and Leopold is around somewhere. Oh, where are you, Leopold?" Now she was introducing him to a somewhat overweight Siamese cat, who stayed close to her ankles. "Say hello, Dave. Leopold is very shy and he will let Dave beat up on him, but don't worry about it. George says to let it happen, it's a natural thing, but it still bothers me. He makes him cry, he nips at his ankles, and poor Leopold has to jump up on the sideboard. Luckily, Dave can't climb very well. He can't jump, I don't think his eyes are so good, because he has to claw his way up onto the bed instead of jumping and then when he gets there, he looks down as if he doesn't know how far it is."

Peter had been in the loft before, at a big Christmas party two years ago when he had just started going with Amy. The ceiling looked like it must be twenty feet high, fifteen anyway and it was made of intaglio metal squares painted cream a long time ago but slightly dingy now, like the walls. It was impressive. First glancing into the room, you were awed by the height, the sheer amount of bare air in there. It had four tremendously tall windows with great black iron shutters all covered with rivets and crossbars so you could lock yourself in and keep out invading armies. The fine old hardwood floors creaked and sagged and dwarfed the two fair-sized kilim rugs that attempted to declare the living room space and that of the dining room. It all ran together, despite the sofas on one side and the rather elegant sideboard and mahogany table at the other. George was with an investment firm and was doing well, or so Amy had said. And he had some family money too, the rumor was. The bedroom was hidden behind a row of tall bookshelves. Along the far wall stood some major hi-fi equipment, with speakers the size of steamer trunks. Definitely not the latest, Peter reflected. Perhaps George had moved on to new interests. Hi-fi was sort of seventies, wasn't it? Anyway, there was a whole wallful of tapes, CDs and old 33s and many rows of books.

"Now, they can go out on the fire escape. We have some wire around it, but George says they wouldn't fall, though I'm not so sure, they make me so nervous standing there and looking over the edge."

Laura showed him the kitchen, behind a screen, and told him for heaven's sake use up the food there, use anything he wanted, they had put away some liqueurs that George treasured and also the good glasses, but anything else was his to use.

He thanked her. Thanked her again as she brought her own suitcases up to the door and formally gave him her keys.

"Where you going, by the way?" he asked during a pause.

"Provence. All over. I can hardly wait. I took the train through France two years ago and I just ached to stop off and see some of those great little villages with the red tile roofs and all that sunlight and the crooked little trees. You know? We spent a week in Paris and it was fine, but I wish we'd had more time in the south, George wants to spend some time in Arles; he loves van Gogh, you know, and he wants to see all those places and get the feel of it. And then we go back to Paris. We have reservations at a three-star restaurant I couldn't care less myself but he says you have to do that at least once or you haven't lived."

"Sounds great."

She waved vaguely at the vast room. "I hope so. You'll love it here. It's so quiet. You'll get lots of work done. And I—we appreciate this so much, Peter. This is really wonderful. I was so worried about the cats. You just can't leave them in a boarding place. Anyhow, it's so expensive and besides, they're—oh dear"—she squatted to embrace Dave one more time; the other cat still hadn't appeared—"they're such spoiled babies. Now you be nice to Peter," she cooed. She started giving Dave a rubdown. Dave looked straight ahead, his crossed blue eyes going all interior.

Peter stole a look at his watch.

"Oh my God. I have to be out of here." Laura leapt up, grabbed her bags and rushed out the door with a final breathy good-bye. Peter closed the door and went over to the large sofa, a handsome, gloriously soft pile of black leather, and sat down. It was going to be good here.

15

For the past year he had been living with two other graduate students in a sort of warren on West Ninety-fifth Street, a hotel that had been converted into a rooming house. He and two friends had moved into a three-bedroom suite soon after entering graduate school at Columbia. The two friends had long since gotten their doctorates in art history and moved on to assistant curatorships at museums far from New York. Peter was now on his third set of roommates, graduate students who spent most of their days in libraries or shut up in their small bedrooms. By this time Peter was no longer the tenant of record, for his finances were not reliable enough to produce the rent on time with any regularity. A law student named Scott—he could never remember Scott's last name— had taken over the job and with it the central sitting room. For a while the roommates' industry had inspired Peter to get back to work on his de Hooch. In his thesis, he questioned the painter's naturalism in the use of light sources: Some of those interiors surely were either artificially lighted or their streaming light had been imagined by the artist, and not always accurately. But Peter's investigation of actual Dutch house plans and photos so far had proved nothing one way or the other, and his energy for the project had soon flagged. Most of this year he had been working with gold leaf in a restorer's studio. He loved gold leaf and was good with it. He loved the venerable tools, unchanged since the days of Cellini, the traditional leather cushion, the membrane of ox intestine that lined the sheets, the ancient names—cutch, shoder—the little wagon with its Moroccan reed runners to cut the sheets of gold when they have been hammered so thin that a steel blade would only ruck them up. He loved the obedience of the tiny sheet when you moved it just so, with a mere breath, teasing it into place with skewer and gilder's tip.

But there wasn't much money in the job, and it was part-time at best.

Tomorrow he would begin on the Hals. Tonight he would explore his new place and the neighborhood. It took him ten minutes to unpack, another ten to make note of all the food on hand—milk, margarine, canned soups, some superb whole wheat bread, and some exotic cheese and sliced meats from Dean & Deluca, plus twelve beers, one of the new yuppie brands. He would find some wine.

A wooden ladder was nailed in place against the walled-in bathroom, which had a low ceiling of its own. Climbing up, he discovered above the bathroom a second bedroom, a neat little berth, in the very center of which lay the other Siamese, Leopold, who stared at him with half-open, sleep-crusted eyes. The room was a real kid's hideout, with a built-in bookshelf and a light above the pillow, in the six feet of space between the bathroom ceiling and the main one. There was also, at the foot, a television set complete with VCR and a handful of film cassettes. He guessed that Laura disapproved of TV and had banished the set to this loft within the loft. It was fine with him. He could watch baseball up here and pretend he wasn't at home.

That night he wandered around the block and found a somewhat scruffy go-go bar, so out of date that it was almost charming but not quite, and a bright, clean lunch counter (not open after six) that featured Chez Panisse cooking and in-house pastries. After dinner at a Chinese place off Canal Street, he came back to watch *The Godfather* on a cassette. Then he moved his things to the berth and claimed it for the duration. He found something slightly threatening about the grand double bed where Laura and her fiancé George slept. She called him her fiancé. Peter had never thought much of the word. *Fiancé:* He mouthed it soundlessly. A couple of his friends had gotten married in huge church ceremonies with morning coats and spats and one even with top hats, and it was all so actory, he thought, as though they were reenacting

17

some ritual that their parents, or more likely their grandparents, had done for real. Those guys would talk about their fiancées. He was perfectly aware that Amy wanted to get married, but he didn't think she would call him her fiancé when he wasn't around. He hoped not.

The cats woke him up shortly after dawn. Leopold climbed into his bunk and Dave waited mewling below. They acted with the self-assurance of cats who ran the house. Groaning, he clambered down the ladder and found that, sure enough, their twin bowls were empty. He filled the food bowls, replenished their water bowl, and was about to return to bed when he caught sight of the journal waiting on the table.

Within fifteen minutes he had bathed and shaved and made himself some powdered coffee from the hot-water tap and stuffed a stale bagel into his stomach. He didn't like the look of Laura's Mr. Coffee machine, complicated and none too sturdy, and she hadn't mentioned it in her pages of instruction.

The book, lying in a shaft of light, beckoned him.

Working with laborious care, he pried up the end of the masking tape and slowly peeled it off, then unwrapped, with infinite respect, the plastic bubble covering. He placed his palm on the blackened old cover, hefted the book gently, set it down again while he went for his legal pad and a pen, then picked it up once more and finally opened the cover.

The inside cover was blank except for some inchoate scratchings, as though someone had been testing a pen nib. The ink was old and faded, except where it had splotched as the point caught on the paper. That single black pollywog still looked as richly dark as it ever had. It was repeated in reverse on the front of the first page, where it had blotted.

Peter turned the page—a blank. No name. He turned another. The paper had gone a lovely soft yellow, almost the color of a butter cookie, brown at the edges. Fine horizontal lines about a centimeter apart covered this and the succeeding pages.

On the third page was a date, written without ceremony in the top margin: 1616. The first line below it was smudged beyond recovery, but after that, Peter saw, the writing marched along steadily in the free and casual hand of a quick writer, controlled with easy skill. The letters kept an even height and never wavered from the printed lines. Some of the words tailed off slightly at the end but never so much that they became illegible. He deciphered them easily.

――――――――――◀○▶――――――――――

. . . day I think it must be April. The sun came roaring in my window this morning and woke me out of a sound sleep. It flares in the window . . .

――――――――――◀○▶――――――――――

A little rush of delight hit Peter and he stretched his neck. His Dutch was holding up fine. He had been worried that he might have gone stale, for he hadn't been reading much of it these past two years, and what he had read was strictly modern, and mostly captions at that. But he discovered that the old Dutch wasn't that different; it came to him almost as naturally as modern Dutch. That word *brullend*—he had translated it as "roaring" without hesitation, for a sudden insight had struck him at the same instant: Why shouldn't the sun roar? It must make an overwhelming noise up close. Curious. For a moment he could imagine he had felt a featherlight touch on his shoulder, the comradely touch of the long-dead author of these words.

It was his mother who had insisted that he keep up his Dutch. Marie, with the ever-blond hair and the lantern chin, leaning over his chair in the hot little sitting room in

Cicero, making him talk, making him read and even write in Dutch from the time he was in grade school. He and Tony, slumped there over the same table, while their mother drilled them relentlessly. I will give you this, she would say, if I can give you nothing else. The fathers came and went, Harry, then Evan, then Wayne, who stayed the longest before he walked off to get a beer and never came back, but the Dutch lessons were as much a part of life as the suppers that Marie always insisted they be there for. It kept them a family.

Marie died alone in a Chicago hospital when Peter was at Columbia. She had told the boys it was a minor operation and not to come bother her. Tony by that time had found a job with a chocolate importer named Diercxk. Within a year Tony had risen to sales director and renamed the firm Dirk Chocolate. Peter had helped design the logo, a piratical scimitar that wasn't really a dirk at all but was more romantic-looking.

Tony was in Washington now, lobbyist for the food-importing business, a rich man with a sprawling estate in Potomac, in the rolling hills west of the capital. All because, he loved to say, he knew Dutch. Not quite true, of course, because he also had tremendous drive and a ruthless singleness of purpose that impressed even hard-nosed Washingtonians and scared a few others, including his wife, who had already left him with their daughter for a spade-bearded rock music critic. It was Tony's five-thousand-dollar "grant" that Peter was living on at the moment, the last grant, he had been warned, that would be coming unless he found some sort of regular work.

"Just do something, kid," Tony had said. "Get a job, any job, if you're not gonna finish at Columbia. I got a kid of my own, pal. Come on."

And then he had gently shoved his knuckles into Peter's

shoulder, a symbolic reminder of the fights they had had as boys, fights that Tony always won. Tony, the classic oldest child. Me, thought Peter, the classic baby.

He shook his head to clear it and bent to his work again.

───────◄○►───────

... day I think it must be April. The sun came roaring in my window this morning and woke me out of a sound sleep. It flares in the window and streaks across the floor and glances over the surface of the highboy. A small diamond of colored light from the pane, sharp blue melting into red. I awoke happy and for a long time could not remember why. The children were thumping around upstairs, or indeed Neeltje. It was the straw. The straw and the Cat Woman. Him and his straw and his herring. I do not like the man. Does he think he is mystifying me? A smoked herring, he says. Nothing but a smoked herring that he would be waving in the air, and a basket of straw. I said, "You are the customer, but will not that make you look like a fishmonger?" He smiled, twinkling, such an arrogant smile, such a pedantic smile. I believe it to be the role he plays in the comedy. I have the straw correct, though. Little underpainting, little black, then slashes, bright on top and musty underneath, and it goes. It is fine.

───────◄○►───────

Reading it over, Peter thought it sounded too stiff, too archaic. Already he sensed the casual air of the author, the loose and slangy style.

From here on he would translate more freely, to catch the spirit of the thing. Right away he felt it was going more naturally.

───────◄○►───────

I got the straw just right, though. A bit of underpainting, a little black, and then I slashed in the straws, bright on top and musty underneath, and it works. It is fine. I went back to look at it this morning. I couldn't wait. I still had a piece of cheese from breakfast and I stood there in my nightclothes munching and looking at it while Neeltje grumbled at me and the world, and it is exactly as good as I had remembered. The hand I am not so sure about.

I saw her again today

———◄o►———

The passage ended with a hasty line drawn across the center of the page.

Peter had been writing at top speed, hesitating for a word every few seconds, but only briefly. He cracked his knuckles and leaned back in his chair. Hmm. It was time to check out the catalog.

He found it immediately, a full-page illustration: the straw, the fish, the man with the uneasy smile. Pieter Cornelisz van der Morsch, painted in 1616. Sure enough, the text revealed that early scholars had assumed the man was a fishmonger, but a more recent study indicated that van der Morsch was a poet and actor who was best known for his role as a sort of wise fool. The fish was apparently meant as a symbol for the part he had played on the stage.

And Hals was right: The straw was wonderful, daringly laid in there with bright slashes of color, while the hand was not quite so successful.

But who was Neeltje? The chronology said his wife Anneke had died the year before. A nurse, presumably. And who or what was the Cat Woman?

Leopold was twining silkily around Peter's ankles under the table. A moment later, when he leaned down to stroke him, the other cat, Dave, darted out from behind the sofa to attack his companion. Leopold simply sprang onto the table with an effortless leap. He purred raucously. Peter ran his hand down the smooth brown spine and returned to his work.

————————————◄O►————————————

I saw her again today. What a face. Standing by the potato stall behind the cathedral. She was staring across the square. At me in fact. It really is a cat face. The nose is small and flat and splayed wide at the base, but not gross at all, a delicate little nose slightly upturned, it is the wide cheekbones that give it that look. I wanted to draw cat whiskers on her. The wide cheeks give her mouth special emphasis, a bud mouth, subtle curves in the lips, strong edges. Supposed to be sensual. And the eyes of course. With thin but very sharply defined brows, indeed ridges, in perfect arched curves above them. Huge round black eyes, deep brown up close. Staring at me bold as a man. There didn't seem to be anyone taking care of the stall.

I said, "These yours?" I knew they weren't. She knew I knew.

She smiled straight at me, her lips curling up at the ends rather satirically.

"And if they were?" she said in a musical alto voice.

"I'd want one. Or three, I suppose." I didn't at all. I still have two bags from last winter.

"Well, I wish I could help you. I'm waiting myself."

Both of us glanced about at the people drifting past, but no one seemed interested in us or the table of potatoes. They were stacked up as high as her elbows. She had black hair, very sleek, pulled back under her bonnet. Proud of the bonnet the way she tilted her head. Or was it the earrings, which looked gold.

No wedding ring. I thought maybe a widow.

Then the old woman came bustling up wiping her hands on her skirt. She must have been at the public latrine. I didn't want any part of her potatoes. The Cat Woman said, "Well, buy your potatoes."

I said, No, she was first. She said, "Why thank you." Nodded as the old woman picked them out for her. Pulled a ridiculous old leather money bag from under her belt and then resumed looking at me. I moved a step closer.

"I'll have three," I said. "My name is Hals."

"I know it," she said.

"Have I seen you here?" I knew perfectly well I had never seen her in my life.

"I'm from here. But I live in Spaarndam with my uncle. I just came back."

"And you are . . . "

Some women would simper because they would expect, or would like you to expect, they are so highborn that they must be introduced. But she had no nonsense about her.

"I'm Reyniersdochter," she said, "Lysbeth." And so I went home with three potatoes I didn't want.

———————

I think I have a miniature. Not really, but a small oval. He wants it on copper, and I can't talk him out of it. It will be too big to set into a box lid. I can't think what he wants to do with it. She is one of twelve! Was farmed out to her uncle, who works in the bleaching fields. Now they want her back at home to take care of her ma, who has some sort of wasting thing.

———————

I saw her

————————◄O►————————

Peter scratched his head. The man did seem to change the subject a lot. He made another cup of coffee, drank it straight down so as not to have it slopping about when he was working with the book, remembering the story about Charles Lamb and the Shakespeare first folios that he left covered with circular stains from his wineglass, even the stains famous now.

I saw her on the bridge this morning staring down into the canal and I went up to her as if we were old friends. This is the first time since Annie. I have not looked at a soul for a year.

"Lysbeth," I said, coming up to her. She was absorbed in the water below. It was windy, it is always windy on the Raamgracht, and the sun was about to disappear behind a great looming black cloud which was bearing down on us from the sea. "May I call you Lysbeth?" I am twice her age. Well, not quite.

She turned to me, taking her time, letting the smile curl up slowly. I already know that smile. Such a strange smile, so full of secrets. "All right," she said. "I am Frans," I said.

"The famous painter," she said.

I laughed. "Oh yes. Famous in Haarlem. Rich too." I stuck my finger through the hole at the bottom of my doublet.

She stared at it a moment longer than she needed to, the white finger extended out the front of me, until I pulled it back in. I suddenly saw it looked like a member, but a small one. She looked straight at me and was on the verge of saying something but couldn't quite.

"Famous in Spaarndam too," she said.

"Ah! Well!" I waved grandly at the trees. Spaarndam has two hundred people at most. I couldn't think of anything else to say, so she hefted her basket and pulled away.

"Good-bye, Hals."

"Frans," I said. "Can I carry your basket?"

"No," she said.

Neeltje attacked me the minute I got in today. All day in that drafty hall and the wind blowing up, and then walking all the way home in the rain, and there she is at the door, her great sheep face poking glumly at me.

"Twenty guilders," she says.

"Let me in my own house."

"Your shoes." I take off my shoes and put on the slippers. She backs off but her skirts fill the hall and with her big fat red elbows stuck out there I can hardly get inside.

"Since March," she says, "and it is May the first."

I know that. I know very well it is May, and I have ten guilders coming from those layabouts which is overdue a week, and they are going to pay me tomorrow. And she won't get that either, unless we are going to eat potatoes for the rest of the month. And yesterday some walnut-faced lawyer from van Backum has the nerve to confront me on the street and tell me I owe the estate four guilders and fifteen stuivers. For a painting I bought! Two years ago! She is looking at me from under her big blond eyebrows and moving her mouth sideways. So unattractive. As if she is munching grass.

I counterattack. "Where are the children?" I say in a loud voice. "They are falling out the window. Margaretha is sick. What kind of a nurse are you?"

I watch her mouth work for a while and remember that I am wet to the skin and push past her, taking off clothes as I go. It makes no difference to her. She follows me into the kitchen with the words still coming out though I don't hear them. Now it is the floors she is talking about. She scrubs them so much the wood is getting waterlogged. Brooms and mops everywhere. I climb the stairs as quickly as I can without slipping. The stairs are so narrow in this damn narrow house. I don't know what I am doing here with these babies and the smell of piss, this stupid woman who looks like a sheep and brays like a donkey at me all the day long and two rooms to a floor so narrow, we could hardly fit the bed into it, and at that had to bring it in the window from the street the way they do in Amsterdam. Oh Annie, Annie.

Sunday. I saw her with her family coming out of St. Bavo. They are all men, louts I mean, the Reyniers, big roistering guys with peasant shoulders, and she is probably the youngest and the only girl not married, so that is why she has to stay with the mother. I can't believe she wasn't married. I will ask her. It is lovely today, the hyacinths are filling the air with intoxicating fumes, really fumes from so many of them, fields of them sometimes I walk through them between the fields and let the smell of them dizzy me. The sun is hot, you can feel it sucking the plants up out of the ground, wet from yesterday's rain. No clouds. Everyone is walking around smiling in the streets.

That silly van der Morsch wore his plainest ruff to the sitting. I am sure because he thinks it will save him time and therefore money. The word has got around that I love to paint ruffs, which take forever. The joke is that I do. So the man creeps onto his chair without a word we are already hardly speaking because of the business of the herring and I see that he is no longer wearing the Sunday ruff he had on before but an ordinary one. I consider mentioning it, except he hasn't paid me yet. At least I have fixed the hand in the straw basket. Still not my best hand, but it is a boring hand in any case. I don't like the considering look on his face, I think he is thinking how to pay me less than a hundred twenty. I have put the look in the painting, which will no doubt please him. He will think it is the look of a philosopher. I will take an extra day on the ruff, however.

Before he goes he takes another good look at the picture. "I don't like that," he mutters, pointing at the straw. My beautiful straw. He steps right up and puts his nose two inches from the canvas. "Doesn't look like anything," he says. "Just a bunch of sticks. It's unfinished. Looks like a sketch."

I patiently pulled him away and back to the middle of the room. Look at it from here, I said. It resolves itself.

"Hmmm," he said. "Maybe."

I would rather have him than the St. George's crowd, I will say that. One man is bad enough, but twelve! Who is supposed to sit where, and which ones get to look out from the canvas instead of

27

being in profile, and what to do with Captain Laurensen's hands. I had them on his chest, but he said it looked too much like pleading, so I put them into a talking gesture. And then old Schout got excited and he had to have his hands changed too because he seemed to be pledging fealty to the other captain, van Teffelen, whatever his name is, and that would never do, of course, oh no. A bunch of old women. They are killing me, they are taking so long to get themselves arranged right. Twice I have had to move a head from one body and put it on another. I have made it into a sort of parody of a Last Supper with van der Meer sitting across the table from the rest like Judas. I am sure no one will notice, but it brightens my day.

It exasperates me that she does so much. Why does she have to take care of the old lady? What about her married sisters? Let them take their turn. Or let all those brothers of yours get together and hire someone. For God's sake, this is stupid.

"Oh don't say that," she says. She is very religious and full of notions that sound more pagan than Christian to me. I can't believe . . .

———————————◄○►———————————

The phone rang.

It stunned him. For a moment he didn't know what it was. He was still halfway inside his cool world of tall, narrow stone buildings with stepped roofs and ancient cobblestone squares and the smell of hyacinths. Reynier, he remembered as he reached for the phone, was the name of the woman Hals married, his second wife.

"Hello?"

"Peter! Where were you?"

It was Amy, her voice tight with anxiety and rage. "You know what time it is? I waited an hour!"

Oh God. He was supposed to meet her for lunch. It was after two.

"Oh shit. I was working here. Jeez, I'm sorry, Amy. You want me to come over there now?"

"No. Forget it. This is the second time you did this."

She hung up.

Peter stared at the phone. He called her back. She would be at the MOMA bookstore. He got Millie, the head saleswoman, but she said Amy had just stepped out.

"Oh shit," he said aloud. Two months ago she got a raise and he had agreed to meet her for lunch. Then he'd lain down for a minute because he had been taking antihistamines for his cold and was falling asleep on his feet. When he woke up it was two hours later and she was furious. And this time he was the one who had made the date.

"Oh shit," he said a third time. He would have to go up there. It would take him half an hour if he was lucky with the trains. He would have to talk to her there in the store. She loved these dramas.

Carefully closing the diary and hiding it under a sofa cushion, Peter put on a clean shirt and his seersucker jacket, with a necktie in the pocket in case he had to go to a fancy restaurant. He might be able to talk her into dinner. He would have to use the AmEx card. Oh well. He could go to a movie until she got out of work.

As he slipped out of the apartment, quickly, for the cats were heading his way, it occurred to him that his whole day had just been totally rearranged. He hated not to feel in control of his time, though he had to admit that when he was in control, he didn't do that much with it. He hadn't even read Dostoyevsky. He was going to read Dostoyevsky this summer and had bought *The Idiot* and *The Possessed* but had yet to open either one. He had read *Crime and Punishment* in college, and Dostoyevsky was a long drink of water even then.

Pushing through the whistling revolving door at the Museum of Modern Art, Peter automatically hurried downstairs to the poster store, where Amy used to work behind the counter. Didn't see her. Remembered she had been promoted to the main floor to work with the books. Hurried upstairs and learned she had gone out for coffee. He caught her as she returned from the cafeteria.

"Amy," he said.

She stared coldly at him. She had had her blond hair done in ringlets to look casual. She was wearing her brick red suit with the little blue neckerchief and looked terrific, he thought. Striking. Arresting. But not casual. Amy could never look casual, not with those sapphire blue eyes, the bluest he had ever seen, and the pouting mouth, a mouth that was always slightly open as though panting a little, eagerly awaiting something, what? Something that Peter was never sure he could give her.

"Hey," he said. "I'm sorry. I was working. The time got away from me."

"Working," she said, busily restoring the two volumes of Edward Weston's *Daybooks* to the shelf.

"I was! I have a translating project. Come on. I'm sorry. I'm sorry. Let me take you out to dinner."

She turned to stare distantly at him.

"You did that the last time."

"Oh hell, come on Amy. Jeez, I'm sorry as hell. The time just got away from me."

He was aware that two other young women were hovering close by with an air of happening to be there. Their heads were turned sideways to him so as to catch every stage whisper.

"I don't want to see you, Peter." Amy picked up an over-sized Imogen Cunningham and stepped over to the *C*'s to shelve it. She managed to look as if no one was talking to her, which meant that Peter wound up looking as if he was muttering passionately to himself. Other customers skirted around him, some elaborately ignoring him, a few giving him the "New York is full of them" glance.

30

"When are you done?"

"Forget it," she said to the shelves.

"Hey." This was his girl. She wanted to marry him, for Christ's sake. "Hey," he said, "I'll be at your place."

He turned quickly and stalked out. He felt great.

There was still time to make the midafternoon showing of *Batman Returns* at the theater in the Plaza Hotel. Amy didn't approve of violent movies, saying they only added to the world's violence to no purpose, and she was probably right. He drew the line at Steven Seagal and Chuck Norris, but he did want to catch Michelle Pfeiffer. He found the movie charming but knew he could never in a million years discuss it with Amy.

Amy Foster lived in a large apartment at Sixty-eighth Street and Fifth Avenue with her great-aunt, a Mrs. Dunaway. Amy never would talk about her relatives, but sometimes he got the impression that her job at the Modern was a favor from some member of the board who knew her family. She had a certain casualness about money. Once, looking for her keys, he had come upon three uncashed paychecks in her purse. All he knew about Amy was that she was from the suburbs of Detroit, had graduated from Cranbrook and the University of Michigan, had two older brothers and was here in New York to get some experience in the real world before going back for her doctorate. Oh, and she loved Monet. That was how they had met, at the painting of the lily pads in the Modern. Both of them had been sitting and staring for some time, on the backless seats along the edge of the room, and when the room finally cleared, Peter had said, "Really, he is grotesquely overrated, don't you think? I mean, this is wallpaper."

It was like touching an electrode to her bottom. She jumped up and started an impassioned lecture that took them down to the cafeteria and out into the sculpture garden and eventually to dinner at Michael's Pub, which she had never been to. He was in luck: It happened to be one of the nights when Woody Allen sat in with the band. There he is! she whispered, and for a horrible moment he feared she might wave or something. On their way out, Peter had nodded politely, seriously at Woody, who was taking a break at the back of the stand, and Woody had politely, seriously nodded back. Amy was impressed.

But that had been two years ago, and now Peter had his hands full lugging a dozen red roses and a black-labeled bottle of champagne whose name he never could remember through the lobby and into the elevator of Amy's apartment building. The doormen knew him well. They grinned. The champagne was really for Mrs. Dunaway, who insisted that she liked Spanish champagne.

He had to ring three times before Mrs. Dunaway came to let him in. She was a little irritated, for she had had to hobble with her cane ("my stick!" she always sniffed) all the way across the living room from her post at the front window overlooking Central Park, where she sat for hours every day playing solitaire and waiting for her bridge partners.

"Oh hi," she said. She was well over eighty. She had flame red hair in a nimbus around her very visible skull, and her long face was drawn with heavy creases from eye to chin, so she more than somewhat resembled Munch's *The Scream*. She had a permanent squint from a lifetime of no-hands smoking, and her voice sounded as though it came from the gearbox of a truck. "Come on in. Oh, lovely." She spotted the champagne right away and took it from him. "Amy's in the shower."

She gave him a quizzical look. "You having a fight?"

"Yes," he said. He shrugged and gave her a significant look.

She shrugged and gave him a significant look in return. "Women, eh?"

"Women," he said. "It's my fault, actually. I forgot a date."

"Oh dear. Well, I don't think it's fatal. You can find her back there. I think she's softened up. She must be, she's been in the shower a half an hour."

That was the nice thing about a great-aunt. She couldn't care less whether you were sleeping together. He had had some pleasant, desultory conversations with her while waiting for Amy. She was a Yankees fan from the DiMaggio days and kept up so fanatically that Peter had to check out the sports pages before going over there so he wouldn't sound like a fool.

He took the roses back through the long living room with its stylishly tattered Oriental rugs, its brass-bound Korean chests and waist-high Chinese vases, its Japanese kakemonos hung from the walls, and then through the study, lined with books to the ceiling, and on to the master bedroom and beyond to the dressing room and beyond that to the master bath. He opened the door cautiously. The room was full of steam.

"Hello?" he said.

No reply. An extra cloud of steam billowed around him. The shower was still hissing.

"Hello? Am I allowed?"

Her voice was startlingly close. "You are a bad person, Peter Van Overloop. What are you doing in here?"

Amy's wet pink face suddenly materialized in a wreath of fog. He reached for it with both hands, forgetting the roses. She screamed a little as the green paper brushed against her shoulder. He dropped the roses and held her face by its plump cheeks. She looked even healthier than usual, her face sleek and gleaming, her neat, straight little nose dripping one elegant drip, her full breasts looking up at him.

"I really am sorry," he said.

"You really should be," she said.

He kissed her and she pressed against him and pulled him to her wet, steaming body. Still kissing, she pulled him deeper

33

into the bathroom, up to the glass door of the shower stall. He could feel her all the way down. He could also feel hot mist spraying him. His good gray cotton pants and button-down shirt were getting soaked.

She ended the kiss and pulled back from him, grinning.

"There," she said.

"You got me all wet," he said.

"It's the least you deserve. You look beautiful all wet."

He grinned back. He was extremely annoyed.

"I'm soaked. I can't go out like this. My God, what if your aunt comes in?"

"No problem. No problem. I'll put them in the dryer."

Well goddamn it, he muttered to himself. He backed out to the dressing room and took off all his clothes, scowling when she handed him a giant towel that was so thick and soft it didn't seem to be drying him when he rubbed it all over his body. She gathered up his things and stepped out of the room, returning a minute later wearing a terry-cloth robe.

They sat in wicker chairs in the huge bedroom and listened to the distant dryer flopping things over themselves.

"Why'd you do that?" he asked, his irritation rising in him with a tingle.

"What?"

"Get me all wet. Jeez, I was gonna ask you out to dinner."

She waved blithely. "Well, I felt like it."

They could hear the old lady thumping about in the front room. He looked up nervously.

"She won't come in," Amy said. "Her bridge ladies will be here at eight."

"So have you had supper?"

"Actually, yes."

"What can I say?" He got up, went into the bathroom, and brought back the roses in their green paper, presenting them to her anew.

A half hour later, still somewhat damp, he and Amy returned to the living room. He found the champagne, which Mrs. Dunaway had put in the freezer, and opened it while the old lady looked on from her card table. She had already brought in a platter containing a superb double Gloucester cheese and Ritz crackers. Mrs. Dunaway was insouciant about her elegance.

"Thank you so much," she said. "You should have fights all the time."

"We do," he said.

Amy bristled. "No we don't. It's just when he—"

"At any rate," the great-aunt interrupted with the skill of long practice, "it is a fine champagne and greatly underrated." To Peter: "Did you wash your hair?"

"I took a quick shower," he replied.

She gave him another significant look, which he returned. "You forgot to take off your shoes."

"Yes," he said.

He said good-bye to Amy at the door. He knew when he was being hustled out. "I wish you would finish your dissertation." She sighed. "I mean, you've done everything else. I thought you said the orals would be the hardest part."

"As it happens, I am having to rethink de Hooch. It just isn't that easy, you just can't dash it off like a letter to the editor. And meanwhile I have to eat," he said.

"Well, I just wish you'd get something permanent."

The way she said it made him uneasy.

"All right," he said.

She gave him a sisterly kiss and closed the door.

When Peter got home the cats reminded him that they had no food, and their box needed to be harvested of its little turds, which he scooped up in a plastic ladle and dropped into the toilet.

In the morning he had to go to the bank as soon as it

opened to transfer the last of his grant money to his checking account. It was not until nearly noon that he found time to work on the diary again.

He had been writing the words down so fast that now he could barely read them. He resolved to write more carefully and went back over the last sentence.

———————————◄○►——————————

"Oh don't do that," she says. She is very religious . . .

———————————◄○►——————————

Who was this now? Oh yes, the Cat Woman. The one he met in the market.

———————————◄○►——————————

. . . very religious and full of notions that sound more pagan than Christian to me. I can't believe that God, if He exists, would object to our mentioning His name now and then. I think people make much too much of Him. We live and we die, we have pleasure and we have pain, plenty of it, and perhaps God put us here, but I can't believe that He is so fascinated with us in our foolishness that He interferes constantly, as she thinks, stirs us about like a boy stirring an anthill with a stick. I have not yet told her my theory that in fact God is a small boy, a mischievous and possibly perverse small boy. Who else would go to the trouble of creating mosquitoes?

We are to meet tomorrow by the Nieuwe Gracht bridge if it is nice. I told her I would take her to the shore. She seems to know someone who runs a boat to Zandvoort. I mean, what is the point of a mosquito? It hums when it is going to bite you so with luck you can swat it. Now that is a foolish bug.

——————————

What a day. She was standing by the bridge with a basket on her arm. She looked radiant in a new cap and a collar but no ruff above her bodice. She was dressed for the country. She is not a widow but calls herself an old maid. Her skirt was a simple dark red, very dark, and the bodice black. She wears dark clothes to go with her rather tanned look, dark-skinned like a southerner.

"This is an old maid?" I said. She is thin but with full breasts that push her bodice out. She is quite short. I found I couldn't help looking into her dark, mocking eyes.

She laughed. "It's because I'm so forward," she said. "Come on, Hals, I'm taking you to the beach."

She will not call me Frans. I have never known a woman of such brisk decision. She was not properly raised. We walked down to the Spaarne where a beer boat was tied up. The thinnest man I have ever seen was sitting on the jetty with his legs dangling down into the boat. He jumped up when he saw us and got ready to cast off without so much as a nod. His face was pocked and sallow and extremely long and narrow. A pinched mouth that looked as though it had never smiled. He wore no beard or hat, a lock of dark hair sweeping down over his face.

We sat side by side on a thwart under the big fat boom. The boat was so broad and massive, its sides bruised by scraping against a thousand jetties, it looked as if it could venture onto the North Sea with no trouble at all. She wasn't talking much, not her usual pert self. In the basket she had a small Edam and some slices of a superb venison pie, a herring or two and a loaf and jug. And a big linen coverall, folded many times. I hadn't been to Zandvoort in years. I remember it had . . .

———————————◄○►———————————

Peter got up, stretched, and went to the bookcase to find the atlas. He could find no Zandvoort on the map of Western Europe but finally located it on an inset map showing Holland. Checking the map of old Haarlem in the catalog, he saw that there was indeed a Nieuwe Gracht bridge.

Well so what? he mused. Anyone could have seen a map

of old Haarlem. Anyone could have had access to the same information that was in the catalog. Still, the narrative didn't seem all that concerned with proving itself, going on and on this way about some picnic.

While he was up he boiled himself a plateful of couscous, which he had discovered at the back of a shelf. It was rather good with just butter and salt. He chewed up three leaves of romaine lettuce from the refrigerator and opened a bottle of orange soda, which he carried to the table. There, leisurely stretching again, he took up his pen and bent over the book once more.

———————————◀○▶———————————

. . . some quite pleasant beer gardens off the high street. I pulled my silver flask out of my coat pocket. I'd had it filled at Piet's with good geneva. Not aged, that's for winter and cold nights before the fire and philosophic thoughts, but the good plain stuff, cooled in stone.

She was impressed. "Is it an heirloom?" she said.

"Oh no, I got it for a painting." It was supposed to be sixty guilders, but the silly man came to me at my house at night half in tears and wringing his hands and said he was bankrupt, he was ruined, and he would have to leave town, and he was devastated, always paid his debts, et cetera, et cetera, and he wanted to make it up to me, and would, someday, by God, but in the meantime he wanted me to have this as a token, just a token, you understand. He'd got it from his father as a wedding gift, and he insisted that I take it.

Well, he had the painting by then. No great painting, but it cost me three solid days of work and I could probably have sold it for at least that. So I took the flask and he went off to Antwerp where he made a fortune with some sort of cleaning mixture he claimed to have invented, nothing but chalk and turpentine, I am sure. I showed the flask to van der Morsch, who knows about such things, and he said it was old, all right, but dipped and not very high-quality dip at that. It does hold plenty of geneva, however.

The sun was intense, burning through the morning mist so hard it made you squint. But there was a steady wind that kept the sail taut and straining, the ropes creaking constantly and the jib flapping in fury every time we shifted direction. I am not a sailor. I was glad to see the village rise up among the alders at last and the boat nuzzle into the old dock.

She used to come here as a girl. The boatman was someone her uncle knew. He seemed to remember her better after we had been going a while, was reminded of her as a little girl fishing from the Zandvoort pier and dancing on the stones in her too-big wooden shoes. He couldn't guarantee a ride back, he said, would have to leave when he was loaded and would look for us, but he had to get back. He had a few barrels aboard but the main reason for the trip was to pick up some empties at Zandvoort.

We climbed out and walked straight through the village to the sea. It was so hot I was wearing my light linen pants and a thin shirt and no hat. When we got to the shore, it was windy. We strolled along the stones for a way. There was no one in sight.

"You look cold," she said.

"No." But I was. We were out of sight of the town. She took my hand like a girl and led me up to the great dunes.

◄◦►

The phone was ringing, had been ringing. It went onto the answering device. He heard the voice of his roommate Scott. "Hey Pete, you better get over here. We have a real problem here. Call me as soon as you get in."

Sighing, Peter returned to his book. Scott always had a real problem. Plus he always called him Pete.

Thickets of dune grass along the top ridges wavered in the steady breeze. The sea was high and a few boats were beating upwind toward the breakwater. I could see a ship on the horizon. But not a soul on the stony beach.

"The wind is too much," she said. "Come on, Hals." And she led me still farther up the shore and through some scratchy bushes, along a secret path so narrow that it was probably made by rabbits, and finally down into a large sandy hollow between the dunes. The wind was cut off instantly and I was hot again.

We stumbled through the soft warm sand to the very bottom, a level place where she unfolded the coverall, handed two corners to me, and together we spread it out smoothly. She sat herself down on it without ceremony. Spread her skirts casually over knees and shins, giving me a glimpse or two as though it didn't matter a whit to her.

Peter looked up uneasily. Better get back to Scott before the guy had a cow. He dialed the number. Scott picked up right away.

"You rang? This is Peter."

"Hey man, we had a fire last night. We had a disaster, a complete disaster. Your stuff was robbed. You better come over."

"Huh?"

"You better get here! Right now. The place is burned up. Firemen are still here."

"I'll be right there."

Aghast, barely taking the time to hide the diary, Peter rushed downstairs and out to the street, took the IRT to Eighty-sixth Street, and trotted the five blocks to his old place.

Two fire engines still stood muttering hugely in the street out front. Some small boys stared from the stoop next door.

Two firemen were rolling up a deflated hose that snaked across the pavement to a hydrant.

The lobby stank of stale smoke and burned plaster. A fireman's air pack lay on the parquet floor and portable wind machines had been set up beside the door. Firemen in gleaming wet boots and slickers stood around fiddling with backpack extinguishers, and several policemen were huddled by the reception desk with Carlos, the day manager. A fat detective, his badge visible on his broad vest, lounged in one of the overstuffed armchairs that were placed at the base of the pillars. He had his glasses up on his forehead and was closely reading the small print on some sort of official form.

Scott was right at the door, talking to another cop. Scott was a head taller than Peter, heavy in the shoulders, and wore a brush cut left over from the fifties.

"Oh great. We need you here," he said excitedly, grabbing Peter by the arm and pulling him to a quiet corner of the big room, whose grandiose carved ceiling and fluted columns hardly matched the stingy poverty of the rooms above.

"Jesus. What happened? What's up?"

"It's a disaster . . . a fuckin' disaster. This, uh, this girl was in your room—"

"My room!"

"Yeah yeah," Scott mumbled, running past the words quickly, "she had to crash there last night, this friend of John's, and she smoked, and she set the bed on fire—"

"My bed!"

"Yeah yeah, well the whole place was goin' up when we woke up, your room, the hall, John's room—"

"Oh shit. Who was this—"

"Wait. Wait," Scott muttered, painting Peter's chest with a broad palm to calm him down, "there's . . . see, there was mostly smoke damage, it wasn't that bad, but we didn't know

41

that. We took all your stuff out of the room, your TV, the hi-fi, the telescope, the bike—"

"Oh good," Peter muttered. "But who was the girl—"

"Wait. We took it all out into the hall, and John's stuff too, he had his word processor and everything. And when the firemen got done we went downstairs to talk to the chief, and when we went up again, it was gone."

"What was gone?"

Scott rolled his eyes, waved his large arms. "Everything. Some fucker cleaned out every goddamn thing in the hall. Even the bicycle. Somebody in this building. Had to be."

"What you mean?"

"It's gone, my friend. Everything."

"Shit. How could that happen?" Peter gaped, unbelieving.

Scott shrugged. "Yeah, right. It couldn't, right?"

"Shit! They stole it?"

"I know it. We were down there couldna been a half hour, and they cleaned us out. We called the cops, but this is a huge building. They probably trucked it out while we were still phoning it in."

"My bike?"

Scott shrugged again. "What do I say?"

He had paid three hundred dollars for that bike, plus the digital odometer thing, and the water bottle, and the electronic horn, and the pedal clips, and the mirror, and he had bought himself a thirty-dollar helmet and the Lycra biking shorts and the special shoes and the gel-lined gloves, and he had ridden it exactly twice in three years.

"And the telescope," he murmured. He had bought that, along with the deluxe stand, because he had had this vision of setting it up on the roof, or maybe at Lake George, where he used to spend his vacations, and while he was peering through it this girl would come up and say, Oh, you have a telescope? And he would talk to her. He had taken the thing up to the roof once, but he discovered that the minute you got it focused on the moon or Saturn or anything, the damn planet would drift out of sight. You would have to keep twisting the knob to make the object stay in the scope, but even then it bobbled all the time, shimmered so badly that you could barely see anything. The other part was that he was going to read up on astronomy so he could talk about it, but he had never even finished the brochure that came with the telescope. So he had left it on its stand in his room, a total waste of money. Besides, he didn't need it, because he had Amy.

"Shit, shit, shit," he said. "What does my room look like?"

"You can't get in. It's all taped up. The landlord has his insurance people here right now. We told him it was the wiring."

"Oh my God. What if they ask the—"

"They won't. Heather spent the morning rubbing the nicotine off her fingers with a pumice stone. She says she hardly ever smokes anyway."

"I bet."

"The wiring is pretty bad, you have to admit that."

Peter took a huge breath and let it out luxuriously. "I don't believe you rented my room out," he said quietly.

"We dint rent it, it was just—she crashed in it, that's all. Shit, man."

Peter stared numbly at Scott's bland face, pale and thick-cheeked from a lifetime of hamburgers and milk shakes. He remembered that he had let his insurance lapse long ago. At least, he thought, he had a place to stay, far away from this hectic scene.

"You owe me, Scott," he said.

"Yeah. But it was shit bad luck. I don't believe this place. I can't look at anybody in the elevator without thinking, Hey, you fuck face, you stole our stuff."

43

"Hey. This is stupid. I have to get up there. What about my clothes?"

Jittery from the adrenaline that suddenly pumped through him, Peter shoved past the shrugging Scott, heading toward the elevator. Angrily, he confronted the plainclothesman on guard there, insisted on going up to his room. The man, balding and gray, looked closely at him and finally nodded.

"I'll take you up, though," he said. "It's all locked up. It's taped shut."

The apartment was not taped shut. Two men were in the living room, measuring things and writing in notebooks. Peter went to his bedroom, which looked quite bare, the sodden curtains and blankets stacked in a wet heap in the middle, the chair and burned mattress shoved away from the wall, the soggy carpet exposed, with black footmarks all over it and a great curving scar where it had burned. His bureau was gone. He found that all his clothes had been removed from the closet and wrapped in a huge plastic sheet and laid on the floor in a large lump. It appeared they were being taken somewhere. He wondered how they could possibly be used for evidence.

"This is mine," he said.

"All that?"

There wasn't that much. Two suits, which he almost never wore, three pairs of jeans, a dozen shirts and four sweaters. Next to the pile was a big cardboard box in which he found his underwear and socks and various odds and ends from the bureau.

Everything smelled of smoke, the bitter smell of painted wood and plastic, the smell of burned curtains.

"This is mine," he said after searching through the other rooms and rescuing a towel from the bathroom and adding it to the pile. "Can I take this with me?"

44

"Have to sign for it," the man said. He didn't help as Peter lugged the stuff to the elevator.

Peter smelled of smoke. He was too depressed to think about anything. When he sat on the sofa to read Laura's *New Yorker,* the older cat, Leopold, climbed onto his lap without asking and curled himself up and lay down. He stroked the silky fur. "Hey Leopold," he said. "Hey Lee."

It was true, he decided: Cats did calm you down. Cats didn't own bicycles. Cats didn't own anything and look at them, how relaxed they were.

Then Dave jumped up beside him and Lee slithered away. Dave, shoulders hunched aggressively, watched him go.

———————◄○►———————

"Sit down, Hals," she said. "Get out of the wind."

"I thought we were going to look at the ocean."

"We did." She was laughing at me again. She watched me as though she knew every move I was going to make. "You want to start the cheese? I have a spoon."

I dug the point of the spoon into the top of the cheese, making a scalloped ring in the wax, and pried it up so it came away as a perfect little cap. We took turns twisting the spoon in and coming up with plugs of cheese. It was perfect, just slightly rubbery toward the center.

We ate avidly. The air had made me ravenous, the air and the tension. I cut the loaf like a patriarch, holding it to my chest and carving off thick slices.

She smiled lazily and stretched back on the blanket. She accepted a glassful of geneva. (She had brought glasses, amazing.) Took off her bonnet and shook her hair free, a surprise, black and shiny, thick long waves of it, luxuriant. I took a deep gulp and lay back beside her. We were quite scandalous, open there to the

45

sky. There was no one for miles. The geneva was still cool, a trace of anise flavor that to me speaks of spring afternoons.

We dreamed on, making remarks about the antics of the gulls overhead, laughing lazily, lying quiet under the sun. She was telling me how she used to play jokes on that skinny boatman. I had a picture of her, very small, with long hair in a pigtail and no bonnet, skipping along the docks and laughing. She murmured something and I raised up to hear better and I was gazing down at her serene face, not a little girl at all, the huge dark eyes, the cat smile that opened now, and to my amazement and delight all at once we were kissing. I could feel the tiny muscled ridge of her lips beneath mine, and her arm was around my neck, her hand pulling me closer, wanting me.

None of this nonsense about, Is it right? Should we? What will God think? And Pastor Leenders? And the Olycans and the people next door and crazy Bobbe and everybody in the world. I had not been with a woman for a year, almost exactly a year. Had not touched one. This was a strange one. I wondered if she was right in the head. I was being seduced! She was touching me, her hand sliding down my back and over the front of my pants. She had known men, I was sure of it. At twenty-three how could she help it even here in prim Haarlem. But she was no whore. My mind was making pictures frantically. All those brothers, did they come into her bed? Those big louts, slobbering over little sister still a girl in her bed. I seemed to be slightly delirious.

I found her bodice and pulled it open. I was panting. She was watching me. I stroked her hair. It must reach to her waist. Her breasts burst free, big rich breasts, surprising on her slight, slim body, with large nipples straining to be kissed. I was thinking of Annie's dear little snow apples with the blue veins. I stopped thinking and kissed one, then the other, like a giant baby, while she cooed and stroked the back of my head. Such abundance. I was quite dizzy. She was panting now too. It is a dance, I was thinking. And me thirty-four, halfway to my biblical allotment, and my deluded member believing he was sixteen again.

Then she was twisting and scrambling under me. I realized she was pulling up her skirts, a fuss and rustle of petticoats brushing against me, my hand working at my pants as we hurried to introduce these two eager hairy strangers to each other. This old business. Now we were joined, with the skirts all around us and the flask somehow loose under her, the blanket rucked and twisted, my elbows digging into the sand, her hands clutching, legs swinging up to embrace me. I am not sure why I am writing this down, it surely is forbidden somewhere. She will say it is the work of the devil.

Perhaps I will read this over when I am bent and white, and I will say, Oh yes, those were the days.

Hello to you there, old Frans! Hello, old man. And did your bowels move today?

We looked at each other. We laughed the silent laugh of delight. Her chest was covered with red prickles. We put ourselves back together. I said, "Have some more geneva, my dear," and she laughed again.

I am not sure how long we stayed there. When we came back into the village I hired a carriage to take us straight home. She said, "I don't mind the boat. Let's wait for the boat." I said no. I was wanting her again, already, breathless to get at her again. She would manage to stand in front of me while we stood on the dock making up our minds, and her hand would stray behind her under cover of her skirts and her fingertips would give him a little flick. So he jumped and I would be embarrassed if I weren't wearing the big loose britches. In the end I forgot I had bought some tobacco that morning, and she had to pay the last four guilders. I was mad for her, sick with her. I crowded over her wanting to touch her everywhere, so sinuous she was, sliding around me like a snake, teasing me there in public without anyone having the least

47

notion what was going on, so prim she looked with her forearm just happening to graze the front of me as she changed hands with the basket.

We walked to her mother's house, which is quite near to mine, across the cathedral square, me not touching but close, rigid with expectation.

"She'll be asleep," she said. She was so calm, business like. "I sleep in a back room on the ground floor to be near her. We can go in the back door through the courtyard." She touched my hand when we came to the alley and there was no one to see. She was growing even more eager now for another, with no sand and no petticoats. We crept up the alley and through the wooden gate into her courtyard, aged red brick, and on into the house.

"She won't wake up?" I whispered.

"No. She is hardly awake at any time. She's all closed in there."

"Maybe you should see to her," I muttered, always considerate of others. If the old creature had to use the pan . . .

Lysbeth nodded, put a finger to her lips, led me into a tiny roomlet under the stairs and slipped away. Space for a bed, not very high, and one chair and a clothes hamper. A blouse was draped over the chair. Stockings scattered on the bare floor. A pair of extremely worn slippers flung recklessly from feet to land where they might. My lady was not a housekeeper.

I heard her across the low-ceilinged kitchen murmuring to the old woman. I heard the clink of a lid. Bare feet stamping about. Someone straining, grunting. She was pushing her back up into her bed. It would be one of those high beds with the curtains all around. High as your chest, some of them. For cleanliness, so you can sweep under them and the cat can't hide there. They are the devil for old people, dwarfs or anyone with a bad back. I fell out of one once and nearly broke my arm.

Finally my cat woman crept back to me and closed the door behind her and bolted it. She was grinning, breathless with gleeful anticipation.

"All tucked away," she whispered. "Lucky I went. She was awake. She'll go right to sleep now."

"Did you shut her in?"

"Yes. It's heavy, it's brocade. She won't hear a thing."

Up to now we had been rushing, pelting through life like thieves on the run. Suddenly everything slowed down. I took a deep slow breath and gazed at her and she gazed back, heavy-lidded. Without a word we began to take off our clothes.

So many clothes. I stumbled over my own drawers, so intent was I on her as she pulled off the bodice, the outer skirt, the first petticoat, the second, the belt for her stockings, until she stood before me in her chemise, gauzy and flowing in the dim light. Then I pulled down my drawers, and her eyes went straight to my soldier, saluting her so ruddy and proud, as if he had just been pinned with a medal. Then with one graceful, negligent conjurer's wave of her arms, she wafted the chemise up and off her to drift down through the air and land on the floor somewhere.

Oh my, her body. She glowed in the dim light. Oh the glory of it.

Slight, I said, and slim. I could pick her up easily and lift her off her feet. But I was not prepared, even after the time at the beach, for the great perfect roundness of her breasts, wider than her rib cage, standing up to face me. Magnificent breasts, making her look almost top-heavy the way they emerged from that narrow waist, with the ribs showing. Too proud to sag. I could see the undercurve. And below them the neat small navel, the creamy abdomen and the hips curving subtly out around the small escutcheon. Haven't painted a nude since I was a student. Her legs were slim, the thighs muscular. Tiny ankles and wrists, as if all this hidden wealth had been tied up with drawstrings, revealing only her small hands and feet. Never have I seen such a body. The skin, perfect, smooth and sleek and slightly brown, almost like a Spaniard's. It is not as fashionable as winter white skin, I know, but I have never liked that frostbitten look with the pink freckles all over. I love colors in skin. She was smiling at me, and I guess my own body is not so bad for my age, except for the beer pockets below my ribs. I stepped up to her. I couldn't believe it was mine. I ran both hands down her flanks and over the slippery swell of her hips, and she pressed those amazing breasts to me, and we kissed very slowly. Himself bumped up between her legs like a dog nosing for attention, and instead of stepping back, as some would, she simply opened her legs a little and let him slip between. I stroked her over and over, everywhere, even the tight fissure between her hips until I felt the heat in there, the inner fires that keep us alive.

Then she was sitting on the edge of the bed, kissing my stomach, and she was kissing him. This ledger is a scandal waiting for someone to find it. Holy Creator, to think of it even this minute.

We went to it on her bed, keeping quiet for her mother (which added a bit, I must say, we were conspirators giggling and snickering under the sheets), and when we were done we talked a while, both of us with an ear out for her brothers. When she told me that four of them still lived in the house with her and her mother I almost lost my lunch. They wouldn't be home till dinnertime, so she said with great confidence, but it put the fear in me. I was more nervous every minute. Oh hush, she said, they won't come in here, they come in the front if they come at all. If they're not at the tavern, they come in and go straight up the front stairs. And you cook for them all? I said. And clean? And take care of the mother? Hush, she said, and took him in her mouth again, and this time he sprang up you would think it was Resurrection Day and Gabriel blowing on his horn.

———————————◄o►———————————

It was past midnight. Peter yawned and closed the diary. He had an erection. He must call Amy in the morning.

He made some notes in the running account that he was keeping of the facts in the narrative. So far, everything checked remarkably well with what was known about Hals. He had even found reference to the portrait medallion. It was a copper oval, later to be set into a wooden panel, of one Theodorus Schrevelius, a schoolmaster in Haarlem and later rector of the Latin school in Leiden.

Copper, Peter read in the catalog, was favored by miniaturists who sought a sleek, enamel-like appearance, though rarely used by Hals. He apparently did not fancy the tiny scale of miniatures, for his brush strokes on the Schrevelius work, according to the scholars, were just as free and unblended as in a larger work.

The Reynier family was duly noted, and Lysbeth Reyniersdochter, or Reynier's daughter, the name usually abbreviated to Reyniersdr. Similarly, the *sz* at the end of a man's name stood for *zoon,* or "son of." Oh yes, and according to one of his historians, cats were considered filthy in those days in superclean Holland.

All these facts could be learned by research. But of the trip to the seaside and the somewhat gamy, homespun details of Hals's life, he found no hint. Still, he had a distinct impression of a personality, so much so that he was finding it easy to put the fluent, informal Dutch into slangy English. *Kerel,* for instance, surely had to be rendered as "guy," not "chap" or "fellow" as his English-Dutch dictionary would have it, superciliously branding the word as "familiar" in any case. He wondered if the word was related to the English *carl,* "a peasant, a churl."

It occurred to Peter that he rather liked this man, whether he was actually Frans Hals or some forger or hoaxer, now presumably long gone and just as dead as the original artist. He couldn't believe that the brittle pages and faded ink could have been faked. But then, he couldn't believe a lot of things that he knew were perfectly true.

2

It had been over a week since Peter had looked at the diary. He had been kept busy filling out theft forms for the police and futilely calling the insurance company with which he had once had a small household-effects policy. It had been Tony's idea, and Tony had paid the first two premiums, back when, following their mother's death, they still had some of her furniture. Peter had later sold his, an enormous canopy bed and a folding mahogany table, to a former roommate who was getting married. He had kept the mattress to sleep on. There was a sofa too, but that had been allowed to deteriorate, the legs breaking off and the springs popping out the bottom, until finally he had just dragged it to the alley and left it there. Someone took it away the same night.

The rest of the time he had been trying to negotiate via Scott with the landlord and the painters who were supposed to fix up his room. Everyone assured him the crew had been laid on to do the work, but they didn't seem to be around. Nothing was happening. Peter had visited the apartment twice in two days, but that just made him more frustrated than ever. The painters weren't there, the landlord wasn't available, and Scott was off at the library.

Meanwhile, the Corwin people wanted him to help with a major gold-leafing project, repairing the frame on a gigantic crypto-Caravaggio, or School of, or whatever it was, that some unscrupulous uptown dealer was trying to foist on the unscrupulous adviser and purchasing agent of a Long Island plastics manufacturer who was undoubtedly unscrupulous in his own field of expertise but who in the matter of buying art was charmingly naïve. Corwin himself had called Peter this afternoon and talked his ear off—Corwin being extremely retiring and unable simply to state the problem and get an answer and hire him—and after a good forty minutes of listening to the whole story including the provenance of the painting, Peter was now committed to spending at least three full days, starting early tomorrow morning, helping with the job.

So the evening was shot. It was almost nine, and besides it was raining a deluge outside, the great hail-like drops splatting against the large windows. For a while he stood and watched them. He liked those windows, which reached to the ceiling and had panes large enough for him to crawl through with ease. He bolted them shut when he went out for the day, but when he was in the apartment he kept the iron shutters open so that light splashed over the dingy white walls and made the place actually cheery.

But now there was a knock on the door. An imperious, impatient knock.

Peter gaped. The diary! Who would know he was here? Who would come through the rain to visit him unannounced? He approached the door with foreboding. Even as he neared it, he heard a key scrabbling at the lock. A key or maybe a jimmy of some sort. A burglar's pick?

Heart beating fast, he pulled the door open.

And revealed Laura, still bent nearsightedly over the keyhole. Her black hair was stringy and wet. Her bags were on the floor beside her.

"Oh!" she said. "You're here."

"Yes!" he said.

"I'm sorry. I tried to call but it was busy."

He stared at her in astonishment. She was soaked. She seemed to be wearing the same jeans he had seen her in ten days ago, but with a man's shirt over them, the tails hanging down around her hips.

"Oh God, I'm sorry," she said, still breathless from the climb. Now she was lifting the suitcase through the doorway and plunking them on the floor. "I, uh, I'm, uh, we had, God. I'm sorry about this."

"You're back," he said, his heart sinking.

Laura stopped moving her arms about and faced him.

"Well, we had a fight."

"You and, uh . . ."

"Me and George. In Arles. I wanted to stay and he wanted he said well, it's um. Well, it's too complicated."

She took a big breath and combed her hair with her fingers, untangling it with amazing skill and leaving it hanging sleekly down the sides of her thin face. She looked hard at him.

"So he was being a complete jerk and I said I was going home and he said, That's fine. So I'm—" She stopped in midsentence, as though she had forgotten she was speaking.

"Have you had any dinner? You want a glass of wine?"

"No, I ate on the plane. I'm—"

"Come on sit down." She had run out of words, so he led her by the hand to the sofa and sat her down. "How about a drink?" he said.

She was looking through the wall. "A drink would be fine. Oh Leopold. Hello Leopold! Oh, Leopold." She hefted the big cat onto her lap, and a moment later Dave skulked out from behind the curtains and jumped up on the sofa beside her. "Oh kitties, are you all right? Are you happy kitties? Mommy's back!"

He bustled into the kitchen and made two Scotches and water. It was the first major drink he had had here.

"So I'm moving back, I guess," she said.

Peter presented her a tinkling lowball glass. "Well, that's great, but there's one little problem here."

She was stroking both cats alternately with one hand while sipping with the other. He waited till she glanced up.

"I, uh, haven't got a place to go, right away. My apartment had a fire."

"Oh my God. Where do you live?"

"Up on the West Side. I lost everything, my stereo and TV and VCR, my bike and everything. Even my mattress."

"Why, that's awful! Was anyone hurt?"

"No, no. But it's burned out and they're just now trying to get it fixed up again."

"Oh." She sat with the glass at her lips. She gave him a quick searching look. "So," she said casually, "you could stay here a night or two."

"Terrific. Great." He was relieved that she hadn't said "crash." Only Scott would say "crash." You had roommates, and no one gave it a second thought. Or was supposed to anyway. He did know of a grad student at the business school who had lucked out by getting three girls as roommates. They all thought they were being pretty cool until one of them found him in her closet when she was undressing.

"I really appreciate it," he said, finishing his Scotch. "You have the main bed anyway, because I've been sleeping up in the loft."

"Oh good," she said. "I'm—"

"I'll get this stuff out of here." He waved toward the tangle of clothes that at one time he had been arranging on the floor, deciding what to keep and fumigate. He had gotten depressed halfway through the job.

"Well, if you don't mind," Laura murmured, getting up and dragging her suitcase into her bedroom, "I think I'll—"

"It's okay. I'll find a place tomorrow," he said, speaking to her retreating back, narrow and uncertain.

"It's all right. No big deal."

Later, she flitted through the big room in her dressing gown while he finished tying his clothes into two bundles. He tried not to hear her sounds in the bathroom. He sat at the table and picked up the diary.

───────◄○►───────

Headache all day. Would have stayed in bed all day, but Neeltje chased me out. Margaretha whining and coughing half the night. Croup. I won't sleep tonight. I am sure Lysbeth wants me to marry her.

───────────────

I have Harmen sleeping with me. Margaretha very sick. She sweats so, like a grown person. The house smells of it, of her sheets.

───────────────

Today I wanted to see her again, not to lie with her but to talk and be silent with her and feel her eyes upon me. It is Annie that gives me the headache. Margaretha a little better. The Guards paid me another twenty guilders and I gave it to Neeltje to keep her quiet. The miniature will go ahead, he likes the design, maybe an advance. I am in bed already with Harmen. Not even dark. Why do I want to sleep all the time?

───────────────

1 June — It is the first of June. I come here for the faces. The shadows make them more striking. The faces. Long bony ones with massive horse jaws. Old wrinkled ones with pointed nose

yearning to touch pointed chin. Fat ones, a round loaf set on a pot, two hemispheres, with small eyes peeking out from the crack between. Foolish pudding faces, cheerful childish faces, all smiles; craggy long undertaker faces. The face that has a series of chins flowing down into the collar. The keen athlete's face, cheekbones and tight skin, eyes slitted as though facing into a wind. The handsome oval face marred only by the interior look of the self-regarding eyes. The potato nose. The stubby cork nose. The arrow-straight nose, breathtaking, and the arrow-straight nose with a bulb on the end, such a disappointment. The Roman nose that planes straight down from the forehead (not a very intelligent look). The staircase nose. The long thin aristocratic nose with beautifully carved nostrils. The nose that is a chunk of putty stuck on any old way. And brows: the ones that go straight across, the circumflex ones that do their little dance of irony upon the face. The bristling angry ones and the bristling kindly ones. And mouths: long, generous mouths that waver and curl and reveal too much, slit mouths that cannot smile, that never stretch (how do they eat? how do they yawn?), pursed mouths wrinkled in their permanent denial of a kiss, thin mouths that lift and pull back to show a row of teeth, and snarl like a dog when they smile. Fat pillows of lips that need to be licked constantly, stern mouths, fierce mouths, timid mouths, determined mouths, mouths that droop open in eternal astonishment or perhaps sheer stupor, mouths pressed tight against the world, mouths that offer, that plead, that mock, that boast, that disdain all comers. And laugh. The laugh that transforms a face, even the homeliest, the brilliant twinkling laugh that sets eyes alight and turns wrinkles into sunny rays of light and makes the whole face blossom like a flower in the morning. She was like that, beautiful at any time but when she laughed she was transfigured. She became a heavenly creature, and so I saw her even in my sober times. I can hear the young trill of her laugh. Annie, Annie.

She arranged it all, shy Annie, went to her family and told them.

I didn't think you could, I was ready to do it myself. But there they were. When we all met, so formally on the cobbles when you came out of the cathedral. Your uncle, smiling above his belly. My parents behind me. Everyone talking at once. You staring at me secretly with fear and hope. Such expectations. You eighteen, is it possible? Annie. I whisper it to myself. I sit in Piet's with my ledger, not at my old seat in the corner but on the settle by the fireplace so I can see. I am not a regular anymore. They don't know me here, can you imagine that, wouldn't you sigh with relief at that, even now, too late. And your grandfather, telling me I should come to work in the brewery.

The night we walked out to the bleaching fields. The stars came right down to the ground. I want to paint that. I want to put that down on canvas so people will always see it, so someone not born yet will see how it was here in Haarlem on this night and me, what I saw. How we climbed the haystack and lay on our backs like crucifixes and looked up into the black, the stars so cold and far, flickering as though not certain of themselves, so shy you have to look to one side of them to see them. How could you paint that and put it on a square of canvas? The way the blackness sucks you up into it. Captures you and draws you up away from your life on this earth and changes you in a few moments, so that you will have that lovely darkness within you forever. So that you know you are theirs, that you are the child of the stars and the night. And they all watching you, the heavenly audience and you alone on the stage, the innumerable host of them up there watching you with their cold flickering eyes.

And the young fool, I said I wanted to paint the stars, I wanted to paint the sun on the water, the million lights, the dance. I am drunk. I want to put this down.

Anneke Harmensdochter is my wife forever. It was decreed by God and your uncle. And my father. You were so frightened, you didn't know what it was all about. How could you if your mother died when you were nine? Only what you had heard, terrible rumors about men. How we giggled together when you told me. It took me two nights to approach you, and then very gently, so gently, and another night before you wanted to take the covers off and see. And another night to decide you liked it after all. Annie. So silly we were. And Uncle Job, who said as a painter I would make a fine brewer. And you, standing up to him, all golden in the sun, curls blossoming out from under your cap and shaking with the ferocity of you, saying in your strongest voice Uncle, I won't have it, he is a master painter, he will paint everyone in town. And I see that heavy face, the jowls pulling the whole chin down in a permanent pout as though he had just tasted shit on his fingers. Yes, yes, we'll see my dear. But he won't paint me he won't.

She used to say that once I painted Uncle Job, Haarlem society would surely line up at my door for portraits. And we didn't care, that was the lovely thing, we didn't care about the portraits because I was going to paint the stars at night and the sea and the bleaching fields with the great shining sheets spread out on them in the sun, all those things I was going to paint. I was going to sit in the fields and paint what I saw when I saw it and never mind the underpainting and the trimming and smoothing and directing the strokes and all that studio stuff.

The beer has made a ring on the ledger. I am drunk. I am sick. How she cried with Harmen, cried and cursed me and every man and herself and Teuntje and the world, and I tried to hold her, smooth her wet hair, I was crying too, shouting at the women. And then with Margaretha, you were so quiet. You didn't want to wake up Harmen, you were so brave. I am making a fool of myself. I am being maudlin. The men are looking at me in plain sight sniffling away. Wish I were in my corner. Drunk, oh my God.

I am putting it down. I hit her. It was the consumption she had and I knew it, her cheeks red all the time, her endless cough day and night, how it drove me out of my mind. I hit her on the back with the palm of my hand. There, I said, that will stop the coughing. I couldn't stand it, and I was drunk. You put your hand up, no, it was all right, stop. And you tried not to cough for the rest of the day, heaving silently into your handkerchief.

It was the night. I woke up and she was gurgling, it was night and she was sitting up the blood was pouring out of her mouth and down her chin, black in the darkness, covering her front and the sheets, pulsing in waves she lurching forward vomiting. I got the lamp lit and the black streaks suddenly turned brilliant red, red all over everything, shocking, and you looked up at me, your blue eyes asking the question. What is happening to me. And I screamed and started to go for help, but you held me, and I held you in my arms and stroked your golden hair with my bloody hands and felt you shuddering, and even when you stopped, I kept on until Teuntje came in and found us. It happened so quickly.

I am writing this, too. I could not pay for a proper burial. The family was scandalized. That's Hals for you, spends every penny on drink, then cries his maudlin tears when his wife is buried in the pauper's yard. I saw her in the canvas shroud before they sewed it, blue eyes shut away from me forever, her little child's upcurving nose and narrow chin, and that beautiful thin, long child's neck. Oh Annie. I put all my sketchbooks in with her. The stars and the million-gleaming seascapes. I put them in there, in her arms. I told her I would paint to make money now, and make a lot, be as rich as Uncle Job. Hello Uncle Job here I am in Piet's and I will have to put this on my account if I still have one, because I have not a penny in my pocket.

———————

She was waiting for me at the tobacco stall.

"I haven't seen you," she said. "I looked for you at church."

"My little girl is sick," I said. A lie. She is fine. I am a terrible liar, though I lie constantly. But now I didn't have to say that the reason she hasn't seen me is that I have been keeping out of her way for the last week.

She knew it, anyway.

———————◄○►———————

Peter glanced back at what he had been writing. This was the other woman, of course. The records showed that Anneke Harmensdr., Hals's first wife, died May 31, 1615. No, was buried. The records showed only the burials. There was a string of burials for those years in the chronology. It didn't say when he had been married to Anneke, only that there were three children, two of whom died early. Presumably she had been married at eighteen. She had been baptized in 1590, which would make her twenty-five when she died.

The catalog item for the burial itself, Peter noted, was quoted from the register of burials. It covered gravediggers' fees for preparing a grave in the chapel of the almshouse. A pauper's grave, Peter reflected. And there was an Uncle Job, a rich Haarlem merchant.

By this time, Laura had gone back to her bedroom and turned out the light. She had waved perfunctorily at him as she left the bathroom.

He felt sad. The writing had gone loose and large in the last passage. He could almost sense the man's drunken presence, his efforts to control himself, his need to write the name Annie over and over like a talisman.

It was time to go to bed. He finished in the bathroom, started up his ladder, but realized all at once that he wasn't sleepy. He wanted to get back to Hals and his Cat Woman. He wished he liked his real work as much as this.

She followed me straight up to the counter and stood by my side while I bought a small pack of Avocaat and watched me dole out the coins. When I backed away into the square she backed away with me. I turned and faced her, and she gave me the curling smile.

"I hear you had some trouble last week."

"I was drunk."

She laughed. "Well I hope so. I would hate to think you were sober."

"They didn't hold me."

"I know."

"You know a lot."

She shrugged. "My brother is a constable."

That was the first I'd heard of that.

"Wonderful," I said. "Have him call you next time so you can bail me out."

"I thought they didn't hold you."

"Not that time."

She walked alongside in silence for a while. I hoped she was done teasing.

Finally she said in a different voice, "You know why I brought water when we went to the beach?"

"Because you heard I was a drunk."

She let that sink to the bottom, hissing like a red hot iron bolt. Then she said quietly, "What I heard was, you weren't."

We were walking south on the Zijlstraat. We came to the bridge and turned right, toward the windmill. There is a little jetty just beyond it, down by the water, and a stone bench partly hidden from traffic by some shrubbery. I used to fish there sometimes. We sat on the bench and looked at the water. It was not even noon and already hot and steamy. This is the stickiest summer I can remember.

She looked young and pretty in a new cap and a startling maroon collar under her lace neckerchief. The red was very dramatic with her black black hair, which shows because the bonnet covers only the back of her head.

"I was thinking of my wife," I said.

"Of course," she said.

"It was the anniversary."

"I am so sorry. I saw her once. She was beautiful."

I wonder how she knew I was keeping sober. I take a little geneva now and then, and wine at a party, but no more beer.

"You know a lot about me," I said lightly.

She smiled, not the curling one but a friendly one. Her feet didn't reach the ground, and she was swinging them like a child. "I don't know half enough."

"I'm not a wild boy anymore."

"Doesn't matter if you are."

"You take pot luck, eh?"

"I take . . . what I've a mind to."

Lord, I used to, all right. I was out every night. I was the talk of the town, or so I heard from Dirck. You jumped in the fountain last night, he would say. You stole a loaf of bread and played it like a flute and pranced around in the water up to your knees. I did? I would say. It was all news to me, except the wet shoes and stockings on the floor by my bed. Dirck was my conscience. Little brother, I would say, you should have taken me home. I was trying to, he would say. But you were determined to make a fool of yourself, and you succeeded. Ah, I would say, I am a success at something. You are a success at something, he would say.

"I eat a lot of sweets," I told her. "I seem to need sugar."

"I love to cook," she said.

That was when my ears went up. Loves to cook, eh? She would love to cook in my kitchen and take charge of it and take charge of the house and me too. But I could not ignore that friendly hand on my arm.

"Oh my God," I said, "I'm late for the Guards. They're all going to be there before noon."

She laughed outright at that. A wonderful abandoned laugh in a low cracked voice. Not ladylike at all. "All right. Go," she laughed. "I'll stay in my own kitchen."

63

I kissed her quickly, and she laughed again and pretended to be looking this way and that. "Go, Hals. You are a child."

I skulked away and went to the Guards, who in fact weren't meeting till after lunch. So I bought a sausage and ate it cold while I was waiting for them.

The Guards were impossible and wanted to change yet again. I said I would have to charge more, and that settled them down. They seem to think I can turn it out like a cartoon.

They still can't make up their minds about the flag. Van Offenberg was going to be holding it, but when they saw how I was using the thing to give them a little depth and breathing space, all the young ensigns wanted to be the standard-bearer. Ensigns get to hold the flag. Captains hold the pikes, lieutenants hold the halberds. That's the way it is. It's all ridiculous — especially as all of these people have served their three years, like me. We aren't even members anymore, officially. I said let it be Jacob Schout, the son of old Lieutenant Schout, because he is the right height, or some such nonsense, and they all agreed instantly. None of us mentioned the real reason, of course, the glaring fact that the Schouts are related to the Coymanses. We are all cowards and lickspittles somewhere in our hearts. They still owe me five hundred, and if they think they are going to work it off by forgiving me my dues for the next ten years, they are tragically mistaken.

Talked to Dirck today. He said Joost has bought a house ...

---◄○►---

Shit. Who was Dirck, the brother? Who was Joost? Who was Teuntje?

Peter shook his head dizzily. It must be time for bed. It was nearly two. He climbed the ladder and fell into his bunk. The last thing he heard was Laura sneezing and blowing her nose in the bed across the big room. She must have caught a cold, he thought before he drifted off.

He smelled coffee. His wristwatch informed him it was exactly six. The smell was wonderful, reminding him of dawn at Lake George, at the cabin, when he would lie in his sleeping bag and hear the early-morning voices of the others, brisk with energy but softened for those still sleeping. It never tasted as good as it smelled. Climbing quickly down his ladder, he found that she had started the Mr. Coffee.

"Hi," he called out. "You up?"

No reply. Maybe she had taken a cup back to bed with her. Maybe she had made it during the night. She wasn't in the bathroom.

He washed, shaved and dressed, poured a cup from the diner-style glass pot and took it over to the table where the journal still lay.

———————————◄○►———————————

He said Joost has bought a house in Antwerp to rent. Down by the water, in terrible shape. He is renovating it.

"He wants me to come down and help him," Dirck said. "What can I do with my family?"

"Why didn't he ask me?" I said.

"Well, you have the children."

"I can go anytime. What's he doing?"

"Everything. The stairs fell in. He's doing it all by himself."

I am done, except for some odd bits here and there. They are paying me the five hundred, fifty per figure minus the advance. We met in our bower yesterday, by the windmill, and there was trouble.

She went straight to it. "Why are we meeting here?"

"Why not?" I said. "It's a nice place and you can sit down out of the sun."

"You're ashamed of me."

"Now that's not true."

"You hide me, you don't want to be seen with me."

"Not true, and you know it. I care for you, Lysbeth, I care for you."

"You care about getting under my petticoats."

She pulled herself into a neat package, wrapping her skirts around her and tucking her hands under her legs on the stone bench.

"Don't say that. I've been finishing up the Guards portrait. And I may have to see my brother in Antwerp."

She awarded me a quick glance. Sometimes I understand her through and through, sometimes she is . . .

———————◄○►———————

It was definitely a sniffle. Peter, head up, listened.

She was crying. She was in the bedroom just beyond the bookshelf crying.

What to do? He shoved the book aside and sipped the last of his coffee. Take her some breakfast. No. Cook himself breakfast and offer her some. Maybe. With bacon.

He started frying the bacon first, then made all the noise he could as he whipped up the eggs in one of her nested aluminum bowls. He was good at breakfast. In a few minutes he had the bacon strips drying on a paper bag by the stove and was wrestling with the pan in the sink. Plenty of noise. He poured out the grease, then set the pan back on the burner with a crash.

That brought her out all right.

She was wearing a navy blue kimono and was blowing her nose. She shuffled across the bare floor in a pair of campy mules with pink fur.

"Oh hi," he said cheerily.

She took a long breath and said "Hi" in a small voice. She headed for the bathroom.

"You want some breakfast?"

"I don't think so."

She closed the door softly behind her. The shower ran for a long time, and when she came out her skin glowed. It became her more than her usual pallor.

"Come on," Peter said. "I can scramble you an egg in two minutes."

She smiled wanly. "Maybe in a minute," she said, scuffing her way back to the bedroom.

When she didn't come out and didn't come out, Peter ventured to the edge of the bookcase and knocked on the wood. There was no answer, so he nervously poked his head in. She was sitting, fully dressed, on the neatly made bed, her back to him, her head down. She didn't seem to be crying, but she clutched a balled handkerchief in both hands. She looked up at him and froze. There was panic in her eyes.

"Sorry," he mumbled. He had never had anyone panic at the sight of him.

For a long moment she sat there, rigid. Then she relaxed. "It's all right. I'm all right."

"Sorry," he said again. "Just thought you might want to—"

She lifted her head abruptly and smiled with effort. "No, I'm just cleaning out some cobwebs here. I was a real moron to go with—"

"He sounds like a prime jerk to me."

She laughed a single sharp laugh. "You got that right. He is a prime jerk. He—"

Then she was turning away again and Peter was sitting beside her on the edge of the bed. Experimentally, he rested his arm across her shoulders. She twitched. He removed the arm and sat still.

With sudden energy she turned to face him, her eyes so close he had to look at them one at a time. "We were in this sweet little place outside Avignon, a little country inn, you know? With about six rooms, and they were going out of their way to make it nice for us. And he . . . he was just awful, he demanded this and demanded that, his food wasn't right, the waiter was slow, he was bullying everybody. He complained about the mosquito in our room. One mosquito! I just wanted to cringe, I wanted to sink through the floor. He said the wine list wasn't good enough for him, so he drove all the way back into Avignon to get some better wine. Imagine. In France."

"Jeez. He must know his wines."

She snorted. "No he doesn't. He gets a wine magazine."

She was shivering. She turned to him and took his hand, startling him. Then she dropped it.

"We went on to Arles, and he didn't like the place we had reservations for, and we were driving all over the valley, and if you know those horrible little two-lane roads they have there, you know what that means. Traffic and trucks and commuters and you name it. We wound up spending the night in a motel."

She sniffed. He put his arm firmly around her now and she pressed comfortably closer. She was talking very low, almost in a whisper.

"Then we couldn't get breakfast at that place so we hit the highway again, and by this time he was blaming everything on me, and he said it was my fault we were missing breakfast and that was why I was so skinny and I was probably anorexic."

Peter was softly stroking her shoulder. "No," he was whispering, "no no, that's not true, you look terrific, what does he know? You look great."

All at once she faced him, wide-eyed, and for an instant he

thought they were going to kiss. But she moved away and sat up straight.

"I used to be," she said briskly. "I was extremely skinny and never ate anything. I was in therapy for two years. I still have to make myself eat sometimes. Speaking of breakfast . . . "

They had scrambled eggs together at the table, chatting like old friends. "How's Amy?" she asked during a silence.

"Oh, Amy's—" He chose his words with some care. "Amy always lands on her feet."

He wanted to take her in his arms but didn't think she would let him. Leopold watched them from the sofa arm. Dave curvetted underfoot, brushing against their legs. After a while Laura said she should get across town to her job at Lovely Lady and take back the rest of her vacation time. Mr. Meyerowitz would let her do that, she said. Mr. Meyerowitz was still rubbing his hands in glee over the way she had redesigned a jacket last month and saved a button.

Peter thought he really should say something about looking for another place, but in the end he decided to let her bring it up. By the time he got the dishes done and the cats fed and their box cleaned out it was almost noon.

———————————◄○►———————————

. . . sometimes she is a total mystery to me.

"You are so thin, Hals."

My God, the way her mind jumps around.

"It's just that I stopped drinking beer."

"I bet you live on herring and bread."

In another minute she would be telling me how to cure Margaretha's cough and asking about their shitting habits. Let me put this down. I do not like Neeltje. I hate to feel her presence in the house. I am tired of the smell of small children. I am tired of eating bread, bread with sausage, bread with gravy, bread with herring in sour cream, bread with berry preserves, bread broken into my boiled egg, bread with butter that has lain around the kitchen too long and has an edge on it.

But I will not marry. I am done with marriage.

"If I want fancy cooking I go to the tavern," I said. I left her sitting there looking across the fields.

Today there was a meeting and I painted in the banquet foods. I am still laughing at old van der Meer, whose stomach is so huge he can barely reach the table to eat. He was putting down one beer after another, his nose getting redder and redder, when suddenly he takes it in his mind that van Offenberg has insulted him. And Offenberg, the most sensible in the bunch, newly made an ensign, had been doing all right too with the beer. In a minute hands were on sword hilts and people were scrambling and shouting as though the Spaniards were at the door, and Offenberg was carving up the air and prancing about and ready to make a fool of him (quite a good sword, I am told, though too young to have fought in the war, of course), and van der Meer was trying to get his sword out of the scabbard. But he was so full of beer that he couldn't. There he was, struggling around, dancing with himself, jerking and tugging at the damn thing by his side, and Offenberg cavorting about him and sticking the air with his point and mocking him. Finally he makes a giant effort, twists himself half in two and at last yanks the sword loose. And at the same instant lets loose the most enormous fart I have ever heard in my life, even counting the time Teuntje's horse got into the bran. An explosion! A cannon! With reverberations and aftershocks that went on for I don't know how long. Everyone screeched and howled. That clown Offenberg reared back, hands in the air, hat flying off, as though blown to bits. And then came forward, bowed low and presented his sword hilt-first in surrender. Would van der Meer laugh? Certainly not. Stomped out mortally insulted.

August fourth. I go to Antwerp tomorrow. Last night I crept to her door and knocked and she let me in without a word and whisked me into her room. We held each other. I told her to write and send me a message by Dirck. On Marktstraat, the house with the scaffolding on it. And I will be on the scaffolding, no doubt.

August seventh. Joost surprised to see me.

"Why didn't you ask me?" I said. "I'm ready to help."

"I don't know. Thought you'd be tied up."

Antwerp is very noisy. I was born here, but I remember nothing. Maybe I remember the smell. You smell the sea everywhere, and the people walk faster and talk louder. The smell of fish and wood smoke and tar and shit. People knock against you on the street. Everyone much better dressed than at home, some of them even in ruffs. The men all in shiny black. The guildhalls were something to see, we have nothing like that in Haarlem. Great jutting buildings, carved stone, very grand, though made of plain bricks behind the facade. The decorations on some of them are fantastic. Gables everywhere. Coats of arms and various emblems carved in relief and stuck up there. Fancy urns and vases of stone balanced on top of every promontory, ready to fall in the next high wind. I thought it was all a bit too much.

There is a great open space near the docks, kind of rough with a lot of sailors there, dark people, Orientals. What a world this is. In the main square, which is huge, bigger even than ours, there are paving stones rather than cobbles, big flat slate squares that give off a hollow sound. It was still wet after the rain, and some of the women had their clogs on, country people, and I tell you, the wooden clacking of a hundred, two hundred heavy clogs, it is an awesome sound, a kind of friendly thunder.

And the diamond market, I couldn't believe it. The shops one after the other where you go in and sit before a table and they lay a treasure in front of you on black velvet. Much quiet trading, merchants very secretive with their little leather bags hardly bigger than my thumb. They stay near the docks — I suppose to be closer to the ships that bring in the stones from far parts of the world.

Pepper! I saw a basket of peppercorns as big as my washtub. What would that be worth? Windows loaded with things of silver, wine buckets, sword handles, I don't know what. Whole table services of silver, whether solid or not I couldn't say.

I bought her an elegant silk scarf in . . .

---◀○▶---

Hmmm. The word was *pars*. Peter didn't know it. He wondered whether it could be an archaism of some sort. Or it could be a misspelling of *paars,* which meant "violet." That must be it. Violet would look great on the black-haired woman he saw in his mind as Lysbeth.

---◀○▶---

. . . elegant silk scarf in violet at a fancy store. Bought a pipe for Joost.

For quite a while I stood around the docks and watched the ships loading and the tackle rising in the air and the men climbing about the rigging. I think about what it must be like in other climates, in hot places with mountains jutting abruptly from the landscape, exotic vines and trees shining in the constant sunshine. And far cities, where the people are black or yellow or brown, wonderful faces so different from our pink puddings. What I would give to go away on one of those ships, sail over the horizon. To Sumatra, perhaps. Wherever that may be.

Joost took me to his favorite pub, the Bulldog, last night and proceeded to get drunk. My treat, I insisted. The beer is darker and heavier and has a sweet undertaste that I don't like at all. I stuck to wine. The place was rank. There is a story that when a taxi barge goes down a river with a full load of passengers, the very foxes are smoked out of their holes in the bank. When we got out, after midnight, my throat was raw and my clothes stank.

Joost was weaving down the street, proud of himself because he thought he looked all right. When we got home he started with the home truths.

"You were the favorite," he said. "Always." And how I always got the white meat, and Ma would take me into her bed when I had a bad dream, and I got all the best commissions. That was what it was really about. I said, What does it matter? You're a painter, I'm a painter, and Dirck too—we're all painters, and we'll have some good times and get drunk a few times and have a woman a few times and then we'll get old and die and be forgotten and so what? The paintings will crack and fade and get burned up in house fires and drowned in floods and no one will remember who they are of and so what? I say make the most of it while we have it and quit wringing our hands over our childhood. Oh, I was eloquent.

Joost thought about it for five minutes, his eyes focusing and refocusing on various objects. Then he said, "You're right, brother. Let's go to bed."

He is a funny guy. I had forgotten.

First day of September. What a day. I have a glorious new hat, black as a cuttlefish, with a great wide brim and high crown. I practice the sweeping Gascon bow. All it needs is a feather. I am young and dashing when I walk the streets now, and I peep in the shop windows to glimpse myself parading past. Walked out to the fields. J had to grind paints for his new commission so no work on the house today. I went out beyond the wall to the fields I came through on the way here. Surprising, there are still patches underwater from the flooding.

Does not smell so sweet as home, rather a relief. Small farms, little squares of fertile ground each with its shock of green. The earth like a gigantic head covered with green hair. The sky like a great curving lens on the giant's eyeball and me a mote in it. I lay flat out on the platform of an abandoned mill (the proud hat carefully braced against a wall so the wind won't get it), the wood gone silvery with many rains, split and curling at the ends, hot under the sun.

———————————————◄o►———————————————

The phone. He was so far off that it actually startled him. When he picked up the receiver a voice was waiting there, didn't give him a chance even to say hello.

"Where were you?" It was a shout.

"What? Who is this?"

"This is Harold Corwin. You were supposed to be here at nine o'clock."

"Oh my God. I was. That's right. Jeez, I'm sorry. Something came up—"

"Forget it."

"I can get there in twenty minutes—"

"Forget it, kid. I got Ettman. He came right over."

"Oh boy. Mr. Corwin, I really—"

"See ya around, kid," the voice roared, not unkindly. The phone clicked off.

Peter sighed and stared across the room, sharply aware that very soon he should get hold of himself and organize his life—very soon.

He ate twenty-four seedless grapes that he found in the refrigerator and an apple-cinnamon granola bar and returned to his story. It was getting so he preferred the life of Hals, or whoever it was, to his own. It made more sense, anyway. But he must look up this business in Antwerp. And was the man born there? That didn't seem right, he being so involved in Haarlem.

But it was true. It was in the book, baptized in Antwerp, apparently in 1582, and his brother Joost two years later, and Dirck after that. Everything checked—except Teuntje, some relative no doubt.

Here in the city you become more aware that times are not so good. More beggars, abandoned mills, flooded fields. She is nothing but a jumped-up peasant woman. She has not written me a word. She has been asking questions about me. I think she would be ferocious defending her children. Ferocious with me too, if I crossed her. But a woman I can talk to.

I put this down September fourth. They are burying little Margaretha this day.

I was squatting in the courtyard, cracking bricks in two and shaping them to the curve of the walk, crooning to myself in the sun, when Dirck walks in. Like that. I can hear the outer door creak in its weary way and he is standing before me, handsome as ever, the youthful beard working hard to cover up the awful fact that he is only twenty-five.

I stand up, delighted. But see his face.

"I'm so sorry," he says. "Got here as soon as I could. Didn't want to send anyone. I have terrible news, Frans."

"Who is it?" I said. Racking my mind. Our mother? Preparing.

"Your little girl," he said, "she took a fever and they couldn't break it, she just burned up with it."

I felt nothing. Nothing. My brain sorted methodically through the facts. And Neeltje?

"She was no help. She called the doctor, the one in the square. She said he knew the girl from before. But there was nothing to be done. She is frantic, you know. She doesn't know what to do with herself. She wanted to come here with the boy, but I said to stay put."

I couldn't grasp it. I sat down on the bricks. Joost came out all covered with plaster dust, his white hands brushing at his pants.

"There was nothing to be done. Neeltje came straight to my

house running through the streets with Harmen in her arms because she couldn't leave him there."

He kept talking and talking. I have no idea what he was saying. I got up and said I would take the next coach back.

"There is one in the morning," he said. "From the square."

I have all evening here to wait. Joost and Dirck have gone out to get some food. They cannot bear to be with me, I think. I sit here at the table examining the worn wood, the gouge made by someone's knife, the circles from beer mugs, the delicate half-moon line burned in by a hot pot. Someone has tried to polish it but the polish has just sunk in. I have only seventy guilders plus the hundred I left back home. Where did it go?

I am weary. I am weary.

Margaretha. Her mother's golden hair, fine as silk, her mother's little nose. I should never have left. It bores into me. I have betrayed them, my family, my Annie. Harmen, his fifth name day only two days ago, I had a toy clay pipe for him to blow bubbles with, left it with Neeltje, and she was going to give him a special feast, a berry tart. I was not there for his name day. I was not there when Margaretha woke in the night crying and sweating and coughing uncontrollably. I have to be here through the night, until the coach leaves. I would run there if I could. If I could sleep! She is in the ground by now.

Home again. Neeltje in a desperate state. At least a decent burial. I took Harmen on my lap. Where is Margie? He is confused. I stroke his blond head and talk quietly, I have no idea what I said. I cannot write about this.

October fourteenth. Neeltje. Why is she doing this? For five guilders!

I am going away again. Dirck says there are accusations that I beat my wife. That I am a scandalous drunk.

What? Impossible.

How can they know? It was nothing, I slapped her on the back once or twice when she coughed. For this I have tormented myself all year. How can anyone know?

Saw Laurensen at Town Hall and he looked strangely at me, so I went straight up to him and said, "Brother, you look as if you'd seen a ghost." He muttered and turned away in embarrassment, but I pursued him. "I hear there is a rumor around about me."

"Well," he said, "I did hear something."

"You heard wrong. You know I'm not a boozer, you saw me at the banquet. Right? I wasn't drinking a thing."

"Yes," he said, ashamed of himself, head hanging.

"Well who is saying this? Where is this coming from?"

"My wife heard it in the market."

Good God. Now I will have to publish an announcement or something. How do these things happen?

"This is really strange," I said. "I haven't even been in town for a month."

"I didn't think it was true, you know," he said.

"So what else is there? That I beat my wife?"

He nodded, and I laughed. "This is ridiculous! My wife died well over a year ago, everyone knows that. Someone is playing games, and I'm going to find out who."

I spent the morning talking to various people, mad Bobbe the fishwife and the girls in the bakery who always know everything, Pastor Leenders at the cathedral. He'd heard it too, and I told him to take some action if he heard it again. He knew it wasn't true, couldn't be true. Said he would do what he could, and for once he didn't scold me about not coming to church. He has forgotten that I never converted like Dirck and Joost. It means nothing to me, though I can't explain this to my mother. She is desolate. Women see more in church than men do.

Everyone admits to hearing it, but nobody says they believed it. I still get odd looks, and I think strangers are pointing me out behind my back.

I thought I saw her coming out of St. Bavo yesterday. I don't want to see her. Then later the same person perhaps, standing in front of me in the crowd at the bakery to get our Sunday meat, just the partial profile, that line, forehead and cheek and strong bulge where the brow began. Uncanny. But it wasn't her. It gave me a start.

It is cleared up. I went to Town Hall and talked to two of the councillors and demanded action. But they were ahead of me. They had heard about it (Pastor Leenders).

They gave me great big smiles and told me: There is another Frans Hals!

Really. I could believe anything now.

They called in the sheriff, a grossly fat man named de Bie with a swollen fiery red face who cannot possibly live another two years, and he said, Yes, you have a namesake, and he lives in this town, and he has been arrested.

I must have looked stupid gaping at de Bie's great fat shiny lips as they spread in a great fat shiny grin. In any case everyone laughed. A great deal of laughter. The sheriff clapping me on the back. Everyone is mightily embarrassed but no one will say so. It is to be a joke. I knew of a Hals family not related to us but never heard of a Frans. My mother is so relieved. So she says. She is relieved! What about me!

I am going out of town. The woman Neeltje pursues me. Thirty-seven guilders and four stuivers. My mother will go to court for me, I cannot deal with this. To pay the woman after she let the girl die.

I say this here, that I let her die too, I was impatient with her sickness and went away partly to get out of the house, simply not to have to hear her coughing and coughing. That sound in that house. I can't think about it yet.

---

15 November. Will it never stop? I am pursued. I haven't painted in a week. My mother went to court for me and got the commissioners to reduce it to thirty guilders (like Judas) and said I would pay that much. It was taken out of what's left from the Guards. They gave her two days but insisted that the full 37.4 be attached, because then Neeltje was ordered to explain exactly why the other seven were due to her.

I was there myself today and had it out with her. I hadn't given her enough to cover the little stockings she had bought for the children. So she said. I thought those were her gifts to the kids. She certainly acted like it, carrying on and simpering and letting them thank her. She said no, I had mentioned the house was too cold and they needed something on their legs and ankles.

This is all too tiresome. The commissioners threw their hands in the air at this childish bickering and said we'll split it. So I am to give her three guilders, twelve stuivers, and the court gets sixteen in court costs. They are all taking my money. My substance is being drained away from me by these vampires. The world is sucking my blood.

She has left town. I watched her house for an hour yesterday until a neighbor girl came out, and she said, Oh Miss Lysbeth has gone, and the little idiot didn't know where or wasn't telling. Maybe I will leave a letter for her. Think about it.

I have a girl for Harmen. He needs someone around him all the time. It is dawning on him. His mother and now his sister. A sad little boy. I draw pictures for him, but he is used to that, I always did that. She lives next door. Her name is Isabella and she is a Berck, some sort of connection of the Coymanses, as her mother let me know right away. No one on earth is so haughty about money as poor relations. She is just sixteen and will work days only — they are nervous about the scandal of her being in the house with me. I said it was all right with me if she took him back to her own house sometimes. Her mother knows I am all right. I suspect she wants to get the girl out from underfoot. Not a very pretty girl, the chin very underslung and the mouth too small, a shy mouth given to trembling.

But sweet frightened eyes. Has probably been filled full of tales of what men will do to her. We talk, shyly. Her schoolwork. Her father was a seaman who went down with his grain ship in the Baltic. He goes off one day and is never heard from again. Awful not to know. Two years ago, but she is still wistful. We have death in common. I do sketches of her, which makes her able to talk because she doesn't have to look at me but can stare at the place on the wall I have indicated. Harmen loves her already.

I am working on the miniature of the schoolmaster Schrevelius, he comes in to pose. She talks to him too, imagine, here she is with these two old bearded men, probably older than her father. She knew Schrevelius from infant school, his classes were in the same building then. I am not happy working on copper. It wants me to be slick and smooth, and I refuse.

We are a jolly little group, though the house is cold most of the time. This is one of the worst winters I can remember. We are having a little school here. Tell me about the Siege, she says, cutting up carrots for Harmen's lunch. The Siege, he says, carefully not breaking his pose. Were you in it? she says. Oh, it was much too long ago for me, he says, and he winks at me. He likes my work. He is writing a history of Haarlem, and he promises to put me in it.

———

Where has Lysbeth gone and why no letter? It is almost St. Nicholas Day.

———

Well! Harmen was up at dawn this day, jumping onto my bed. The sudden sharp ache that there were not the two of them. I put it away. He is valiant. He does not talk about her.

"Happy Saint Nicholas!" And he gives me my present, wrapped in fancy printed paper all the colors of the rainbow, from the East I suppose, where on earth did he get it?

The present almost makes me cry. It is a stand for my pipe, made of clay and baked at the bakery and painted a rather spectacular red. It is shaped like a goblet with a base nicely scalloped with his little finger marks all around and a sort of nest for the pipe to be set into, bowl-down. "So you can leave it there while the pipe's going," he said, leaning over my shoulder to help me admire it as we sat in the bed. I am forever trying to smoke when I work, but I get absorbed and set the pipe down, and it spills ashes. And then goes out and I get paint on it when I pick it up to light again. I have nothing but good briars. I hate these clay pipes. They stick to your lips and break in three weeks.

Then I got up and brought him his, unfortunately wrapped only in the flimsy boxes they came in. I had hidden them on top of Annie's armoire, an enormous ornate thing of tortured oak with Corinthian capitals and naked nymphs and grape leaves and twining carved branches, all varnished half to death so it gleams like a mackerel.

He got back onto the huge bed (we used to call it our boat, it is so big, the four of us all jumbled on it in a tangle of blankets on a Sunday morning, tickling and laughing, Margaretha's little-girl rippling laugh, o silvery madness! and Harmen trying to climb the bedposts) and under the puff because of the cold. He opened the first box ceremoniously. It was lead soldiers, forty of them I think, and in the other were two wooden ships designed to hold them. The ships have flat bottoms so you push them across the floor. With real cloth sails that go up and down. He was speechless.

81

"They're all Dutch," I said, "but you can play Spanish wars anyway."

He picked up one figure after another. They are quite well done, some firing muskets, some kneeling to load, some marching. He hugged me. He comes to me often these days, wants to be held, even picked up. Dirck says it will make him babyish. I don't care.

We didn't go to church. I had bought some Brussels cakes for breakfast, with jam. He had a lump of sugar dipped in my coffee. It was always a treat for being brave when he got cut or something. We worked together, Harmen and I, to get past all these little hidden traps, things that would suddenly remind us. He would see me hesitate over some small detail, the way I buttered the cake for him perhaps, the way it used to be, and he'd chirp out some funny remark to distract me. He touched me more than usual. I hugged him once because he was being so brave.

I sluiced the tiles and brought down the upstairs rug to make the kitchen look more like a parlor. It was the only really warm room in the house, and with the sun streaming in through the diamond windows on both sides and my landscapes on the walls, four of them, nice bright scenes if I do say so myself, one of them from when I was sixteen and dreaming of being a painter, it was as pretty as any Coymans drawing room.

———————◄○►———————

Peter shook his head. He was getting fuzzy. The narrative had carried him along at top speed, but now he became aware of the fading sun as the light gradually shifted in the big room, light that was softer and more sensible than at noon.

He checked the records for 1616, September fourth, and found the burial notice for an unnamed child of Hals's first marriage. And there, just below it, was an item about a debt owed to one Neeltgen Leenders, five guilders for expenses, and the lawsuit that arose from it. Several documents from the Court of Petty Session followed in the catalog, ending with the information that Hals finally paid three guilders and twelve stuivers. The commentary concluded with the fact that, according to these court records, Hals visited Antwerp before August sixth of that year and returned between the eleventh and fifteenth of November.

It all checked. It checked uncannily. No doubt the hoaxer, if there was one, had used the same sources as the catalog. But Peter had the impression that most of this scholarly commentary was very recent. Apparently a good deal of work on Hals had been done by an art historian named Abraham Bredius, published as early as 1913. A hoaxer could have used antique paper and homemade ink and could have stored the books for several years to let the ink age. But how reliable was Bredius? And did he have access to the Court of Petty Sessions records? Someone would have had to do a lot of research here. It was hard to imagine a hoaxer content to do his work, then simply to hide the books and finish his own life without making sure he would be around for the great discovery.

3

When Laura came home Peter had chicken breasts, rice and string beans ready, and a cheap but nice California wine. She seemed somewhat cheered to find him still around. She said he shouldn't have gone to all that trouble, that she was just planning to make a tuna fish sandwich. He said it was nothing, it was the least he could do. They sat over dinner for some time, finishing the bottle and digging into the partly crystallized quart of ice cream from her freezer.

He told her about his boyhood in Cicero, in the upstairs apartment with the bay window that looked exactly like the gangster apartments in those thirties movies with Edward G. Robinson and Paul Muni. He recounted the rise of his brother Tony, who received a sculpture in solid dark chocolate from Switzerland every Christmas, and one year a perfect copy of a Henry Moore mother and child. He also described the life and death of his mother, whom they always knew as Marie. He skimmed over his academic career, of which he was not proud, but talked for several minutes about Hals. Then he remembered that he wasn't supposed to tell anyone and so swore her to secrecy.

Laura said she came from way upstate in New York, a place

called Utica, which was full of Italians. Are you Italian? he said. My mother is, she said. The name was Hauss before it turned into House. Her father was with a big insurance company and her mother was a docent for the local art museum, the Munson Williams Proctor Institute.

That was how she had gotten the job at the Modern, she said. But she had quickly discovered that she was a fabric designer at heart and got the job at Lovely Lady over in the Garment District. This last year, she said, she had been getting interested in the economics of the thing. Do you have any idea how much you save if you have two buttons instead of three? And when he shook his head she went on and told him at some length. I love it, she said, her eyes glistening. I can hardly wait to get to work, and I work right through to six or seven sometimes. I can believe it, he replied, though really he didn't, for he had never had a full-time job of any sort.

Then they adjourned to the sofa with espresso cups and started to talk about George.

"What really did it," she said finally, "was like I say, we had this fight over whether I was anorexic. He was really getting into it. He was looking at me like I was a frog he was dissecting, and he didn't like my hair, he didn't think I shaved my legs enough, and he said I had garlic breath. I just suddenly realized that this guy not only hated me but hated all the women he'd ever gone out with. He had garlic breath too, you know, everyone has garlic breath in France. It just came to me: This one is not for me. So that was it. I said, Take me to the bus station. We were still in Arles. We were lost, been driving in circles, but I saw the bus station a few blocks back. So he took me to the bus station and I got out and he drove off."

"Charming," Peter muttered.

Leopold lay between them, and Laura was stroking him

idly. Peter reached over to pat the cat but found Laura's hand and stroked that instead. She looked at the hand being stroked.

They were kissing. Her lips were fuller than they looked, and softer than the softest pillow. Peter was thinking about cool roommates who lived together for months without touching. His hand was caressing her hair, the sleekness, the fineness of it, the way it ended just above her shoulders in a soft brush, so soft that you could gather some of it between your fingers and brush her skin with it. She was leaning back into the sofa pillows. His hand was on her breast, very small but beautifully rounded, cuppable. His elbow was caught between the pillows and he pulled it out; now she was lying on the sofa beneath him.

She squirmed and brought up her forearms. Her hands crossed before his face. "Wait," she whispered.

He pulled back, surprised. She sat up. "Sorry," she said. "I'm sorry. I can't do this. I have . . . "

He moved to the far end of the sofa.

"Peter, I'm sorry."

"It's all right."

"It's that . . . "

"I understand. Forget it. I'm a jerk."

"No you're not, Peter." She was still breathing hard. "You're not. I have . . . it's just that I have to work out—"

"Forget it. It's okay. It's okay."

It was that goddamn George. He got up, went to the table and picked up the book. She watched him as he bent his head to it, trying to read. After a few minutes she went to the bathroom, and he was able to make sense of the words before him.

———————◄◦►———————

I stepped out before they came. The air was so cold it crackled in your nostrils when you breathed. The sun was blinding, flashing off the new snow. Everything was beautiful, the sheds, the outhouses, the pollarded trees, the rain barrels and various other ungainly things all transformed into lovely smooth-curving white creations. A few people were out, and everyone nodded and smiled and tipped hats. Me with my new hat. I walked down to the canal, which was frozen and snowed over. The gulls would come down and land on it and skid. They would keep swooping down and doing it again. Do birds play? I think so. Mrs. Berck came over with Isabella. They are alone too, the older children staying in Amsterdam with her sister. And later Schrevelius dropped in. He lives by himself, and I insisted he have dinner with us. So glad that stupid Neeltje is gone. She cast gloom over every meal.

Mrs. Berck came in carrying an enormous covered dish, Isabella holding the door open for her. She is stout, with a slight, fragile face that has started to go to fat but is still pretty in a wan sort of way. They were both dressed for church, caps and ruffs and elegant starched cuffs. They must have been working for days to cook all this. The St. Nicholas cake came on the second trip, a glorious cathedral of white frosting with spires and turrets and a ring of nicely executed rose blossoms around the rim. And pots of creamed onions and vinegared beets and potatoes fried in disks thin as a coin.

I was in charge of the booze. I had laid in ale and a magnum of pretty good Bordeaux, allegedly French, and lemon geneva. This is a day drink, sharp and acid and strong, yet light on the tongue and never bites. I had left the bottle on the sill in the shed to get good and cold. The aged stuff I prefer warm as the air.

"Have a drop," I told Mrs. Berck, and she said indeed she would, which surprised me. I had taken her for a Calvinist. While we toasted one another, Isabella came back in carrying a large wooden shoe filled with gingerbread men. I haven't seen that since I was a child.

"She made them herself," her mother said. Harmen headed straight for them, but we only let him have one for now.

Schrevelius arrived about noon, stamping his boots at the door, bundled in a fur hat and greatcoat. He is getting bald but still has quite a bit of light auburn hair and a somewhat stringy beard. High forehead, bulb-ended nose, quizzical expression that seems to me more skeptical than anxious. He wanted me to call him Theodore and he brought a full bottle of very old brandy from Cognac. It was superb, and I should know.

Well! The old man and Cornelia Berck hit it off from the first minute. "Mijnheer Professor!" she sings out. "What makes the whales come and die on our beaches?" Her daughter stands there aghast, mouth open in horror at this familiarity. But Mrs. Berck has spotted a sparkle in those watchful eyes.

"What?" he says. "No idea. I'm as baffled as you."

"But you're a professor!"

"Ah." He chuckled. "You have me there. You are tempting me. I could give you a whole lecture, and it would all be made up."

I said perhaps it was the cold winter. No, he said, we have been having whale beachings for years, all up and down our coasts.

"Let's reason it out," he says. "Whales are big as ships, correct? They need deep water. Now, whales have eyes on either side of their heads. The eyes don't work together, they never see the same thing at the same time. Now, to judge distance, you need two eyes that focus and make a triangle with the object, correct?"

"Right!" says Mrs. Berck, smiling in triumph at getting a free lecture, knowledge being dispensed exclusively for her. "If you close one eye, it's harder to tell how far away things are. I had a brother in the fleet with one eye, and he could never —"

"Exactly. Precisely," says Schrevelius, the bit in his teeth now, "if the whale can't judge distance with his eyes, he must have some other means. As we know, whales roam the seven seas and surely know perfectly well where they are going."

Mrs. Berck stopped stirring the gravy and concentrated on his intent face. He raised a pedagogic finger.

"So they have some other way of triangulating. Wouldn't you think? What it is, I have no idea. But doesn't it sound logical?"

"Like homing pigeons," Mrs. Berck offered.

"Wonderful. You're brilliant. Some organ we know nothing of, correct? Now, the thing is, suppose this organ requires deep water to work in. And suppose the whale wanders up on our shallow shores. All along the Zeeland coast it is very shallow and gradual, you know, like a shelf."

"So the whale—"

"Exactly." He beams. He is teaching. "The whale swims along there, and he can only see out of one side of his face at a time, and his special organ—"

"It's blocked. It needs deep water, so it can't work. Like a farsighted person."

"Precisely, my dear Mrs. Berck."

"Oh, do call me Cornelia."

He grew more elfin by the minute. By the time dinner was ready his nose was red as a hot poker and his hair stood out in all directions in a fine nimbus. He has a strong basso and led us in some songs, the children piping up boldly. They have trusted him from the start. We were well into the geneva when Mrs. Berck announced that all was ready.

We sat down at the best table. I had brought out my family silver, what there is of it, a dozen spoons and assorted forks from three different sets of ancestors, and some very old wooden-handled knives that were Annie's. An arrangement of mistletoe and holly as the centerpiece (the children in charge of that). My old tablecloth with the burn hole nicely concealed under a serving dish.

She swept the cover off the platter, and there sat the biggest goose I have ever seen! A beautiful goose! Cooked in her own oven, which she is so proud of ("the baker always overcooks everything, and never bastes!"), and magically tender. The stuffing was rich with hazelnuts and chestnut mash, and the gravy was studded with sour currants, a delicious surprise.

Oh how we tucked in, passing the onions and beets and celery and curried rice, the haystack of crisp little potato wafers, a prune pudding that worked magnificently with the meat. Everyone chattering. I carved. It has been years since I carved a goose, and they are the devil to manage, the joint sinews strong as wire, but with plenty of advice from the professor and Isabella, on my right, I did a fair job. I felt like a patriarch, handing the plates down the table to this one and that one, all the faces turned up toward me, or rather toward the goose, watching it gradually disappear.

Schrevelius asked us conundrums and puzzles. "A boat sits in the harbor with a ladder hanging over the side. The ladder steps are eight inches apart, and there are six steps visible above the water. The tide rises twenty inches. How many steps are visible now?"

We scratched our heads. Impossible. Too hard. Would call for pen and paper. Until Isabella shouted out, her mouth full of rice, "Six! It rises with the tide!"

It was the first time I ever heard her shout.

Then a quiet spell while we gazed over the wreckage of our feast and Isabella cleared. The goose was nothing but a skeleton, its bones dry as parchment. Schrevelius had brought a small tin of flavored ices that the confectioner hawks at this time of year, and we each had a very genteel helping, for it is quite dear. "Clears the passages," he announced.

We talked about skating and agreed we would all meet again for a grand skating party. Schrevelius told stories of his boyhood in Amsterdam, his wild days at university. Then Mrs. Berck spotted the old mandolin on the wall and brought it down and sang "The Rose Garden" in a tiny, sweet voice. The big logs in the fireplace had by now crashed and crumbled, spitting sparks at each new collapse, and I put on a new one, so heavy I had to heft it on my thigh to set it in there right.

At last it was time for the cake, as Harmen had been remarking for some time now, and what a cake it was. I removed the steeple, which turned out to be a separate cake on top of the main one, which was big as a cheese wheel. The cake itself was white and fluffy, laced with layers of nuts and sweet cinnamon. I was afraid Harmen would burst.

"You must take some of this home with you," Mrs. Berck said when Schrevelius volunteered for a second piece. There is enough for us all for three days. We were exhausted. The room was so warm I had to open the windows.

The cognac went around once or twice, followed by strong mocha coffee that I had brought back from Antwerp, bought out of a barrel right on the docks. We ground it in the pestle, to great hilarity. Coffee was new to Mrs. Berck, but I told her with the air of a world traveler that in some countries it is taken daily. The children drifted away, Harmen to play with his soldiers (I found him an hour later, fast asleep on the floor in his room, surrounded by his armies) and Isabella back to her house with her mother. Schrevelius attempted to sit up and make conversation with me, but he was nodding, as was I, so I insisted that he take a nap before struggling out into the cold.

It was nearly dark by now and a raw wind was rising. When I slipped out to the outhouse I could see the powder snow being blown off the top of the shed in a fine white curtain. I gave him the big bed and stretched out on Neeltje's bed upstairs. He was so grateful. He was not looking forward to going back to his empty house. I know he is married, but he doesn't talk about a wife. So many solitary souls out there.

I woke up an hour later (an hour! I never nap!) and went down to sit before the fire with my pipe and my new pipe stand. The ladies had taken the dinner away, leaving a semicircle of cake, and the dishes and silver were stacked neatly in a washbasin.

91

I filled with my Avocaat, a rather expensive but wonderfully smooth tobacco, not sweet but with perhaps the slightest touch of anise. It also has a streak of perique in it and a pitchy dash of Turkish. The smoke makes me think of wood fires and boyhood. I settled back and let the wind whine outside. I wonder whether blind men smoke. I thought about the day and the sound of laughter in this house again, and after awhile Schrevelius stole into the room, all but rubbing his eyes, and we passed the cognac back and forth a couple of times and smoked and looked at the fire, which was almost out, little winking points of bright light in the blackness, a miniature city at night.

1617

The year is two days old. Did I deserve this? Last night I was coming home from the Town Hall, where I had some business, when I saw two hulking men in my path. I had just turned into our street and was approaching the house when they seemed to pop up from nowhere, blocking my path. It was totally dark, no moon, not a sliver of light from the houses around. It was snow all about, which gave some lightness, but not enough to see who they were — aside from the fact that I didn't know them, or wish to.

At first I tried to think they had nothing to do with me and I began to sidle past them, but they sidestepped and faced me squarely.

I thought, Oh God, the other Hals. What has he done now?

One of them crossed his arms and blocked my path. He stood about a head taller than I. Big rangy guy with a slouch hat and soldier's boots.

"You Frans Hals?" he said.

I said, "Yes."

The other one stood at his shoulder, just as tall. Younger.

I said, "I think you have the wrong man."

"No," he said. "You live here?"

"Well, yes."

"Frans Hals the painter?"

I shrugged. "What is it?" I said. I thought, Who do I owe now?

"Our name is Reynier," the younger one said in his higher voice.

"Ah."

"Lysbeth is our sister."

"Ah." If they thought they were going to keep me from her they were sadly mistaken.

"You know her."

"Yes. I haven't seen her since I got back from Antwerp. I don't know where she's gone."

The first one leaned close to me. Lantern jaw, no beard but stubble whiskers, heavy cheekbones, burning eyes deep in their sockets.

"You don't know?" he growled. I was baffled, and my feet were getting cold. Harmen would be waiting.

"No, I don't know what this is about. I wrote her and she never answered."

This seemed to stagger them temporarily. They exchanged a glance.

"She can't read," the younger one said accusingly.

Now I was staggered. I had no idea. Annie could read and write as well as any man. I shrugged again.

"So where is she?" I demanded, feeling that the initiative had passed to me. I was wrong.

"She's having a baby," the older man said with great clarity, his breath making a cloud.

I forgot what I said. I asked how I could see her. I wanted to see her. I think about her all the time.

"And why do you tell me?" I said, or something along that line.

"We knew where to come."

"Well," I said, "why didn't she let me know? How was I to know, if she left town like that?"

"You going to ask her?" asked the older one, his deep eyes fixing me like a snake.

"I beg your pardon."

"You heard me."

I shrugged. "This is the first I knew she was pregnant."

"Well?"

"Well yourself. I haven't asked her."

"So, when you going to stand up with her?"

"That's up to her, isn't it. What you think I am?"

His face broke into a slight smile. I could have run him through. He put his hands on his hips. "She's at Zandvoort with her aunt Colterman."

"On the Heerenstraat," the other chimed in. Both watched me closely. I'm not sure what they expected me to do.

"Well I'm certainly glad to know that," I said boldly. "I'll go find her."

"You do that."

I walked there this morning. It is only six miles or so, time to think. My doom seemed to be closing in on me, marriage again, she has taken me nicely, I thought. Very neat.

I make no promises, I told myself. I'll see her, we'll talk, and that's as far as I go.

I found the house on Heerenstraat, a trim plaster facade with a ziggurat top like all the others in the row. A pleasant open street with a line of young elms down it, leading to the breakwater a couple of blocks away.

An elderly woman, sharp-faced with a wedge chin, opened the door. Yes, Miss Reynier was there, and who should she say was calling?

When she heard my name, she shut the door. I stood there with my mouth hanging open, and then I knocked again several times.

She opened it again, her face changed now, stiff with anger. She wouldn't look straight at me. "Bang on the door like that, I call the sheriff," she said in a hard, quacking voice.

94

"I must talk to her," I said. "She wants me to talk to her."

The door swung nearly shut while the woman turned to speak with someone out of sight. "She won't see you," she said with finality. And the door closed, also with finality.

What now? I stood there for some time, baffled. What was this? She sent her brothers to scare me up and now she wouldn't talk? I knocked once more, politely. It opened on the fourth knock.

"I'm sorry," I said. "Miss Reynier sent her brothers to my house to demand that I see her. Are you sure she won't let me in?"

This was ridiculous. I looked up and down the row. No one in sight. Did a curtain move across the street? The air was thick with sea fog. No snow here, but it had been raining. It was almost warm. I began to swelter in my greatcoat. All right, I thought. She doesn't want me, fine. What do I need with a woman in the house anyway? Finding fault, ragging me at every step, objecting to my pipe, and then the screaming matches every two months — who needs it? Who needs it?

The woman came back at last. Her face was neutral again. Lysbeth stood beside her, just inside the door.

She was big as a house.

And her face — oh lovely. Glowing. I thought I had forgotten it, but now it was back with me as if it had never left me. The shape I remembered so well, every curve and plane of it, softened and broadened by her condition, her dark eyes radiant. She was glorious. She was so beautiful, I was absolutely stunned.

My face must have lit up like a lantern, because she smiled then, and even though it was a distant smile my throat closed on me and my eyes welled.

What was happening to me? I couldn't understand it. I didn't care. I held up my hands.

"Your brothers told me," I said.

A sudden frown. "I told them not to."

"Not to?"

"I didn't want you to know."

"What?"

She shook her head with that abrupt defiance I knew, the long hair flying out behind her. I forgot to say, she was bareheaded and her hair not put up, and wearing a house robe of dark blue silk. Dark blue makes her look magnetic and mysteriously powerful.

"You weren't to know. I'm moving to Amsterdam."

"Lysbeth," I said. I made a wide gesture indicating the open street, and she bowed and pulled back the door to let me inside. My God, discussing our private affairs on the stoop, what will the world think? Not that it mattered at that moment, not really. Suddenly I was hilarious, dizzy with joy. I didn't understand.

I stepped in, wiping my boots on the mat. A short hall, white walls, several landscapes and a round mirror.

"This is my aunt Gabriela," she murmured, and the aunt, who was taller than I, shook my hand with an embarrassed smile and a certain deference. She led us silently into the parlor and slipped away. We were in a surprisingly large room, more paintings on the walls, beamed ceiling of dark oak, a brisk fire going in the fireplace, which was tiled in blue Delft. These people were not poor. Lysbeth sat at the table and I sat across from her. She pulled a heavy brocade coverlet over her knees and tugged at the collars of her gown, folding them closer to her.

"I didn't want to see you," she said rather crisply.

"Why?"

"I don't belong to you. I'm not going to spend my life sniveling at your feet."

"What? I beg your pardon?"

"Being slapped around. If you ever dared to slap me, which I very much doubt."

"Wait a minute. Wait a minute. That wasn't me."

She stared at me.

"That was another Frans Hals, the other Hals family, on the Prinsengracht."

"Oh? Indeed?"

"Yes indeed! Believe it!"

"Believe?"

"Do I have to say everything twice? Ask the sheriff. It wasn't me. I don't hit women."

Her shoulders relaxed a bit. She almost smiled. "Ah. Well. I'm glad of that."

"I should think so."

"Didn't sound like you at all."

"It wasn't. It wasn't me."

"All right." Tentative smile.

"With the troubles I have, I don't need a doppelgänger going around creating scandals."

Her smile widened. Her eyes danced.

I said gruffly, "Well, if that's all the problem is —"

"No," she said, adamant again, but her voice came softly now. "It's not all."

"Oh."

"It was a game. Everything that happened, you understand that? A very nice daydream. And now I get on with my life and you get on with yours. You owe me nothing."

"Lysbeth, you are not listening to me. I don't care about owing."

"I have relatives to help me. I will start a new life. And you —" She gestured toward the door.

"It's not about owing!"

"Stop shouting," she said. She stood up.

"I'm not shouting."

"I am moving to Amsterdam."

"You are not," I said.

She opened her mouth to speak. She looked astonished at this reply. For some unaccountable reason I beamed. I couldn't help it. My hands floated up into the air all by themselves, like a conjurer's.

"Will you listen to me? You are going to marry me, Lysbeth."

I said it. I was as surprised as she. I heard myself talking on. I still do not know where it all came from.

"I can't live without you. I think about you all the time. I want to feel you next to me in bed and hear your footsteps in the street and know the sound of you opening the door to come back to me, every day, even when you go just to the market, I will listen for the sound of you coming home, the rustle of your skirts, your humming to yourself in the next room, your call to see if I am there. I want to make love to your hair. I want to draw cat whiskers on your face."

That stopped her.

She looked at me for a long time. I looked at her.

Then she smiled, very slowly, the cat smile.

And said, also very slowly, "Oh Hals."

The banns are to be published next week.

She has gone back to Spaarndam to get her things together. I think they are fixing a chest of linens and things for her. I have met the huge brother, his name is Claes, and we shook hands like fast friends. Her sister is to stand up for her.

Fifteen January. The banns are out. We are to be married in the Reformed Church. I said it was hers to decide. I don't give a damn about churches.

Met Hillegond today. I thought all the sisters were married. She is going to get the mother now. A curious thing. She has the same kind of face as Lysbeth, the short nose flattening out to a broad base, the sharply defined circumflex eyebrows, the curling smile and muscular mouth. But Hillegond doesn't believe she is pretty, so she isn't. Lysbeth does, so she is. Tomorrow I see Dr. Bredeman.

I lost a hundred guilders today. I went to see Bredeman at his grand house on the Spaarne. Not one but two servants ushered me in, wearing my good-luck hat and my best vest and the brocade coat and the Antwerp shoes, which are too small.

It is five stories high and has a formal garden in front, with marble statues. I was led through room after room. Paintings everywhere. Gold-leaf frames. Massive. Good stuff. Finally found him at bay in the biggest reception room I have seen yet, you could hold a ball in there. High-backed chairs along the walls.

Vaulted ceilings, the beams gilded and the plaster in sky blue. More paintings and an enormous fireplace with silver and crystal things on the mantel, my impression anyway, I didn't have time to look. A spinet in the corner. There is a row of Delft . . .

──────────◄◦►──────────

A rustling from Laura's bedroom. Peter looked up. It was after one. The rain sluiced down steadily outside.

Her light went on, then off. She shuffled out like a ghost. She had on a baby-doll nightgown of silk or satin that gleamed in the soft light.

"I couldn't sleep," she said.

"Ah," said Peter.

──────────◄◦►──────────

There is a row of Delft tiles at the bottom of the wall all around the room. And the floors, you could skate on them.

A very tall man stood at the far end by the spinet. Leaning back so he could point his nostrils at me.

"Hals?" came this deep voice.

"Dr. Bredeman," I said. A stranger in the room would have got our identities wrong. An odd custom.

"I am told you do a fine portrait."

"I have done some."

"How long do you take?"

99

"Depends. With concentration, perhaps a week. From beginning to end."

"I wouldn't want you to rush."

"No sir," I said.

He didn't offer me a seat. Looked me over like a horse at the fair. "Hmm," he said. He had a long, brushy soldier's mustache, carefully combed, and a little beard. Black satin pantaloons and slippers. A most elaborate ruff, you would think it would make him sneeze. I yearned to paint it.

"I will pay a hundred," he said. "How soon can you start?"

"I'm getting married in two weeks. I could probably work you in before, but I'd rather not make any plans beyond that."

He drew himself up. He was going to make a pronouncement. I did not like him.

"I would like to start soon," he said. "But not to hurry. None of your slapdash stuff, Mr. Hals."

"I don't understand," I said.

"I want it smooth. I don't want to see brush strokes. I have seen your work, and some of it looks a little slapdash to me."

I took a long time.

"That is how I paint, sir."

"Not for me, Mr. Hals. A hundred guilders, I guess I should get what I want."

I looked right at him. I bet he made his fortune in slaves.

"That is how I paint," I said, omitting the sir. "Slapdash. Too bad we can't do business. Good day."

And I turned quickly and left the room before he could call me back. When I told Lysbeth, describing him with some venom I confess, she said, "He sounds awful. He won't come after you, will he?" What a thought. Her people have always been poor, I take it, day laborers and that. Quite squalid, really, her childhood. I envisioned one of those tumbledown houses out beyond the wall with packed-earth floors and goats peering in the doors, and little Lysbeth, with her bright button eyes and skinny little frame running all over the place. Her father used to beat her, she says. Mother too. She was a tomboy, always getting dirty. Her mother caught her playing with herself when she was six and held her fingers over the fire. Imagine. She laughed, said it didn't work; her mother burned her own hand worse than hers. I can see her, that bold little soul. Brave. She was always.

She is somewhat awed by the Hals family, my father being in the clothing business and a lieutenant in the militia. The Reyniers are country people from outside of here. It surprised me that she can't write.

---

12 February! We are married! In the Reformed Church at Spaarndam, a spare little box of a building with a woodstove at one end only, which was little help against the cold. Bright but bitter out. We all wore coats up until the ceremony. Harmen wore his first real ruff, he looked like an elf. Dear Lysbeth, simply enormous, her rear hems trailing like a train. We kept laughing.

"You two," said Claes. I take it back. He is all right, a little protective of his baby sister.

Hillegond gave her away, and afterward they fell into each other's arms. Poor Hillegond. She's only twenty and two. It is she who will take over the house on Smedestraat and the four brothers and the moribund old mother. Maybe the downstairs bedroom with its private back door will bring her luck.

We had the party at the Spaarndam uncle's house. My mother too sick to come. I brought the geneva as usual. Claes gave me a father hat that has been in his family for years. Everyone laughed because it looks like I'll be wearing it any day now, she is so huge. I have my own bonnet, with a gilded crown, but it is nice to be making a new start.

On our wedding night we held hands. I gave her a picture. It was a surprise. I put a small canvas on a wooden frame and stuck it in my satchel with some paints and thinner, and I went out to the place in the dunes, our secret place, and painted it. Sat on the sand and painted it! The waving grass and the sky and the wonderful flat calm line of the great sea, just that. Didn't worry about finishing it. I was so excited, working outdoors. To see the sun on the sand, right there while I am painting it! I must think about this.

I did the last bits at home. She was so pleased. It hangs over our bed. Very small, hardly a foot long and quite narrow, and up close it looks like nothing much, but from across the room you can see the whole thing. You can almost smell the salt air.

She is so beautiful. Her eyes so sentient. And bright. And full of mischief. Those smooth round cheeks, so smooth, a miracle of smoothness. It is a miracle that she loves me.

"I've been in love with you since the first minute I saw you," she whispered to me, two heads on the same pillow. "Talking back to the town councillor, right out there in the square, and he laughed and you laughed, and I said any man who can talk up to a town councillor and still have that merry look in his eye, that's for me. You jaunty man! Jaunty man!" And she rubbed my shoulder. I don't remember talking to any town councillor lately, certainly not making jokes with him, but I smiled modestly and permitted myself to bask a bit in her fond gaze. Such scoundrels we are.

———————

Lucky I have the new father bonnet. Her water broke last night and she sent me off to fetch Mother Vooght, but when I brought her back, panting and complaining, there was Lysbeth with the baby on her lap, still wiping off the blood.

I should have known, she was so calm all the way through it. Wakes me up very gently, tapping my shoulder, and gives me a big smile and says, "I think we're ready now." She was the one who had to calm me down. I couldn't get into my pants legs and all but put them on backward, typical joke father, all in a panic, and then rushing through the streets with my shirttail out. "It's all right," she kept saying, "It's all right, Hals."

So there she was, and all the old lady had to do was cut the cord and wash up and get rid of the mess. It was a girl, nearly nine pounds, and suckling like a colt almost before she was dry. Slight pang—don't chew on it so hard, there. That's mine. The sweet little perversions of our daily bedroom life.

She was baptized today, nine days after the wedding. Some sort of a record, I am sure. Is it worse than nine months minus one day? Sara. Lysbeth asked nicely whether I wanted to call her Margaretha. Politely, a friendly gesture. I said no.

Spent the day cleaning. Some of my brushes have sat in turpentine so long it has dried up and they are crusted and curling. I am to see the great van Mander next week. What he can teach me, I am not sure. I went to school with his son, and he was here for his wedding.

Ask about canvas. Have had trouble with the ground layer recently. I restretched a canvas when the primer wasn't quite dry and noticed a peculiar scalloping effect. I don't know why this is happening now as I have done this before. Also remind myself to ask about the new canvas. I hear people are using broader weave. Maybe it will give me more depth.

At least my brushes will be clean. I haven't had a job to speak of since Schrevelius. Lysbeth is worried.

In bed this morning she said, "Will you talk to Bredeman again?"

I was amazed. "Certainly not. Not after that."

She was quiet for a while, getting ready to break something to me. She always does that, lets me stew while she prepares her statement.

"We have only two hundred left."

Ah. I knew it. Not to worry, I said. There's always a job. Van Mander will get me something.

103

"Well," she said. Staring up at the ceiling. Hands folded on her breast like a corpse.

"Well," I said. "I'm seeing him next week."

"Just the same," she said, "I wish you'd go back and talk to Bredeman."

"Bow my head to that idiot?"

"A hundred guilders," she said, "is a hundred guilders."

———————◄O►———————

4

Peter opened his eyes. Light was streaming in, but it was still early morning. Last night came back to him gradually in a succession of revelations.

She had slipped out of the bedroom in that baby-doll thing and then had gone back out of sight, to reappear moments later wearing a silk kimono on top of it, saying nothing but smiling shyly at him, and he had closed the book and gone to her.

She shrugged and her smile faltered. "Hi," she said.

Did she want to do it? His hopes rose like a rocket and dived straight down. No. The smile wasn't right.

"Hi."

"Peter, I, uh . . . "

"Yeah, I know."

"You do?"

"It's George, huh."

"I just—"

"You don't have to explain."

She took both his hands. "It's just that I can't, you know. I mean, I was engaged to George. I had a ring and everything. And I feel terrible if I just . . . "

Peter had no idea what to say. He shrugged his eyebrows and shoulders in unison.

"I mean, I need a little time. You know?"

He nodded.

"I like you a lot, Peter."

Yes, hmm, and I am so considerate and wonderful, and I would love to take you down on that big bed and tear everything off you right this minute, but I am not going to, no.

"It's okay," he whispered. His voice had left him for the moment.

He had an image of Hals cavorting with Lysbeth in her little bedroom, but then it came to him: No, Hals wouldn't put the make on this lady either. Not yet.

"I would love it if you could stay on here a while," she said brightly. "If you want to."

"Sure. Of course."

She leaned into him and kissed him like a sister on the cheek. He took hold of her upper arms and pulled her closer and made it a real kiss on the mouth.

"If I can stand it," he added. He retreated to the big room and picked up the book. To his amazement, he found himself on the last page of the volume. He had been so absorbed he had barely noticed how near it was.

And here it was morning again, and it was going to be a nice day after all. I am done, he mused, realizing he was beginning to speak to himself in the rhythm and manner of Hals. Five hundred dollars and it's not even three weeks. Should he wait a week before taking it back? No. Get the money now and go on.

Systematically, he started a list of possible discrepancies and the confirming data he had found in the big catalog. He mentioned the dates of Anneke's death and the baby's, the names that checked out perfectly, the lawsuit by Neeltje, the trip to Antwerp, the brothers, the father bonnet which, he had discovered, was a tradition of the day to make the new father feel special. Something like giving out cigars.

She came from the bedroom while he was thumbing through the catalog. Already he knew the outline of Hals's life and the names of his subjects. All those men in the Guards portrait were correct too, the names and the elaborate conventions of who was supposed to hold the spear and the flag and who got to look out of the frame. He had even found an essay on canvas stretching that tallied with the artist's remarks.

"Hi," he chirped as she shuffled toward the bathroom. For some reason she was wearing a wrinkled lightweight raincoat.

"Have you seen my kimono?" She sounded hoarse.

"The one you had on last night?"

A little electric charge passed between them.

"I can't find it."

"You want some coffee?" he said.

"Why, do you have some?"

"No. I was just gonna start it."

Jeez, he thought, we sound like an old married couple.

She disappeared into the bathroom.

Peter turned to a fat paperback that Silverstein had given him. It was Simon Schama's *The Embarrassment of Riches,* a study of Dutch culture in the era of Hals and the other great painters whom people loved to call old masters. He hadn't read the book. It was long, but it looked interesting, and it covered the political events of the time.

He had been on the lookout for references to major historical occurrences, because he suspected that they would be a clue to phoniness, though not necessarily. Diaries just don't talk about such things, he reflected, unless they are thrust upon the diarist, like Pepys and the great fire. So far, Hals was doing fine. A few cryptic references to the wars with Spain and that was about it.

He didn't know exactly what he expected to find. He remembered seeing some old engravings of whales when he had riffled through the book.

And there it was. "Whales, beached."

The year was right, 1617 or around there. An epidemic of beached whales along the Dutch coast. He smiled. Good old Hals, or whoever he was.

Laura came out as the coffee finished dripping.

"You want breakfast?" he said. "There're some croissants."

"Yeah, in a minute," she said. She padded up to him and laid a warm hand softly against his cheek. "You okay?"

"Sure."

"Don't mind me," she said, smiling. "I'm still mad at him, but, you know."

"Yeah, well. You got a right. You were engaged."

She swished past him in the quiet, bemused way she had, and he could feel himself getting, as Scott would say, chubby. He caught her arm and pulled her around, which she seemed to have expected, and kissed her very deliberately. She ruffled his hair a little.

"See ya later," she said. Hmm, he thought.

He ate one of the croissants and called Silverstein, who was in though it was barely nine. He said he was bringing back the first volume. As he went out the door, Laura appeared from her bedroom dressed in a severe but smashing dark blue suit.

"Hey I found the kimono," she said. "It was down behind the bed."

"See you tonight," he said. He gently shoved Dave aside as he opened the door.

Silverstein was in a receptive mood. "Come on in," he said cordially, glancing critically at Peter's jeans with the fashionable tear at the knees. The sky was yellow and lowering, already steamy, with the promise of a thunderstorm later. Few people were about on upper Madison Avenue, and no one was in the gallery. Silverstein led him quickly to the office at the rear.

"The owner called me yesterday," he said. "Getting anxious. What you got for me?"

"Well, here's the translation. And I have some notes on all the stuff I found. Everything checked. Everything. Names, dates, history. There wasn't much history, but what there was he had it right."

"That's fine. I sent one of the books out for dating, but they said it wouldn't help much. You can't be that precise. But then I showed it to Dr. Smith and his people, and he turned it over to some lab over there. They said it could very well be seventeenth-century paper. The cover is right, too. It's very old, in any case."

"But you mean someone could just have found some blank notebooks and filled them in."

Silverstein nodded. "That happens a lot in the hoax business. You get a diary that's supposed to be Napoleon's or something and the first few days are torn out, you can bet it was a real nineteenth-century diary that someone started but lost interest in, then they sold it, and later the hoaxer bought it at an antique shop. We're looking at the ink now. All they could tell me was that it's not a modern ink. I asked 'em to analyze it, see what that turns up."

Peter nodded in his most knowing way.

"Tell me this, Peter. How did it feel to you? I mean generally. The way he put the words together. Does it sound old? Does it sound antique to you?"

"Well, it sounds like I would imagine they would sound in the seventeenth century. Although he's very laconic in his style, very spare with his words. I can't describe it. You have to see it."

Silverstein sat down at his desk and waved Peter to the other chair. Peter handed him the volume itself and the thick folder with the translation. He laid his few pages of notes on top.

"You wanted me to put it into modern English, and what I found was that it wasn't all that hard. I mean, it seemed to go right into American English without any trouble. He was a very slangy guy. I had to move his verbs around some."

Silverstein flipped through some pages.

"Now Peter," he said, "I've been going through these other ones looking for Descartes. As I said, we know he painted Descartes around 1649, and you would think he would mention that. Unfortunately, there doesn't seem to be any diary for that year."

He opened a drawer of the desk and pulled out another of the buckram books.

"Been keeping these in the safe," he grunted. "Now take a look at this one here, it has no date on it. It seems to be all one essay. I was combing through it just looking for that name, and I found it. But I can't tell what he's saying."

He shoved the book toward Peter. "Look. Have you got a few minutes? You got half an hour or so?"

"Your time is my time," Peter shrugged. Really, he felt so easy with this casual man.

"Okay. What say you take a look at this passage while I read over what you got here. Maybe that's all we need. I would love to get the owner off my back."

"Okay. What am I supposed to be looking for?"

Silverstein scowled. "Not sure. I found the name but no dates. If he definitely says he painted Descartes, and if there's a date in there, that's one thing. If it's the right date."

Peter pulled up a chair at a corner of the desk with a pen and pad of yellow legal paper that Silverstein gave him.

"It's right here," the dealer said, pushing the open book toward him. The page was marked by a torn slip of paper. "There's the name halfway down." A long, articulate finger pointed, shaking slightly with coffee nerves, at the scribbled name Descartes.

Peter bent over the book. The paper was slightly springier than the other, and hadn't been worn flat by months of daily writing. He checked the front pages first. It was just numbers.

───────────────◄○►───────────────

Van Ostade Friday. With hat.

65

37 supplies.

──────────

28

12 to Dirck

──────────

Hoornbeeck. Ask 75.

──────────

The man is amazing. He speaks thirteen languages, or so he says. We talk of churchly things. He talks, I grunt. Insists on the book. Nails quite dirty. "Just the way I am," he says. "The truth." I will paint his nails dirty then.

──────────

Sara is betrothed! Can't believe it. To a Friesian sailor. We will see her tomorrow.

──────────

July the sixth. In bed for two days with my back. Couldn't straighten up, had to walk to the privy bent over like the Crooked Man. Thought my back was broken. Hot compresses. L minding me like one of the children. I have not time for this.

68 less house 55. Dirck 25.

Peppercorn thing a bust, ship almost lost, cargo thrown overboard. Dirck says we will recoup, he ruining me with his brilliant . . .

Peter saw that the numbers and cryptic entries continued for about twenty pages and ended with a torn-out section. At least five pages had been ripped out. There were several more blank pages, some badly water-soaked and streaked with faint pen markings, but beyond them the writing resumed on un- damaged paper, this time in a more flowing hand, as though the writer was taking his time and putting it all down at one sitting.

He started at the top of the marked page.

. . . in his grave forty years and she had no picture of him, she had forgot what he looked like, imagine, the whole world changed around her, and the aches and pains, the bad stomach and the broken hip that never mended right and all that, but still she would say she wasn't ready to go, that she was afraid. She hated to go to sleep every night because she might not wake up."

Judy sipped her water and studied me carefully. "I am afraid to go to sleep," she said calmly.

I tried to think of something to say.

"You'll laugh," I said. "Did you know I joined the church?"

"No!" She did laugh. "Hals the famous skeptic? Hals the cynic? Hals the philosopher? I don't believe it for a minute."

I shrugged again. "I did it, all right."

"I heard you painted the Frenchman who thinks that he thinks. I hope you didn't tell him."

"Oh yes. We discussed the human condition and the future of the world. It was a great dialogue."

In fact I hardly spoke to the man, or he to me. It was arranged through a dealer friend of mine and Schrevelius, who had known him on account of Leiden. He came there to lecture—what a sensation! Descartes himself at our university!—and then stopped to visit Schrevelius and I painted him there. He spoke barely a word of my language and I only twenty of his. He spoke very little in any case. He would greet me at the door and I would say, Bon joure, and he would say, It faite beau aujoourdwee, and I would say, Oui, oui, sa va, and then I would put him in his seat and get to work. An interesting face, not what I would call knife-sharp with intelligence, but calmer, slower, wiser. An old face, very French.

After a while, she bid me leave. She was tired.

———————◀○▶———————

Peter scanned down the page and onto the next but found no further mention of the Frenchman. Silverstein suddenly looked up.

"Hey," he muttered. "What's this?"

He was at the end of the pile of pages. He put his finger on a line and stared intensely at Peter.

"Landscapes? He was doing landscapes?"

"Why not?"

"Hals didn't do landscapes. Not that I know of."

"Well, he mentions some paintings or drawings he put in Annie's shroud."

"That was when he was a kid. Student stuff. But there was no money in landscapes. You could do historical stuff, allegories. But the money was in portraits. I don't know of a single picture by Hals that wasn't basically a portrait."

"Well. Looks as though he did that one for a souvenir. A present for Lysbeth."

Silverstein shook his head. "I don't know. I don't know. And look at this. Look at this stuff about catching the moment. Painting *en plein air*. That's not right! That sounds like some damned Impressionist. That's a nineteenth-century painter! That sounds like something Monet would say."

Peter sighed. It was as though he had just caught Hals taking money off the bureau. "You mean that would end it?"

"Make him a phony? I don't know. It shakes my confidence. And who was this Teuntje you mention?"

"Oh, I found her. She was the wife of Annie's uncle Job. She was Harmen's godmother."

Silverstein gave him a long look, which Peter deciphered hopefully as admiring.

"Boy oh boy, you do have a good line on this guy, I have to say that."

"Well it's in the book."

"Okay." He dug in the drawer again and came up with the other volumes. "I think we should keep going. I looked into this one, must be the second, it has 1626 on it. It's badly damaged."

Peter took the little book. Something had gnawed the corners of the covers and had tried to dig out the glue of the binding. The first pages were half-eaten away, and one hung in shreds, whether from termites or some larger predator it was hard to say.

But there was a date at the top of what was left of the first page: 1626. On the next ripped page he could make out the words: " . . . finally made up their minds. It is definite. Eleven figures, including the servant, I suppose Jake Coets . . . am to get fifty apiece plus the . . . "

A few more words were tattered into illegibility. On the following page he could read more:

Cold! Blinding bright sunlight! What a morning! Every breath crackled in the nostrils and the snow crackled underfoot. Every sound magnified. The trees in the alley cracked like musket shots. Far down the block a giant icicle suddenly broke off from an eaves and crashed to the road. Every surface caught the sun and sparkled and glittered like jewelry. The cobbles were filled in and frozen . . .

Silverstein was talking to him. Peter raised his head.

"Peter, I'm going to give you all three of these. I'm taking a chance. I hope you're keeping them in a really safe place."

He didn't wait for Peter's nod but hurried ahead impatiently. "I been keeping these in my safe most of the time. But I just have to get a decision one way or the other on this. Can you get through all these in a month? Some of them aren't so long."

"I'll give it a shot."

"And of course the minute you come across anything that settles it as a fake, let me know immediately."

"Of course."

"Meanwhile, I will turn this over to Dr. Smith. And your notes. I think they'll be impressed."

"Thanks," Peter said. The phone rang and he turned back to the book, already absorbed.

I felt like a kid. A boys' day! Boys were all over the streets, shouting and skidding on the ice. Lysbeth packed lunch for me and Harmen and Dirck and we started off with our skates. She is having trouble with the veins in her legs. They swelled up when she was carrying that great monster Jacobus and haven't been right since. Might meet us along the bank this afternoon. She walks every day with the two babies on a sled and Sara and Frans, her lieutenants, trotting alongside. She is teaching Sara to watch my purse and cluck at me when I buy tobacco. My guardian, age nine.

There was ice all the way to Amsterdam after the floods: an event. It's one thing for the canals to freeze up, but when all the fields and country roads are covered with it and even the square in town is a lake of glass, well, it is not a regular day. Before I knew it we had a party, with Joost, who has moved here from Antwerp with his brand-new wife, and Isabella and her Pieter. I can't believe she used to tend Harmen when he was little. That shy girl, and now actually married. We arranged to meet outside the gates after breakfast.

And so did everyone else. There must have been fifty people standing along the bank, talking and laughing, putting on their skates. It was a carnival. Before I could set my things down, Harmen was on his blades and off, careening skillfully back and forth, carving great circles on the ice far from the bank. I haven't skated in years, but Dirck had a pair for me, the blades freshly squared off, deadly sharp. They were so cold the skin stuck to them. I made a few circles by the bank while we waited. Already the ice was crowded, and smooth all the way to the dike a mile away. Then Joost and Maria showed up with Pieter and Isabella, who is suddenly so pretty.

Bustle and chatter and laughter. We finally set out, knapsacks on backs, for Amsterdam. People were everywhere. What a mob! Ladies in ruffs, gents in their Sunday hats and pantaloons, fishermen looking for a quiet spot to saw a hole, kids by the score, hot-chestnut salesmen, a horse that some fool was trying to inveigle into drawing a sleigh. Several rowboats had been caught by the flood and were half under, drawn up on the beach by the bow, with the stern hidden beneath the surface. They made good resting places, because you could sit on a thwart to fix your skates and then simply stand up and glide off.

What a scene! The sun was still bright, though clouds on the way. A throng of people darting this way and that, the lovely metallic arpeggio of blades scraping on ice, like a sword being drawn. Whick whick whick! Laughter and shouts. People falling, to their friends' great hilarity. Petticoats flying. Here and there a rather grumpy old man would trudge across the ice in his boots as though God had created ice with the express purpose of making us look foolish. (Typical of Him.)

Isabella and Pieter set out confidently, hands crossed, skating in unison, a pretty couple in their trousseau clothes, her honey-colored hair pulled trimly back under a coronet, he in a dashing gray hat whose side brim he had pushed upward. Joost and Maria more cautious, struggling along separately, talking to each other about their new house. She is half his age, about twenty-two. They are not close.

We worked our way steadily east. It was more crowded now, with horse-drawn sleighs, fancy ones on great curving runners that sweep up in a gigantic S to form the bow, coming out from Amsterdam. Bells jingling gaily. Women bundled in high collars and warming their hands in fur muffs, the men gallant in tall hats (ears freezing; not me, I wore my wool cap even if I do look like a peasant) and greatcoats. The ice is thick enough to hold a dozen horses. Busy salesmen had put up tents on the ice to serve hot chocolate and pastries. There was a hot baked potato stand. Harmen finally circled back to join us.

After a while the clouds lowered and threatened and the air smelled of snow. I began to need to sit down. My ankles hurt. I headed for the bank where some people had a fire of driftwood. Pieter and Isabella joined me thankfully and we sat on the frozen bank with the back edges of our skates jammed into the rough slurry at the very edge of the ice.

Their cheeks were brick red. Pieter is tall, with pudgy good looks, a long oval face with long wide Dutch nose and a heavy chin. He is learning to use his natural air of authority, now managing a wholesale fish market. How he got into that tight little

117

world of Coymanses and Schouts I do not know, perhaps something in the direct friendly way he looks at you and shakes your hand. And towers over you, I might add. A vast advantage. Not brilliant, but the fish business does not require brilliance.

I passed the flask around. They are buying a house in the South End with Mrs. Berck's help, and she would sell the place next to ours and move in with them. Sad, the Bercks gone after all these years.

At last, moving again lest we freeze right on the spot, we stood up, wobbling and rubbing our knees. We met Isaac gliding in for a rest, and Pieter was delighted to be introduced. "*The* Isaac Massa?" he said, impressed. They talked about Russia and about the language, which Isaac speaks, and about the book he is writing. I knew nothing of this, and I have known him since we were children. He stood up for Adriaentje in fact. I wonder how many other people I knew in school are famous and I never heard a word about it. I must get out from behind my canvas!

Now we really covered ground. The ice spread across the entire world, an endless sheet of it reaching to the estuary and making little islands of the groves on the banks. The great barge canal project was nowhere to be seen, buried by ice. Pieter announces it will open in two years. Well. He is very young.

Suddenly we rounded a bend and saw Amsterdam, its bulbous towers slightly Oriental, looming against the darkening sky. Harmen swooped back from adventures far ahead, and we stopped by an abandoned hut on a promontory where a cheerful crowd had already built an enormous fire. I shucked off my skates and headed for the men's bush (a bigger one, modestly remote, for the women), stuck my head in the hut but found it packed with young louts smoking and laughing their braying laugh while they took off their boots. A homey smell of wood smoke, tobacco, wet wool and feet. We made a circle on the bank and I broke out my chicken and Genoa sausage, the sharp kind with the heavy paper that you peel back, and a generous chunk of Gouda. Joost had some first-rate Spanish wine through his Antwerp connections.

There was some sort of commotion behind us, a fight among the young toughs over the hut, I suppose. Dirck wanted to join in but I said it was time to move along. You can't let an unpleasantness like that ruin your day. So we all got groaning to our feet and headed for home. My boots were soaking wet and cold and my backside sodden. Besides, as I pointed out, the geneva was getting low.

Then Harmen proclaimed that he was skating all the way to the city, a good five miles in the distance, its lights going on as the afternoon faded. I forbade it. He insisted. "I can make it," he said. "I know you can," I said, thinking of the ruffians we had just left behind us, "but why do it so late? Why not tomorrow and make a day of it with Jan?"

Jan is a friend of his from the academy. Taking his father's place in the rope walk next year. Harmen wants to work there, which I have told him is a stupid idea. My mistake.

"However," I added casually, "if you must do it, you better take a nip of geneva."

The wind was rising to a dull whine. We were all too cold to stand still, so circled constantly on the ice.

"I guess not," he said in a gruff manly voice. "Thanks." So we started home. You could still hear the silvery swish of skates on all sides but not much laughter anymore. Faces a bit grim and pinched. Snow was drifting down and on the banks people stood around the fires. Many new fires now. I pushed one foot ahead, then the other, my arms swinging in rhythm like a farmer with a phantom scythe. The thighs tired, the calves sore, the feet colder than I thought possible. And as the light dies and the wind cuts through your clothing, the cold seeps under your collar and up your pants and down your mitten wrists to where little bangles of ice chafe the skin red, you feel the dull weight of winter evening settling onto you, a great sadness that leaves you infinitely weary of the cold and the wind and the dark and wishing only to be sitting in front of a crackling fire in your own snug parlor.

It was full dark when we arrived. A hot mutton pie with winter vegetables and a tray of anise cookies to go with our chocolate. It was heavenly to lie down, off my feet at last. I want to paint the ice. That lowering sky.

———————————◄o►———————————

Two pages were eaten nearly to the spine, then the narrative resumed with a darker shade of ink, perhaps a stronger mix. It seemed to be another day. Peter relished the distinct sensation he had of that hot, low-ceilinged room with the fire in the corner and the smell of anise and cooked meat and healthy sweat. And the high children's voices all about as their father sank gratefully onto his chair, rubbing his bare feet, grunting with the sheer pleasure of not moving.

———————————◄o►———————————

What was I supposed to do with four Evangelists? I sold them two weeks later to a man named Bout who has a big house behind the van der Meer brewery where they say Mass. (Supposed to be a secret but everyone knows where it is. I myself have directed a stranger there on a Sunday morning.)

She was in the parlor jacking up the fire when I got up. Bedsheets were draped everywhere: on the doors, on the highboy, on the backs of chairs. She turned and stood in front of me, glaring from under her brows. Some women put hands on hips to fight. She folds her arms.

She was going on about my purchases. She started to shout at me so loud that the music in the next room stopped short. (Sara and Frans were learning a song with the mandolin and recorder. Sara plays the recorder remarkably well.)

"We are poor, Hals! We are going to the poorhouse! We need

money! You understand? Money! And you play around with these — stupid pictures — "

And she grabbed my canvas right out of my hands and smashed it over her knee. It was long and narrow and it cracked the first time and bent almost double. She whirled it in the air and threw . . .

———————————◄ o ►———————————

Silverstein was off the phone. He was in a hurry now. "Call me in a week, all right? You're doing great. Keep looking for mistakes, okay? There's got to be something. This can't be real. I mean, can it?"

With a curious beckoning gesture he motioned Peter closer. "Tell you a secret," he muttered. "Whatever it is, it's gonna be worth a bunch. Someone went to an amazing amount of trouble to get this thing right. Of course, if it's real . . . "

He reached into the top drawer of his desk and brought out a large checkbook. Silverstein quickly wrote a check and tore it off and handed it to him with a little bow.

"So far so good." He smiled cordially. "Oh, and don't forget. Not a word. You understand? My God, if the press hears even a whisper of this before we're ready . . . "

The check was for five hundred dollars. It was one of the brightest moments in Peter's year.

At Canal Street, he climbed the steps up from the train two at a time and walked briskly along the bustling street past an endless succession of stores that erupted onto the sidewalk, stores where they sold radios and cordless phones for suspiciously low prices, stores that handled nothing but coils of wire, stores blossoming with bolts of fabric, with stacks of china, with tray upon tray of little glass beads and trinkets, with basketfuls of hammers, screwdrivers and pliers stapled to cardboard, with bags of poisonous-looking candy and stamped-out cookies and fruits and vegetables in beautiful towers. He loved Canal Street.

All at once someone stood directly in front of him, a skull-faced Asian man with the tight skin and slitted eyes of the concert hall assassin in *The Man Who Knew Too Much*.

"My friend," the man said, his smile tight.

Peter tried to flow around him but was blocked by a rack of dresses that suddenly loomed up on his right. He was stopped cold.

"My friend, I have them for you."

"What?" Peter mumbled, still trying to slip past.

"Your slacks! Perfect for you! Thirty-two waist, right? Thirty-inch inseam, right? I am always right."

It was as though the hot wind that had been blowing him down the street with such vigor had abruptly stopped, leaving him becalmed. He remembered Silverstein's glance at his jeans. He remembered the check in his pocket, soon to go into his account. He remembered that just the other day he had been thinking about his new life on upper Madison and how he really should try not to look like a delivery man. It was the first time he had given a single thought to his clothes in three years, not counting the momentary panic after the fire when he counted the dozen shirts and wondered why he had them and how he had ever managed to collect that many because he usually wore polo shirts.

"What?" he said, his attention now partly on the intent figure before him. The man, never taking his eyes off Peter's, reached for some trousers on a rack beside him and, maintaining the hypnotic stare, held them up in his face.

"Perfect," the man said in a lower pitch, his voice turning soft and intimate. "Your color."

The pants were hospital-attendant white. They shone in the dull light of day.

"They're you, my friend. For you, sixteen-fifty."

"Sorry," Peter muttered, attempting once more to push past. The man danced in front of him again.

"From Hong Kong. I guarantee it. Hong Kong tailor. You heard of Raffles? Raffles of Hong Kong. The greatest tailor. Make you a suit in an hour. You heard of him? This is his work."

"Sorry, I—"

"Look. Beautifully tailored. Handmade in Hong Kong. This wasn't run off on some machine, my friend. This is tailored goods. Look at it. Raw silk. You don't find that uptown less than three hundred. Come on. What can it do you?"

Peter gave him a hard smile. "No thanks, not this time," he muttered.

"Okay. Fourteen-fifty. My bottom."

"I got pants," Peter said feebly.

"Fourteen dollars. That's it. I'm getting killed here. What do I think I am, Sunny's Surplus?"

Peter remembered from somewhere that his inseam size was indeed thirty and his waist thirty-two. He thought about Silverstein in his superb gray lightweight with the fine lines down the flat lapel.

"Oh hell. Fourteen dollars. Okay."

The grin barely widened. "Good for you. My man. You won't regret it, I tell you. Now I got a great jacket here, would go just—"

"No!" Peter said too loudly. "Pants only."

To his astonishment he discovered that buying clothes invigorated him. When he got back to the apartment he pulled the trousers from the flimsy bag, cut off the tags and slipped into them.

They were perfect. He studied himself in Laura's full-length mirror. Just a tiny bit high over the shoes. Oh dear. Yes, as he walked back and forth, he could definitely see an inch of sock. Oh shit.

With sudden decision he took some nail scissors from Laura's bathroom cabinet and snipped the threads holding up the little fold of extra cloth at the trouser bottoms. When he flattened out the pants he had an extra inch. The crease was still there, but it looked somewhat like a cuff. From a few yards away you couldn't tell a thing. It looked great.

Great, he told himself. He swaggered before the mirror again. Great. Upper Madison. A little shiny in the hard light of the loft, but certainly Upper Madison. He threw the jeans up onto his bunk and felt chic.

———————————◄○►———————————

She whirled it in the air and threw it into the fireplace.

I was absolutely appalled. She has never done anything like this. Shouts and fists and once a shoe. But this was new. I could actually feel the wrath rising in me. I went for her. She ran across the room and yanked one of my old landscapes off the wall. I stood there frozen. Shocked. My picture! It was like a rape.

A spring scene with the new leaves, that lovely light young green, and a breeze ruffling the water. I was proud of that green, and the delicate baby leaves almost tender enough to eat

———————————◄○►———————————

What was this? Landscapes already. Major works. Was Silverstein right? A gray disappointment with Hals settled on him.

———————————◄○►———————————

. . . tender enough to eat. She threw it down on the floor. It was big, almost four feet long, and she kicked at it where it lay and it lifted off the ground a little and landed close to the hearth, where the other one was already blazing up dangerously.

"What are you doing?" I shouted something. I don't remember what. "Are you insane?"

She yelled something back and started toward the next landscape. I ran up and grabbed her arm and we struggled. Her face was a hate mask, and I suppose mine was too.

She tore loose with a terrific jerk. I didn't know she was so strong. She ran toward the hearth and kicked the frame farther into the fireplace and the flames reached out and gobbled it up. Suddenly the whole hearth disappeared in a flash as the oils ignited. A great yellow blossom of fire exploded into the room. I could see her staggering back, arm up to protect her face. A roiling cloud of greasy black smoke belched from the fireplace.

In an instant the sheets hanging nearby took fire. It was all happening at once. Lysbeth screamed. Flames rushed through the whole room, leaping from wall to door to chair as they enveloped the sheets. The sharp, acrid stink of burning linen. The thick smell of burning oil — the stench of disaster.

All this in a moment. I still stood with my mouth open. She screamed again, a different scream. I saw that the flames had caught her skirt. Her arms flailed to beat them out. She spun around in panic, fanning the fire.

I rushed to her and threw her to the ground and rolled on her, covered her, ran my hands over her body, patting and slapping in a blind fury to stop the brilliant darting flames. I pinched out the last sparks. Her skirt turned to filmy black ashes. Traceries of soot clung to me like a spiderweb. Her face. Her face! I was crying as I tried to calm her. She was still madly beating the air around her, hitting me in the process. Her face was dark red, smeared with soot across forehead and cheeks. Her eyes closed tight.

I sprang up, aware of the roar around me. The children! They were shrieking in the next room. "Stay there! Stay there!" I yelled. I ran for the bucket that stands by the hearth. Threw the water in a long splashy tongue at the wall where flames were climbing to the ceiling beams. It seemed like nothing, like spitting at the fire.

But the next moment — as suddenly as it had begun — the fire died. With the sheets burned up, there was nothing left to attack. I took a broom and went about the room beating to death the small remaining blazes—on the doorjamb, on the mantel, on the rug we had put down for the babies. Soot covered everything. I brushed the sweat from my face with my sleeve and it came away with a great smear of black. My throat was parched and I seemed to be hiccuping. I realized I was sobbing. The fire burned merrily now in its proper place as though nothing had happened, crackling away on the last of my canvas frame. I glanced at the others on the walls. They were hideously darkened with a uniform mist of soot.

Someone banged on the door.

"It's all right!" I shouted. (I have no idea what I meant.) I opened it. Mrs. Berck stood there with a wet mop in her hand.

"Help the children," I said. "In the bedroom."

I went to Lysbeth. She groaned and sat up. Her blouse hung in tatters, exposing her chemise. Her skirt looked like Cinderella's rags. Skin had peeled from her forehead and cheeks and the ridge of her nose.

"Salve," I muttered.

"Not butter," she whispered, gripping me urgently.

We keep a pot of ointment near the bed. We use it for the childrens' scraped knees and cut fingers. She gets it from some herb woman she knows. I know about butter. She didn't have to tell me that.

The crying in the next room stopped and I could hear the calm voice of Mrs. Berck saying something in a soothing monotone. The air stank. I opened the front door and pushed out a window, cold though it was. Shoved the charred sticks farther back into the fireplace with my foot.

She cried when I gently spread the ointment on her face.

"What do I look like? What do I look like?"

"It's all right. Just some blisters. It's not bad." But her skin was still that angry red and scraps of fine surface skin hung on her cheeks like sunburn peelings. Shocking. I tried not to let her see anything in my face. I feared for her so.

"My hands," she murmured.

They were blistered too, the backs of the fingers and knuckles. I smeared salve on them.

"It hurts, Hals," she said. She seemed weak and weepy.

"I'll go see de Vere."

"No, stay a minute." She clung to my hand. It must have cost her to open her fingers. She winced.

I stroked her lovely black hair. The front had been singed, leaving her with rough bangs. I got my hands under her and lifted her from the floor. She put an arm around my neck and nestled her head against my chest. I hugged her close for a moment, I was so glad to have her with me safe. I took her into the bedroom, where the children were huddled with Mrs. Berck, and laid her carefully on our bed. They all watched me with big eyes. Thank God the little ones were upstairs in their room. I could hear them tuning up.

"Mrs. Berck," I said, "I'm going to the doctor. Would you stay here with my wife? Sara, you go see if the boys are all right."

Sara needs a job to do. She is so bright. And jealous. She needs to be singled out and given little rewards.

Lysbeth was gingerly touching her face.

"Don't do that," I said. She was feeling better, though lying flat on the bed.

"Hals," she said.

She put her hand on my arm. This time I winced at the stiff way her fingers moved.

"I'm sorry," she said.

"It's all right," I said.

"I shouldn't have done it. Terrible."

"No, it's my fault," I said, "I spend all the money. I know . . . I know." Stroking her head.

"Paint whatever you want. Paint your landscapes."

"I am a thoughtless fool," I said.

"No, no," she said. "Forgive me."

"If anything happened to you . . . "

She ran her small hand down my cheek and our eyes sought each other.

Tuesday. She is so much better. De Vere gave me a powder to mix into paste and spread on her face and hands. Very uncomfortable last night. But it took all the sting out, she says. Not so red today. Mrs. Berck is here all day to care for the children. Must do something nice for her. Since Isabella left she hasn't much to do. She gets me in the parlor when she's heating up their lunch and she talks and talks and talks, mostly about Isabella and Pieter. Yes, there is a baby coming. They will just make it, nine months even. Not like some people I could mention, I told her, and she laughed. Berck would have been pleased with Pieter. He will make their fortune. She has an oven in her house.

Went to see de Vere. Dr. Tulp in Amsterdam actually goes around to his patients in his carriage. Described Lysbeth's skin as best I could. The blisters are gone, two angry raw spots on her forehead where the skin burned off and along her nose, which luckily is not a big one. Her eyes are fine, eyelids. He asked particularly about . . .

He knew the smell of smoke in a house fire, so different from when you are camping out. Hmm, why is that? Oil paints and bedsheets. Nothing smelled worse than a burned mattress. Someone was scrabbling at the front door, someone who wasn't as skilled at finding the keyhole as Laura. There was a metallic sound, a key. Scrabble, scrabble. Finally, someone pushed furiously against the door and it flew open, slamming against the bookcase by the wall.

The guy was big, six feet four at least. His curly dark hair formed a big bush on top. It was George.

Dave and Leopold, who had draped themselves on either side of Peter on the table among his papers and books, each lying quietly on an Appalachian macramé doily, leapt down instantly and disappeared under two different chairs.

The guy stood there like a Japanese warrior statue, staring furiously at him, arms also furiously akimbo.

"Who the fuck are you?"

"Uh, George, I think we met a couple years ago."

"Get the fuck out of my place!"

"It was a Christmas party. It was right here in fact."

George advanced on him with great deliberate steps, both hands out front like claws.

"Peter Van Overloop. That is. You know. I met—"

The claws closed on his shirtfront and grabbed handfuls of cotton mesh.

"You. Are in. My place. Guy."

"Hey." Peter could not retreat without tearing the shirt. He noticed that George was wearing French corduroys with an extra wide wale. He wished he wasn't wearing his shiny new white pants.

"Hey!" he repeated, because George had stopped shouting and was merely glaring. The claws were starting to lift the shirt up to his face and Peter with it. Possibly he was nearsighted, Peter thought.

"Cut it out, George. Laura asked me here."

"Laura. Where's Laura?"

"At work, of course."

He was being set down, but the glaring continued.

"Who do you say you are?"

"Peter Van Overloop. I go with Amy. I met her here, you remember that. Jesus Christ, man."

"So what you doing here?"

Most of the time Peter's rage surfaced long after the appropriate occasion, but once in a while it came up right on the money.

"You hired me, you dumb shit. I'm house-sitting your stupid loft."

A certain red glimmer went out of George's eyes. He stepped back one step and surveyed Peter calmly.

"Oh," he said.

"Right," Peter said, rearranging his shirt.

"So where's she stay?"

"Well she's here. She came back, remember?"

"And you're staying with her?"

Peter shrugged. "It's a long story. I had a fire—"

"She putting you up, huh? Is that it?" George advanced farther into the room, his elbows winging out and his fists clenching. "So what the hell is this?"

"My place was burned out. No big deal." Peter began to get the feeling that now he would never have another chance with Laura. He wished he had had time to cash his check. The banks would be closed by now.

George was standing quietly in the middle of the room, possessing it the way a chessman possesses the center of the board and forces the opponent back into the corners. Peter sidled around by the table where he worked, feeling fragile.

"Well, I think this is all very simple, my friend," George said, leaning ostentatiously on the last two words. "I want you out of here in ten minutes."

"Look. Laura invited me. Let Laura tell me to go."

George smiled menacingly. "Laura can tell you what she likes. I'm telling you to go. You got that? This is my place, and I am telling you to leave."

Peter sighed. "What if I don't?"

"What if nothing. I can call the cops. But I don't think I'll

130

need to. I can just throw your stuff down the stairs and you with it."

He could, too. Peter saw that immediately. He loomed over Peter and his pectorals were all but bursting his shirt. A most unattractive look, Peter had always thought.

After a pause of perhaps twenty seconds, Peter turned his hands out. "Okay, George," he said calmly. "If that's the way you want it. I'll go now, but I'll call Laura. I want to find out what she says. It's her place too, as I understand it."

"You do that," George said. He turned on his heel and strode behind the bookshelf to the bedroom. Peter pulled his suitcase from the closet and threw his things into it. He had to climb up to his aerie to fetch a few books, and he took special care to wrap the Hals books in some shirts before placing them reverently on top of the pile. The suitcase would hardly close. He couldn't believe he had more stuff than before.

As he was dragging the load toward the door George came out of the bedroom.

"I'll be back," Peter grunted, lifting the heavy luggage as he opened the door.

"I don't think so," George said.

"Glad I could help with the house-sitting. It's been delightful."

Apparently unable to think of a riposte, George showed his teeth. But a minute later, as Peter struggled down the three flights of stairs, bumping at every step, George opened the door again and called out, "And where in the hell did you get those ridiculous pants?"

"Fuck you, George."

———

At the hotel the lobby still smelled of smoke. Scott was out. The porter manning the desk said the room had not been

131

fixed yet. Peter asked whether there was another room he could use for tonight. No, there was a waiting list for apartments as it was. He left his suitcase behind the desk, irritating the porter by insisting on a receipt, and headed over to Broadway.

The first thing was to find an ATM and withdraw his last hundred. He stuck the twenties in different pockets, leaving one in the wallet. Then he sat on one of the benches that stand on the Broadway midstrip. Most of the benches were more or less permanently occupied by old people who sat there with their small dogs and smoked and sometimes talked. The women sat with other women and men, sat with other men. The women talked more than the men, who seemed to read the papers more. It was a beautiful evening, now that the sun had sunk into New Jersey. It was as though a heat lamp had been turned off: not cool by any means, but not broiling either. The city seemed to have taken a gigantic breath and let it out in a wonderful relaxing sigh. The people who went home had gone home and the people who lived there were stirring about in their apartments or roaming equably along Broadway, headed for the nearest Korean grocery or Chinese-Cuban restaurant. The old people on the benches must eat early, Peter figured. The rows of benches stood perpendicular to Broadway, hash marks on the midstrip. From thirty feet up it would look like some enormous open-air bus. The Broadway charabanc, going nowhere, but a pleasant place to sit and watch the sky turn orange and then brick red and then a lovely dark magenta.

Later he went back to the hotel. This time there was a different porter on duty who told him that Scott had gone to visit his family in Arizona while the work was being done on the apartment. No, it would be impossible for Peter even to camp there, because the floorboards were taken up and the walls stripped and the bathroom being overhauled.

He went out to Broadway again. It was deep dusk by now. He wandered up and down the street for several blocks before deciding on a bar called Dunnigan's. He loved Irish bars but refused to have anything to do with one called Paddy's or the Blarney Stone or the Shamrock.

Dunnigan's was just right. Not too dark, and with a generous space between the door and the beginning of the bar, a dark spot where a person could stand for a moment to get the feel of the place. There were no shillelaghs over the mirror. The bartender glanced at him, nodded and went on swabbing the broad mahogany bar. Three patrons also gave him a quick look, then went on talking about hockey. There were booths along the left wall and a few tables at the back. A couple sat at the far end in the gloom, eating dinner, and a slim waitress hovered near them.

Peter slid onto the end stool. "I guess a Jameson's," he said.

"Jameson's," the bartender replied. He was a heavy-jawed man in a white shirt and bow tie, his hair clipped extra short to disguise the bald top. He picked a bottle from at least five other Irish whiskeys in his little army of bottles.

The men, well-dressed, pouchy, in their fifties, started in on hockey again. One of them was remembering a team called the Comets from someplace in upstate New York.

"World-class," he said. "Just local kids. They beat the Rangers."

"Bob. It was an exhibition. Had to be."

"Nope. Nope. They beat the Rangers. . . . "

Peter called for a second whiskey, studied the wet circles on the varnished wood before him. He was trying to decide whether this was the worst day in his life.

When he ordered a third, the bartender gave him an extra look and asked whether he would like some dinner.

"We got pretty good food here," he said confidentially, man to man.

"Not Irish food, Skip," said the attentive Bob. "Don't ask him to eat Irish food."

Skip ignored him, tilted his head toward the back. "It's Italian. This one's on the house." He slid the drink toward Peter, who thanked him and clambered off the stool. He was definitely dizzy. He was glad to sit down again in a padded booth.

The waitress had merry eyes that turned up at the corners. Her hair was green as grass.

"You have green hair," he said.

"Yeah," she said.

It was beautiful hair, too, as far as he could see. Short and wild, sticking out but not spiky at all. Soft like feathers.

"I think I'll have the lasagne," he said as he perused the dog-eared, sauce-spotted menu. "No. The veal parmigiana. And a little salad. With the, uh, house dressing."

"You had some bad news," she said.

"I beg your pardon?"

"You had a bad day."

"You got it," he said, looking at her more closely. She had a narrow face, very white skin, a ski-jump nose, and big eyes full of concern.

"I'm a little psychic," she said.

"So I see. So what do I do now?"

"Eat some dinner," she said, and walked off stuffing the order pad into her belt. She wore a long black skirt and a man's white button-down shirt open at the collar. She moved like a young cat.

He decided that possibly the worst day in his life had bottomed out.

His head was spinning when the basket of Italian bread arrived, with very thin squares of butter on cardboard pats. He tore at a thick slice of bread and ate it dry. The whiskey sat in front of him untouched. He saw that he had already drunk his water, but before he could look around for the waitress she was there, pouring him another.

"Thanks," he said. "What's your name?"

"Suzanne."

"My name is Peter."

"That's S-u, Z-a-n. Two words."

"Ah. Su Zan. Great. How did your hair get green?"

"I like it."

"Good for an Irish bar."

She shook her head. "Nah. It's seasonal."

Later she came back with the veal. It was covered with red sauce and lay alongside a large heap of spaghetti. Peter had never seen such a feast in all his long life. He dug in, searched around in this dim booth and reached for the salt, reached for the small squat jar of hot pepper seeds, reached for the tall jar of grated cheese.

How nice, he thought, free cheese. In a fancy place the waiter doles it out with a teaspoon and winces if you nod for more than two spoonfuls.

He shook down a blizzard on the spaghetti. But when he started to devour the feast in earnest, he reared back. It was sweet.

The tall jar contained sugar.

Oh shit, he thought. Oh shit.

Su Zan was watching him. He beckoned her over.

"You know what I did?" he said.

Oh shit. This was stupid.

"You know what I did? I thought this was grated cheese."

She looked at him.

"I, uh, poured sugar all over it."

She lowered her head and peered at him over what would have been glasses if she had been wearing any.

"I'm sorry. Can you take this back and get me another? The same thing? It looks delicious."

135

She gave him another inquiring look. "I was right, huh."

"What?"

"Bad day."

He sighed. "I'll pay for it. That's no problem."

"No, I'll say—"

"No, it's okay, Su Zan. Don't get in trouble."

When she smiled her eyes grew even larger and she showed her teeth, which were very white and very short, with a lot of gum. She habitually looked as if she had just had the most wonderful idea.

She brought him his duplicate dinner and a bowl of grated cheese which she left with him. He said, "Hey Su Zan. When do you get off?" He had never said this to a waitress before.

"Eight o'clock."

Nobody else was eating dinner at eight, so she sat with him while he finished his cannoli. Skip glanced at them a couple of times and finally walked back to the booth to offer Peter a Sambuca, looking him over carefully. He also studied Peter's credit card and listened to the story of the hotel fire. He knew about it.

"So you live in the neighborhood. You never came in here before," he said quietly.

"No. Not much of a drinker."

Skip nodded his agreement.

Su Zan had just finished her shower when Peter arrived at her place with his suitcase. She made him wait outside the door until she had her clothes on.

The apartment consisted of a large cluttered living room with two tiny bedrooms off it. In the living room was a sofa and an armchair and the biggest table he had ever seen, a bare wooden tailor's table with a sewing machine on a stand next to it. Peter noticed some brilliantly colored cloths draped over

136

another chair and some more hanging from tacks on the far wall. He couldn't make out what they were.

She made a pot of tea for them. Peter said he had had enough coffee, though he didn't think anything could keep him awake much longer. Her name was Kurek. She had on a much shorter skirt, blue to go with her hair, and a T-shirt that said BALTIMORE INSTITUTE, COLLEGE OF ART. They talked about the Kureks and the Overloops, about Baltimore and Chicago, about what they were going to do. She was an artist. Everyone in Baltimore is an artist, she said. She was part of a show in the Village once with her sculptured pots, and now she taught ceramics two days a week at a West Side senior center. She did bowls with crazy rims, rims that had been interfered with. There were some around her apartment, fine thin bowls whose rims had been gnawed and chewed and wrinkled in the name of art. "But that's not what I do for the ladies," she said. "What they want is molds. They make things out of molds and paint them. I can't get them to throw pots." Her roommate was staying with her family in Ohio, she said, because her father had just died.

She didn't really want to talk about the bowls with the wrecked rims. She was restless, crossing one leg over the other on the sofa, then reversing legs, then jumping up like a child to pace about the room.

"So you translate from Dutch? What exactly? How does Dutch sound? I never heard any, I don't think."

"It's not at all like German. It's sort of brittle, like very small twigs snapping."

"Twigs! What is French like?"

"Leaves," he said. "Walking through leaves in the fall."

She was delighted. "Walking through leaves. And can you kick them?"

"Oh no, it would never do. The French are very precise.

It's why they have all those marks on their words. You have to say it just right."

She laughed her light girl's laugh. "And German is the forester clomping through in his boots."

Her hair stood out like a sprite's hair. In a minute he would be looking for small cellophane wings on her shoulder blades.

It was suddenly after midnight. Peter noticed that he was extremely tired. The plan was for him to take the roommate's bed, but when he politely went to kiss Su Zan good night something happened. They were standing in the doorway of the roommate's room doing the polite kiss when she put her hands at the back of his head and turned it into a real kiss, and then his hands were slipping down her thin back feeling ribs and then hips, and before he knew it he was panting and she was too and the skirt was on the floor along with his pants, and they left them behind when they went into her bedroom, she leading him by the hand.

She was deft and quiet in bed. For someone so thin she was smooth all over, and so deliriously, erotically soft that he had trouble holding back.

In the morning, in the light of the new sun, he saw that her hair was truly as green as the grass in one of those china Irishman's heads. He told her that, and touched it, and stroked it, and pretty soon they were kissing again. Now he could see her breasts, quite small but full, pearly in the daylight, and he discovered that her pubic hair had been dyed fire-engine red and clipped into the shape of a heart.

"A valentine!" he said, and kissed it.

"That was for Bradley," she said, starting to squirm a little. He glanced up. Her chin looked big from below and her eyes heavily lidded.

"Bradley."

"My boyfriend. I threw him out."

"Oh good."

"He was getting to be a wuss."

"Ah."

"I hate that."

He propped himself up on one elbow and gazed at the valentine, so dramatic against the white of her abdomen. "Did it hurt?" he asked.

"Oh no," she said, "I used nail clippers."

They had breakfast well after eleven. Su Zan always had canned tomato soup for breakfast. Peter ate a piece of toast. Afterward he wandered around the living room looking at the strange cloths. One looked like an enormous pair of butterfly wings, tall as the ceiling. Another appeared to be a gigantic green caterpillar with fantastic foot-long hairs growing from it. There were photos on the wall, but he couldn't make much out of them.

"All right," he said when she came from the bathroom dressed in her black skirt and an extravagantly frilly white shirt that seemed to be exploding in her face like popcorn, "what is all this?"

"Oh that. That's Bananas." She pirouetted serenely in front of the big butterfly.

"Bananas."

"Bananas. That's our name. We do parade art."

Peter knew instantly from her eyes that it was this, not the ceramics, that was Su Zan's true art.

"Okay. What's parade art?"

"Well, we have this group and we go around to parades wherever we can find 'em and we march. And we wear these things. It's performance art."

Peter returned to the photos. Now he could see a wonderful procession of exotic figures prancing down a city street before a sidewalk crowd. There was the butterfly. There was the caterpillar. There were wild twisting shapes with several people under them. There were monsters on stilts and a row of soldier dummies without heads dangling from a rack like dresses and carried by one soldier in the middle, and a strange fluffy pink sort of valentine heart waving in the breeze and a variety of peculiar nondescript hopping things. Leading them all was a person in a gorilla suit with a huge top hat.

"The gorilla is our trademark. He's in all our shows. He always leads. He also passes the hat."

"Who is he?"

"Anybody who's left over when we go out there."

"What do you wear?"

"I made a vulva. I'm gonna wear that."

"Ah," said Peter.

He watched her dart gracefully about the room as she collected her things to go to work. She would get lunch at the bar, she said. There was some tuna fish in the fridge. It was understood that he would be there when she came home.

"Oh, and some guys might drop in to work. It's okay."

"What?"

"They're okay. They just want to use the sewing machine."

With that, she waved her thin arm in a bizarre angular farewell and flitted out. He was totally baffled. He adored her.

He did the dishes and set up his books on the broad table. It seemed a long time since he had been involved in the quiet world of Haarlem. Hals was talking about eyelids.

———————◄○►———————

. . . but she says they are fine. Must have got her hand up in time. Amazing how the body protects itself in sudden danger, long before the intellect knows what is going on. The intellect, so full of itself.

The children love Mrs. Berck. I hear them when I am working in the next room, jumping about on the tiles, some sort of game, and laughing their wonderful laugh. (I tried to make a picture of

140

that laugh with Frans. It almost comes off, I think.) Lysbeth sits with them, her chair as far from the hearth as she can be. Addie is all over the place. Jacobus wants to follow her but still has to learn the basics of walking (not that Addie is what you would call a master of this skill). Sara takes him about the house, walking above him like a giantess, his tiny hands holding on to her fingers as if they were udders, his stubby little legs working so hard, putting this foot down, then that foot, his face screwed up in concentration.

Lysbeth is always at her. "Look out, don't take him so near the fire!" "Sara, you're pulling his arms!" "Don't go so fast!" Sara turns and glowers. Her hair was dark at birth but now a flaming red. She is tall already. She will be a beauty.

We talked calmly today. I took down the other landscapes, leaving white patches on the walls. She was so contrite, wanted me to have them cleaned at all cost, but they are ruined. I took them under my arm and went up to van Weilinck and sold them for Fl 10 apiece as is. But they're not signed so who cares.

I told her I will concentrate on my real work. She is right, of course. Reminded her that I have not been exactly drumming my fingers. Schrijver and his wife. The Olycans. Heythuysen last year. And Isaac. What else, I can't remember. Then I told her the Guards are postponing. Jake, the dandy, going to Copenhagen for his father. I told him I thought his father was so rich he didn't have to travel anymore. He said, "True, he just sends me." I think they get special wood for their barrels up there.

The Olycan clan—I have had my fill of them. Their smiling easygoing ways, all of them, lubricated by the serene assurance that they are who they are, always have and will be, by the will of God, oh it sours the juices of my stomach and turns my mouth to brass. And Jake, the ineffable Jake, our self-appointed leader from earliest boyhood, turned to at all times, sucked up to even before we understood what it meant to suck up, following our parents and grandparents and uncles and cousins and business partners and in-laws and hangers-on. Oh that greasy grin, that soft mouth spreading like molasses on a tile floor, lifting the little mustache so it seems to be joining him in his boundless self-satisfaction, his complete confidence that whatever may happen, whether the Spanish fall upon us, or a hurricane smashes the dikes from here to Groningen and tumbles us from here to Ararat, or a volcano explodes in our midst and buries us like some ancient city, whatever may happen, he Jacob Olycan will survive and prevail, still smiling, still handsome, still rich and therefore admired and bowed to and asked for his opinion on things he is not competent to judge.

God forgive me vomiting up this venom. It burns like acid. I swallow my own bile and lick my chops at its bitterness. God forgive my vile thoughts. Nod at me like a servant will you. I wish you in hell Jacob Oilcan, you eel. I smear my bitter shit across your shiny smile.

Sunday. She went to church to give thanks. There is only the ridge of her nose and two spots on her forehead. The cheeks healed completely. Her herb woman has given her some mixture.

I can't wait to get back to the new Isaac. Went to his house for lunch and set up shop in his study. I don't see him often for any length of time. His quiet smile is most attractive. I almost caught it last time. He was digging his pipe into an elegant wooden humidor and he pushed it over to me. "Danish," he said. "Very sweet." I tried some and it smelled like face powder.

He wanted a different pose from the last one. We sat him this way and that, with his hands resting on lap à la statesman or supporting head à la philosopher. He was restless. I was getting cross with him when it came to me—he is restless? So paint him restless.

We were talking about Addie (to whom he gave a fine silver

porringer for the christening) and what a little lightning bug she is, climbing up to the attic and having to be rescued because the stairs are so steep. And the time she pulled the curtain down. And what she did in the warming pan. (Lysbeth furious but I said, It's better than in her pants.)

I noticed he was sitting sideways in his chair with his arm resting on the back of it, absorbed, listening, and I saw him that way. I blocked him in, to get the arm right and the angle of the head, slightly to one side. It will be good. Restless but attentive, a high intelligence at work.

He saw me working fast and said, "What? This?"

I said, "Of course, why not."

He thought a while, then said, "What if I don't like it?"

"Isaac," I said, "you'll like it."

Silence.

I laughed. "If you don't like it, I'll do it for free. I'll give it to you."

Now he laughed. "But if I don't like it, I won't want it."

"What? A genuine signed Hals in your own house? Save it for your grandchildren, they'll make a fortune on it."

"Bloody likely," he muttered. But he held the pose. He looked comfortable. I wanted him before an open window, so I could work in a slice of Haarlem scenery, but he insists on putting his Molijn into the background. He just bought it, a Russian forest landscape. Has Molijn ever been to Russia? I doubt it very much. So I will have to do homage to Molijn and copy his silly painting. Oh well. I'm putting holly in Isaac's other hand. Because he's a friend of mine.

———————

Another afternoon. More sweet tobacco. He can get it for me, he says. Douceur it is called. He talked carefully about Lysbeth. I think he was shocked about the baby so soon after the wedding. A difference between us that we try never to show we know. That merchant morality. Girls: Sew it up till you

get married. Not her! Or me, luckily. Those people see everything as some kind of goods, to be kept in perfect condition until
sold.

Easter. To St. Bavo with Lysbeth and her sister and new swain.
I was always wrong about Hillegond. I thought she would never
marry, but she is a widow already. To a fisherman who drowned
ignominiously when he caught his foot in a net and was pulled
overboard. Hillegond quite consolable, to say the least. All she
would say was, Oh, Jacob, always stumbling over his own feet.
We do say such strange things about our own dearest dead
sometimes.

I still think she is unattractive, though clearly Roelant is
bedazzled. Hangs around her all the time, sniffs the back of her
neck, clutches at her hands. She ignores him. Brushes him away
now and then with an exasperated but melting smile. I think it is
serious. He is a weaver. Handsome and lean, beardless but starting
a dramatic mustache, long neck with enormous Adam's apple, and
long legs and arms. But quick on his feet, I note.

She was concerned about Lysbeth's scars. Still the two spots on
her forehead, they seem to change from day to day. They are more
like pimples now, splotchy, red and somewhat puffy. And they
don't get smaller. Lysbeth worried.

Hillegond (standing right over her and examining her at the
table): What are you doing for it?

Lysbeth: Henrietta has a salve I use.

Every night she puts it on before bed. It smells of sulfur.

Hillegond (squinting closely at them): What is it? Looks angry
to me.

Lysbeth: I don't know. Henrietta says it will cure anything on
the skin.

At this Roelant's ears perk up. "Henrietta?" he says. "Yes," says
Lysbeth. "In the alley by the Raamgracht."

He sits up, all attention. "Henrietta Wetselaer?"

"I don't know. I never knew her name. She sells me things for the babies."

Roelant leans forward, elbows on the table, face grave. "I hate to tell you this," he says, "but if that's who I think it is, she is not straight."

"What you mean?"

"That salve is my mother's. She gave the formula to Henrietta and they were going to sell it together."

Lysbeth very delicately passed her fingertips over her forehead. "So?"

"Henrietta took it over and said it was hers and she was going to sell it herself."

"What did your mother do?"

He shrugged. "Nothing. She had a job taking care of old Schout, she was too busy. She had enough to do."

That was when Sara spilled the kettle. But it worries Lysbeth. She says the stuff stings her skin and keeps her awake. What next? What next?

Had a visit from Schrijver. His portrait is splitting, he says. I told him impossible, that ironwood doesn't split. He insisted that I come over and see it. That was the panel that was cut with the rings instead of across them. Why I charged him less. I did tell him to keep it out of the sun.

It can't be splitting already. I am positive I oiled it.

Sensation! Roelant at the house today to fetch Hillegond, who has been minding the boys. (Lysbeth gone to see Dr. Wath. Sores are hurting worse, probably because of all the fuss.) There was a knock on the door and I opened it. It was Henrietta, a short, fat woman with a cross face and a woolen hood that makes her look like some old goose woman. She stepped up to say something, but at that moment she saw Roelant standing behind me. So she just turned on her heel and walked away. Without a word!

Roelant saw her and shouted, and at that she started to run down the street.

"What was all that?" I said.

"She knows who I am," he said. "She cheated my mother."

But he wouldn't say any more.

Then Lysbeth came home, and she was full of news. Dr. Wath knows all about the woman.

"Soon as I mentioned her name he said he knew who she was. He said he is going to sue her. There're other cases, Hals." She was quite breathless with excitement. "And he says there is definitely something wrong with that salve."

He had the apothecary make her another ointment.

"He says a salve shouldn't hurt, whatever it did."

She was not only excited but gay. Rushed around the room tending to the children and the dinner, inviting everyone to stay, and so forth.

Saw Schrijver's picture. It's a hairline crack. All that fussing. Offered to paint it over, but now he doesn't want to change it. Says he loves it just as it is. He is afraid I will charge him more.

I haven't been out for days except to go to the outhouse or the market. The weather acts more like March. We walked over to Town Hall today with Roelant and Hillegond. The doctor already there. Magistrate a youngish man, clipped pepper-and-salt beard, small bright eyes like a mouse, shiny black and opaque, and an impatient manner. As if he was in a hurry to get on with his (illustrious) career.

The woman is mad, of course. Even before the magistrate came in, she fidgeted in her seat and cast great owl eyes at us. Smiled to herself and appeared to be knitting the air with her bare fingers, which tugged and picked at each other aimlessly on her lap. The magistrate bustled in and took his seat surreptitiously, as though he thought we wouldn't notice him arriving late, though we were standing there before his dais having been duly called to attention by the bailiff, who turned out to be dear old Willem Vetters, a friend of my father. I thought he died years ago. He didn't recognize me until our names were called, and then he peered in my direction like a sailor looking through the fog.

The magistrate's name is Vreese. Very brisk. "Now what's the trouble here?" Addressing Dr. Wath, clearly the only reputable-looking person in the bunch. Though I wore my new ruff. I am doomed to spend my days on this earth looking like a slightly untrustworthy frequenter of taverns. Something in the eyes, I think.

Wath stood and the rest of us sat back on our bench facing the dais. The wind had died down, and the tall windows were open to the fresh May morning, really a bright day in spite of the cold. Not a cloud in the sky, and the light filled the hall, a truly impressive chamber with beamed ceilings two stories high. Enough room in there to sue an army. Elegantly patterned tile floor, paid for by us citizens. Wath explained about the burns and gave the whole chronology of salves, from the stuff I put on the first day to de Vere's powder to Henrietta's sulfurous nostrum. He spoke slowly and clearly, with great precision, just the way you would hope a man of science would speak. How I wish I had that kind of presence. Then he sat down and Vreese looked from one to another of us, there in our indignant row.

Henrietta was fidgeting worse than ever, and Vreese stared at her for a full minute before he said, in a voice that somehow conveyed both impatience and resignation, "Madame, and what do you say to this?"

She popped up like a marionette. "Sir!" she said. "Yer Honor!" She took off her wool hood and held it in her hands. "I been giving this salve to everybody, I never heard no complaint."

"Selling," Lysbeth muttered. The magistrate, without deigning to glance at her, nevertheless picked up on the point.

"You sell it," he repeated. "You sell it for profit, right?"

"Yer Honor, I'm a poor woman and I have to make my way as

best I can—" Inexplicably, she rumpled her hair with both hands, stirring up a great frizzle of dirty ivory white hair, so that she resembled an astonished poodle.

"Madame—"

"Why, I give my salve to babies! True!" She turned to glare briefly at Lysbeth. "Yer Worship, little babies have had my salve, all over their faces and hands and bottoms, begging your pardon, and never in my life have I heard a word about it."

"How long have you been selling this salve?"

"Why, I been giving it to babies—"

"Truth, now," he snapped.

"One year, Yer Worship."

"And where did you get the formula?"

"The what?"

"The recipe."

"Why," frizzling her hair anew, "from a friend of mine."

"And who is that?"

Studious pause, eyes all but hidden beneath brows, followed by sudden wide-eyed inspiration. "Cornelia, Yer Honor."

"Cornelia what?"

"Why, I don't know. Never knew her last name."

At this point Roelant frantically raised his hand. The judge calmed him, raising one palm in a sort of benediction. He turned back to Henrietta. "And would this Cornelia be in fact Cornelia Jansdochter of Raamstraat?"

Henrietta shrugged glumly. "You say so. I never knew it."

Then her face lit up. "Wasn't nobody ever complained about my salve," she cried in a voice that gathered volume until it filled the chamber. "If she got hurt it was something else. Not my fault. It was her doing! It was the devil did it!"

At this, a certain unquiet silence fell upon us. Henrietta sat down. Vreese gave her a sardonic glance, then pursed his lips and studied his papers. Roelant raised his hand again.

Roelant: Sir.

Vreese (quickly referring to his notes): Mr. Laurensen.

Roelant: Sir, my mother has made this salve for as long as I can remember, and I have helped her make it many times.

Vreese: Yes.

Henrietta: Yer Worship, this man is not to be trusted. He —

Vreese (louder): Go on, Mr. Laurensen.

Roelant: Well, I've seen the stuff that this lady, this person has used — that was sold to Mrs. Hals. It's not the same. Definitely not the same. It is not made the same way.

Vreese: How do you know that?

Roelant: Much more sulfur. You can smell it. It can't be the same formula. It even feels different. Rougher.

Henrietta (something like a shriek): The devil! It's the devil's work!

Vreese (cold as a tuna): Madame, kindly take your seat. . . .

He fined her fifty guilders, plus three more to be paid to Lysbeth directly for the salve she bought, and she . . .

———————————◀○▶———————————

The lobby doorbell rang. Wildly searching for the speaker, Peter found it by the apartment door after the third ring.

"It's Bob," the metallic voice announced confidently, then he hung up. Peter obediently pushed the button that opened the outside door. A minute later there was a knock at his door. He opened it to two tall, extremely thin young men. The one in front was almost bald, with a few long brown snakes of hair running forward along his narrow skull. He had rings in both ears, rings a shade too large to be piratical, and a neckerchief pulled tight, like Yves Montand in *The Wages of Fear*. He wore a plain tank top and jeans. The man behind him had lots of brown hair and a pointed beard and wore a batik guayabera from which protruded the boniest arms Peter had ever seen.

"Hi," said the front man. "I'm Bob and this is Waverley. And who might you be, if I may be so bold?"

"I might be Peter. Su Zan picked me up last night."

"Oh good. I love a scandal. Whatever became of the dashing Bradley?"

"I think she said he was a wuss."

Bob clucked his tongue and ran it around the edges of his mouth. "Dear dear. I could have told her that."

Waverley silently entered the apartment carrying a large roll of fabric, which he set on the big table.

"Not Peter O'Toole, by any chance?" Bob asked brightly. "Such a charming name. So suc . . . cinct."

"If a bit repetitive," Peter retorted. Bob flashed him a look and laughed a single burst.

Waverley, who had already hoisted the sewing machine over to the corner of the table and set a folding chair before it, cleared his throat.

"Oh dear," Bob whispered confidentially, "I am dawdling again, and himself wants us to work. To work, to work."

Peter laughed. "To work, to work," he said. He moved his own books across the room to a coffee table. It was only now that he realized he had left his Dutch history behind at Laura's. The two men spread out a giant wing-shaped crimson, yellow, purple, silver and black sheet on the table and began expertly to run it through the sewing machine in long bursts, attaching it to a narrow strip covered with green polka dots.

<hr>

. . . and she is enjoined from selling or distributing any ointments or medicaments of any nature subsequently or hereafter. One day in court and I am talking like a lawyer.

So we went home in a grand mood, despite Roelant's dark warning that the woman is vindictive and to watch her carefully.

When we got to the house, who was waiting here but Joost's Maria, that quiet girl, all distraught but trying not to show it.

I took her aside in the vestibule while the others trooped in out of the wind (which had risen again, it was that kind of a day) to start supper.

"He's gone off somewhere," she said in a supercalm voice. "I can't find him in his usual places."

She was so afraid of upsetting anyone, yet was frantic, I could see. She would keep controlling her face muscles, smoothing her forehead, but the anxious frown would keep returning.

"He went off yesterday and hasn't come back. I've asked everywhere."

I said, "What do you think it was? Did you have a fight?"

She was mortified. I patted her shoulder. A little too upholstered for my taste. Straight blond hair that is unusually coarse for a blonde.

"Yes," she whispered at last, "and he said he was leaving."

"Did he take anything with him?"

She shook her head and blew her nose.

"Did he have money?"

She nodded into her handkerchief. "He got a payment on the house. They owed him some extra and he said he would sue if they didn't pay, with interest, and it came day before yesterday."

"How much?"

"Forty guilders."

Enough for a thorough drunk was my first thought. I told her to go home and wait for him there and I would go around town to look for him. I am going to stop here as it is very late and Lysbeth is calling

---

To finish last night. I grabbed a piece of bread and some sausage and headed out. Lysbeth not pleased at all. Dropped in at all the bars I knew myself, all in the old neighborhood, but no luck.

Maria said she had done the ones around their place, so I decided to try some in the poor section of town behind St. Bavo. I had forgotten how many bars there are in this town. Some are just a basement room with steps down from the pavement, no tables or chairs, just a crude bench along the wall, and the only bar is a door laid across two barrels. The rotgut they serve is what you would expect. Homemade, and not very lovingly made at that. I have had my share and I am lucky I'm not blind.

He was in the fourth one. It wasn't one of the very worst, but bad enough. He sat in the far corner, head on arms. I thought he had passed out, but when I sat down by him, he stirred and finally lifted his head to look at me.

"So," I said.

"So," he said, his chin on his hands. He wouldn't look at me. "You better pay."

"You don't have any money?"

The tears started now. He put his face in his hands. "I'm no good, I'm no good." It was so muffled. Two old guys in the corner looked our way. I let him cry it out, and finally he stopped and put a hand on my arm.

"I can't do it," he whispered. "I can't do it in bed."

Now we were getting to the heart of things. "Well, that's nothing," I said. "Happens to me all the time."

I told him he was thinking about it too much. Women take these things much more calmly than we do. Besides, what do they know about it? Tell them a man misfires like a cannon now and then. This cheered him up at last.

We left the place and I steered him to his home.

Harmen had another fight with Lysbeth. He came in at dawn, messy drunk, with vomit on his shoe tops. Demanded breakfast.

"Go to your room!" she shouted. "I don't want to look at you!"

He mumbled something vile, for which I grabbed him by the

collar and propelled him to the stairs. "Up!" I said. "I see you again like this, I'll beat the pants off you."

He stamped out of sight, and the minute I turned around Lysbeth was upon me.

"He insulted me! And what did you do? You should have slapped his face!"

"I did enough," I said. "He's drunk."

"You always take his side! I can't stand the way he glowers at me. Looks like murder in his eyes."

She folded her arms, a sign that we are in for a long siege.

"Lysbeth, he's only fifteen years old."

"So? He can control himself, can't he?"

"It's a wild age. You know that. At fifteen, I was—"

She shook her head violently. "Don't give me those anecdotes of yours. He's living in my house, he will be civil to me."

"Whose house?" I said.

"Don't you roar at me."

"Look. If he insults you, he insults me too. I dragged him out like a puppy, that's enough. I say he knows he did wrong. He'll come down and apologize, you wait."

She subsided. "If he will, fine. I want him to apologize. That's all. He should be reminded. He can't run roughshod over the world."

"Agreed," I said. She tucked back a long lock of hair that had got loose and had been waving back and forth like a dark oriflamme. She was magnificent.

"We have to talk to Dirck," she said calmly.

It was very simple. Dirck, it seems, is looking for a cheap assistant. Harmen was intrigued with the idea of working for a painter. The romance of the rope walk has melted away like the dew. So I brought them together and they sized each other up (had always got along fine anyway since H was a baby), and yesterday he moved in. He will be paid as an apprentice, that is, mainly bed and board.

I dropped in today just to check, I thought the boy might be feeling somewhat homesick. Not at all. There he was, cleaning brushes in the shed, whistling away. I asked him how things were, and he turned to me, his red hair bristling and his round boy's cheeks ruddy with good health, and said Dirck is taking him fishing tomorrow and Agneta is a wonderful cook and he is learning how to stretch a canvas.

I was about to point out in my defense that I was continually offering to take him fishing but that he would never go. But I said nothing. I looked at him afresh and remembered little Harmen. Coming to me to be hugged.

He no longer has Annie's uptilted nose, but he does have her sunny face.

I said remember to keep them moist after you've cleaned them, and I patted him and went away with a hollow feeling in my stomach. I realized that I was the one who was homesick.

Lysbeth much relieved but quiet. Last night, she turned to me in bed and said I was looking sad. I said no. She said, It's Harmen, isn't it? And I said, I miss him, that's all.

We held each other for a long time, saying the things you say that have no words to them, and after a while we began to get interested in the other thing.

It's been a week now, and she is more cheerful than I have seen her for some time. She is very beautiful today. Those huge eyes, drawing me in. Her smile is full of mystery.

She is pregnant again. I knew it. I knew it. Lucky we have Harmen's room. Someday I will knock out the partitions on the top floor and make a dormitory for all the boys.

They think I am made of money. Now it is Mother Vooght. She

is hinting she should get more for an older woman. I hinted right back that Lysbeth's must surely be the easiest she has ever had to deal with. She pops them out like kittens.

Joost again. Dr. Wath is sending him to some sort of quack who is supposed to have a marvelous potion for men. My advice for nothing. Evidently this is all beneath Wath's dignity.

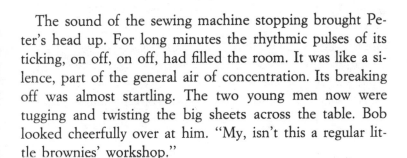

The sound of the sewing machine stopping brought Peter's head up. For long minutes the rhythmic pulses of its ticking, on off, on off, had filled the room. It was like a silence, part of the general air of concentration. Its breaking off was almost startling. The two young men now were tugging and twisting the big sheets across the table. Bob looked cheerfully over at him. "My, isn't this a regular little brownies' workshop."

Joost actually cheerful, if rather jittery. He wanted me to go to Piet's with him. Why can't he find someone at the tavern? That's what taverns are for. When do I get my work done? These people are devouring me.

Peter lifted his head. Right. He was being devoured, all right. What was he doing here anyway? What was happening to his life?

He was living in three different places and had been thrown out of two of them and wasn't all that sure about the third. What if someone wanted to reach him on the phone?

What would Hals do?

Joost is gone again. Maria too embarrassed to come to me but sent a neighbor child. I can't keep doing this.

We are worried about Joost. He has not come back. Went out two nights ago, very depressed.

Very early this morning there was a knock on the door and I opened it and there stood this skinny boy from the fish market. I know him, his name is Jan and he belongs to one of the fishwomen with a stall down there, his father is with the safety brigade. The minute I saw him and his long face I knew everything. But you have to let it all unfold at its own excruciating pace. So I said, What is it? And he said (also knowing everything already, I think, but acting his part in this ponderous drama), It's Mijnheer Grober, he wants you down at the Marktstraat bridge.

So I said, Thank you very politely and formally and turned to Lysbeth, who was coming up behind me, and said, I have to go down to the bridge. They want me there. And she (who also knew, of course, instantly and completely) laid a gentle hand on my shoulder blade and said gravely, All right.

I followed the boy's tousled head, so blond it was actually white, through the narrow streets. It had rained all night and the cobbles were slippery. The sky was still full of rain, dark and lowering, clouds hovering just above the rooftops, it seemed. The air smelled of salt and deliciously clean.

Turning the corner to Marktstraat, I saw what I had known would be there: a little clump of men huddled glumly together talking in low tones. They looked up as we approached. I recognized the chief of the night watch, Grober, a rangy broad-boned man with the rough, patchy red skin and faded eyes of a veteran drinker.

He nodded curtly. "Hals," he said in that curious way we have of identifying ourselves with one another's names. "Grober," I

156

PIETER CORNELISZ VAN DER MORSCH
(MAN WITH A HERRING)
Courtesy of the Carnegie Museum of Art, Pittsburgh

"Him and his straw and his herring. I do not like the man.
Does he think he is mystifying me?"

LAUGHING BOY
Courtesy of Mauritshuis —
The Hague

"The children . . . laughing
their wonderful laugh. I
tried to make a picture of
that laugh with Frans. It
almost comes off, I think."

ISAAK ABRAHAMSZ
MASSA
Courtesy of the Art Gallery
of Ontario

"I wanted him before
an open window, so I
could work in a slice of
Haarlem scenery, but
he insists on putting his
Molijn into the
background."

RENE DESCARTES
*Courtesy of Statens Museum for
Kunst, Copenhagen*

"An interesting face, not what
I would call knifelike with
intelligence, but calmer,
slower, wiser. An old face,
very French."

MALLE BABBE
*Courtesy of Staatliche
Museen ZU Berlin*

"I have been watching
the mad witch. . . .
Those quick, violent
movements. I have
been thinking how to
paint someone in
motion."

ST. GEORGES GROUP
Courtesy of Frans Halsmuseum de Hallen

"It was just a face among many, toward the edge of the group, but it looked straight at the viewer with the measuring eyes of a painter."

ALMSHOUSE REGENTS, 1664
Courtesy of Frans Halsmuseum de Hallen

"I forget everything, my fingers grow nimble again. . . . Today it was Westerloo's eyes, which must seem intelligent but not too much, caring but not too much."

said. The other men stood aside a little, and I saw the tarpaulin with the long lump under it.

"Sorry to bring you here at this hour," the man was saying in a harsh voice not accustomed to the amenities of formal talk, "but we may need you to identify this man."

"Where was he found?" I say.

"Under the bridge. Wedged against the post there, or he would have been seen earlier."

Meaning he would have surfaced and drifted, facedown, inert, ghastly, right through the town and past the docks.

"How long has he been there, you think?"

A slow shake of the bare gray head.

"Don't rightly know. Not too long. Sometime the last two days, I would guess."

I nod, gazing at the still form. I am not sure what comes next.

"Uh." The man clears his throat. "We weren't sure if it was your brother — we thought — "

"We thought it looked like, uh," mutters another man, "a family resemblance." He doesn't want to say it looks like me. The man's name is Kuiper. I have known him all my life, a town fixture, night guard, member of the fire brigade, onetime brawler with his cauliflower nose and gnarled hands. I didn't know he knew my name. There are dozens of them around town, part of the landscape you've grown up with, are vaguely aware of and perhaps nod at in passing. It is always such a surprise to realize that you are part of their landscape too.

"May I see," I say. It is not a question. Without a word, stepping back to surround the tarp, conscious of their minor role in this pageant, the men seem to present the body to me. Gruber peels back the glistening corner of the tarred cloth.

First I see hair, long gray strands flung crazily across a pale forehead. My eyes don't want to organize this sight into something I will understand. For a moment I see only the separate features, livid and splotchy, beaded with water—a thick nose, bruised cheekbones, waterlogged beard. The eyes are closed, have been closed for him, but I can see how they bulge beneath the stretched lids.

Then, abruptly, I see it is Joost. It is Joost. Not peaceful, not frantic, just somewhat harassed.

"That's my brother," I say. "That's Joost."

The corner is laid reverently back, covering the face. I want to see the rest of him, to get another look at his long, bony form, but then I don't. It would be twisted and contorted, misshapen by the hours in the water.

I feel nothing. We agree to take him to my house for now. It is good to have them here, impersonal and competent. They roll the body into the tarp to make a tight package, and Grober commandeers a delivery cart. We walk slowly behind it, drawing covert stares from the early-rising women with their market baskets. A couple of kids gape openmouthed and follow at a distance.

When I see Maria she shrieks and covers her face and runs back into the house.

———————————◄O►———————————

They were folding up the sheets.

"Okay, Peter, we are out of your hair. We are on our way. We have completed our task."

Bob's brittle, scratchy voice shattered Peter's gloom. He was still seeing the men carrying the body through the gray streets of Haarlem in the grim morning. He leaned back and stretched.

"You got it done?"

"As done as it's going to be."

"May I ask—"

"In fact you are a sport not to have asked before. Isn't he a sport, Waverley?"

Waverley nodded.

He and Bob continued to fold the painted sheets this way and that, like soldiers folding the flag at a military funeral, until it was a mere armful, whereupon Bob tucked it under his arm. "It is," he said grandly, "not a wing. It looks like a wing, but it is not a wing. It is . . . Waverley, tell him what it is."

"A sail."

"Correct. A wonderful, phantasmagoric sail. Without a boat. We will have a man on stilts for the mast and six people on either side of it to be the boat and another in the middle to be the sailor. A conceptual sailboat, you might say."

"Lapstraked?" asked Peter.

Bob jumped in amazement and joy. "Lapstraked indeed! Lapstraked exactly! What a delightful mind you have, young Peter. And what a spiritual experience it has been working here with you in Su Zan's magical workshop."

"My pleasure."

"And so we leave you. Until parade time perhaps."

"Who knows?" said Peter.

"Indeed. Who knows but Su Zan?"

He was still chuckling when he closed the door on them. It was several minutes before he could get back into Hals's mood.

I have been thinking about Joost all day. We put him in the ground this morning. I never knew him well. Hard to say this when he was only two years younger and we were together day and night for the first twelve years of my life. I knew him then, I suppose, but when we met again, me freshly married, he was so different. Even more so when I stayed with him in Antwerp. A brooding man, silent and sullen. His stomach bothered him. He would say he was in pain all the time, and he looked it.

One time when I was twelve — it must have been just before he went to live with Carel — I took him out on the river in my boat. This was an old rowboat I had found on the bank some miles out of town and had mounted a mast made from a piece of driftwood, and I had a sail that was real canvas, so rotten you could poke your finger through it.

———————————◄○►———————————

The antic image of Bob and Waverley in their human sailboat made him actually stop and glance about, stretching his neck. The afternoon was wearing on. Pretty soon he would stop to do some checking and make himself some coffee. As he riffled through the pages of the thin book he saw that he was nearly at the end of the writing. The last several pages were blank. My God, he thought, maybe I better slow down. Give the man his money's worth.

———————————◄○►———————————

I would cast off and drift with the current and pretend I was sailing the thing, which was the nearest I ever came to sailing.

I'm taking you sailing, I told him, and like any ten-year-old he was game for anything. He jumped in and I pushed off and we cruised down the river with a pole for a rudder (it didn't steer; you just poked yourself away from the shore with it). I took it out in midstream where the river gets wider, farther out than I had before because I was showing off. Got out there and of course I had no control over our direction, and we were swept along to the widest part.

The water was high after the rains, and we began swirling in circles, and he could see I was getting nervous. Then it sprang a leak, and another one, geysering up between our feet. It looked like a mile to shore (probably fifty feet or so). There was no one in sight except some barges far upstream.

"Can you swim?" I said casually. "No," he said casually.

"It's all right, the boards won't sink. We just stick to the boat."

But we didn't. It sank lower and lower and began to break up, so we cut out for the closest shore. I knew enough about swimming to paddle and kick, and I tried to keep him calm by pretending this was a sort of lesson. "It's all right," I kept saying. "Just kick and move your arms like this and you'll stay up. Like a dog," I said, "like a dog does."

He was sobbing with terror but he kept thrashing, and when he saw that he wasn't sinking he relaxed some. Later I was able to get hold of his shirt and pull him after me. We climbed out on the far bank with a four-mile walk ahead of us to get home.

"That's good," I said. "Now you can swim."

He didn't say anything but he knew perfectly well that I had very nearly got us both drowned. We never talked about that time afterward. I would visit him at our half brother's in Amsterdam, but he wasn't one for jolly reminiscences, even as a kid. Carel's Mary would tease him, but he wouldn't tease.

They lived by the Rooden gate, water on all sides. Once I asked him if he'd ever learned to swim and he said no. I think he said no. That was what I remembered. I think about him splashing along beside me that time, his face, the urgency to live.

St. Nicholas Day. All content. Took Lysbeth to bed though she is huge. One glass of wine only.

1627

11 February. The baby was baptized today. His name is Reynier. For his mother. He is enormous with hair red as a brick. Lysbeth thriving. Thank you God, you have a warm spot for little boys I think, being one yourself.

Talked to Jan van de Velde after. We had the witnesses at the house for geneva and cakes. He has been making prints of some of my work. He is doing Pieter Verdonck.

"You are just encouraging him," he said about Verdonck. "Now he's going to think he's inspired by God."

Because I showed the man with the jawbone of an ass. He got into trouble for bothering some Mennonite preacher . . .

—◄○►—

The rest of the page was chewed away and several other beneath it had been torn out completely. The next full page picked up some time later, apparently.

—◄○►—

Took Frans to see Harmen today—at Dirck's. I haven't seen him since the funeral. Nothing like a funeral to improve the quality of your social life. Harmen acts so much older. So serious. Barely had time to shake my hand, he was so busy with the canvases. To Frans he is the king of the world. Sixteen years old! Frans watches every move he makes. Tries to walk like him. Not so long ago Harmen couldn't stand the kid, always underfoot. But father, he's so childish! he would say, and I would say, Well he's a child, that's why. Then suddenly Harmen was sixteen, a man, and he could afford to be tolerant of his nine-year-old audience. Especially when the audience hung on his words (including curse words, which I had to warn him about) and swung his arms the same way when walking.

Frans had been rummaging in a trunk and came up with a great old fur hat. He put it on and looked like a bear cub. At that moment Harmen, who was off somewhere behind him, began to haul on a pulley to lift a heavy frame into place. Frans turned and stared at him.

What a look. Mouth open, totally absorbed. Whatever he was doing is utterly forgotten as he gapes at his hero. I will get that look, I thought.

Dirck was watching in his quiet way. "That's Agneta's old hat," he said. "Show him, Harmen."

162

Harmen went to a cabinet and pulled out a small canvas and shyly presented it to me.

It was a still life of the hat and a wineglass. It was quite competent.

"We're working on the look of things," Dirck muttered, glancing over my shoulder as the boy held up the frame.

The look of things, eh? Oh, that. Maybe you could give me a lesson too.

I studied the brushwork up close. "This is very advanced stuff," I said. Such a surprise to see your talent in someone else, especially your own child. Fur, long-haired fur, is impossible to get right. You have to slip in between the clumps of hair, bring the light in there, yet without making it look like a bunch of sticks. He had some lights and darks playing in there, was on the right track, but I sensed that he wasn't grasping the main thing, to see it all as light.

Harmen beamed. Dirck moved in beside me to examine the small square.

"The glass is fine," I said. "I think you have been doing a lot of glass."

Harmen smiled and glanced at Dirck, who chuckled. "He's done every jar, glass, pot and bowl in the house. I may have him do some work on my next commission."

Sixteen years old. What was I doing at sixteen?

Harmen frowned at his creation. "But it doesn't look right. The fur. It looks dead."

Dirck looked at me frankly. "What you think, big brother? What would you tell him?"

Exactly what I hoped would not happen. I can't teach. It is in my eye, then it is in my hand, then it is on the canvas. The people I teach (if they are good, and so few are) end up painting just like me and no one is happy.

But it was raining again, and I had no special desire to go home, where I have nothing going right now, and Frans was having such a good time with all these men around. Besides, I smelled something wonderful bubbling on the stove. So I said, "Let me try."

What I had in mind was that glimpse of Frans in the hat gawping up at his hero.

"Aw, you don't want to . . . " Dirck made polite noises, but he was pleased. So they bustled about to get me set up. I sat Frans on a soft chair. Harmen brought out a board he had prepared for one of his exercises, underpainted a caramel color, and Dirck presented me . . .

<hr>

Peter felt a shiver of delight. Caramel underpainting, a Hals trademark. Where had he read that?

<hr>

. . . with his own, extremely cluttered palette, the one he had been using to touch up a little village scene when we came in.

"My God, how do you find your way around on this thing?" I said. It was darker than mine, all browns and grays and gloomy umbers, dabs and blobs and great mounds of paint scattered in a sloppy circle about the central plain, where the real business takes place. He set a pot of white in front of me and a freshly mixed jar of a brilliant yellow, oh lovely, a clear rich dandelion yellow that hurt your eyes. Harmen ceremoniously stood the easel in front of me where I sat on a high stool.

Dirck nodded expectantly. They both nodded expectantly. Oh well. I quickly sketched in the boy's head, complete with gaping mouth and yearning eyes.

"The white. You put it right on the nostril that way?" murmured Harmen. It was a sharp little hook of near white done with a loaded brush to give it a bright edge.

"Stand back and you'll see."

He did and hummed with sudden comprehension. I don't need

to stand back so much anymore. A touch of white on the inner eyelid brings out the delicacy of that young skin. The smallest touches of white on the lower lip suggest the moistness of its pads and the slight cleft between them. All this with the lightest blips of the brush end. I have done these things so many times, but I still try to see every face as though it were the first.

Enough of the face. I blotted in the dark brown form of the hat, a massive frame around three sides of the face. Then, with the small brush, I mixed some dandelion, just a dab, in with an olive brown and a touch of magenta.

"Now we get to the good part," I muttered. They pressed closer, as if some magic thing was going to happen.

One, two, three, four, five, I struck in the feathers of color, ranks and ranks of them, standing up at the center, falling away at the sides, each stroke slightly curved. Coming to the front I loaded the brush with a bit of white and made another row. Then down the sides past his cheek, where the streaks of light were actually brightest yet mixed in with the darkest parts. Blacks, grays, whites, individual strands. Then out around the edge, delicate tips of brown to show the shape of the hat coming through the thicket of hairs.

We ate the stew with pieces of good wheat bread. I always feel content after a day with my brushes, when I sink into my chair and breathe deep and think of nothing in particular.

I am being sued by my dairyman. He wants seven guilders for some cheeses I bought in April. I paid him at the time, I am sure of it. I remember him urging it on me and me reaching into my purse to pay him the extra. This ridiculous business. He has a cast in his eye, a sly thief if ever I saw one, and has tried to shortchange me before. More than once I have caught him in that quick sidelong glance to see if I am paying attention as the money is being . . .

Where is the money to . . .

. . . is the worst in memory, and coming after two bad summers of nothing but rain and hail, and that on top of the floods in '25, was it, when cows floated across the meadows. Now the farmers are desperate. People are beginning to drift into the town in their wagons with all their possessions on top. I can't imagine what they expect to find here. The price of bread is tripled already. The herring fleet . . .

1628

It is only getting worse. Fish of all kinds are very dear now, and the market is down to a handful of stalls. You see no chickens or game (it is treasured in secret, I am sure, by anyone lucky enough to bag a squirrel or woodchuck), and the baker makes bread once a week, an occasion. Everyone lines up, one loaf to a customer. The Council stands guard in person. Last week a ship brought a small load of rice from somewhere in the Orient (Sumatra?) and we bought a large bag. It will keep us going for several days. There is milk for the children, from the farms, thanks to the Council again. It is worse than during the siege.

She blames me for the famine. She believes that I personally am the one who is keeping the food from the children's mouths (and my own too, I might add, I have lost several pounds and am rather svelte at the moment though hungry all the time).

"It will get better," I say. "In the spring."

"In the spring? There are no crops."

"The ice breaks up, my love. The ships can come down from the north."

"And they have bread."

"I suppose so," I say. "I hope so."

Still she scowls accusingly at me.

I find that . . .

We went fishing, Sara and Frans and I. Walked up the Spaarne a couple of miles, past all the other fishers. There was still snow on the ground, but the thaw has nearly finished it, and with last week's rains I figured at least a few of the fish would be stirring down there.

I bought some worms from a very small boy who had a stand in the meadow beyond the big mill. Paid him three pennies, and Sara objected. She is going to be a dazzler. Very affectionate. She clings to me just for the sheer pleasure of feeling a warm body. Lysbeth is always at her, and I have to mediate.

We put our hooks in over a bank where an old alder has fallen down and lies half . . .

◄○►

The writing ended at the bottom of the page. Some pages were torn out and the rest were blank.

Peter turned without pause to the catalog and checked it against the names and dates he had listed as he translated. There, on February 11, 1627, was the baptism of Reynier Hals. There was the painting of the St. Hadrian guards and the St. George's too.

Isaac had to be Isaac Abrahamsz Massa, a merchant fluent in Russian who stood witness to the baptism of Hals's daughter Adriaentje, who must surely have been Addie, in 1623. It was all there, even the forest landscape by the artist Molijn that Massa was known to own, even to the comments on the unusual pose that Hals invented for his subject, a pose which was, in fact, "the earliest known single portrait" of a model with his arm on the back of a chair.

With mounting excitement, Peter tracked down the herb woman named Henrietta, cited in the Haarlem town records as one Hendrickje Wetselaers, who was sued by Hals for giving his wife a damaging salve. The records also mentioned a twenty-four-year-old weaver named Roelant Laurensz., who testified that his mother had given the woman the recipe for the salve but that the herb woman had changed the formula. To Peter's astonishment it even spoke of Roelant's visit to the Hals house and the appearance of Henrietta and her panicked flight upon spotting him.

And there was the split frame and Schrijver's complaint. And van de Velde making prints of the Verdonck portrait. What about the food shortage at the end? He could find nothing in the records. Schama reported that in general the Dutch were prosperous during the seventeenth century but that there were a few local famines and even food riots. There were four such in what Schama called "the dearth year of 1630," and also some disturbances in 1628, but no mention of Haarlem. Perhaps Hals was poorer than usual that year.

The dairyman was there in the records, too, a Cornelis Dircksz., who had demanded payment in May of 1627 for butter and cheese, suing Hals first for seven guilders, then for an additional three.

Thumbing through the glossy pages, Peter came suddenly upon a large reproduction of a laughing boy wearing an extravagant fur hat. He yelped aloud. There it was, the fur hat described in such beautiful detail, stroke by stroke, in the diary. Peter went over the passage again and found it matched, every dab of white, every slash of brown and "dandelion."

A great surge of relief swept through him: This had to be the man's own book, his own handwriting, his own personality shining out of the pages. A sardonic man, as ready to snicker at himself as at anyone. A kind man who adored his children and who stuck faithfully to his illiterate peasant wife. A disappointed man, but one who could laugh at what was happening to him.

Peter tried to explain to himself why, after all, he was rooting so hard for his Hals. It just didn't seem right that some skulking literary con man would be writing all this stuff, pouring out all this energy.

Further along, Peter found a picture of Hals with the St. George Militia, one of only two he was known to have made of himself—Hals, the portraitist!—and the only one still surviving. It was just a face among many, toward the edge of the group, but it looked straight at the viewer with the measuring eyes of a painter. A face worn down by life but nevertheless alive.

Someone was at the door. It couldn't be eight o'clock already.

But it was. It was after eight, and Su Zan would be rushing in to take her shower. Never in his life had he worked with such concentration for so long. He had eaten nothing but some tuna straight from the can. Maybe she would be bringing a steak or something in a doggie bag. He had known her for twenty-four hours. Peter closed his books and looked up expectantly.

5

Not only was the gorilla suit hot, it itched. And it had no pockets. Every time Peter passed the enormous top hat through the crowds, he fielded a few quarters and dimes and the occasional dollar bill. Then he had to pour his booty into his hand, unzip the suit at the collar and reach all the way down to his Skivvies to insert the money inside the waistband. Some coins had missed and were scraping his ankles where the suit went into the tops of his sneakers. Sweat was running down his face so heavily, he was having trouble seeing out of the eyeholes. And he had to go . to the bathroom in the worst way.

Oh come on, Su Zan had said. It's not hard.

She had found a small parade that some French group had organized for Bastille Day, going up through Central Park.

You'll have fun, she had said. The hat brim was chafing his sweaty temples. It was too small for the giant head, which no doubt was on purpose to make it look funnier. Peter took it off as often as he could. He bowed frequently to the crowd, which seemed to consist, at least the ones he could make out through the eyeholes, of children with nannies walking beside carriages and strollers. It was a superb day, and everybody was beautifully dressed.

They had assembled at the corner of the park by the Plaza, unfolding their fantastic wings and great canvas caterpillars and stilts and people-sized condoms and the conceptual sailboat and gigantic hats attached to helium balloons which hovered over them on the march. Preceded by a band made up of French musicians, some quite good and others not good at all, they were to parade past the Children's Zoo, over to the Lake and down to Columbus Circle, where they would meet Waverley's pickup truck.

Su Zan was up at the head in her vulva outfit. It was really quite beautiful: a suit consisting of delicate large pink silk petals arranged in fluttery ranks, with her head in the center, wearing a silver bathing cap with purple spangles, as the clitoris, or so he supposed. He hadn't asked.

He finally discovered a slit in the left wrist of his hairy Dr. Denton's. You simply fed the money into the left paw and let the paw dangle. He began to step higher.

Some children shrieked as he approached them, the whole crowd that lined the roadway giving way in a wave before him. He doffed his hat. He waved it in a cavalier's bow. Children laughed. Suddenly grasping the fact that no one could possibly know who he was, he began twirling on his toes, attempted an entrechat, achieving a leap that he felt was quite graceful considering. He jumped up and clicked his heels. The children howled and clapped. The mothers smiled. He pushed the hat to the side of his head, Maurice Chevalier–style, and strutted. Picking up on the band's rhythm, he cakewalked to "The Washington Post March" until, getting so twisted in the suit that he lost the eyeholes, he careened into the crowd, evoking screams.

It came to him that he was enjoying this. He could be anyone he wanted. He felt dangerously liberated. Maybe, he thought, I should be an actor. Maybe this is my new life.

171

Then he thought, What am I thinking about? What is happening to my life? What am I doing here?

All these women, he thought. And Tony's grant running out. And de Hooch the next thing to forgotten. And Corwin would never hire him to do gold leaf again in a million years.

He whirled, paws in the air, to do a bravura Spanish dance step. Coins showered down his left arm, past his chest and stomach, to collect in his pant leg. Damn, he thought. He took off the hat again and balanced it on his nose. Didn't work.

What would Hals think of him now?

They were past the Children's Zoo now and turning west. Some elegantly dressed people had drifted in from Fifth Avenue to watch. He did some complicated shuffling, pushing his arms back and forth like pistons. It was the way he normally danced to rock music.

Out of the eyeholes he saw a tall woman, an extremely old woman with hair as red as fire and carrying a cane. Very distinguished. One of those Fifth Avenue matrons who shopped for Fabergé eggs at La Vieille Russie.

Wait a minute. He grabbed his furry head and turned it to get a better look through the eyes.

It was Mrs. Dunaway. He walked over to where she stood at the edge of the roadway. She appeared to rear back a little when he approached.

"Hello Mrs. Dunaway," he said.

Her mouth opened, then closed. She held her ground.

"How do you do," she said rather formally.

"It's me," he said. "It's Peter Van Overloop."

"Oh," she said, brightening. "Peter! Is it really you? How delightful!"

He doffed his hat. "I really should take my head off, but it's zipped on."

"You look marvelous. This is a new talent."

172

"Yeah well."

"Peter. We haven't seen you in ages. Amy has been calling you."

"Oh dear. My apartment was burned up and I moved."

A lumbering four-man turtle was waiting behind him, so he waved it ahead.

"I have to go," he said. "I'll call."

"Oh do. She's quite impossible. Do come for dinner next week."

"Okay, if I can."

"What's your number, Peter? How can she reach you?"

"Uh, my number. I don't know. I'll call."

She looked with concern into the nearest eyehole. "Peter," she said quietly, "are you sure you're all right?"

"No I'm not, Mrs. Dunaway. I hate my life."

He waltzed away. Really, what if he fell down right here and had to go to the hospital with heat exhaustion or something? How would he tell them where he lived? And what was Su Zan's last name anyway? Mrs. Dunaway faded back into the crowd, still looking worried.

He hadn't thought about Amy in weeks. She would want to talk about de Hooch again. She would expect him to make a decision or something. Furthermore, he had to get back into Laura's place to rescue his history book which didn't belong to him. Goddamn Scott to hell, it was Scott who had let the firebug stay in his room in the first place.

He trudged on through the park, no longer cavorting. He wished he could talk to someone about Hals. He didn't dare even discuss it with Su Zan. One day he had told her he wished his life were like Hals's. "Imagine, doing one thing all your life. Painting. Painting nothing but heads. Just the one thing. Boy, I'd love it."

She said, "No you wouldn't."

173

The next day, he made a date with Henry Silverstein. Silverstein was excited.

"Been trying to reach you," he said the minute he unlocked the door to let Peter into the closed display room. "Things are happening."

"Well I finished the second book. I have some notes too. He talks about landscapes at the beginning but his wife burned them up. Some of them, and he sold some. I don't think—"

"Wait'll you hear," Silverstein interrupted, guiding him into the back office. "Remember the Barnett kid?"

"No." Peter sat down in his regular seat beside the desk. Silverstein stalked up and down past the Mapplethorpe flower photos on his walls and the fine Hiram Powers bust on top of the file cabinet.

"The kid, Don Barnett's kid who found the books. He told his teacher about it, and the teacher called the papers. Things are beginning to fall apart."

"What?"

"The *Times* sent someone down here. I told her we were still checking. So she says fine and goes away, and I think that's all. Next day some editor from *Art in America* calls me up and demands an interview and pictures and the whole thing. I say it's much too early and besides everything is out of my hands right now. The lab still has the first book and you have the rest. They are okay, aren't they? I really worry about them floating around."

Obviously he had a picture of Peter's student digs with the empty beer cans and the basketball hoop on the wall and the floor ankle-deep in socks and disgusting underpants. Peter hadn't worried a bit.

"Well you have the second one back now. I'm taking excellent care of the others. I'm on the wing these days," he said. "I got burned out of my place and I'm sort of staying with friends. But I want to get back to work. I like this guy."

"Another thing is that Dr. Smith's people at Columbia are having a ball with this. They greatly admired your translation—especially your notes."

"Have they told anyone?"

"Not the press. Barnett says someone called him with an offer the other day. He'd like to sell but wants to wait and see if it's real. Of course, if it's not, the whole deal would be off."

"Couldn't you find someone who would buy it in any case?"

Silverstein shrugged. "That's what his wife says. That Mrs. Barnett." He shook his head. "Anyway, Smith's people are very worried about those landscapes. Everything else checks out perfectly. In fact, Smith says it looks too perfect to him, it looks like someone had the catalog in front of him and wrote it from that. Though strictly speaking that's impossible because the catalog was done in '89."

"Well, there's more on the landscapes in the second one. As I said, he lost some in a fire and then he sold the others. But he says they weren't signed. So they could be out there right now in some little museum somewhere, listed as Dutch School. No one would pay any attention to them."

Silverstein nodded. "Anything more in that line that you find, give me a call. Things are speeding up here. Oh, and they're still checking on the book itself, the paper and the binding, the threads, the glue, everything."

He gave Peter a long, speculative look before abruptly reaching into his top drawer and bringing out the checkbook. "You're working faster than I thought. I was going to cut you back a little because this was all getting expensive, but Barnett came through with some money to pay for the lab work. So I'm giving you the five hundred anyway."

"I'll take it," Peter said.

"It's for speed. I would love to have the entire diary translated before somebody forces our hand."

"Well if it is a hoax," Peter mused, "why haven't we heard from them?"

"Maybe they died. I've thought about that. The crate was under some old hay, and we haven't checked exactly how old that was. Five years, twenty years, who knows. But the crate could have been there long before the hay. Stuck away in a corner there, you never can tell what you're gonna find in a barn. It was addressed to some art dealer in New York who went out of business almost a hundred years ago. And Barnett says he can't find any connection between the dealer and Amagansett."

"Well a bunch of artists used to hang out near there years ago, didn't they? Pollock, people like that?"

Silverstein shot him a keen look. "Very good. Very good. Peggy Guggenheim had some connection with the place too. Any number of ways it could have been left out there."

"So someone does the hoax, wraps it up with some paintings and plants it in the barn. And then plans to come and find it, or get someone else to find it. But he dies."

"Before he can tell anyone." Silverstein smiled. "I already checked out the Kitterman company. The Kittermans all died before World War One. There was a sister, but she died of influenza in 1918. Far as I can make out, they were reputable dealers, serious people." His eyebrows flew up as he grinned and raised his hands. "But who knows? Maybe old Sol Kitterman was a kook. We'll never know."

He stared across the room at the Mapplethorpe and mused, more or less to himself, "And then there's the possibility that it's quite recent and that someone found the Kitterman package and somehow inserted the diary into it."

"Barnett opened the package himself, right? It could have been tampered with and he didn't spot it."

"Or tampered with it himself. But in that case it seems to me he would have taken some precaution to see that he wasn't suspected. Like have a witness to the opening."

———————————

Peter called Laura's place from his bank downtown but got no answer so went back uptown and let himself into Su Zan's apartment. The subway had been impossibly crowded and noisy and had left him exhausted. But the apartment was a haven. He could hardly wait to get through with his peanut butter sandwich and start on the third volume.

The date on the front page was 1634.

———————————◄○►———————————

Judy is coming to live with us when we move to the new house. Every week I watch them leave the house when the lesson is done, Molenaer tall and skinny, politely chatting her up, both of them walking slowly down the street, eyes on the ground. I watch them till they turn the corner. Sometimes she laughs at what he says, and I am stabbed to the heart.

I called her by that name for the first time last week. After four years. It was Miss Leyster at the christening, of course. Lysbeth's young friend from the school, I understood some sort of teacher. Brought up short when I commented lightly on this. Teacher indeed! Assistant to the director! I was humbled.

Then she comes for lessons, introduced by Molenaer, my one surviving pupil, and it is still Miss Leyster until I see her work, an oil she has done of her father, whereupon, with the shock still visible on my face, I bow low before her and say, "Judith Leyster! I salute the future!" Some such nonsense. (I am full of nonsense when I am around her, it is humiliating.)

So it has been Judith until last week, when I was calling her

to me to inspect her treatment of an eye — where all of us need a
little luck — and she was bent over her tray of pots stirring up
some colors, and I could see the side of her face with a lock of
auburn hair trailing down from beneath her cap, and she looked absolutely sixteen years old, and I couldn't help it, I said,
"Judy . . . " and even as my voice choked itself to death in my
throat, she turned, unconcerned, oblivious, and said, "Yes?"

I could not speak. It has been my secret name for her ever since
I caught sight of her standing straight-backed and proud, holding
little Maria there in the church and saying the holy words in her
low, dusty voice.

The new house is to be vacated the first of April. It is a
comedown. I saw it in L's eyes the first time she set foot in it. I
winced for her as I took her down Groot Heiligland yesterday for
her first look. It is not exactly the Olycans' neighborhood. Two
places down from us is a truly ramshackle hovel with dirt floors
and chickens all over. The houses are big but plainly made,
without even an attempt at a stepped roof or facade of any sort,
just a steep peak to keep the rain and snow off. The street is wider
than Peuzelaarsteeg, but that is because it is a thoroughfare of
sorts. All kinds of commercial wagons rumble through at all hours
of the day (and night, I suspect).

The one thing about the house is that it is bigger. I particularly
looked . . .

Peter turned to the map of old Haarlem in the catalog, with
Hals's various homes spotted here and there across the city.
He had indeed been living in Groot Heiligland Street as of
March 1636, had moved there from Peuzelaarsteeg, just a
couple of blocks away, where he had lived since January 1617.
Peter shook his head in wonder and excitement.

But no mention of Joost's suicide in the records. Just that

he had died sometime before October 1626. Wouldn't a suicide show up in an official archive? Every time he seemed closer to Hals, the man dodged away and turned into the hoaxer.

———————————◄○►———————————

I particularly looked for one with more room on the lower floors and wider stairs. Her legs give her pain all the time, she shows me the veins standing out on the calves and up above the knees even, ugly swollen blue knotted things. She wraps them in flannel bandages, pulling very tight, and that helps, but she says climbing stairs is agony.

"Hals," she says, "you're going to have to carry me about, one day." I laugh. Right. She's small enough and still has her waist (after nine!) but somehow I can't see my imperious Lysbeth directing the world while cradled in my arms like a cat. Like Devil, the cat Sara had, who would ride around in her arms with one black paw resting imperially on her forearm and the other raised in a sort of papal blessing. Devil disappeared one spring. L much relieved. "Cats are filthy," she says. "The way they slink around, like rats with their tails swaying, and you never know where they've been." So much for cats. We have never had another. I like them, their regal indifference, their silence, their sudden leaps of pure fear as though still in the jungle.

There is a huge main room at street level, with a wide hearth and a bench along the side wall ("like a tavern," she sniffed) and a long table that has been through the wars. I have an eye on that for my workroom, which is out back and hardly better than a shed. But warm. And a fine window on the south side, where we back up to a small yard, not ours. Our land (land! estate!) stops just beyond the shed, which seems to have been added some time ago. Barely room for the outhouse. On the second floor we have a good bedroom in front for us and the baby in her crib, and two small ones off a hall in back, and the top is one big loft. We will have the little ones by us, and the older ones will make do in the loft. I will have to build some more pallets, as I am tired of seeing them all rolled together in one bed. They are getting too big.

Sara has been fussing to get more privacy for herself. She actually volunteered to sleep with Maria and Nicolaes so she wouldn't have to be with the older boys. She is becoming quite conscious of herself. She will be like her mother, with that elegant small waist and magnificent swelling above. She pulls her middy tight to show it off, which isn't necessary at all, I could point out (but do not).

Of course, when Judy came to us with her proposal, Sara was ecstatic. She will sleep with Judy and the little ones will be put together in the other small room. Everyone is happy. L is delighted to get two guilders a week, Judy escapes from an impossible situation at home, Sara gets a companion and the big sister she has always yearned for (Judy about twenty-four, I think), and I get to have her in the house day and night.

Which I do not admit to myself. Panting like a schoolboy. I will not look at her. A sickness. I watch whenever she is in the room. The slash and swirl of her skirts when she gets up from her chair. My eyes follow her every move—unless I look firmly away, whereupon my brain does the work for them as I picture her walking across the room or sitting by the hearth or bending intently to her easel.

I am mad to have her here. To allow this. Should not even have her as a pupil. I lust for the mere sight of her, for the brush of her fingertips (unintentional—she knows nothing of all this), the honey smell of her. Like a miser I gloat over her comb when I find it left behind on the table. I sniff it. I press it to my palm. I imagine stroking the lush brown hair, so sleek and shining, when she wears it tied behind with a ribbon so the long flow of it falls straight down her back. (Once I touched her head. I was directing her to see a vase in a display for a still life and she was obstinately looking in the wrong direction, so instinctively, unconsciously—I swear it — I put my hand on the back of her small neat head and turned it slightly to point her right at the thing. She giggled a little but didn't seem upset. I remember exactly the feel of her round head, the slick softness of the hair, like satin it was, and the way I let my hand gracefully disengage, stroking gently downward, savoring the touch of smooth hair against my fingers.)

This squalor! Franszoon the baker is taking me to court again. I will never go back to him. His enormous fat body with his floury apron and sausage fingers and his horrible fat cheeks with the little pig eyes all but hidden behind them. Such mean eyes, dishonest eyes. Never have I seen such a dishonest face. He is demanding twenty-three guilders, seventeen stuivers, and two pennies. Two pennies! I told him that would pay for half a year's bread and a basketful of sugar buns thrown in. Sure I have paid him something within the past half year. Gave him a painting on account, the one of the boys, and now he is at my throat for more.

So. Have paid him and he is to return the painting. The magistrate had the gall to give me the fish eye as if to suggest that I was not quite honest and said, "We see you again, Mijnheer Hals."

"You see Franszoon too," I pointed out. Said I considered the man paid when I gave him the painting, which is worth certainly more than a barrowload of oversalted, undercrusted rye bread.

Imagine this: He then appoints Suycker and Grebber to appraise the painting! "If you as court appraisers find this work to be valued at less than twenty-three guilders, then that amount will be deducted from the debt." The mills of the gods, I tell you. As if those two old duffers could paint a privy.

Should have reminded the court that they see me far more often as plaintiff than defendant. I scared up Hillegond last year when she tried to tell me she didn't have the canvases that I left with her.

The Amsterdam militia again. I have told them I will do it here in Haarlem. I can't possibly afford to go to Amsterdam again. Already owe me for two nights' lodging.

———————

We have moved. In one day, miraculously. We were all sad to leave, but poor little Pieter didn't understand and had to be torn away from his place in the corner. He thought, well I can't imagine what he thought, poor creature, but he knew enough to know something was going to be different. He was bellowing even as I took him on my shoulder. I never knew it was possible to make so many sounds without making a single word. He has no words at all, not even *Mama*. But he gives no trouble and sits peacefully by the door and gurgles when the other children play with him as if he were some sort of toy. Lord guide me what to do with him when he gets older.

What a saga. I hired a wagon to take the big things, and the boys helped to haul the pallets down those awful stairs, good-bye stairs forever. I was afraid the man would fall at any moment, his giant boots on those narrow steps, but he survived unscathed. We made a procession behind the wagon, the Magi themselves, L carrying her precious vases which she will not trust to anyone, especially not a swarthy half-Moorish lout with leather wristbands. I brought my painting things and the new canvas, luckily not very big. I hate to have people gawking at my work in progress let alone handling it. The finished ones I don't care about. Frans followed with some private objects of his, and Sara carried the baby. The little ones perched on the wagon with the Moor, who never spoke a word and seemed to begrudge us his time.

Judy has gone to fetch her belongings. Her mother is dead, and her father uses her like a servant, refusing to hire a nurse for the younger ones. There are six. I gather she is expected to cook for the whole brood and cope with the youngest, still in the creeping stage, and keep the house clean. A life as a painter is out of the question for someone in that situation. She stood all this until a few weeks ago, when her father tried to get into her bed. Heard this from Sara, who is already becoming her confidante. They are charming together, sisters, heads bent close in conspiracy as they peel potatoes or shuck peas, squealing as they clean a chicken — the other day Judy picked up a chicken foot and pulled the tendon so the claws grabbed at the air, and she went after Reynier and Nicolaes, crowing maniacally and snatching at them with the clenching claw like a fiend from hell. Oh how they laughed. And took it up themselves, fascinated by the marvelous construction of God's creatures.

L hesitates to give Judy work to do around the house, but I tell her not to worry, that she is not a guest and will expect to do as much as anyone else. One thing I am glad of, Lysbeth goes easier on Sara, more patient with her. Sometimes the very sight of Sara infuriates her. ("Why does she name it after the devil? It's sacrilege. What put that idea in her head?" I said it was nothing, it was that the cat was black, and so she saw him as an imp perhaps, with ears sticking up like horns. "Well I don't think it's funny at all. Your own daughter trucking with devils and Satans. Whatever made her think about them? She shouldn't be thinking that way." I said I thought we were supposed to think about the devil now and then so we would know what not to do. She didn't find this funny either. She belabored the thing for days. Even after the cat ran away.) It is a hard life, to be a woman. The baby work never stops. I have done it a few times myself, when she was sick or too tired to roll out of bed. Many a napkin have I changed, many a sugar lump dipped in milk, many a walk around and around the room trying to rock a teething baby to sleep. But I get thanked for it.

I must say, Judy does not take kindly to this arrangement. She works as hard as any of them, but she defends a certain line that you do not go beyond, man or anyone.

Example: Last week she was working at her easel as always —

she paints straight through from breakfast to midday—when I needed her to hold a violin for me. Difficult to catch exactly the way a violin is held, the left arm twisted under so awkwardly, it would appear, yet the hand and fingers poised so elegantly above the strings. I called her over.

"Sorry," she said, "I can't now."

"What?"

"I'm doing this bottle. I'll be there in a few minutes."

I was shocked. After staring at her innocent, busy back for several moments I said, jocularly. "The master is calling his pupil. Come."

At that she deliberately laid down the brush and palette and came over to me.

"I'm your pupil," she said rather formally. "But if I weren't, I wouldn't."

Ah. I gave her a look. She gave me one back.

"My time does not belong to you. I wasn't put on this earth to be your handmaiden."

I got her set up with the fiddle properly under her chin and the arm fixed in place and stepped back to paint it. (The picture is of Frans, but I could never have got him to pose that long.)

Finally I said, "Time is time. Doesn't belong to anybody."

What insanity. If time were worth money you'd have to pay all sorts of people. You'd have to pay philosophers to think. Pay the baker for the time he spends making the bread. Pay a slow carpenter more than a fast carpenter.

Without budging from her pose, she said, "It's worth something to me. If I spend all day cooking and cleaning, when will I paint?"

"Well," I said reasonably, "you are a woman."

She didn't say any more. She sat there making silent music on the violin and smiling grimly as if she had made her point.

We now live just down the street from Gans, so I am taking up with him again. He is the best butcher in town, but we have been

184

going to the one on the square since the lawsuit. Went in yesterday to see him. A huge person with a great stomach that goes before him and makes him tilt his head far back. Great broad head with sparse black hair, broad forehead and broad nose, wide-set eyes and massive thick lids that always stay halfway down over the eyes. His lips are extraordinary: extremely thick and shiny, but the thing about them is their color, they are almost purple. Like a piece of beef that has sat in the sun for three days. Behind them, broad, spade-shaped teeth set wide apart. He grins like an ogre.

"Gans," I said. "I'm back."

He had his cleaver above his shoulder. With one mighty swing he planted it in the block (which is an oak stump fully four feet across and as high as his waist) halfway up to the hilt. The poor lamb chops he was operating on shuddered visibly. Wiping his vast hand on his thigh, he pushed it forward to shake mine.

"Delighted to see you," he roared. "We are forgiven."

"You are forgiven," I said. "Am I?"

"You are," he said. "The past is past."

He continued to pump my hand. His skill is amazing. I have watched him chop ribs one after the other from a side of beef, making them all exactly the same, without an instant's hesitation. He cleans a chicken, breaks it and joints it in moments. He can bone a turkey while you watch, his fat fingers deft as spider legs as he works his blade under the skin, through the muscle, over the bone, humming to the poor naked bird all the while. You get the impression that if the turkey was still alive it wouldn't feel a thing.

We discussed his cheapest beef cuts. I was celebrating the new house, also the auction sale. He slices the ragged edge of flesh off the ends of the ribs and rolls it up and calls it a skirt.

"Tastiest meat on the ox," he says.

"I'm sure," I say, careful not to ask any tactless questions about its age. The last time, he sold me a shoulder cut that was so rotten you could see the worms in it. He denied it, but they looked

185

enough like worms to make Lysbeth scream. Took him to court to get back the price of the roast at least and make him pay a bit for the scream too. It was three guilders, but the weasels on the Council reduced it to two. They have to go to the butcher themselves, after all.

At last I have received the Fl 34 from the auction. First money in two weeks. What are we going to do if I can't find a real commission? L says I grind my teeth at night. My back is hurting again. Monday I couldn't stand straight for most of the day and had to lie on the bed curled like a lobster.

This is too much. Sara was out again last night. Judy takes her side, insists she was in the room the whole time. But Lysbeth saw her come in through the shed in the dawn. Says she had the runs, but L not satisfied, points to the mud on her shoes. They wrangle till I can't finish my supper. Those cawing voices. Like fingernails on slate. On and on, the same words. I am beset. No work for three weeks.

Off to Amsterdam tomorrow, at last.

L last night, "You have to talk to her. I can't get anywhere: Everything I say she turns and combats me over it. You have to take some part in this, Hals."

All right. So this morning after breakfast I took her into my workroom. Her pretty young face was already set. I sat her down on my old couch and sat beside her.

"You know what this is about," I said.

She nodded.

"What, then?"

Sara's eyebrows are like her mother's, not thick but clearly marked and very mobile. They went up now, ironic, defiant. "I was out on Sunday."

"You were out. You were gone from the house. All night."

We sat there considering each other. Her lovely red hair shines out from under her cap and down her back in some sort of pigtail, the fine strands gleaming in their broad braids. Her eyes are jade green, very light, and she has L's upturned nose and fine cheekbones. The lips are her very own, though, beautifully articulated, a perfect bow with the little ridges on top sharply delineated and the lower one full and generous.

"You are a child, Sara," I said quietly. "You could be hurt. Kidnapped. Men can mistreat you, you know. You know all that."

She nodded, giving me an amused smile that made me feel like a simpleton.

"If I am a child, well, other children I know are free to do what they want."

"I know that. I know what happens to them."

"I was safe at Anneta's house. We were just talking around the fire."

"Anneta, eh?"

"Oh Fa, don't start that."

Anneta is the rope walk manager's daughter, a pert little mink if ever I saw one. She moves as though she itched down there.

"Who was there?" Now we were getting down to it.

"Oh, friends of hers. You don't know them." She bristled. "You want their names? I don't even know all their names. What business is it of yours?"

"It is my business. I am to raise you in the fear of God. You are sixteen, you have to be protected against the world."

She sneered.

"Yes. You don't know as much as you think," I said. "I can't stop you from having friends. You will have to live your life on your own soon enough. I'm just asking you to be sensible. Can I ask that?"

Now I really felt like a fool. Sensible! Who ever acted sensible on cue, young or old, in the history of the world? What do you do with these young people? How can you tell them? You can't, that's the thing. They have to go through it all for themselves. Tell any person the plaster is wet, the stove is hot, tell them and tell them, and still they will put a finger to it. Or the human race would surely have improved in these thousand years. But here we all are, still as foolish as Saxons in bearskins.

She said she would come in earlier, and be careful with her friends. I am so afraid that she will go off with some wild boy. She's so full of love, and no one to receive it. When I let her go she hugged me and smiled her sweet smile for me alone, a smile that says she knows how I feel about her (including the odd secret twinge of lust), she knows her mother can't help being jealous of her smooth young skin, and she forgives us for being ourselves. And that she Sara is going to be what she Sara is going to be, like it or lump it. The smile of a grown woman. I suspect she is not a virgin.

We are settling into the house. First rain yesterday and discovered that the roof leaks in four places. Also water collects in the path to the outhouse. I will get some slates from Pieter.

It is the solstice. L seems to think there is some religious significance to this. I tell her that is a pagan notion and that she is probably a pagan by nature. She is, too. I still have to remind her to keep her nails short, because she rakes my back with them when excited in bed.

"When am I going to get you to church, Hals?" she says.

"When Calvin brings himself back from the dead," I say. She used to take fright at this and say I would be struck by lightning, but no more. There are many worse things I haven't been struck for, so far, and she has almost given up hoping.

Marriage makes one efficient in conversation, I will say that. We can get along for days with barely a word between us. "Do you have the thing?" I say, bending over the hearth. Now, there are hundreds of things in this house, but she is unerring. "In the pot," she will say. Whereupon I, also unerring, reach among all the legions of pots for the old retired flower vase (it leaks) we keep on the mantel . . . and take from it the long fork we use to lift the lid from the kettle so I can check on it without pulling it from the fire.

Then she will say, "Do you want?" And I will say, "No, not now." A stranger in the house is baffled. We think nothing of it. She is going to get me into that church if it kills her.

The truth is I get my best work done when they are all out of the house Sunday morning.

Saw crazy Bobbe today, hobbling up the street. She must live somewhere near.

I should not write this. I saw her leg today. She was turning all in a whirl to climb the stairs, and I saw a flash of her bare foot with its neat high-curving arch, gentle sweet foot, articulate foot, trim, elegant, feminine foot, and the little pointed anklebone, the long thin tendon up from the heel with the delicate violet hollow beside it, and the calm swelling gently above, bulging slightly in a refined way as she put her weight on it. I pore over this sight like a picture in a book, though just as remote from the real thing, just as unsatisfactory. Why is this? What would I do if I had it before me now? Stroke it, revel in its smoothness. Kiss it, lick it, rub myself against it. Mostly I think simply feel its sleekness and gloat over the smooth perfection of that long thin shadow by the tendon and the subtle harmonies, the silent joy of its gradual merging into the curve of the calf. I am mad. I must put her out. I search for her every morning when I come down to breakfast. Not to stare at her, of course. Barely to glance even. Perhaps. To wave a cheerful hand. Just to sense her presence there beside me. I grunt hello. To which she replies with her own careless good morning. Unsuspecting.

They are all unsuspecting. L has no idea, I am sure. Except

possibly to wonder at my renewed vigor in bed. Oh I sin. I put Judy's face on her when we come together, it is Judy's face just beneath mine as I squeeze out my pleasure. Sara may have an inkling.

I have been watching the mad witch. She trudges past the house every day on her way to her favorite dive, I suppose. She seems to be drunk day and night, or perhaps it is some ailment she has that makes her limp and stumble. Talking to herself full blast. Tremendous energy in her. Those quick, violent movements. I have been thinking how to paint someone in motion.

"Lady Bobbe," I called. She turned in the street to glare at me.
"Man talks," she croaked.
"Buy you a tankard."
She brightened. "Buy me?"
I said no, I wasn't going to buy her, I just wanted to talk.
"I want to paint you," I said, coming up to her. She smelled of goats, and the heat was no help. We have had nothing but sun for a week. My head aches when I go out. I hope the tulips are happy.
"With Bezom."
"With Bezom?"
"Bezom."
I gaped. She grinned anew and shrugged her left shoulder.
"Your crow," I said.
She nodded one violent nod.
"All right," I said, "with Bezom."
Why I do this, I cannot say. There is no money in it. No one will buy it even at auction. Lysbeth will rag me. She thinks my talent will run out, like potatoes in a cellar, and she hates to see me waste it.
It was half through the afternoon when she banged on the door. She had her crow on her shoulder. I led her through to the

workroom and sat her at the table and poured out the big tankard full of Piet's best ale, which I rarely touch these days.

"Now you sit there that way," I said.

I had the canvas all ready. She peered about her for a while, settling in, and took a giant gulp of ale, leaving a large mustache of foam under her considerable nose. Right away I saw that the crow was wrong, much too small. I blocked in a shape there for balance. I will put an owl in there, for obvious reasons.

Her eyes are solid black, like southerners' eyes. She stared at me madly. I wondered what was happening inside her head.

Long silence. Another enormous gulp. Swinging her elbows, feeling more at home. She has a curious way of ducking her head like some crafty person. She looks like a conspirator plotting.

"You come to this house from a better," the old woman suddenly burst out. "Work and fly. See the waves you have sausage?"

"Certainly," I said, in my distraction jerking so badly that I smeared. I had fixed a plate for her. It is good pork sausage that my friend Gans mixes with a minimum of sawdust.

She ate furiously, with her hands, tearing the meat in her mouth like a dog, stuffing gobs of bread as if wadding a cannon. I said a wordless prayer of thanks that the children weren't here.

We worked in silence, I painting, she chewing. She let a long resonant fart. Drank some more ale. Set the pot down with a clang and stared at me with new insight.

"Flowers make them mad. Dead people on the street and no one cries."

She was getting restless and I had no more ale to give her. I raced through the bonnet, dashes of white to catch the light. But it wasn't coming right. To paint motion without making a blur. At the end I was simply splashing it on, as though the very slash of my brush would somehow capture the life in her.

Suddenly she stood up in a shower of crumbs.

"Good sausage," she said, grinning. She clapped a hand on my shoulder like a man and strode toward the door in her off-balance gait. At the door she turned and said in a pleasant feminine voice as though this whole episode had been a clever piece of acting, "Thank you." And left with Bezom clinging desperately to her shoulder. I looked at the painting later. It was better than I thought. The children caught three large bass, which L baked in fennel.

———————

Took little Pieter to see Dr. Wath. He is definitely feeble. We knew it. Poor creature. He sits by the hearth and stares at the air with his mouth open and the spittle dripping out. I can't understand it. All these bright children with their raucous play and cunning minds, and Pieter. God's joke. They are kind to him and delight to get him laughing. They are quite sweet with him. But what happens when he gets older? Stronger? I worry about him coming to manhood.

I have never had a pupil like her.

———————◄O►———————

Peter put down his pen and shook his head to clear it. He checked the chronology in the catalog and found as usual that everything happened exactly as stated. The nickel-and-dime lawsuits, the appraisal he was so indignant about, though he didn't mention that he won that suit. The date was right for the Malle Babbe picture too, the Witch of Haarlem.

He should call Amy. She would be back from work by now.

Mrs. Dunaway answered. He figured she would follow up on the dinner invitation. She was punctilious about such things. But she sounded apologetic.

"Oh hello Peter, so glad you called. All is not well. Amy wants to talk to you, I'm afraid."

Then Amy picked up on another phone.

"Peter, how could you."

"What?"

192

"I am so embarrassed."

"For heavens sake, what's the matter?"

"I am humiliated. A clown! I can't believe you did it. A gorilla! In the park!"

"Amy—"

"And you talked to my aunt! In Central Park!"

"You weren't even there."

"I don't care. It's an insult."

"Amy, you weren't even there. You had nothing to do with it."

Long silence. The line hummed. He presumed Mrs. Dunaway had hung up.

"And," Amy began in a deeper voice, "I hear you're staying with Laura."

"No I'm not. I—"

"I saw her, Peter! Don't try to wiggle out of it. She came back from France and you were there and—"

"Yeah well. I left. The next morning. I was there because my place burned up. Nothing happened."

"Yeah, likely. I saw your little beady eyes on her. So don't call me back. Okay?"

"My God Amy. Calm down, will you?"

"I don't want to see you. Anyone who wears a gorilla suit in public in Central Park, I do not want to see. Just forget it, Peter. Don't call me back."

She hung up.

Peter stared at the phone. He had always liked Mrs. Dunaway better than Amy anyway.

———————◄○►———————

I have never had a pupil like her. She seems to see it inside, the way I do. I had her working on the fur hat again, and she objected but she did it.

"What if I don't want to?" she complained. Standing there in front of her own work (a portrait of me) with white paint on her knuckles and yellow paint on her forehead where she had wiped the sweat off. She is not a china doll, my Judy. She sweats. When she works hard in the heat she has dark crescents under her arms (I have seen the hair there, a quick glimpse when she raised her arm in the loose-sleeved shirt, a girlish little patch, the hairs fine and straight, just a dab of dark moisture that roused me for hours and I still slaver over the memory of it like a monster) and her smock is garish with streaks and blobs of paint.

"It's an exercise. Everyone does it."

"But it doesn't interest me. Why should I work on an old hat that doesn't interest me?"

I am more patient with her than the others, but when she sets her mind to it she can drive me into a temper. She has been working on me all day.

"Because it has weak thingness."

Now she laughed out loud. Her teeth are white and perfect, not far out of the gums. "Thingness!"

"I'm serious. If it has strong thingness it's easy to paint. A box or an apple, anything with strong edges and definite shape. The shape tells you what to do. But when it's weak, you have to paint the light around it."

She looked at the hat speculatively. "But it has a shape. Everything has a shape."

"But it's weak," I said. "If you were to draw it literally, every spike and every hair, it would look like nothing. It would look like a hedgehog. You have to show what's between the hairs because that's what makes it fur."

Her mouth curled up. She turned to her picture, pursed her lips and pretended to be studying it. It is very good. Though it does look like my own work. Oh well, she could do worse.

"You don't understand," I observed finally in a friendly tone.

"No," she said.

"What I said about light. Everything we paint is the light that

194

strikes objects. You don't paint the object itself. In a dark room the object looks black so you paint it black even if you happen to know it's white —"

"All right, all right." She waved impatiently. "I know that speech."

With the tip of her long brush she pointed at the nose, which at that range was nothing but a dash of white on top of some beige strokes.

"Right," I said. "Good. So do the fur, will you? Just to please the old man?"

At that she chuckled. "All right. For the grumpy old man who sits in the corner."

We work back-to-back for hours on end, standing in the middle of the room because the light is best there, and those hours are the delight of my day, both of us silent in concentration with maybe a word here and there. But sometimes I go off to the bench to clean brushes or grind paint, and I will sit there and simply stare at her straight back and young hips, her proud intelligent head with tendrils of hair flowing out from under the bonnet as she leans forward to touch the canvas with the brush in her delicate, sure fingers.

I felt a thrill of fear when it came to me that she knows I am watching her.

I have a new pupil, Willem Woutersen. About sixteen. A pudgy lad with crafty eyes, not very energetic. He wanted to be taken on as an apprentice, but I said we would see. Obviously I have an apprentice already. Unless he takes her for a journeyman painter, which she nearly is. I am thinking ahead to the time when she leaves me. A dark day that will be.

Today we were working in heavenly solitude at our separate portraits. The workroom is remarkably cool, it seems to pick up a breeze from the water somehow, though we are not that near.

The heat outside was unbearable. I had sent Master Woutersen to the wharf to buy us some whitefish. She claims I hum when I work. Sometimes I can hear her breathing when she is bearing down on a difficult passage, peering close to the canvas, frowning (this I can only imagine, for she keeps her back to me) in concentration. I wouldn't mention it to her for the world, it is too dear to me.

About midday I broke off and strolled over to see how she was doing. It was the picture of me. She is good. She is good.

She muttered to herself. "Still can't get the nose, I think."

She is beginning to talk like me, too.

"I don't know. Looks fine to me. A little big maybe."

She paused, dabbed at it with the white, stepped back to consider it.

"No," she said. "It's wrong. Too much thingness."

She glanced at me. I laughed.

And the door opened.

There was Lysbeth with the baby in her arms and Nicolaes and Maria underfoot.

"I hear merriment," she said politely. Confusion. Both of us dithered a bit in sheer surprise.

———◄○►———

There was a metallic scrabbling at the keyhole. The door burst open. A big paper bag pushed into the room, followed by Su Zan, tottering, panting as she set the bag down on the table.

"I brought us a couple of little steaks."

"French fries?"

"French fries."

"Let me fix you a big fat gin and tonic." Peter bounced up from the table and headed for the kitchen. Su Zan slumped onto the sofa, wiggled out of her sneakers, then leapt up again with a new surge of energy.

"Let me take a shower," she said, already peeling off her blouse. "Honestly, the smoke in that place is a real turnoff."

He had the drink on the table for her when she came back wrapped in a white terry-cloth robe that she somehow managed to look sexy in. She sank onto the sofa again, sipping the drink and contemplating him seriously.

"I got a call at the place today," she said. "Carol's coming back. My roomie."

"Oh hell."

"Sometime tomorrow. She didn't want to surprise me."

Peter sighed. He must find Scott and get him to do something about the room. "I can get out of here by then. It's all right."

"Will I see you?"

"Of course."

Dinner was quiet. She hardly spoke until he got her on the subject of her pottery.

"Actually, I hate pottery. I used to do pottery because Jake did pottery. Until he broke everything up. There's so fucking much of it in the world. I used to bite the rims, but you couldn't see it when I fired them. So I tore pieces out of them."

"So, what do they say in the ceramics world?"

He didn't want to know who Jake was. Or why he broke everything up. Something about Su Zan made him a little nervous.

"They love it. Everyone's doing it now in the Village, that's what I hear."

Her robe had fallen open during the speech. There was not a hair on her smooth body except for the little red valentine. That was the moment that he first began to suspect that Su Zan was playing in a different league and maybe a different game entirely.

Possibly, he reflected later, it had something to do with the

197

picture of the leather biker on her dresser, signed "Karl." He didn't want to find out who Karl was either.

In the morning she was sad. She didn't want to go.

"I won't see you again," she murmured. She smoothed his collar, her long, elegant fingers deft about his neck, and looked into his face.

He said, "I'll call. When I get moved."

She smiled gently at him.

"Of course I will. I like to hang out with you. I love to be with you." He kissed her lightly. "And be a gorilla."

"I think we should graduate you to something else."

"Maybe a condom."

They sat quietly a while. He was as sad as if he had already gone. She said, "Hey, it's been fun."

"I'll see you," he said.

"Come around to Dunnigan's sometime."

"I'll call."

"Yes."

She left hurriedly. He was so upset he made the bed and did the dishes.

After a while he tried to call Scott but got no answer. It didn't matter. He packed his things anyway. He would go over there later and figure out something. Goddamn it, how was he supposed to work if he didn't have a place to stay?

———————◄○►———————

She swept into the room, where she rarely does intrude, and the children followed, with Pieter shambling behind. When she saw the picture her eyes grew round.

"Oh, but this is wonderful! She's a marvelous painter, Hals. She's really got you."

"Except the nose," mumbled Judy.

"The nose is fine. It's exactly right. Perfect. Don't you think so, Hals?"

"Don't ask me," I said. "I can't see it."

I thought this was a pretty good retort.

Said Lysbeth, shifting Susanna to the other arm, "Hals, I have to run to the market. Will you watch them?"

We ate the lunch in a somewhat guilty silence, facing each other over the table while Claes herded Maria about the room in a complicated game of his own invention. It was a potato soup with onions and milk and a great sprinkling of dill. It was superb. I don't appreciate her. She does so many wonderful things for me.

"I should have offered to take the baby," Judy said.

"No. Don't worry about it."

Willem now returned, knocking on the door to be let in, though he has a latchkey. He is not too bright. He had a fine whitefish, which he had wrapped in his handkerchief.

"Didn't they give you a wrapping?" I asked. "did you go to the place on the bridge?"

"No. They were out. It was one guilder."

That was all I had given him. "That's not so cheap," I said. "They were sixteen stuivers at the bridge." I regretted this immediately, for his face sank. This is how I spend my life, discussing pennies and stuivers with adenoidal errand boys.

"I'm going back," said Judy at last. Willem joined her, shambling toward the workroom in his knob-jointed adolescent stride. He lists to one side slightly, the way a dog will trot sometimes, at an angle.

I sat with the children. I took Pieter on my lap because he likes to be high up. Addie and Reynier came down from their naps, and that great lummox Jacobus thundered into the room from where he had been playing in the mud. How did he find mud in August? I made him take off his boots and wash them at the standpipe. I organized a penny-pitching contest. They love to pitch pennies against the wall.

———————

This morning in bed L turned to me and said, "You'll be painting all day today?"

"I don't know."

"Do you guide her hand?"

Presenting a picture of me standing behind the girl, holding her brush hand in mine while I encircle her, enclose her, with my lusting big body. I had thought of it.

"Of course not, Lysbeth. What do you mean?"

She hesitated, staring up at the ceiling. "It looks exactly like your work to me."

"I never touched her, if that's what you mean."

"Fine." She sniffed, still looking at the ceiling.

"I never touched anybody. You know that."

She dropped it there. We had what was left of the whitefish in a magnificent chowder with some late leeks, which always give me the runs.

All Saints' Day. I have been in Amsterdam again. Left my ledger at home. Those people are impossible. Reael does his best, but I have never seen such a bunch of gadabouts. First the one had to be away on business, then the next wanted off to get his hair trimmed, then a third raised a fuss about wearing his hat, which he had bought specially for the occasion. And on and on. I told them I simply cannot afford to keep running up to Amsterdam to work on the thing. I am so tired of their shouting.

So I return and find Miss Leyster has been usurping my place while I was gone. She has taken it upon herself to teach young Willem the rudiments of painting. More to the point, when I got back I told him he needn't pay the week's fee because I had been away. He reacted politely, as always, but without enthusiasm.

"I hope that'll make things a little easier for you," I added, for he lives with his mother, who is widowed.

He hummed and hawed, not knowing what to say. "Yessir. But I had the lesson anyway, so I paid Miss Leyster."

"Ah," I said. Judy was across the room daubing away in her own world.

I went over to her. "You took his fee," I said quietly.

"I've worked with him every day. We did the color wheel and I started him on shading and showing depth."

"Good. That's good. And what have you assigned him today?"

She glanced sharply at me.

"He's doing some bottles. Why? Was it wrong? I spent two hours with him every day."

"You're still a pupil," I snapped. "Don't forget it."

"I'll give it back, then."

"No. You say your time is worth money. So be it. My time, nobody cares what my time is worth. I trust you finished the hat."

We have never resolved the argument about time. I fling my hours and days about like water. I spend three hours on a single white ruff, making it gleam, making it stiff and crisp, and how much is that worth? And who decides?

She brought me the little canvas with the fur hat. To mock me she has painted it draped over a bottle.

It was brilliant. She had brought the spiky fur to life, catching its shiny vitality. The way it poked up thinly at the top where the bottle's mouth pushed it and the individual hairs jutted separately. The way it bunched together in a fold at the bottom. "I thought you didn't want to do this," I said at last.

"I didn't." Her face shone.

"It's just right."

"Thank you."

"It's good."

"Thank you."

Oh Judy. It is a little miracle. It leaps out and cries at one and all, "Here I am! I am a fur hat! I am all the fur hats in the world." I turned away and walked back to my own easel. Then came back to her.

"I can teach you no more," I said sternly. "There will be no more fees."

Her pretty face paled. "I beg your pardon?"

"I have taught you all I can. I go no further with you."

Her face widened in delight and she flung herself at me. Hugged me. Arms around my neck. I grasped her waist, small as a child's, firm, warm under the linen. It was over in an instant. I had the memory of her brown hair brushing my cheek, her agile, slim body soft against mine, the honey smell of her.

Later we agreed that she would continue to pay for her room and board. I am to advise her when she asks. We are to be colleagues.

Jan Molenaer came to the house last evening. She was ready for him, sitting in the parlor. I realized he was paying a call on her. I had forgotten.

Yesterday she was collecting the bowls for the stew and her foot slipped and she stumbled forward over the table. For an instant her blouse fell away and I saw one breast, the right one, perfect, round and white, not dangling but hanging there firm and neat, with the little dark button of the nipple. I could not take my eyes away, actually was unable to move them. Luckily she was unaware and straightened immediately. I have no idea whether L or Sara spotted me gaping, all but drooling. Another precious memory to be fondled and rubbed like the miser's coin.

The curves, the delicate curves of the breast and hip and thigh. What is their magic for men? What is this power they have to stir our blood?

She saw Jan again today. He is clearly dizzy with her. She wants me to sell her portrait of me. What does she need extra money for? They hold hands in private. I note the new brightness in her eyes and am desolate.

Took the picture to Obersteyn's today. Winter is early this year. There was a smell of snow in the air and the trees are already as bare as you would expect them to be in December. She had some difficulty at home. I gather that her father has left, at last, disappeared or just walked out, and she is making arrangements with a cousin to take care of the little ones until something can be decided. A bleak outlook. They have no money to speak of—she considers me rich!—and she will probably try to sell the house. Assuming the old scoundrel doesn't come back. Which everyone hopes and trusts.

She wanted me to take the portrait in right away, to sell it as fast as possible. I said she didn't have to worry about any rent or anything, and we haven't thought about the painting lessons for a long time. L will be annoyed when she finds this out, I am sure, but it can't be helped. I am not going to be the one who sends her into the street to beg or worse.

———————◄○►———————

Scott answered on the sixth ring. "Hello?"
"You're there!" Peter said.
Scott was not a subtle person. "Hello?"
"Scott, I have to get back into my room. Tonight."
"Well, they just finished painting it."
"That's all right. I'll be over in an hour."
Scott sputtered. "You—you coming back?"
"Well yes. You didn't put another girl in there, did you?"
"No, no. But—"
"But what, Scott? Goddamn it. Did you give that room to somebody?"
"No, it was just that we didn't think you'd be coming right now."
"Well I am. And that room better be ready."
"Oh it is."
Peter slammed down the receiver. Goddamn. That was his

room. Some people had no sense of what was right. Only one month behind on the rent. Well, two.

He glanced outside. A light summer rain was falling. He would wait for it to stop, because he didn't want to lug his stuff through it unless he had to.

———————————◄○►———————————

Obersteyn was impressed. "A fine likeness," he said in his professional murmur. He lifted it out of the wrapping and stuck his nose up to it, then held it at arm's length, then walked it to the door. He set it on an easel there by the big window and stepped back to admire it.

"Unfinished, but still, I can see you there," he said finally. "You look as though you were about to speak. I like it."

"Thank you," I said. "She's really got it, I think."

He mumbled something as he turned toward the back of his store. Like a fat mole he is, happier in the gloom and dusk. You never see him in the front, always at the back of his place. Looks rather like a mole too, the eyes close together and constantly blinking, the sloping forehead, the bent little nose that appears to be sniffing at all times. And he walks with a curious shuffle as though he was wearing slippers.

"What you think?" I asked. "Is thirty too much?"

He shot me a strange glance. "Thirty? I'll ask fifty."

"Really! And get forty."

"And get fifty!" He shrugged his lower lip.

Someone came in then, and he waddled away to meet him.

"When's your next auction?" I called. "If you don't sell it before?"

"Two weeks." He was speaking over the newcomer's shoulder.

"All right. If you haven't sold it by then, put it in the auction."

"Really?"

"Yes," I said. I had an odd feeling we weren't connecting.

When I got home last night Lysbeth was in a state. "Sara went off with a man!" she cried. "She's gone! She almost spat in my face!"

Good God. One thing after another. The children were boiling around because they hadn't had their supper.

"She said she was sick of it here, sick of me, sick of everything, and she was going to go away with somebody."

"Who?"

"How should I know?" She raised her feathery hands from the chicken's little corpse. "One of her young men. Henrick or somebody. And when I put my hand on her she slapped it away and I thought she was going to spit at me. I really did." She angrily rubbed the tears away with her forearm.

"Well," I said.

"My own daughter," she said.

Jacobus, sensible child, also fearless in these family dustups, picked up the chopping knife and started on the carrots. He spends a great deal of time thinking about his next meal. Sweet, softhearted Jacobus. He is the one who will take care of us in our old age. L finished the chicken with a final furious tug that all but pulled off its wing with the last speckled feathers and plopped it on the table. She took up the cleaver and whacked the creature into pieces. I hoped she had remembered to clean it. She hadn't. (This has happened before.) Even as she split the breast she yelped in exasperation, and she had to fish out the insides and scrape them off the ribs where she had smashed them. She flung the meat into the kettle.

"And when she went out the door, there was this man waiting for her. An older man! Never saw him before." She glared at me as if I had done it. "Right outside our door!"

After a while I said, "Did she take anything with her?"

"I don't know. She just flew out the door."

I ran upstairs and rummaged through the room where the girls sleep. Things were tossed here and there, bedclothes scattered on the floor. The good basket was gone from the hearth, the soft-sided one that she can hitch on her shoulder and hold under her arm like a purse.

"What can we do?" Lysbeth cried.

"Nothing,"

"You would say that."

"I say let's get supper and then think what to do."

Of course we did nothing after supper either.

Judy came back today. She kissed me. Walked straight up to me in front of the family and kissed me on the cheek as the children and Lysbeth stood all around rejoicing at her return. I instinctively clamped an arm around her. Felt her young ribs, her slim firm waist, warm and—what? what was I thinking?—crushable, ready to be pulled to me with all the strength of my madness. For a moment, a moment only. She is selling the house and in the meantime has found a cousin to care for the little ones. Our whole establishment perks up when she is around. She has something to say to everyone, teasing fat Jacobus, who grins, tickling Anthonie and Nicolaes, who giggle and scamper, murmuring some quiet comment to our silent Frans, who glows for a while before retreating back into himself.

Tonight over the brushes (we clean them together after work, a ritual more precious to me than she will ever guess) I asked her casually if she had any idea where Sara might have gone, or with whom. She has been away for a night twice before, but now it is two nights and Lysbeth wants me to notify the guard. I hate to because it will mark Sara in the public mind, which loves a label. She is just a wild girl.

"His name is Johan," she said. "He works in the bleaching fields."

I felt privileged. Almost light-headed with a sudden sense of intimacy and camaraderie, I said, "Have you met him? Is he all right?"

She looked speculatively at me. "He's not as old as he looks. A bit of a rough one, I think. But he seemed to care for her very much."

I grasped at this straw. Maybe Sara would be the making of the man. I found myself almost wanting to like this invisible Johan, partly no doubt because Lysbeth had found him so frightening. We delude ourselves with such ease.

All is well. Sara was back at dawn with a timid knock on the door. I would have slept through it, but Lysbeth heard. The girl stumbled in, her blouse dirty and slippers scuffed, and wrapped her arms around her mother. They both cried.

"He said he was going to Antwerp," she sobbed. "He just went off."

"I know," said L. "I know."

"He said I could go with him, and then he just left."

"When you were asleep?"

Lysbeth constantly amazes me. I thought she would have ripped the skin off her daughter for this, but she was as warm and open as I have ever seen her. I was the one who was starting to paw the ground.

"Where is he?" I said. "The son of a bitch. Where can I find him?"

The two of them turned on me. "Forget that," snapped Lysbeth.

"Where did he take you?" I roared. "By God—"

A soothing motion of that elegant young hand. "It's all right, Fa. He's gone. Let him go."

I felt an idiot. The classic seduction. The classic weeping daughter and ranting father. Sara came to me and put her arms around my neck and pressed her red hair against my neck. Here I was with another young body in my arms.

"I am sorry," she whispered. "I made you worry. I was so — I'm sorry I was so angry at you."

"It's all right," I said, "all right, baby, you stay here as long as you want."

She pressed my arm warmly.

"Your mother didn't sleep," I added. She removed her hand.

"I'm sorry," she said again.

Well, more tears and reconciliations. The children all gathered shyly around and we wound up having a glorious gala breakfast with the Gouda that I had been aging and slices of ham and cinnamon biscuits for all. Judy came down in her new bonnet with her hair newly trimmed. She looked radiant. I was quite inflamed with all this young flesh about. Lysbeth sees me eyeing her across the bed. She has that greedy smile.

This is the coldest December I can remember. The canals are frozen already. Today the sky is yellow, hanging low. I hate a yellow sky. A prescience of doom. I brought an extra load of wood in from the shed. Tonight we are having the ham that Massa sent us. I asked her to have it baked in mustard and Demerara sugar.

I confess this. It was snowing this morning, has been all night, and we are enclosed in it. I could hardly open my shutter, and when I did look out, all I saw was white. The children went out early to play, and Lysbeth built a great fire to take the damp off the house. It was the fire that inspired Judy to boil water for a grand bath.

She brought the tub into an alcove off the kitchen and strung a curtain across the opening, as we all do, but being not one of the family she was a bit shy about it and pinned the edges to the wall. Usually we are rather careless about this in the family, no one pays much attention to bathers in there. I retreated to my workroom. I have seen naked women before, not many I will admit, not more than most men who have been to a whorehouse in their youth. But never one that didn't intend me to see. I was sharply aware of what was going on in there, heard the kettles of water splashing into the tub and the cloppings of her clogs, for it is a cold stone floor in the alcove.

At one extra loud splash I glanced up—and noticed a ribbon of steam wafting through the wall. I went over to investigate. And found a crack. My heart was already beating fast. I knew what I was going to see, and I was so crazy with the knowledge that nothing could have shamed me away. She was down to her shift. As I watched, gulping because I had forgotten to . . .

———————————————◄◦►————————————————

Damn. The phone.

It was a man, for Su Zan. He sounded large and violent. "Who is this?" he demanded.

"I have no idea," Peter replied calmly. "How many guesses do I get?"

The man made a noise like the MGM lion.

"I came over to use the sewing machine," Peter said. "Is this Bradley?"

"Bradley who?"

"Never mind."

"You tell her Ray called. Tell her to call me." The man hung up.

The rain had stopped. Peter left her a note. He didn't mention Ray. He didn't want to know even the first thing about Ray. He smiled to himself. Hals aways made him feel better.

Scott was standing in the center of Peter's room, wrestling with a queen-size mattress. The walls and ceiling were hospital white and smelled of rubber-based paint. The floor was covered with new gray wall-to-wall carpeting.

"Hiya," Scott sang out. "I got this from downstairs. They're gonna have a chair for you by tomorrow."

"Great." It really was finished. Peter peeked into the bathroom, but it was unchanged. Doubtless the toilet still hissed. "Thought you'd rented it out," he confessed.

Scott wiped his smooth face. "No no no. I just thought you were still downtown."

"No, that fell through. I've been homeless for the past week."

"Yeah, I was in Arizona. You owe me some rent. I had to pay the whole thing this month. Even John didn't pay."

John was the third roommate, a truculent and mostly invisible economics grad student who spent his days in some office on Wall Street and his nights in the library.

Peter set his suitcase on the floor, opened it and took out his checkbook. He made out the rent on the spot.

"That's last month," Scott said.

"Come on."

Then Scott was gone and Peter could concentrate on his work. The bare walls and gaudy pink mattress with the sleeping bag flung onto it depressed him. He set his papers on Scott's desk in the small living room they supposedly shared but which was in fact Scott's study. He had had a portable electric typewriter, but that disappeared in the fire. He just remembered it now. He didn't use it that much.

———————◄o►———————

As I watched, gulping because I had forgotten to breathe, she grasped the two sides of it at her waist, with arms crossed, and pulled it over her head. In one breathtaking instant she stood there naked, not two yards from my avid eye. Her stomach was sucked in from the effort, making her leaner than she really was, but even when she tossed the garment aside and breathed out with a sigh, she was still childishly slim and neat. The stomach flat, the navel just a delicate whorl—God's fingerprint. The breasts small with boyish little buds that stood out in the cold. Perfectly rounded, not a shadow beneath them, the skin so white and fine and smooth. Below, she had a dark tuft for her escutcheon, a girl's narrow patch, not even a full triangle, and the hair appeared downy rather than curly. Her legs, oh, long and finely tapered, elegant as a deer she was, when she stepped high over the tub's edge and into the hot water, crouching, slowly lowering herself with hands on the rim. I could see her sleek rounded bottom touch the surface, the legs separating and revealing more hair, then the final plunge as she sat firmly down, gasping at the heat.

I had stopped breathing again. I was frozen to the spot, abandoning shame, drinking the sight like a drunkard in the desert. Now she was rubbing the lye soap on a cloth. Now she was washing her breasts, caressing them familiarly as they bobbled slightly, slick with suds. She was looking at them complacently. My member strained against my pants, and when I adjusted it the thing shot straight up and though I had barely touched it, I was on the point of my pleasure. And I confess this. Like a boy, I gave in. Held it tight as it bucked and throbbed and jetted, all as I stared through the crack at her slender body, watched her soaping between her legs with an absent smile as though she too were pleasuring herself, as though we were somehow together, implanted in each other, rocking, joined in the same moment of delight.

Abruptly I turned away and went back to my work. A great wet spot stained the front of my pants. I would have to sit in the workroom till it dried. Almost without thinking, I took up a large sketch pad and a fine brush and set down what I had just seen. I filled in with a gray wash. I caught her in a few minutes, working with hot speed, her newly short hair hardly reaching to her shoulders, pushed back, with lovely wet tendrils curling forward below her perfect small ears to accentuate the curves of her neck. That bare neck, with its soft shadings, its young cords and veins, its long aristocratic throat. I got her eyes too, the lashes bright with droplets of steam, the dreamy look of the bather, content and warm and inviolate.

The thought of her, trustful in her solitude, suddenly overwhelmed me with guilt. My Judy. I had invaded her. I had had her without her knowledge, really against her will, for she had never shown me anything but the purest friendly affection. And I, the slavering lecher wetting his pants over her. Still, I couldn't bear to throw the sketch away. I stuck it in the back of a portfolio just in time. Lysbeth burst in on her way to the shed. I will think of a place to hide it for good.

I must not let this scene fill my mind.

Judy's picture has sold. For fifty! It is still snowing.

I am in trouble. She went to Obersteyn's to get her money and came back ten minutes later in a spitting rage.

"What did you do?" she shouted. Rushing into the workroom where I was stretching a canvas. Slamming the door behind her. "You told him it was yours!"

"What? I certainly did not!"

"He says it's not mine! He refuses to pay me."

"What? Nonsense," I retorted. "I told him it was —"

"You said it was your work and he sold it as your work. How could you do this?"

"Do it! I did nothing of the sort! Didn't you sign it?"

She stopped short. "No." The anger ebbed, then rushed back into her face. "No I didn't. You knew it was my work. You should have —"

"Well I always sign mine. He would know it wasn't mine. He would look."

She glared at me, eyes wide, nostrils flaring. "You didn't tell him, did you?"

"Of course I did. I did."

I was trying desperately to recall exactly what had happened in that shop. I had walked in, had set it down on the counter and opened the paper, and he had exclaimed over it. I am sure I said it was her work. But she caught the hesitation in my look. When I say I am sure, I actually mean I am not sure.

"You didn't!"

I waved my arms at her. "I did. I remember talking about you. I don't know if he heard me."

"Oh, right! It's his fault."

"The man lives in a world of his own, Judy. I know him. He doesn't hear half of what you say."

I move toward her, put a hand on her shoulder. She bristles but does not move away. "Let's go there together. Let me introduce you to him. Look, he sold the painting for a lot of money. That's what he thinks about. He'll be delighted to have a new artist."

She hesitates, scowling at me. I make a basket of my hands, inviting her to be nice.

"All right," she says. She still frowns at me.

"Why wouldn't I want you to have every success?"

"I don't know," she mutters. "What about Willem?"

"The boy? What about him?"

"I was teaching him and you couldn't stand it."

"Not at all. I was merely surprised."

"No, you were furious."

"I wasn't."

She turns away. "Let me get my coat," she snaps.

"All right," I snap.

I didn't tell her that the boy has asked me to apprentice him. His mother has some money from somewhere, and she thinks he will make his fortune with me.

Obersteyn was at the back as usual, sitting behind his counter on his special wide chair, upholstered in a charming antique Flemish pattern. He lives in that chair, keeps his disgusting used handkerchiefs in the crevices. He squinted at us.

"Ah," he said, eyes darting keenly from me to Judy and back.

"Yes," I said, "Miss Leyster is here for her money. A fast sale, I must say. I congratulate you."

"Miss —"

"Judith Leyster." I bowed toward her, court-style. "The painter."

"I beg your pardon?"

"She painted it, I say."

"It wasn't yours?"

"No. As I told you before, she's been working with me."

"I thought it was yours."

"No," I said. "If it was mine I would have signed it."

Obersteyn growled. "Man bought it as a Hals. Paid me a Hals price. What am I going to do?"

"Well, it's simple. Give it to Miss Leyster. It was fifty guilders, I understand."

He takes twenty percent, which means he sold it for over sixty. I do not understand why this is not considered usury.

"What do I tell the man? He bought it as a Hals. Otherwise it would have been thirty at the most."

Judy was getting her sardonic look.

"Tell me who it was," I said, "and I'll write him a note. I'll make it up to him."

Judy, hackles rising: "What will you make up to him?"

"Why, I don't know, the fact that he thought it was mine and it wasn't."

"And what will you make up to me?"

"What?"

She faced me, bold as could be, ignoring Obersteyn, who watched this exchange in astonishment. "Are you going to tell him it was mine?"

"Certainly, certainly."

"And I will personally go to his house and put my signature on it?"

Obersteyn: "But the fifty guilders. What if he wants it back? What if he says it's only worth thirty?"

"I'll pay the difference," I said.

"You will not," said Judy.

"It was my mistake. I should have made it clear."

I would not call this a tactical retreat as much as a feint to the flank.

"If it was worth fifty guilders, it's worth fifty guilders," she announced, drawing her slim self up. "It's a Leyster."

To my amazement, Obersteyn chuckled. He spread his fat fingers like God quelling the Flood.

"The man is from Amsterdam," he rumbled. "However, I will write him and explain the misunderstanding. If he insists, I will take back the painting and give him his money."

"But no thirty guilders," Judy added quickly.

He stared slowly at her. "No thirty guilders."

"Thank you."

He continued as though there had been no interruption. "I will tell him he is lucky to have an early work by a rare young painter in the great Haarlem tradition."

Swinging his massive body to one side, he delved into a drawer, found a metal box, delved into the box, found a leather packet, delved into the packet and found a velvet sack, delved into the sack and came up with a handful of glittering guilders.

"Fifty," he said. He stacked them on the counter and graciously—and it is hard to do this graciously, but he managed, pudgy fingers and all—pushed the stack toward Judy.

"Thank you," she said quietly.

"I do hope," he said, "you will bring me any future work you do. But do sign it."

She bowed. We walked out of the place and it wasn't until we were well down the street that she turned to me and said, "Thank you."

"Not at all," I said.

———————

I am slow about these things. I was thinking in bed this morning how generous that was of Obersteyn to give her the full amount instead of making her wait till he had heard from the buyer.

Then I realized that he had no intention of writing the man. That portrait is going to make its way through the world as my work.

I think I won't mention this to Judy.

Getting ready for St. Nicholas Day. The children bustle about the house. The little ones are working on something together, with Judy's help. An artwork, I suspect. Sara is knitting in the attic. There will be slim findings this year in the good saint's sabots.

---◄O►---

Peter checked the catalog but found nothing about this portrait. Somewhere presumably there was floating about the world a fine likeness of the artist in his prime, unsigned but done by Judith Leyster.

---◄O►---

December Fourth. I do not know why, but I am fated to have my every sin and failing exposed to the world. I cannot let a fart without someone happening by.

This afternoon Judy beckoned me into the workroom, her face set. I thought one of the children had spilled paint on her work.

She closed the door behind her, latched it and turned to face me. "I want to show you something," she said, her voice taut. She strode to the corner and plucked a large sheet from a portfolio that leaned against the wall.

My heart fell.

"I found this," she said in a low voice, holding it up in front of her. The sketch I had forgotten to hide.

I said nothing.

"I found the hole in the wall too," she said.

I looked at her. I went blank.

"It's a fine picture," she said.

"Judy," I said. My voice cracked.

There was a silence. She looked straight at me, or through me. Like an arrow.

"I didn't think you were that kind of man."

Nothing in my life, nothing my mother ever said to me, or my father, or Lysbeth or even poor Annie, struck me as hard as that mild sentence. What kind of man am I indeed? I sat down heavily on one end of the old sofa that we use when studying our work across the room. I closed my eyes and rubbed my forehead up and down with my fingertips. I felt her sitting down on the other end.

"Listen to me," I said.

"I'm listening."

"I can't help it," I said. "I can't help myself with you. I think about you all the time. It is a craziness. I see you in the hall, in the kitchen, on the street, I work next to you, and I can think of nothing else. I am mad, Judy. I am too old, I have no hope you would ever look at me, and Lysbeth is like a part of myself, I could never leave her, but I am out of my head with this thing. I confess it. I would never have said one word of this. And now you can have nothing but contempt for me."

"No," she said at length. "It's pathetic, that's all."

I am pathetic. It is true. I nodded, unable to speak.

In spite of everything I felt closer to her than before, and it excited me to know that she knew that I had seen every inch of her.

We sat in silence. She rolled up the sketch.

She was going to keep it. She was going to keep it. My eyes brimmed.

"So I'm going back to my father's house," she said at last, rather briskly. "I have a lot of business there, and I won't be getting in your way."

"Will you stay for the holiday?"

"Oh yes. The children have a surprise for you." For a moment she was her merry self. She got up and walked to the door.

"I leave in the afternoon. I have my own family, after all. And Jan."

"Jan?"

She smiled. "Jan my friend. Jan whom I am going to marry."

Molenaer. That lanky scarecrow. My cup of gall was full. I swallowed it.

"I wish you the best," I said.

1635

A curious thing last night. I was strolling down by the docks when I heard a rumbling of wheels on the cobbles, and horses. As I watched, two guardsmen rode by, followed by a closed coach, and then four more riders. They were trotting fast, their faces hard. No small talk. They barely glanced at me as they passed. The carriage driver leaned forward on his seat as though to urge on the horses. They headed for the bridge and straight out of town.

My impression was that some important personage was being escorted through the city. But at night? Secretly? some Spanish envoy going to Amsterdam? Prisoners being transferred?

This morning I roamed about the square and talked to the hangers-on at the Town Hall. Cautiously, for the incident smelled of guilt and conspiracy. No luck. I will go back tonight.

"Did you see the fire?" Willem said. "There was a fire by the docks last night."

"What? The docks?" I would certainly have heard of that.

"No, not the docks themselves. A house down there. Burned right through, front to back."

There are some shanties along the river, a wonder they didn't all burn.

"The fire company was there," he said. "They saved everything around it but the one house was gone."

"Anyone hurt?"

"No," he said, "nobody there. I was watching."

He lives in that area somewhere, it's full of rats. When we were done I walked back with him to stretch my legs. It was a fine cold moonlit night, and I was stiff from standing in front of the easel. I smelled smoke, and he said the house that burned was just over on the next street. We turned the corner and there to my amazement was another house afire! And the fire company standing there watching it! Now and then they worked the buckets and splashed water around the edges to keep it from spreading, and they wet down the adjoining buildings, making clouds of steam rise from the roofs.

We ran up and joined the handful of onlookers. "Why are they letting it burn?" I asked. "Is anyone in there?"

"It's empty," shouted a grizzled old longshoreman over the general clamor and the rising roar of the blaze. "There was a family here but they left."

Another guy said, "It was a wreck. Let it burn."

It was hardly more than a shed. The men had attacked it with their pikes and yanked the wall boards away from the one next to it where they were almost touching. Brilliant yellow flames billowed up amidst greasy strings of black smoke. As the walls began to fall inward and turn the building into a mere bonfire, the firemen started herding us away.

Coets died two weeks ago and now I am being sued for an ox. I knew him when he was the steward for the St. George's, and he was a tricky one even then. My brother went shares on an ox last December, and I paid something to him so we could have a roast for St. Nicholas. But ninety guilders!

---◄○►---

Peter did a quick check of the catalog: Yes, Coets died March 1, 1635, which would make this entry mid-March. He was indeed steward of the militia, and there was something about going shares with Dirck on the purchase of an ox and also something about the Coets's other customers. Interesting, Peter thought, as he reviewed other items in the chronology: There were a lot of entries concerning Hals's work, deals he was making about this time for painting military groups and individuals, haggling over price and little lawsuits and the eternal debating over whether he would go to Amsterdam to do a group or they would come to him. Almost none of this appeared in the diary.

Why would this be? Maybe it was simply that he didn't need to write his daily business down. If this was a hoax, wouldn't there be more about the art? Or could it be the hoaxer hadn't had the information about the workaday side of Hals's art?

Scott bustled into the room behind him, carrying a tall white bag. Scott always brought extra lunch home with him. This time it was enormous croissants with custard filling.

"Hey, you got some phone calls, did you know that?" he said, offering Peter a giant sugary horn. At the first bite it oozed filling all over Peter's hands.

"Who called?"

"Some art gallery. Some professor. I didn't write them down."

"Oh thanks. Was it Dr. Smith?"

"Yeah, that sounds right. Some weird name."

"You told them I was coming back?"

"I said you were gone and I didn't know where."

"Great. Did any girls call?"

"Just the one at the Lady place. Something Lady."

He must call Laura as soon as she got home so he could pick up his history book. He wished he could charge somebody mileage for all these trips up and down Manhattan.

Went to Town Hall to settle the Coets thing and ran into Adam Kuiper who works in Lot's old office of Weights and Measures. Adam's hair has gone entirely white including the beard, which he has let grow down to his breastbone. With that huge nose and the pouched bloodhound eyes he looks like a prophet, but he is a timid man and a gossip.

"Have you heard?" he whispered once we had exchanged our news such as it was.

"Of course not," I said. "Why would I have heard anything?"

"They burned three houses this week."

"Ah," I said. "On purpose, then."

Sometimes there is an infestation of rats down by the docks and the town councillors get so many complaints that they actually do something about it. But I never heard of them burning a house down.

Adam stepped close. We were in the great hall, with its figured tile floors and grand windows. I have never understood why governments have to build buildings that are too big for people. Doors so tall you can barely reach the handle, let alone open them by yourself. Ceilings high enough for us all to wear stilts. Is this supposed to make us all feel like midgets? If so, why? The officials are no bigger than the rest of us.

He presses his wiry beard close to my ear. A bit of egg has dried on the end of a bristle.

"It's plague," he murmurs.

"Oh, right," I say aloud. "So where are the dead people?"

He frowns in alarm and hushes me with a finger to his hidden lips.

"They've been burying them in the potter's field and taking the families out of town."

"Nonsense. I would have heard."

He rolls his eyes. "Well, you're hearing now."

I thought of the carriage the other night. But not a breath of it anywhere, or someone would have heard, surely, Lysbeth, Sara, Frans, even young Willem, who roams the city all day. On my way home I stopped off at the market stalls, picked up some Avocaat and two enormous turnips that will do us all tonight. I said nothing, just asked the ladies what the news was. Nothing. So much for Adam Kuiper. But I worry.

I settled Coets widow for twenty-five guilders. She is suing the whole St. George's gang. Good luck. Dirck paid forty.

It has happened. This morning a madwoman ran screaming down our street waving her arms and yelling, "It's the Judgment! It's Judgment Day!"

A crowd ran after her and brought her down. I watched from the stoop. Then, most extraordinary, they suddenly drew back from her—left her lying on the cobbles still waving her arms and legs but no longer shrieking—and everyone scattered.

"What is it?" I called to a man sprinting head-up past the house like someone in a bad dream.

"Buboes! She had buboes!" he shouted. And was gone around the corner.

So. There is plague. The thing to do is keep calm.

Last night I gathered everyone in the house and told them, even the littlest children. I said, Don't go talking to strangers. Don't have any contact with anyone you don't know. Clean yourself well after the privy. Close the windows at night.

Lysbeth bought sprigs of a gum tree in the market, it comes from the New World and the leaves are long as fingers, brittle and dry, and they smell most aromatic. She will burn some tonight on the hearth.

Today Willem came back from the docks with a story that a ship came in from the far sea with a crew of just six men. They had escaped from Venice, they said, where the plague was laying people low in the very streets, collapsing where they stood in the squares. Bodies heaped in the alleys, floating in the canals. Everyone is fleeing, they reported.

◄○►

Peter looked through his books for mention of a plague but found nothing for 1635. Schama had a reference to "the terrible plagues of the 1630s" in Venice, but the bad years in Holland appeared to be in the fifties.

He marked the spot. Was this a break? Wait. Here was something in the chronology. "1635–37: frenzied speculation in tulip bulbs; Haarlem struck by the plague."

So. Tulip bulbs. Hmm.

◄○►

My father used to tell me about this. You feel weak, with headache and chills. Your groin aches and you stagger about, barely able to walk or even to speak, confused and weary. In three days the buboes start. In the armpits, on the side of the neck, in the groin. Then your heart beats wildly and your skin darkens and you may do all kinds of strange things, maddened by pain. Then the skin turns black and you stink and you die. It takes five days. But there is another kind that can kill in hours, even in minutes. Go to bed well and die before morning.

So far there is no panic here. We hear of terrible things in Amsterdam. People stay in their houses and do not move about more than they have to.

We have a cat. His name is Goliath. Willem found him in the fish market. He is fully grown but very young, a tabby, striped brown and black with amazingly large ears. I have always heard that it is the rats that carry the plague, which is why I asked him to find us a cat, any cat. The children are swarming all over him, but I have forbidden anyone to feed him after tonight. Tonight we make him feel like a king. Tomorrow he works for his living.

He is thin enough. He is a stray, I am sure. I am not confident about Willem's education in biblical matters. Suggested he would be better called David.

Our old neighbor Mrs. Berck is dead. We are not sure whether it is the plague. She was well past fifty. I will get a message to Pieter and Isabella in their grand house by the park.

Lysbeth does not approve of Goliath. She thinks cats are dirty and is not in the least impressed at the way Goliath cleans himself by the hour or by his dainty habits. Of his first rat he left only the tail. Now he is getting bored with them, I fear, because he eats only the choice bits and leaves the rest for me to sweep up. L won't go near it.

I cannot write this.

They are all gone, all of them.

I walked through the park this morning to the house though Lysbeth urged me not to go. I met no one anyway. The streets are empty most of the time.

That fine house, newly built across from the green. A black ribbon on the door. I knocked and no one answered. Silence. I stepped back and saw someone watching me from two houses down. An old woman in a bonnet leaning out an upper window.

"They're dead," she called.

"Mrs. Berck?" I said stupidly.

"All of them."

"But I know Isabella and Pieter," I said, my voice trailing off. "And the three children."

"All of them," she said. "The mother died first, then the babies, then they themselves. There is no one even to lay them out."

I walked to the Town Hall where a sanitation office has been set up. I gave the address. Someone will go and fetch the bodies and bury them, I was told. I don't remember who told me, man or woman, old or young. I can't remember at all.

L is devastated. Mrs. Berck was her dearest friend for years. I remember how Isabella came over to mind the babies, hardly more than one herself, and the funny times we had with Schrevelius. We saw little of her after they moved away. In the square I would see her and Pieter now and then, arm in arm, strolling about as though they had all the time in the world.

To church with the family. Everyone goes to church these days. We count heads to see who is missing. Old Pastor Leenders reads the names some days, of parishioners at least. Sixteen dead yesterday alone. He has services every day, matins and vespers. It is nothing like the old days, when whole processions of people roamed the countryside beating themselves and each other with whips and brambles. Or so I was told. They must have been quite hysterical, knowing only that the Death was killing half the world for all they knew, and supposing that God was angry at all His children.

You don't see much of that in our time, enlightened by philosophers as we are, but I must say people do crowd into the churches.

The women wear black shawls and some cry aloud. No one smiles these days. No one works, either, except at the fisheries and bleaching fields, where a man can be ordered to work so another man can wear satin breeches. The breweries are going full tilt. Bad enough to die, but to die with a hangover is simpleminded.

I am not sure I can bring myself to love a God who limits our intelligence but not our stupidity.

After the service everyone scuttles off home in all directions without talking, afraid to catch one another's effluvia. One school of thought embraces all the noxious smells and tastes in hopes of shooing the monster off in sheer disgust. I have heard of people breathing deep in privies, bathing in urine, surrounding their beds with pots of excrement.

I believe the opposite, as does L, luckily. We envelop ourselves in perfumes and aromatic smoke day and night. The house smells beautiful and I will say this: We have not seen a mosquito for weeks. We may not stop the plague but we have conquered the mosquito.

Forty-six dead yesterday. The most so far.

The cat is a champion. He gets at least one a day, and now he has to slip out into the alley to catch them, because there are none left in the house. I watched him last night. He crouched in a tuft of grass behind the shed, his hunting blind. When I called to him he refused to so much as turn his head. I realized that I was disturbing him in his work, so stopped. After a while he tensed, ears forward, great shoulders sticking up. I could see nothing but darkness out there. Then he leapt, in silence. A squeak, a tiny scream, small swishings. He carried the rat, thoroughly dead, around the corner of the shed to be private with it.

The children think he is sweet.

Lot Schout is gone. I saw his wife at the fish market. We are so matter-of-fact about it these days. She came up to me and laid a hand on my arm (which she never does unless she knows you well) and smiled sadly.

"He died two days ago," she said quite calmly. "He had a chill but thought it was a cold coming on. Then he found a rash on his leg."

It is like a target, they say, a small black itchy sore surrounded by a ring of little red pimples, the famous rosy ring. So far I have never seen it.

"And you know what he did?" She peered at me, head slightly tilted. "He said good-bye. He blew me a kiss, he wouldn't even come near me, and walked out of the house."

"Oh God. Where did he go?"

"Oh, he didn't get through the door. I brought him back and

put him to bed. He was gone in two days, but we were together. Can you imagine? He wanted to spare me."

That would be Lot. That would be Katerina, too, staying with him all the way. There are stories of people boarded up and nailed into rooms to die.

I have not worked in two months. It is getting better. Four deaths reported today. Leenders's wife, who was my teacher in infant school once. It is so commonplace now that you don't feel much. Old fixtures in town, close friends, you say, Oh dear, too bad, and carry on. Going to church I stepped on a patch of ice, surely the last patch left in the entire city, and twisted my right knee. It is swollen so I can hardly walk on it.

Spring! The tulips are up early. It is going to be a great year for them, according to Massa, who is supposed to know about these things. Lysbeth took the children on an outing today. They have been prisoners in the house for so long. Sara enjoys taking them too. The girl is bursting with love.

Last night L was in a jolly mood. As we were going to bed, she took hold of me and kissed me as though she were sixteen and said, "Still here, Hals. It's gone, and we are still here."

"So far so good," I said. I hate to give God a chance to play one of His little jokes on me.

"And the children," she said. Her arms are wiry as ever, strong as a snake she is, winding herself around me. She is all the woman I could ever want. She has never said a word about Judy. I know she was aware that something happened.

Speak of the devil. Tonight I went to the door expecting to let in the boy for his lesson, and it was Judy Leyster, wearing that set face of hers. "Hello," I said. "I thought it was Willem."

"You stole him," she said.

"I beg your pardon?"

She moved right up to me, standing on the top of the stoop so her blazing eyes were level with my chin.

"He was my pupil."

"Oh? He's been coming to me since before the . . . " (We don't say *plague*. We don't give it a name.)

"He was mine, and you lured him away. And I won't have it!"

Why, what nonsense. She knew perfectly well. Lured him away, indeed. As though we were competing for his services. Competing over Willem!

———————◄○►———————

It was evening already, the light outside fading and the noise of traffic increasing three flights below. Peter stretched and took a turn around the room. Scott had a hot plate in his bathroom where he sometimes cooked revolting little suppers, but now he was plunging about looking for a clean shirt because he was going to eat out.

The phone rang. It was Silverstein. He sounded excited.

"Listen. Bad news. Barnett's dead."

"Who?"

"Don Barnett, the guy who found the diary. Had a heart attack."

"Wow."

"He was fifty-two. Man."

"Uh, sorry to hear it. Uh, what does that mean?"

"I don't know yet. But Mrs. Barnett called and she was very upset. She wants to sell it."

"Now? But we don't know—"

"Of course. She wants to sell it anyway."

Peter thought about this. "So what does that do?" he asked. "You want me to stop or something?"

Silverstein paused for a long moment. "No," he said slowly, "I would keep on going. How does it look? Still look all right to you?"

"Oh yes. Every detail is right-on. There's almost too much. I got hold of that little book you gave me, you know? The one about the militias, and it has the names of all the people in them, everybody, left to right. And those names are all over the diary. He talks about 'em like real—"

"Good, good. Will you be at this number a while? I'm expecting to hear from the lab."

"I'll be here."

"Don't go away. Things might be coming apart."

"Okay."

The man was a lot older but acted as if he were the same age. He had never felt he should call him Mr. Silverstein. What if the woman sold the thing? What would happen to his job, such as it was? When was he going to call Laura? He was nervous about calling her because he might get George instead.

———————◄O►———————

"Furthermore," she said, "you never registered him with the guild. I checked."

"Well no, it was no formal thing. He just came around—"

"And you just took him up without a backward glance."

I didn't understand why that bothered her so. She was furious.

"Well let's ask Willem," I said.

"It's not the point." She seemed to have a little spasm of rage, shaking her head and shoulders at me. "Oh! You are just the most—" She wagged a finger like a schoolteacher. "You get away with everything! You just take what you want and go right ahead with that innocent face."

"What did I do? For heaven's sake."

She was not herself. I had never seen her like that.

"You assume the world belongs to you and you can do whatever you please and everyone will say oh yes that's fine Mijnheer Hals, whatever you want."

229

"My dear girl, the boy came to me and asked whether he could apprentice with me and I said all right. Starting with some lessons and maybe we'll get to a real apprenticeship later on."

"But don't you remember? The time you were in Amsterdam? I told you about it. The color wheel and all. Don't you remember any of it?"

"I remember that. I remember that you took his fees, too. Which I didn't appreciate since you were my pupil yourself."

"You'll hear from me," she said in a cold voice I had never heard from her before. "I will speak to him myself. And please. I am not your dear girl."

She spun around and marched off. I am baffled.

Haven't seen Willem since the Tuesday.

It seems Mrs. Berck left me some land. I was so touched. It is only an acre, out by the Little Houtwech, but it is in hay. I told Isaac about it and he was enthusiastic.

"Tulips!" he said. "Put it in tulips!"

Now, I know that tulips are all the rage this year. I hear people are making a lot of money on them. But I am not a farmer. When I told Lysbeth she wanted to see it. I said it was just a little patch out there where people have their garden allotments.

"I never knew you were a gardener," she said rather accusingly.

"I'm not. It was just a nice thing to do."

The will said, "In memory of his willingness to share with us when there was little."

I am going to be in the tulip business after all. A man named Cardoes came to the house this morning. He had seen the publication of the probate and looked me up.

He was a young man, hardly thirty, handsome, clean features. A driving look about him. A frown lies perpetually grooved between his sandy brows, giving him a look of concern, but the lunging way he moves, head forward, makes him seem rather disagreeably avid.

"Mijnheer Hals?" he said, smiling in the doorway with a friendly irony, for who would I be, answering my own door, but myself? "My name is Cardoes. I would like to talk to you about your land."

My land? Good heavens, I had only owned it for a day. Yesterday I went to the town hall to look it up on the plat. It was so lost among all the other bits and patches on the Houtwech that I copied out a little map for myself so I could find it.

"Do come in," I said. He was carefully dressed in ruff and satins, hat in hand. His beard was sandy too, neatly clipped to a point, and his mustache brief but thickly bristled. Even his hair had an air of energy. His fingernails were split and black-edged, the fingertips etched with dirt so the cracks and lines stood out.

"I raise tulips," he said. "I'm a grower."

Ah, I thought, dismissing the mystery of the nails.

"Perhaps you know of Pieter Bol."

"Oh yes," I said. "Of course." I knew Bol when he was a barrow boy. Now he sends his bulbs to England and Italy and is too grand to nod at me.

"I was Bol's chief gardener," Cardoes said. "I left him two years ago to be on my own."

"Ah," I said carefully, this being my second day as a country squire and landholder. He sensed my puzzlement, his nostrils widening as he frowned with sheer acuity.

"What I am saying is, I want to buy your land."

"My good sir," I said, "I haven't even seen it yet."

Now he chuckled. "Neither have I. I spend all my days looking at land on paper. Why don't we go look together?"

"Right now?"

"Right now."

So there I was, at midday, riding in a carriage with a stranger while half the town gaped as we crossed the square. I had planned

231

to walk out there one day soon. It's hardly a mile. We found the patch after close study of my map and his copy of the town plat. I felt sharply aware that I was in the hands of a purposeful man who had given hours and days of thought to all aspects of this business. I also had the distinct impression that he had been there before. He led me straight to it.

The land stands along the bank, extending back to make a perfect square. It was a lovely summer day before it clouded up, and the sky was deep blue, studded with little round juicy clouds. The widow Berck had had it in hay, cut and reaped by a neighbor, a van Loon, who paid her half the profit. I learned this from her lawyer. As the new owner, I could continue this arrangement and make perhaps two hundred a year on it. Not a thrilling prospect.

Side by side we tramped the boundaries, weaving along a narrow path beside the rustling grass, which stood thigh-high and was if anything overdue for the first haying. There was a series of vegetable-garden allotments on one side and a pasture on the other, complete with a picturesque gathering of holstein cows. I love cows and their triangles. At the back my property fronted (I am getting the language already) on a gorgeous carpet of tulips. Beyond that, more tulips on both sides, a sea of them, reds and yellows and flashy striped ones and even some that looked purple in the sunlight.

"You see," he said, waving to the south, "your land will give me access to the river. I'm landlocked now, I have to bring everything in and out by wagon. You can see why I'm anxious to buy. I'm being frank with you, Hals. I need your land."

He paused and fixed me with his searching eyes.

"I'm offering you a thousand," he said softly. "It's way over the market. I pay in gold. All I ask is that you think about it."

I struggled to keep a dead face. I am not good at this sort of thing. A lot of these deals are done in cows, sheep, horses, jewelry, other pieces of land and so on. Or so I hear. Gold was something I could understand.

He drove me back to town and I went straight to Isaac Massa. Isaac said the man is a shrewd dealer but honest. "He's right. You could get maybe four hundred, possibly six hundred, no more. He told you why he wants it. Seems reasonable to me."

"But he'll make more, I take it."

"Oh yes. Tulips are booming. He's probably buying up all the land he can afford and then some. He'll make it back in the fall."

I took my news home tonight. Lysbeth was cautious as usual. Two hundred a year, she reminded me. And you have the land besides.

"Why don't you plant tulips yourself," she said, "if there's so much money to be made?"

I laughed. "I wouldn't know a bulb from a horseball. I wouldn't know which end to plant up."

"Sleep on it," she said.

I don't know who else to go to. I am not entirely happy with Isaac's vague recommendation.

Woke up thinking about a thousand guilders in gold. We could move to a better house. I talked to Isaac again, he is investing in bulbs. He says it is a big business. You don't even buy the bulbs anymore, you buy a note promising delivery of so many aces of such and such a bulb. You can buy them by the pound now. I always thought you had to buy a whole bed of them, or at least a thousand aces, which can be a hundred bulbs if they are small. But now it's all broken down. You can buy a basket of them!

Isaac says he knows of someone who paid four hundred guilders for a single bulb. For a tulip? I said. A tulip? And he laughed. This is not just a tulip, it's a Semper Augustus.

<o>

What? Time to hit the books.

Schama had it, the whole story. An ace was one-twentieth of a gram, and tulips were sold by the thousand aces during the boom. Yes, and there was the Semper Augustus, red flames on white, and a bunch of other names. There was indeed a Cardoes and a Pieter Bol, big names in the tulip business. There was a Dorothea Berck, who married a Coymans and had a daughter named Isabella. But his Mrs. Berck was named Cornelia.

As Peter pored over the books the phone rang again. It was Silverstein.

"Peter." A hurried voice, cracking with tension. "Can you get over here by any chance?"

"Now?" It was after eight.

"I'm sorry. It is important. I'll be here. Knock on the door with a key."

He took a taxi across the park to Madison. The gallery was dark, but Peter obediently rapped on the glass door with a quarter. Silverstein bustled out of the back room and ushered him inside.

"I didn't want to say over the phone, but we have definite word here about the books." Photos of the first two volumes were laid out on the desk alongside some eight-by-ten blow-ups of the bindings and the spine and a typed report.

"It's French," Silverstein said. "The books are French, made in Paris. The paper is French. The covers are some kind of sized fabric stiffened by heavy paper, and that's French too."

Peter was stunned. Both of them stared down at the books, which exuded an aura of shame and dejection.

"Well couldn't they be exported? Couldn't he have picked them up at some big bookseller—"

Silverstein shook his head and smiled sadly. "It wasn't like that. You didn't have the EEC. Anything exported had to be really valuable. And unavailable. Coffee and spices and silk and stuff like that. Things that the very rich would buy. You wouldn't put your money in a shipload of notebooks. There wouldn't be the demand."

"Well couldn't he have—"

"Gone to Paris and bought 'em there? I don't think so. As we know well by now, the guy didn't have a nickel to his name."

Peter slumped into a chair.

"There's another problem. I heard from Dr. Smith. He says Descartes was in Holland for twenty years."

"Yeah?"

"So he would speak Dutch, wouldn't he? He doesn't seem to speak a word of it in the diary. And there's no mention of Schrevelius in this connection. Apparently it was a Catholic philosopher named Bloemaert, in Haarlem, who commissioned the picture."

Peter stared at the Roman bust across the room. It was of a particularly disagreeable-looking senator or merchant, the mouth drawn together in a peevish pout. Impossible that the voice in his diary was not the real Hals, or anyway somebody real. He had come to know this person, with his ironic asides to himself, his many foibles, his unending struggle to keep his huge family going, his war with creditors and, seemingly mentioned in passing, his work. The references to specific painting projects came less frequently as the man moved into his most productive years, but Peter could understand that. He could imagine the diary being set aside for months, years at a time or picked up simply to record some event in the artist's life that he needed to remember for one reason or another.

He felt as though someone had died.

"So," he said wearily, looking up to find Silverstein watching him. "You want me to keep on going anyway? I'm so far along."

Silverstein pondered. "I'm supposed to hear from Mrs. Barnett tonight. She's hot to sell it no matter what. She's really bearing down here. A translation would be imperative whatever happens. But the thing is . . . " He glanced quickly at Peter.

"You can't pay me."

Silverstein chuckled. "I'd love to. Wish I could. But I've already invested a lot in this, and at this point I think it's really up to Mrs. Barnett."

"Well I'm gonna keep on. I still think it's real."

Silverstein nodded. "Terrific. After all, someone is going to want that translation somewhere down the line. And they'll pay for it. But right now, I'm afraid you're working on spec."

It was after ten when Peter got back to the apartment. The light was on beneath John's door, but Scott had gone to bed. Peter returned to his work numbly. It was better than trying to sleep. For a moment he thought of calling Su Zan, but already Su Zan was fading from his mind, like a dream he had waked up from.

This is not just a tulip; it's a Semper Augustus. It is a superb creation of red fire on a brilliant white background. Like a ruddy painting, he says.

I am going to ask fourteen hundred and accept twelve. Lysbeth throws up her hands and says do what I want, that I always do anyway.

It is done. Cardoes paid out twelve hundred gold guilders. Now I have cash to invest. Isaac says he will advise me. It is late for this buying season. They will be planting in October, and I will have to wait for the lifting next June.

Isaac says he'll go in with me on some futures. We no longer have to wait for anything so mundane as plantings. The market goes ahead regardless of the seasons. We will buy bulbs that don't even exist yet. But they will be lifted in the spring, and by then they'll be worth so much more. We are buying Pieter Bols and Viceroys. The growers name them after themselves, which is a good sign, I think. I am putting up four hundred. Lysbeth shakes her head until I remind her that Massa is in this too, and look at him.

I knew it. She is suing me. By God we are a litigious people. I have the notice today: Judith Leyster, member in good standing of the Guild of St. Luke, asserts that Frans Hals took Willem Woutersen as his pupil eight days after said Woutersen had started studying with said Leyster.

The guild wants to fine me three guilders and pay the apprentice fee. I will do nothing of the sort.

She was there with Molenaer, who I strongly suspect put her up to all this. Though on second thought she is feisty enough to take satisfaction from this on her own. We sat on two benches before the board of wardens, three of them sitting solemnly on their dais. Judy and Molenaer on one bench, I on the other next to it. I asked Harmen to come for support, but he is busy.

She was wearing her best, a rich maroon velveteen — it has been cold all week, the first signs of autumn — and an elaborate snow white collar, extra crisp, curving up from her bodice like a great petal. A new cap, more severe than the old one, pulling her hair back tight and emphasizing those big dark eyes and the strong mouth. I used to watch her lips, so firm yet pillowy, the way they would delicately move with her feelings: the tiniest push of muscles, a tightening, the minute ridge that formed along her upper lip when she was determined, the sensuous slow relaxing as her mouth opened ever so slightly in moments of concentration.

None of that today. She was glaring at me even as the wardens took their seats. A Dr. Heemius was the chief judge. White hair clipped so short that it stood up straight, black mustache but no beard, keen blue eyes that flickered from face to face.

"What have we here?" he muttered, glancing down at the papers. "Hals. The artist." Pause.

"There are several Hals artists," Judy piped up. This was not really like her.

He went through the facts of the case, speaking in a dead monotone while the other two wardens looked on, glazed. Finally he seemed to reach a decision.

"Who, may I ask, is tutoring Master Woutersen now?"

Judy looked at me. I looked at Judy. "He's yours," I said.

"And you," the judge said, turning gravely to me, "will from this moment cease and desist to tutor the boy or to claim him as apprentice or to take money from him on any pretense?"

"Right," I said.

"You will pay her half the tuition so far incurred, and each of you will pay half the apprenticeship fee dating from the first day that you agreed to tutor him."

That was that. We met at the cashier's desk, where I paid out a few guilders and she paid hers, brushing aside Molenaer when he tried to pay for her.

"We could have settled that ourselves," I said afterward.

"You never would have."

"I'm not a cheat. You know that."

She glared at me. Such rage! For this! We were walking three abreast toward the big double doors.

A cold smile. "I'll do it again, too. Unless you behave."

I had to laugh. "Me behave?" I said. "I always behave."

She gave me a look.

"Good-bye, Judy," I said.

She didn't answer. She stood there and watched me until I turned away. I thought she would have said something.

<hr/>

It was very late. Peter's head felt heavy. He didn't want to think about money. He didn't want to think about Amy or Laura or Su Zan or guys who roared. He didn't want to think about anything. He went to bed on the mattress in his paint-smelling room, with the sleeping bag zipped open like a comforter on top of him. After a minute of lying there he got up and went into the living room and took one of the sofa pillows back to bed with him.

The phone woke him in midmorning. Anyway it seemed like midmorning, for the sun was fully up and he could hear traffic sounds outside.

It was a woman, a hard, flat Brooklyn voice, a smoker's deep contralto. "Mister Van Overloop? My name is Evelyn Barnett."

He cleared some phlegm.

"You know what I'm calling about? I got your number from Professor Smith."

Thanks a lot, Dr. Smith.

"I talked to Henry Silverstein but he wouldn't tell me a thing. I told him I didn't think that was any way for you people to act. He was very uncooperative."

Peter nodded at the phone. He wished he had some coffee.

"He said you're the one who's translating the diaries. And you say they're authentic."

"Mrs. Barnett, I can't say anything like that. I'm just the translator."

"Yeah, but you're the only one who knows what they say."

"No, I turned over the parts I finished to Dr. Smith. He's the one who's supposed to know."

"That's fine. But I'm the one who owns them. I want them back and I want all work stopped on them."

239

"Ma'am, you'll have to talk to Mr. Silverstein. I can tell you that he's had to stop payment for now."

"Well that's the first good news I've heard all day." Her voice came down to a normal conversational tone. "I don't want any more work done on it, you understand? But I might want to resume later, and I would probably want to hire you again. Can I reach you at this number?"

"Probably," Peter said. He hung up and reached for his pants.

In the living room Scott was taking the last cup from his thermos. "Hey," he said, "I need the rest of that eight hundred."

"You'll get it."

"I mean yesterday. Bateman came to the door and gave me a lot of shit."

"Okay," Peter said. "I can give you two."

"Hey, why should I have to take all this shit for you guys. John owes me two and a half, you owe me four. Shit!"

"Okay, okay."

It was shaping up for a nice day.

Peter glanced at Scott's *Times* while waiting for his coffee. Just below the fold on the front page he read:

FRANS HALS DIARY REPORTED FOUND

The story described the whole sequence of events, including Dr. Smith's role. It also mentioned that the diaries were still being translated but didn't say by whom. It wouldn't take long for someone to track him down.

There was nothing about the lab findings, nothing to indicate new evidence that the books were looking more and more like a hoax. Then he realized that Mrs. Barnett was almost certainly the main source for the story. She was going

240

to try to sell it before anyone found out about the French paper.

Which meant that as of right now, he was the big expert. Should he tell them about the lab? Maybe he should get out of town for a day or two.

That's what Hals would have done, he was sure. Take off for Antwerp or Amsterdam. Let them spin their wheels for a while.

———————————————◀◎▶———————————————

I am not going to be a painter anymore. I am a tulip investor. My 400 has turned into 780. I have put that and some more into a large order of Goudas, which are plain red and yellow and very small bulbs, weighing only about ten aces each. Massa says it is time to get into the big wholesale market, and Goudas are perfect for that. The little growers are getting into this in a big way, and Goudas are affordable.

———————————————

Today I went with Isaac to Van Dyck's, a pub that everyone calls the Bourse, because it is where the tulip investors meet. What a scene. What an uproar. It was almost cold enough to snow, and everyone who came in the door brought a great rush of icy air, which made everyone else shout at him. A fire was blazing on the hearth (much earlier than I would have one at home) and at least fifty men stood around in the tiny room, smoking and lifting their glasses and talking. The ceiling was so low you could touch it. This did not help. Smoke was so thick people kept having to wave their hands before them to see.

Every so often a deal would be made. One man holds up his open hand as if to slap the other in the face. The other shouts, "Done!" or whatever his literary taste runs to, and holds out his palm for the first one to hit. Then the second one slaps the first one's hand, and you think they are coming to blows. As soon as this is over, the buyer buys a drink for everyone within earshot. How anyone can do business in a carnival like this is beyond me.

"We'll just listen a while," Isaac murmured as we cruised through the crowded room toward the bar. I bought him a lager and we stood there with our backs to the bar watching the antics of the speculators.

There is a rumor that someone paid a thousand guilders for a single bulb, no doubt a Semper Augustus. Growers are trying to duplicate its sumptuous colors and patterns, and already there are various other "Augustus" tulips on the market. But no one has matched the original so far.

"I might buy some futures in Scipio," Isaac said. "It's doubled in three weeks. Up to sixteen hundred for a pound."

"How far ahead can you buy a future?"

"The general principle is that the closer to delivery date, the higher the risk."

"Why is that?"

"Because you're getting closer to reality." He chuckled. "The grower has to come through, and who knows if the bulbs are going to be a success or are rotten or if they never germinated at all or the grower has absconded to England?"

"Well then, why doesn't everyone cash in sooner?"

"Because the closer to delivery the faster the price rises. Don't ask me why."

———————————◄○►———————————

It was Silverstein again. He sounded agitated. His voice was high and sharp.

"Peter, has she called you?"

"Yup. This morning. Wanted to know if I was still working on them. I said no."

"Good, good. Thank you. You see the papers?"

"Yup. No mention of the lab."

"Well, I'll tell them myself when they call me. This is very important, Peter. If she sells that diary and gives the impression that I stand behind it, it would ruin me. You understand?"

"But she doesn't have the books. We have them. Besides, anyone would have to be a fool to buy something like that without checking the hell out of it."

"Of course. But there's always someone who'll buy just to have it and then check later. And then if it turns out he has lost a lot of money on the deal, he'll start looking for someone to sue."

"If they call me I'm gonna tell about the French paper. And also that we've found some discrepancies."

"Great. Great. I'm expecting her to call me any minute and demand to have the books back."

Peter set the phone down. He had moved it beside him on the desk where he was working. Scott had left with the check for four hundred, scowling.

◄○►

"It's insane," I said, appalled.

"Nevertheless," he said, winking, "people are getting rich on this. All it takes is capital and a lot of nerve. Even you've made money."

And so I have. But I am uneasy.

Went back to the Bourse by myself today. Met a banker named van Damme who wants to loan me money to buy futures. Everyone is doing it, he says. You absolutely cannot lose, because you sell out the minute things look bad. But in the meantime things look wonderful. Prices are going crazy. I have made two thousand guilders in three months.

Told Lysbeth that I have invested three thousand in Viceroys and Bols. She said, "I thought you only had two thousand."

"I did. But the price was so low on the Bols that it is sure to double by the end of the year. So I bought them on the margent."

She didn't like the sound of that. I explained that I buy so many futures at the current price but don't have to pay for them for sixty days. By then the price will have gone up, so I can sell a few shares at the new price and use that money to settle my debt.

"Hals," she said, "what if it goes down?"

I tried to explain that it can't go down. She doesn't believe me. But she can hardly write her name.

1636

Pieter is getting worse. He put his hand in the fire last night. You would think by this time that even an imbecile would know about fire. A big boy, almost as big as Jacobus, and still messing his pants and crying when he can't work the door latch. What do we do when he grows up?

The banns are set for Judy and Molenaer.

Went to the Bourse, the "college," as some wits call it. Van Damme nervous. Everyone nervous. Men standing around in small groups whispering. No hand slapping.

"What is it?" I asked him. "It's the rains," he said. "The planters are worried."

I almost forgot that we are actually dealing with a real crop here and not just numbers on paper. This is the wettest . . .

"Peter?"

It was Amy.

"I can't talk now, Amy."

"I read about the Hals diaries. That is you, isn't it? What you're doing?"

244

"Amy, I'll have to call back. Yes it is, and I'll call you later. Sorry."

He hung up, then took the phone off the hook. She would call him in two seconds, furious. She had never been hung up on in her pleasant little life.

When he restored the receiver five minutes later, the phone rang instantly.

"Peter Van Overloop?"

"Yup."

"My name is Carter Johnson, with *Newsday*. I understand you . . . "

He hated being in the paper. They always made you sound like an idiot. He had an inspiration. He called his brother.

But Tony was out of the office.

◄O►

This is the wettest January I can remember. I have seen the fields myself, ankle-deep in standing water.

By noon people had cheered up. There is a rumor that Coymans sold an order of Semper Augustus for 4,100—plus a coach and pair! Should have bought those, but they are already so high.

The gloom was returning as the place closed for the day. I heard one man say, "If Coymans is selling, it's time to get out."

I reported this to van Damme and he smiled wisely. "Not to panic," he said. "Not to panic. The market's going up. Lots of room for expansion."

He suggested I get into Switsers, which doubled in three weeks and now have gone down again, to 820. I would do it but everything I have is tied up. I told him to give me until tomorrow. I might sell my Goudas (for a neat profit but nothing spectacular) and get into Switsers.

Market down. Spent the day at the Bourse. Young Bol may buy my Goudas. He is waiting.

––––––––––

No buyers at all. The men stand around waiting for something to happen. I do not like the quiet.

––––––––––

We got some prices today at last. Some bulbs you can't get a price on at any level. But Goudas and Viceroys are being bought in small amounts and with great caution. Van Damme came up to me, his face the color of slate, and said, "My friend, I'm going to have to call you."

I didn't understand. He reminded me that the price on my investments has gone below the level of my loan. I have to make up the difference.

"You borrowed three thousand for the Viceroys and Bols, and they are now down to twelve hundred. So I will need the other eighteen hundred."

"Oh," I said, like an ass.

"Immediately, I'm afraid. I'm in trouble myself."

"My dear sir," I said, "where will I get eighteen hundred guilders from? All I own and more is in futures."

He stared at me. The friendly Mijnheer van Damme had turned into a different person, the eyes wide open and glittering like icicles. Such a scouring look. I could have been a chicken that he had just beheaded on the chopping block but which was still inexplicably flopping about.

"I will need that by the end of the week," he said. "Do you understand?"

"I would sell my other stock if I could find a buyer."

Long pause. "I think," he said finally, "you mentioned your house."

"What happens if I can't raise the money?"

He shrugged. "You know that, Mijnheer Hals. I go to court, and you go to the workhouse."

"Ah," I said.

I left soon after. I don't know what I will do.

––––––––––◄○►––––––––––

"Peter?"

It was Silverstein.

"She's going to be calling you. I told the *Times* about the paper the diaries are written on, and they called her, and now she's fit to be tied. I think she wants you to defend their authenticity for her."

"Me! I'm just a grad student."

"That's good, that's good. Tell her that. Whatever you do, don't make any judgments one way or the other. You can say you've been given instructions."

Peter turned from the phone to the scrawled pages before him. He felt Hals inexorably slipping away from him, this man whom he had come to know so well. How could it be a hoax? Could all this passion, all this unexamined miscellany of daily life be invented?

All the objections Dr. Smith had raised were ambiguous: The failure to mention the war much, the lack of stuff about paintings, Descartes not speaking Dutch—all of that could be read either way. Maybe the man just hadn't liked to speak Dutch. Maybe he hadn't talked much anyway.

Everything was ambiguous except for one thing: the paper from Paris. That was hard physical evidence.

He had never felt so disappointed in his life.

———————◄○►———————

Where will we go? I will have to rent some hovel and all my children and goods thrown together. I do not seem to learn. The little ones, depending on me. And Lysbeth. All these years, trudging along with me in this ridiculous life I lead. And now Judy, yet another weakness, me, the sturdy one, the oldest brother. Though I have done nothing but yearn for her, have never gone with another woman. Thinking myself so right and perfect, and now to turn simple over money. Tulips! Of all the stupid things. I can't understand it. I have watched people make and lose

247

fortunes in ships all my life, seen old Bergman bring in half a million from one shipload of peppercorns and silks, and Lot, investing in the very same fleet, half-ruined because his ship was the one that went down. And I stood by and laughed at their idiocy.

I am going to tell her tonight. She already knows something is off because I am so cross. I need a keeper. I cannot work in this misery.

Home again. I think it is Thursday. She threw me out.

Harmen came for me at Piet's tavern. Piet is dead and his grandson runs it. He never heard of me. He demanded to be paid and then he called the night guard and they sent for Harmen. Evidently I was making a fuss. The grandson is nothing like the old man. Hard young people who think of nothing but the profit.

We are in a very pleasant but small place across town, in an alleyway off Lange Bagijnestraat. At a rent of Fl 99. We are no longer freeholders. The children are in two rooms, boys and girls. Sara will be leaving someday soon, I trust, and Frans is already . . .

"Mr. Van Overloop? This is *The New York Times*. Mr. Gordon is calling. Would you hold, please."

Shit, the editor or something.

Peter answered the barked questions with yesses and noes. He was tired of this. Yes, he had translated part of the diaries. Yes, he had found they mostly checked with his references so far. No, he didn't know whether Descartes spoke Dutch. Yes, he would suppose he did, after twenty years in Holland. No, he was not a Hals scholar. And would you please talk to Dr. Smith, he's the expert, not me.

"We already did," Gordon drawled. "And he referred us to you."

Gordon hung up after ordering him to stay near the phone. Hands shaking, Peter took the phone off the hook so he could finish this section. He was nearly at the end of the third volume.

. . . and Frans is already apprenticed to de Keyser in Amsterdam. My workroom is part of the storeroom, so I work with the smell of cabbages and hams in my nostrils. Very touched that Isaac has asked me to do another portrait. My leg is worse than ever and I have been flat on my back for two days. It was the moving, I think, getting all that stuff up and down the stairs. Aggravated the knee. Sometimes I walk without a hitch, but on certain days the knee stiffens so, it is agony to bend. It feels sore most of the time, like a pulled muscle, but at certain times the pain shoots up into my thigh and I walk like an old man.

Our Pieter fell into the canal, but before he could do any damage to himself Jacobus jumped in after him and pulled him out. I took Jacobus up to the fancy baker on the square and let him pick out any tart he wanted.

This morning I found Pieter under the covers with Goliath. The cat was mortified. Wriggling frantically and starting to scratch, and Pieter was holding him down between his legs. I knew this day would come. Didn't think so soon.

They are married. I was not invited, but I sent her a platter she always admired, a rather fine one with a gold rim that came from

Annie's family. Lysbeth was incensed. "She lived in our house! She was like one of my own!"

"It was a small wedding, no doubt," I said. "Besides, she doesn't speak to me, you know. She brought the guild down on my head."

"So you send her our best platter." The arms folded, the eyes narrowed.

"It was not. It was just a platter."

She let it go. I never mention Judy around the house. The children miss her and speak of her now and then. She has moved to Amsterdam with Molenaer.

She has sent me a painting of a tulip. A Leiden yellow-red. Sent without comment from Amsterdam. A mean gesture. I didn't think she could do such a thing.

The writing ended halfway down the last page. Faint markings were imprinted on the endpaper where he had shut it when the ink was still wet.

Peter needed a break. Tony was surprised but pleased, anyway not displeased, to hear that his kid brother wanted to visit for a day or two. Peter said he would take the train to Washington, where he would call. Tony would send his driver to take him out to Potomac.

6

It was raining. Peter had found a window seat and now sat there comfortably reading the diary as the train waited in Penn Station while late arrivals bustled aboard, storing luggage in the overhead racks and shaking themselves out of their raincoats.

He had told Tony he would be getting in around six but he had left the apartment before noon just to get away from the phone. He had gone to a movie and now, at last, was able to draw a deep untroubled breath and concentrate on this final volume. Somehow it was restful to be spending four uninterrupted hours on one thing. Like Hals serenely painting ruffs: white fold after white fold after white fold, seeing only the marching patterns of lace that could take up his entire day.

The first section, dated 1645, was what he had already read at the gallery. Among the lists of figures he found a few notes about Sara. She was married to a Friesian sailor named Sjoerd and had gone to live in Amsterdam. One entry said in passing, "Sara formal and distant. She has not forgiven us. It was my fault, I did not speak out."

Mention was made of portraits of a Coymans and a man named Hoornbeck, a lawsuit involving Lysbeth. A quote:

"Another dandy, a man named Schade. I am doing a picture a week. I am a factory. Still nothing in the bank. This one talked about clothes through the whole sitting." A date: "July the sixth. In bed for two days with my back. Thought it broken. L minding me like a child. No time for this. What am I to do?"

Some blank pages followed, some pages ripped out, and a section written in an even hand. There was no year given. Peter settled in to read it.

◄◉►

I did not plan to write any of this, but it is time now.

Some weeks ago a note was delivered to the house, folded upon itself and sealed with wax. It was from Judy Leyster and said only, "I am thinking of you and would like to see you."

I had no idea what this meant. I had not seen her for over twenty years.

◄◉►

Ah, Peter reflected. She had left the scene in 1636. That would make this the late 1650s. Hals would be about seventy-five by this time. What had happened to all the missing years? If this was a hoax, why would it skip all the way to age seventy-five?

◄◉►

She moved to Amsterdam soon after marrying, and I would see their work from time to time, Molenaer in particular, both of them making a moderate success. Some years ago I heard that she was a protégée of the great Rembrandt. But then nothing. I have been busy enough merely keeping my head above water.

I found myself rubbing the letter between my fingers as if it held something of her actual presence, and it made those times come back for a moment, that lovely face and slim body. She would not be slim now. She would be nearly fifty. Those days pleasant to remember but so remote to me now. Lysbeth and I clasp each other in bed, enjoying the warmth and closeness, and we happily press our bare bodies together as well as we can—me with my stomach and my leg, which hardly bends at all, or when it does bend, won't straighten, she with her sore veins and the pains in her back—for comfort against an oppressive world and a God who seems irritated to find me still roaming around alive.

Even as I held the letter, musing about what it meant and what I should do, there was a knock on the door. I was alone in the house, L having gone to market, and it took me a few minutes to reach the door. There stood Jan Molenaer himself. I was astonished.

"I just got this," I said, holding up the letter. "Amazing. Do come in."

Now he was astonished. "I didn't know she'd written."

We stared at each other.

"But she asked me to look you up," he added.

He was quite grizzled, his hard angular chin bare, his hair thin and dark gray, lighter at the temples, combed across a shiny liver-spotted pate. He was as tall and lean as ever, though somewhat stooped now, with lines of hardship coursing down his cheeks to his mouth corners.

He was looking around at the room, seeing how far we had come down in life. The one room where we live and cook and paint, with only the curtained alcove where we sleep to count as a second room.

"She wants to see you," he stammered. "She is very sick."

Oh. Sick. We are all sick. Half the mornings I can hardly get out of bed. Now and then I think about putting my head under the water and drawing a deep breath. What could he mean? Why call on me after all these years? Why kick a sleeping dog for that?

Then I looked at his face again and everything became clear.

253

"Tell me where you live," I said. "You're in Heemstede now, is that right?"

"Yes," he said, surprised that I knew. A former apprentice of mine had run into them a year ago. What surprised me was that I remembered it. Most of what I am told slips clean through. Only the shapes of things stay with me now. I rarely go to Heemstede, though it is just a fair walk from us. In fact I rarely go anywhere, what with my leg and no money for a carriage.

"I'll be there tomorrow," I said, and his face brightened pathetically.

"Thank you. She really will look forward to it. She really will."

And he turned and blundered out of the house. Extraordinary. She was so near, yet she might as well have been in the New World for all I saw of her or thought about her. She had been erased from my life since the time she took me to court and then insulted me with a picture of a tulip just after I lost the house in the panic.

So. Next morning I set out for Heemstede, talking my way onto a barge that was headed south out of town. The bargeman turned testy when I wanted to get off—because I could see the canal was headed in the wrong direction—and made me scramble ashore from the moving deck. I barely kept my footing. Not that I would have minded a dip in the canal that day, it was steamy as June. We had a late summer this year, or rather autumn, the crops all in and nothing to do in the fields, so the country people could sit around for once and simply enjoy the soft air.

Their house was on the outskirts, small but neat, with a garden in front—unheard of in Haarlem, where every inch is built upon—and a pleasant meadow with a grove of willows by a stream at the back. He met me at the door, beaming, and led me through the narrow front room to a sort of study at the back with a door open to the meadow. Two landscapes stood on easels and three or four smaller paintings hung on the walls. She was lying on a Roman couch.

254

"Frans," she said, holding out both arms like the prodigal. "Frans."

She looked like an old woman. Her hair had gone white, her face thin, the cheekbones sculpted above the hollows, fine wrinkles below the eyes and faint ridges across the forehead. Her eyes were the same, candid and arresting and clear with the radiant honesty of her searching mind, but they were sunken deep in the shadow of illness. Her arms, her lovely strong hands which even now beckoned impatiently to me, were thin and white.

"So glad you came," she said in the familiar strong husky voice, "so glad to see you. I've felt so badly. All these years."

"My dear," I said. I don't remember what I said. I was stunned at the stillness, the narrow smallness of her body under the crocheted wrap.

"I have a terrible feeling," she said briskly, "that you must have been offended by a little picture I sent you. You remember? It was of a tulip."

I nodded.

"I sent it because I was so touched by your wedding gift. After I had snubbed you so, you and Lysbeth. Such a silly child I was, I should have been spanked."

We smiled at each other rather sadly. How distant that day was.

"I sent it in friendship. It wasn't till a year later that I heard you had been ruined in that awful tulip scandal."

"Ah," I said. "That's what Lysbeth said. It wasn't like you."

She chuckled. "A tulip was not exactly the thing you wanted to see right then."

Jan reappeared with a pot of chocolate. I was touched again, for chocolate is much too dear for the likes of us. I gave L a small jar of it last St. Nicholas Day. Jan sat with us a while as we talked rather haltingly about the old days. Then he excused himself to work on a commission piece that was near deadline. It was a saint for a church and had to be ready for the saint's day.

Judy and I were left alone, whether by accident or plan I am still not sure.

"I started to have headaches last spring," she said abruptly. "I had double vision and strange lights in my eyes. Zigzag shapes. And then one day I was walking to the market when I lost my balance. I couldn't keep straight up. It was as though everything had tilted."

I nodded dumbly. She looked hard at me. She sounded as though she was discussing a brush technique.

"I was frightened. I came home, and it got worse. I was confused for days, Jan says, didn't know where I was. At first it was almost pleasant, you know, like being slightly drunk. Where am I? Oh well." She waved her hand airily. "But then I began to be frightened."

"You went to a doctor?"

"I went to Amsterdam. They said it was nothing. It was the climacteric. It was a rotten tooth. One of them even hinted it was from too much geneva."

We smiled at that. She never was a drinker. "Then this summer," she said quietly, "I found this bump." She turned her head and put her fingertips just behind her left ear. "Feel it," she said in her matter-of-fact way. I leaned over and shyly touched the back of her head. It was there, all right, big as a walnut, hard, just under the skin. A sinister lump, an alien thing growing out of her. A foreign growth, drawing nourishment from its host like a living creature.

"I see," I said softly. "It's not like a boil."

It was not, not at all. It had an ominous air of permanence.

"The surgeons won't touch it. It's not a goiter. They called it a tumid feature."

"Is it painful?"

"No. But it grows."

We sat together looking at each other.

"I'm frightened," she said at last.

256

What do you say?

"Perhaps it will stop," I ventured. "Sometimes these things go of their own accord like warts."

She smiled.

She was tired that day. I left early, but only after promising to come back. I had not expected this. I stood up to go and made some remark about trying to get back in a week or two.

Then she said something that truly brought me up short.

"You're my best friend," she said. I didn't know what she could mean. They had no children, it was true, but surely they were in the thick of the art world, both of them painters and fresh from Amsterdam. And she a friend of Rembrandt: Of course she had been caught up in the whirl of his life, whether or not she went to his bed, which I doubt very much. I wondered whether she had met the famous van Uylenburgh woman.

"We don't know anybody here," she said, reading my mind. "We moved only two years ago, and I don't get out, and Jan is a solitary sort of person, you know. I have been thinking about you so much, and Lysbeth and Sara and Jacobus and the little ones."

I told her that Jacobus had died. She was appalled.

"Ten years ago," I said, "maybe eleven, I don't know. We couldn't believe it."

It was the last day of May. I have never written this down. We were moving Annie's old highboy to the upper floor to give us more space downstairs. Jacobus and Claes and I were struggling up those awful steep stairs with the thing, tilting it laboriously around the corners, lifting it clear over the banisters on the landing. A hot day, already muggy as June, and we three sweating and puffing and swearing. When Jacobus, who was on the bottom end, set it down carefully on the landing, said, "Just a minute," turned, sat down heavily on the step and curled up as though he had a cramp.

I was above, mainly directing the operation because of my leg, and I saw how red his face was and had heard him puffing and

257

heaving, but thought nothing of it. He was taking most of the weight there. He stayed hunched for so long that I grew worried and called to him. "You all right?" I never knew if he heard me.

At that moment he slowly rolled over — I can see it now, like an instinctive attempt to keep from tumbling down the whole flight — and lay facedown on the landing beside that terrible damned highboy. I knew he was dead even then but refused to believe it. Something stabs into you, something you see in the queer abandon of the attitude. That unbearable moment of knowing. The enormity of it, this outrageous invasion of eternity into the comfortable small chaos of your daily life.

Jacobus, fat, laughing Jacobus, who a minute before had been making some droll remark about the angels on the cabinet, there he lay with the sweat still beaded on his pimply face, the eyes gone blank. Dear jolly Jacobus, who always said he would take care of us in our old age. He was twenty-four.

A dreadful long day, one of the worst. The demeaning physicalness of it all, carrying him down the stairs, calming Lysbeth who was perfectly hysterical at the sight of him (she had poured mugs of ale for him and Claes and me and was actually on her way up to us with them), and most ridiculous of all, our having to finish lugging that monstrous cabinet the rest of the way up the stairs that very day because it blocked the passage. That was the worst part. Both of us pouring down tears as we shoved and wrestled and lifted and jimmied the thing to the top. To this day I am reminded whenever I look at it and its silly wooden angels.

I went back to see her on the Sunday. Lysbeth wanted to come but simply cannot travel any distance, and I have not the money for a carriage. She sent her love and a gorgeous strawberry tart, which I carried in an old cheese box that had been thoroughly fumigated by time.

It was yet another beautiful lazy afternoon, with plump white clouds sailing majestically by in a perfect blue sky and a gentle breeze that stirred the poplar leaves, making them flutter softly, twirling like round yellow paper coins. We sat in the garden at the back, where Jan had moved her couch, along with a table and a chair for me.

No chocolate today, but coffee with the tart and later good water from the spring that feeds the stream, cold and iron-tasting. She was livelier today, sitting up brightly, color in her face, a smile for me. I brought her a little oil-on-paper I did of Sara a few years ago.

"Wonderful," she murmured, peering closely at it, framing it with her hands as she studied it propped on her knees. "It's just the way I remember her. We were conspirators, you know."

She wanted to know about my work, so I recounted the big years, when I was doing two and three commissions at a time and people were standing in line for me. It was fun to remember. She wanted to know if I was working and I lied and said I was. She wanted to know about Sara.

"Married now," I said. "Settled down."

"Hmm. You say that with a certain relief, I think."

I couldn't tell her. Even if she had heard the rumors, it was not in me to confess.

The girl was completely out of control and was fast becoming the town whore when we finally took action. L came to me in my workroom one day unable to hold back another minute.

"She's having another baby!" she cried. "What are we going to do?"

I was already getting strange looks from the men in Piet's, and I finally understood that her whoredom was no private sin but very much a concern for the whole town, this town being what it is.

What people do in Haarlem in these cases may seem strange in another place, but it is what we do.

So L gave the nod, and the Council had to ratify it. Sara had already had a little girl by that layabout Abraham Potterloo, and

I trust that it was Potterloo who started the second one. The girl, named Maria, stayed with her mother, though she was only two. I think it was best, for Sara was really a sweet mother.

"We have two grandchildren," I told Judy. "She's married to a seaman, a man from Friesland, all white eyebrows and pink freckles. They moved to Amsterdam and they seem quite devoted."

I didn't mention poor Pieter. The city moved him to the workhouse at one hundred a year. Sometimes he would saw brazilwood in the saw-house, but other times he just roared and tried to attack everyone in sight. I don't understand it, that quiet baby.

For a while we sat contentedly in the little garden. The bees were humming in the hollyhocks that Judy had planted by the stone wall. Beyond it the meadow shimmered and rustled with the busy life of autumn, insects whirring above the grass as they skimmed this way and that on their tiny errands. The sun fell on her face, so I fetched a bonnet that she had left by the door with the pile of trowels and rakes. She looked like a girl with the cotton shade framing her face.

"Lovely garden," I said, settling into my chair again.

"Better next year."

We sat in silence.

"It's not the pain," she added quietly.

"Is it bad?" I said, like a fool.

"Not yet. Not much. There are herbs I take. No."

I thought of that thing behind her ear, working away.

"It's in the morning," she said. "I wake up, and for just a moment it is a glorious new day and the sun is coming in the window and I have my Jan beside me. And then I remember."

I groped for her hand and we sat together like that. A locust sang its metallic song in the poplars and died away in a rattle.

"What will happen?" she said.

"When?"

"After."

"What do you think?"

"I'm asking."

"What do I know? Maybe it's a gradual thing," I said, not knowing where this was coming from in me. "Look how long it takes to get born. I think after, we stay around for a while, invisible, and then gradually let go."

She contemplated this for a minute or two, then burst out, "What if you're not ready to let go?"

I felt like some huge obscene excrescence, alive and hearty at my age. She looked at me with such profound reproach that I bowed my head.

Of course, fifty is a long life. But I could never think of her as fifty. To me she was still the girl I had known, in her twenties, when no one deserves to die.

"They could be wrong," I said. "Doctors are wrong all the time."

She didn't respond. A breeze rattled the poplar leaves again. We sat there for some time. Finally she said, in a ruminating tone as if contemplating some philosophical conundrum, "I wonder if there is nothing. Just nothing. Like sleep. That would be the worst, I think. To have it simply end. Drop off into darkness. You wouldn't even know, would you?"

This great adventure that all of us are plunged into, willy-nilly, even the most timid.

"I had a great-aunt who lived here in Heemstede," she was saying. "Lived to ninety-eight. Nothing left of her but bones and skin you could see through and gray old veins. She had no hair left and only a few teeth, and she couldn't hear a thing. But she could see, and her mind was good. I used to talk to her when I was a girl, and she would say it was terrible, to live beyond your time, all her friends dead, her husband in his grave forty years — and she had no picture of him, she had forgot what he looked like, imagine, the whole world changed around her, and the aches and pains, the bad stomach and the broken hip that never mended right and all that, but still she would say she wasn't ready to go, that she was afraid. She hated to go to sleep every night because she might not wake up."

Judy sipped her water and studied me carefully. "I am afraid to go to sleep," she said calmly.

I tried to think of something to say.

"You'll laugh," I said. "Did you know I joined the church?"

"No!" She did laugh. "Hals the famous skeptic? Hals the cynic? Hals the philosopher? I don't believe it for a minute."

I shrugged again. "I did it, all right."

"I heard you painted the Frenchman who thinks that he thinks. I hope you didn't tell him."

"Oh yes. We discussed the human condition and the future of the world. It was a great dialogue."

In fact I hardly spoke to the man, or he to me. It was arranged through a dealer friend of mine and Schrevelius, who had known him on account of Leiden. He came here to lecture—what a sensation! Descartes himself at our university!—and then stopped to visit Schrevelius and I painted him there. He spoke barely a word of my language and I only twenty of his. He spoke very little in any case. He would greet me at the door and I would say, Bon joure, and he would say, Il faite beau aujoourdwee, and I would say, Oui oui, sa va, and then I would put him in his seat and get to work. An interesting face, not what I would call knife-sharp with intelligence, but calmer, slower, wiser. An old face, very French.

After a while she bid me leave. She was tired. "It was good of you to listen," she said. There are things you have to say, even if no one is ready to hear them.

She didn't ask me any more about joining the Reformed Church. I gather she has turned from church. Or anyway finds little help in it. I gave in five years ago when Lysbeth was so sick. She had a frightening flow of blood from her bowels, she was terrified. So much blood. And I had not the money to buy her red meat. Pray, she said, please pray. So devout herself. I did pray. I went into St. Bavo's at midday and prayed on my knees on the bare flagstones. Leenders saw me (how, I do not know, he has the milky eye disease) and came right up to me when I rose to go, and said, "Mijnheer Hals, a man was just asking for you. Just this morning."

And that led me to Councillor Berckx, who had been trying to find me at the Oude Gracht house which I had left years ago. He wanted me to paint a vanitas with globe and skull in memory of his son, who had died at sea. It was for his wife, still mourning the lad after a year. Generally I don't like these didactic works, but he paid me well enough to cover the doctor and the cost of a good shoulder of ox. L said it was clearly a miracle, and I didn't argue with her. She did get better right away. The flow stopped on a diet of cream and eggs and various herbs. I wouldn't let them bleed her.

"I'm costing you a fortune, Hals," she said once.

"I'm rich," I said.

She wanted to see Judy. We arranged to go together in a carriage the next week, but she fell sick with a heavy cough. Then I caught it and spent five days flat on my back. Everything takes longer when you are old.

I am constantly cutting myself, scraping the flesh from knuckle or elbow, because the skin is less elastic, and the scab is part of me for a month. And a cold takes its own time in making its laborious passage from throat to nose to chest and back. And I go to bed, when a few years ago I would have shrugged it off. So boring. I become so cross that she refuses to visit me on my couch except to bring food. Once she stormed out and left me alone in the house for the whole day. It was quite peaceful, really. I tried my pipe but found it revolting. She came back at dusk refreshed and friendly. She has a close friend across town, the widow Schout, and they spend hours muttering together over their tisane. I can't stand the woman since Lot died. She has changed so, turned bitter, always greets me with a quizzical look that says, What, you still around? For some reason she makes Lysbeth cheerful.

By this time winter was setting in with an early snow, and I was becoming anxious, so I went by myself, bearing a special cheese pasty that she is famous for. (I rarely have it, it binds me, but she makes a meat version for me when we have meat, which is not often.) It was another of those ominously still days when the sky seems to lie just above the treetops, sullen and yellow and pregnant with snow. Jan met me at the door.

"So glad," he said. "We thought you must be sick."

She lay on her usual Roman couch, only her head raised, the rest of her flat. I was shocked. She was smaller. Her white hair, which she combed out loose, had spread and swelled in volume, it seemed, so now it looked like a huge, exotic headdress, with her face a narrow, gaunt shape in the center. Her hair was swallowing her up. I don't say she looked older, but more fragile, more remote. It was like seeing her from a distance. Her voice was distant, too, clear but faint, with the lovely husky quality that reduced it almost to a whisper.

"I missed you," she said.

"Lysbeth wanted so to come. We've both been sick."

She patted the chair by her head. She was calmer than before. She seemed infinitely wise.

"Tell me about Sara," she whispered.

Isn't that amazing? Such a soft expression on her face, such kindness. She raised one hand in a sort of absolution.

"It was terrible," I said. "I hated Lysbeth, Lysbeth hated Sara, and Sara hated both of us and herself."

It wasn't so much when we had the scene. That came earlier. Sara turned up at the house after being away for at least three whole months, and I for one had given up on her. She went to Leiden, we learned later. But there she was at the door, right in the middle of supper with her belly so big that the little ones stared. Lysbeth took one look and threw the kettle top clear across the kitchen. And screamed at her for a minute or more, even as the kettle top clanged and rattled and reverberated with a racket painful to my ears. In the middle of it Sara started screaming back.

"Yes I did!" she shouted. "Yes I am! And so what!"

I headed off Lysbeth as she was making for her daughter with a mop. Far from cowering, Sara was looking around for something to throw back at her. She never was afraid of her mother. It used to scare the britches off me. I shoved her into the front room and took Lysbeth by the shoulders and calmed her down a bit, and we had peace for the moment. The real thing came two days later. L went to the Town Hall by herself. When she came back she wore a peculiar grim expression.

"I have done it," she announced.

"What?" I was shoveling ashes out of the hearth. It was spring.

"I have requested that they take her into the workhouse."

I dropped the shovel. I never thought she would actually do it. It is true, many women are sent there to have their bastard babies away from the sight of the rest of us virtuous citizens, all honest and pure-hearted as we are. Sometimes they are adopted, sometimes they go to the orphanage, a few are absorbed into the mother's family one way or another. (I remember Jacob Steen discovering when we were in school that his older sister was in fact his mother. For some reason he found it terribly exciting, or so he confided to me.) The trouble with this system is that the townspeople cannot decide whether the workhouse is a sort of hospital or a sort of jail. One school of thought wants the inmates to suffer physically in addition to the abject humiliation of being there. The other says the shame of it is enough.

I said, "Can't we send her out of town?"

"Where? That would be worse."

"Can't we find the man? It was Potterloo, I suppose."

She drew herself up. She had thought it all out. "He would have come around the first time if he was going to. It might have been another one. Who knows?"

Eventually she wore me down. I thought it might do some good, the shock of it. And besides, little Maria could be with her. I would have been willing to take on the child for a while, but Lysbeth stamped her foot so hard it made her cry. "Enough children!" she cried in a biblical roar. And I had to agree with that. So I said I would talk to Sara that evening.

She knew something was up when I brought her into the parlor. The beans were on for supper, and Lysbeth settled the fire down before wiping her hands on her apron and joining us. I sat on the bench in front of the table. Sara condescended to sit at the far end. She looked magnificent, by the way, her head defiantly high, her red hair flowing in fine soft waves down her back. (She always hated caps and bonnets, and she is right, they bind up a woman's beauty like a bandage. Modest it may be, but as a design for apparel it has the mark of the Calvinist.)

"Sara, we have made a decision," I said in my most formal manner. L stirred in her seat across from us. "This can't go on. You are becoming known in town."

Her lips curled.

"I have told you, your mother has told you. When you had Maria you swore it was all over, it would not happen again, you had learned. You were done with that way of life."

"If you knew," Lysbeth said, "what it did to us, coming home that way."

"So?" She shrugged dramatically and rolled her eyes. "So I am living my life. I am old enough to take command of my own life."

"Obviously you are not," I snapped. "No one is in command. You don't seem to understand, these are real live people you are bringing into the world. They are not dolls."

Her face seemed to draw in at the sound of me. I strike out in that way so seldom. I have watched the face of a child in his dying moment and seen how the cheeks collapse, how the skin sags as the heart stops pumping and the vessels go flat. It was almost like that.

"The fact is," I said, "we have asked to have you committed to the workhouse to have the baby."

She didn't gasp. She simply stopped breathing. For the first time she looked straight at me.

"You did," she said.

"We did."

"You mean mother did, and you backed her up."

She was a valiant fighter always. I took this contemptuous slap in stride, the way one shrugs off a bloody nose in a fist fight, but it stung, all right. Lysbeth, however, exploded in one of her special tantrums that Sara alone could inspire.

I didn't burden Judy with all these details, how the girl finally broke down and ran upstairs and sobbed herself to sleep, how we completed the arrangement the next day, with the understanding that we could take her out at any time. I did tell of the scene at the workhouse itself, a suitably depressing brick structure with high walls and mean windows.

We stood at the gatehouse, the four of us, Maria holding her mother's hand and sucking all four fingers as she stared up at us with round eyes.

"I didn't believe you would do this," I remember Sara said.

"It will come out best," Lysbeth replied calmly.

"I'm sorry," I said.

Sara looked at us both. She had grown up in the last two days.

"This is really what you want."

"Not at all," I said. "It's the last thing I wanted. It's terrible. But what else can we do?"

Her mouth corner curled.

"We've been over this already," muttered Lysbeth.

I was going to tell her it was for her own good, but I didn't have the stomach for that classic hypocrisy. So I said it was really for the sake of her child and the other one, which wasn't much better.

"You're only thinking of how it makes you look," she said calmly.

" 'Keep a strict watch over a headstrong daughter,' " I reminded her, having looked this up in the Bible the night before.

She shamed me utterly. Looked me straight in the eye and quoted the rest of the verse. " 'Lest she make you a laughingstock to your enemies.' "

I wanted to tell her that we loved her and would always love her one way or another. What I said was, "If it weren't this, it would be something much worse later on. You know how people are."

"I'm finding out," she said.

We watched her go in past the blank-faced old sexton, through those big dark doors with Maria and their small satchels.

Telling Judy about this was the worst. "I did it," I confessed, "put my own daughter in the workhouse. I was the worst kind of self-righteous pharisee. And yet I thought this was the best thing for her. It was like dashing cold water in the face of someone raving hysterical. Can you understand that?"

She nodded slowly. "You could have done nothing, and then you would feel even worse."

She was right. That short stay in the workhouse with all the other young mothers and assorted miscreants and castaways from our tidy society, the terrible hard birth of little Frans, the daily pain of seeing Maria in that place an innocent prisoner, it all changed our Sara. We met her when she came out, and I gave her half my commission from a small portrait and put her and Maria and the baby on the stage for Amsterdam. She had friends in Amsterdam, she told us. I gave her a couple of names, and Lysbeth reminded her of her cousin Reyniersen, who was living there.

"She named him after me," I pointed out with a pride so visible that Judy actually laughed.

"So she forgave you."

"I think so."

"And you forgave yourself."

"I think so."

She laid a thin hand on my arm. "I'd like to go outside," she whispered.

"It's going to snow again."

She said, so casually, "I will miss that. I will miss the trees."

I would have carried her outside if I could. Years ago I dreamed of holding her and lifting her light, lithe body in the air and clasping it to me. I used to imagine the feel of her, the softness of those modest breasts, the young thighs pressing against mine, the intense firm curve of her hips beneath her skirts. (Once she passed close in front of me and my hand brushed her hips, and at the sheer round solid beauty of her under my touch, a sudden flash of lust absolutely dizzied me, sent my head spinning.) I could not leave her that afternoon.

"I was fierce," she said. "I was going to become a famous painter. I was better than the men."

"You were."

"I wanted to say, Here is a woman who can do what a man can do, so pay attention."

We used to argue about whether God was a man. She insisted He was above all that, since He had created both sexes. I was never very successful in these debates. Isn't He our father? I would say. God as a woman—what an idea. What would Pastor Leenders say?

We talked until nearly dark. Or rather, I talked a lot. She got me going about the big years. All those Coymanses. Those impossible Friesians with their Moorish boy: They insisted on his being in the picture to show how rich they were and were

269

scandalized when I talked with him at some length. That glowing dark skin, so much more interesting than ours. He was far more intelligent than the old man, spoke the language so fluently that I could hardly believe he wasn't a native. Caesar, his name was, insulting. I wanted to ask his real one but was too shy to.

She loved my accounts of the apprentices (we slid smoothly past the sore business of young Willem) and their slovenly ways and lack of talent (with exceptions) and especially about Pieter van Roestraten, the pick of them all, who married Adraientje, much to my surprise but not at all to Lysbeth's.

And the deaths, so many deaths, even poor crazy Bobbe in the workhouse, fallen through a hole in the ice on one of her attempts to run away. (Run away to what?)

And the money, how it slipped through my hands, how I had to work free for an entire day and pay Fl 60 as well when Harmen came to me in disgrace for not paying his rent. And the time I got excited and bought a bunch of paintings at an auction and couldn't begin to pay for them and Dirck had to bail me out. How I chattered on.

At long last I thought to ask about her pictures. She had one fine portrait, virtually complete, and a sheaf of oil sketches. I fetched them from the corner and we looked at them together. More tulips, vibrant with life. Some dashed-off faces that were full of character and reminded me of my own earlier work. Several studies of hands. She was wonderful with hands.

We talked shop. Her love affair with greenish blue. The idiotic ways of the patrons. Rembrandt and Vermeer and all that bunch and the money you can make in Amsterdam, or could, before the hard times. I told her that the guild had exempted me from my dues because I couldn't pay them. I am becoming a character in the town.

The light faded quickly that day, the sun shrouded behind the heavy snow clouds.

She was getting tired, though she kept urging me to stay. Finally I stood up. I didn't want to walk home in the dark. As I opened the door to go, I smelled snow coming, a fresh, sharp smell in the laden air. A few heavy flakes, fat as flannel, were drifting down.

She called me back once more from the other room. I went to her.

"Come soon. Come this week."

"If the snow lets me."

She clasped my hand. "Dear Frans," she said in her velvet whisper.

"Dear Judy." I leaned down and kissed her on the forehead. It was cold. I knew her so little.

"I wish you a good journey," she said, and I left.

When I got home Lysbeth was excited.

"I found the slip for Hendricksen!" She was breathless, waving the paper at me from her chair.

"Where?"

"In the blue vase."

I don't know why we didn't look there before. Maybe we did. We put everything in the blue vase, an imitation Delft I had bought for the real thing many years ago when I was even more foolish than now.

"Wonderful," I said. "What do we do now?"

"I'm going to go talk to him."

"And what good will that do? You think he's going to give it back?"

She shrugged. "He might. At least he'll know I was right."

We still have the chest of drawers Hendricksen sold us, but I had to practically rebuild it because it kept falling apart. Imagine, the nerve, to sue her for nonpayment when he must have known she had indeed paid.

Later the snow came and I couldn't sleep. I lay and listened to it settling softly on the window, thinking of the things I had not

271

told Judy. I should have stopped it. I should have said, Of course we'll take you in, as long as you want, you and Maria. Of course. Of course. My defiant daughter, so eager to love, so yearning to be loved.

I thought of all the times Lysbeth had ranted at her—the beautiful young woman she herself no longer was—and I had sat silent or drifted off to my workroom. And the whippings when she was little. L did the whipping. She didn't think it decent for a man to.

Not enough that I would bring her bread and cheese in the night. Not enough.

I thought I would go back the next day, which was a Friday, and lay my confession before her as an offering. I went to sleep with that happy thought. If the snow would stop. Your journey, she had called it. What a strange word.

That morning the promised blizzard broke. Wind tore at the corners of the house and drove the snow against the lintels and piled it up in each frost-crusted frame. I could barely open the door. I was frantic. I tried not to listen to the urgent voice inside me.

We didn't get out until Monday. Snow lay in great white waves, waist-high in the alleys and against the fences. A narrow path had been worn through knee-deep snow up the center of the street. I have not seen such a snowfall since I was a boy. There were no carriages about, and Lysbeth held my sleeve to keep me from starting out.

"Let me go," I said. "I have to."

She made me put a small Gouda into my pocket and my flask of geneva. I rarely ever drink it now.

It was a magnificent clear day, as so often after a storm. Patches of snow clung to the sides of trees and houses, driven into the surface by the wind. A few citizens were out and greeted me with the joy of the survivor. I plunged on, down one newly pioneered trail after another, my boots crunching the crisp snow with the sound of someone eating carrots. Despite the cold I was not limping. My knee appeared to thrive on the dry brightness of this fine day.

I passed beyond the wall of Haarlem and across the bridge and into the warren of poor streets on the outskirts of Heemstede. Small boys romped on the ice of the canal. All along the banks they had built slides and were taking turns, yelling and shouting in sheer excitement, riding down the slick chutes on the seat of their pants to slither across the polished ice of the canal, all the time shouting.

Through the center of town, out the other side, as the houses thinned out and the fields and orchards and pastures gradually contested the space with them and began finally to win. My knee twisted itself again. I wished I had brought my stick. I hate it.

Ahead I saw her house. Two women were coming out of the front door, one of them carrying a loaded basket. They nodded to Jan, who stood on the step. I saw their faces. Suddenly I didn't want to get there. The distance seemed so short. I would be there too soon.

The women departed in the other direction, stumbling through the snow.

He looked down the street and saw me. He didn't nod. I reached him and looked up at him, standing still on the stoop.

"It was yesterday," he said.

"Ah." Not wanting to understand.

"Early in the morning, just before dawn. In her sleep."

"Oh no."

"I'm so sorry."

"I came as soon as I could," I said.

"Thank you," he said. "Won't you come in?"

She looked like a statue of herself, an extremely clever likeness but not quite right. I had thought she would look as if she were sleeping, but she didn't. Sleepers have an innocence. A presence. She was not here. He let me borrow a stick, a good ash with a carved knob head, to get home with. I have it still.

———————————◀◉▶———————————

7

Potomac, Maryland, a sprawling suburb northwest of Washington, was full of estates built by people who wanted it to be known that they live in Potomac, Maryland. They seemed to prefer houses that looked like the modest bungalows or even trailers that they came from, but blown up to enormous proportions. Even with the seven-window facade and the three stories and the succession of additions on either side, Peter could see the bungalow design, the trailer mentality, at the center. Many of the estates had actual acreage, too, but often the owners did not seem to know what to do with it. They chopped down all the trees and sowed a vast lawn, or they built a pool out back and ignored the rest, leaving the land in the raw state that the developer had left it. A strange community.

Tony's estate rested on a pert knob of land just beyond the woods that extended all the way down a long slope to the Potomac River. He had built a New England traditional, with the five windows on the second floor and the classic symmetry downstairs of a central porch and a door flanked by tall windows. On each side, however, he had added wings virtually the same size as the main house, and on the ends of the wings he had stuck screened porches. Since he was living in the house with just a cook, maid and driver, he used only about three rooms of the twenty-four. The windowpanes on both wings still had their stickers on. His wife Beverly had left some time ago with their daughter, Dulcet.

Tony greeted Peter with a hug and a shout when he piled out of the Alfa-Romeo ahead of the driver. "Been awhile," he chuckled, taking in Peter's curious white trousers with the cuffs let down. "I've been getting calls about you."

A cold hand gripped Peter's insides. "What?"

"Newspapers, magazines. *Time* and *Newsweek*. You're a celebrity."

"Well, that's why I'm here. I hope—"

"I told 'em I hadn't seen you in three years."

"Thanks."

If he had hoped to get away from Frans Hals for a weekend, he was drastically mistaken, for Tony wanted to know everything. He was fascinated by the idea of a lost diary and quizzed Peter sharply about its provenance.

Peter explained that the thing was now pretty well shot down and did his best to cool his brother's enthusiasm. Sipping his Bols Dutch gin in the cavernous family room with its outdated sixties conversation pit, Tony eyed his brother shrewdly. "You have a lot invested in this, dontcha? In him being real?"

"I dunno. Just so I get paid."

He felt himself blush.

Meanwhile, the brothers were living high. They ate steaks on the terrace overlooking the muddy hole that was to have been a pool and watched Dutch movies on the giant TV screen in the evenings. Tony said he needed them to keep up his Dutch, since he rarely visited the Netherlands these days. On Saturday he, Peter and the driver, whose name was Jeff, went to Gettysburg in the big black Lincoln and roamed the battlefield. There was a girlfriend somewhere, Peter understood, judging from the women's things left lying around the enormous ruffly bedroom beyond his, but the subject never came up.

Tony was in such an expansive mood—"I was made to be single, it's the only way"—that he even gave Peter an extra two thousand to tide him over until he could "find a buyer for those translations."

"We gotta stick together, kid," he told Peter as they said good-bye outside Union Station on Monday morning. "You're the only family I have."

Settling down on the train, he felt sure that the calls would have tailed off by now. The first thing he had to do was reach Laura. He needed that history book, which didn't even belong to him. He also wanted to check out the deaths of Jacobus and Judy, and the fate of the idiot son—did they really saw brazilwood as punishment? It sounded too crazy not to be true. And the extraordinary story of putting Sara in the work-house.

On the trip north, he started to read the last section. It was quite different: The handwriting was less certain and there were dates. The man must have had a lot of time on his hands. As usual, the year was inscribed at the top of the first page: 1664. Hals would have been about eighty-two.

————————◄○►————————

January 6. Sunday. She demanded that I do this so I won't complain so much.

I count my days. This day was rainy, the steady rain of winter. Canal ice is covered with sheets of water. Will melt soon. Cheese-and-onion pancakes for dinner. She knows I am worried.

January 7. To the Town Hall this morning. I have exactly a week's worth of peat left. She needs the heat for her rheumatism. Rained in the afternoon. Depressing.

January 8. Thaw continues.

January 10. Spoke to Councillor Wolleswinkel this morning. So hard to get through the bureaucrats to someone who can actually make a decision. So important to them to seem to have power. Wolleswinkel a wise old bird, passing seventy, I knew his older brother. Face like a cheese, perfectly round, yellow, smooth above insignificant gray beard. But old eyes. Watches me. Fat fingers drumming on his desk, very broad, blood-gorged nails.

"The artist," he says, bowing his head graciously, waving me to the chair beside his desk, which is bare except for a single file. To show me that he delegates mere work to underlings.

I sit, a laborious process because of my leg. I used two canes, not strictly necessary. Showing off. But it was bad today, as always in wet weather.

"Thank you," I say, meaning the chair. Last year some insolent child let me stand for half the interview.

"You signed for your January payment, I see." Looking down at the paper in front of him.

"Right."

"You are up to fifty guilders now."

"Can't complain," I say. "The city is as generous as a city could be."

"I would say." He nods pleasantly. "From now on it will remain at two hundred a year, but I don't expect it to go up from there. Times are hard, as you know."

He is wondering why I am here, trying to head off a request for more money.

"I should know," I reply. "And I appreciate all that you do for me. There is a small thing, though. It has been a terrible winter for us, we suffer from the cold more than we used to. The place we have is so poorly built that we get drafts all the time."

"So," he mutters.

"So I am requesting some help with the fuel. Could you let me have some peat squares? Could the city spare a few?" Subtly, I fan myself with one hand. In fact it is blazing hot in the hall. They must keep the furnaces roaring until May.

Wolleswinkel smiles a hard smile.

"Frans," he says, instantly making an enemy of me, "we have been through this before. This is precisely the reason that the city supplies fuel to the almshouse. There is absolutely no need for anyone like yourself to lie about in a drafty rented place. We have suggested this several times, as I recall."

"The answer is no," I say.

He lifts a hand as though I was shouting at him. "Let me finish. It would be no credit to Haarlem if its most famous painter were to be found frozen by his easel one day. This is why we have begged you to come to the almshouse."

"No," I say.

"You would have the pension and everything. Rooms for both of you. Friends — "

"I've heard this," I say. "I will not go into the almshouse. I have said it and I have said it. Now, the pension is wonderful. We are able to get along if de Geest doesn't raise the rent. But I would starve before I go into that place."

For a long time he studies me. I wonder what he sees. At least the smile is gone. Frans indeed.

"All right, I'll take it up," he sighs. "Come back in a week."

I attempt to stalk out with my canes. Almshouse! One room for each. In separate buildings! We had potato-and-cabbage pudding, I love it but would like it better with a bit of bacon.

January 11. She is very low. The cough is at her lungs, she cannot clear them. I brought her some horehound drops.

January 12. A caller today. I should have expected him. Raps briskly on the door, bent and bearded, fixes me with a bright eye. Name is Smoot. From Doctor Westerloo.

"If you please sir, Dr. Westerloo would like to talk with you, if you could arrange to meet with him."

"What does he want?"

The man shrugs. He is some sort of majordomo over there, I suppose. A glorified servant.

She calls from the other room where she is still in bed. Who is it?

"Westerloo," I say. "He wants to talk to me."

"Westerloo at the almshouse?"

"Right."

"Don't go," she calls feebly.

"No, I will go. Does he want me right now?" I ask the messenger. "I'll go with you." Better to get this over with while I am already angry.

"Oh no, that won't be necessary," he says stiffly. "Dr. Westerloo will see you in the morning."

It was a summons. I nodded the man out of the house and went to see her, sitting up pertly in the bed, flannel wrapped around her neck.

"I'll tell him what he needs to know," I said. "When I get done with him he'll never need to ask again."

"Don't be hard on them."

"Hard on them! They put him up to it!"

"Who, now, who?" She loves to bait me.

"Why, the idiots over at the hall. That smirking Wolleswinkel."

"What, because you went and asked for some peat?"

"They're trying to get us into that damned pesthouse. You know that."

We had nothing today but turnips with a bit of butter. I am becoming a fair cook. If it turns cold again I can't last the week with the miserable chunks I have left.

January 13. Been past that building a thousand times, but it never looked so ominous before. Dark leaden gray brick, tall windows with mullions and the smallest panes I have seen anywhere. Great slabs of chimney, four of them, with crumbling red pots on top. That is the part that you see from outside. I walked into the courtyard and found myself ringed with more tall windows and smaller ones on the second floor.

There was a gatehouse in the passage, and a decrepit old man hobbled out to overtake me. "Dr. Westerloo," I said. "He wants to see me. My name is Hals."

An extra bow. Was that a sneer I saw on the gnarled face? Was this old toad going to be one of my cellmates whom I would have to hear snoring and farting and coughing through the night? He was the kind who would pester me to play draughts and have the board all set up whenever I came by.

He led me into a grand reception room, dragging a foot as he went. I had my one cane, after long debate over whether to use both and look truly crippled or to bring none and risk not being able to get up from the chair and causing all sorts of concern and anxious looks. The first room had an elaborately molded ceiling at least twenty feet high and a long table with two rows of fine spindly dining chairs and a series of portraits of solemn people on the heavily molded smoked-mahogany walls. I thought, Someone is making money from this place.

The second room was half the height and a third the length, but still elaborate, with an enormous rug covering the ubiquitous inlaid floor of black-and-white checkerboard. Only a small table here and several armchairs grouped around the fireplace, which stood twelve feet high and looked long enough to accommodate the Cross itself in one piece. I cannot imagine why, but churchly thoughts pursued me in this hushed place with its unctuous smell of laundry starch and floor wax.

The third room was smaller still, a working room, with a littered desk at the center, two chairs, a brazier (filled to glowing) and, behind the desk, my quarry in person. I have known him for years, or seen him anyway. Dimpled chin, long straight nose and soft eyes that examine you while giving away nothing. The mouth, visible now that—thank God—we have given up the beards, reveals nothing either but simply lies there calmly unsmiling, pushing out slightly from beneath the feeblest mustache I have almost ever seen.

"Mijnheer Hals," he said cordially. "Appreciate your coming. Do take a seat."

I did. It was a bad day for the knee.

He studied me across the desk, long articulate fingers making a steeple under his mouth. He is a surgeon, I think. One of our most eminent doctors. I sat with my mouth shut waiting for him to make the first move.

"It's my understanding," he began in a discursive way as though about to tell a long, cozy tale before the fire, "that Mijnheer Hals is the finest painter in Haarlem."

I hate to be addressed in the third person. "Was," I replied.

He smiled at last, a carefully considered smile that gave his face a kindly look for a moment. "Not at all. I have been in touch with Amsterdam. In fact I have been looking for someone to do some work for us, and I naturally went to Amsterdam." Impressive pause. He leaned forward. "Imagine my surprise when they sent me right back here."

"What sort of work?"

" 'Hals is your man,' they said. 'He can do it better than anyone.' "

Ah yes. Flatter me with some bauble and then when I am slavering for it, point out that, well of course, I will have to live here in the almshouse.

I said, "What are we talking about?"

He had been prepared for a rude old character. Still staring, moving only his fingers to point the steeple at me, he snapped, "Painting, of course. What else?"

"I beg your pardon?"

An impatient sniff. "We want a portrait of the regents. And one of the regentesses too, if it works out."

I was too stunned to speak. He must have thought I was still being fractious, because he added dryly, "Why else would I ask you here, Mijnheer Hals?"

"Right," I said, wiping the sputter off my lips, "right. You want a painting. You were thinking a group portrait?"

"Yes. Something for the grand hall."

"And the women in the same group?"

"Oh no, they would be separate. We have two separate houses, you understand. They are an entirely different board."

He hesitated a beat or two, then said, "But I will be handling them both. The budget is for three hundred."

I started to cough. Put a hand up. Something was tickling my throat, probably the dry rusk I had had with my morning cheese.

"You don't agree?"

"No no," I gasped. "It's fine. Fine." And coughed again.

"Each, of course. Three hundred each."

I stopped in midcough. I stared at him in the ringing silence.

"Of course," I said.

"You will do it?"

I counted on my fingers and rubbed my chin. "I think," I said finally.

He waited on my words.

"I think, I do think I can work it in. Yes. Yes, I'd be delighted to do them both."

"Good, good." He grinned now, a grin of amusement that he struggled to turn into a grin of triumph, his dead eyes piercing straight into me. "We'd be most grateful indeed if you could work us in."

I do not understand it. Either I have a secret friend in Amsterdam or these people do not read what the critics say about me.

I went home in a dazed state. I told her I had a job, but not the amount. I am superstitious. She said to read the contract carefully. I said I didn't think there would be a contract, it would probably be done with a handshake in the old style. I haven't had a job big enough to require a formal contract in ten years at least. I was in danger of crediting Dr. Westerloo with being a gentleman. I talked so much about him that she mumbled, as I joined her in the bed, "He's going to get you there, that's what it's all about. Well, he won't get me."

I had to laugh. She would follow me to hell. Complaining every step of the way.

January 14. This morning I woke up and the first thought that came to me: Three hundred! I turned to her and found her looking at me wide-eyed. I couldn't help myself.

"Three hundred!" I said. "They pay three hundred for each, and there are two pictures."

"I don't believe it."

"It's true."

"For two pictures?"

"Two pictures. Maybe ten heads, twelve heads."

"I want to see the contract."

She is impossible.

January 15. There are five of them. I shook their hands one by one. Dirck fixed the canvas for me, underpainted just the way I need it. He said he would charge me Fl 20, but I suspect he will forget. Only a pauper knows the sweet bitterness of this sort of forgetfulness.

Westerloo goes in the center. A beer wholesaler named Johannes Walles on the right, a nice bland face with competence behind the eyes. He said very little, but, as I recall he is well placed. The others tend to defer to him a bit.

Deinoot is going to be a problem. He has something wrong with his face, and there is some kind of cast in his right eye. I set up the canvas and marked in some figures. Five people, nothing fancy, they are not interested in poses. They want Smoot in it, which pleases me. So it will be six heads, which is fifty per head. Not bad. Not the top, but not bad. We celebrated with a goose sausage and the last of the apple jelly. So good, but it will lie on my stomach tonight.

January 16. Talked to Smoot this morning. The regents decided to have a private meeting, seeing that they were all collected together, so I was sent off to the dining hall to find myself some coffee and a bit of cheese. There I ran into Smoot, a sly old codger who still wears the ruff. And beard. Knowing old eyes. He introduced me to the cook, an enormous woman who was thin in the face, hair pulled sleekly back under her cap, but generous at the throat, mannish about the shoulders and mountainous from there on down. He and I sat at the end of a long trestle table with our coffee and a sugar pancake.

"Be careful of Walles," he muttered. "He's a smiler. He tried to have my job once."

I found out about Deinoot. He has had a stroke and the right side of his face is paralyzed. Makes him smile crookedly, so he tries not to smile. Also, according to Smoot, who says he went to school with him, his right eye was damaged when he was a kid, some hot oil spilled on him and there is scar tissue on the lid. He will want to be in profile, no doubt.

They took so long I had little time to work. De Jong wants a Bible in it. He is a lay minister. No banquet scene here. Simple, solid figures, and they want it dark. Everyone wants chiaroscuro. I am getting famous for my blacks. Wonderful effects. A touch of Prussian blue when I can get it. Expensive. The way the faces gradually emerge from the gloom. The longer you look, the more you see. It makes you take your time and study the picture. I like that.

Will need color. What?

January 17. Things looking up. Just as I was starting out to see Westerloo and his friends, a team of workmen shuffles up to the place, their blue smocks all dusty with peat. They are delivering three cartloads from Town Hall. The carts are at the end of the street and they want to get into the alley to dump

285

their loads at the back of the house. I have to inform them that we have no house, only a room and a half with a shed out back. This cheers them up visibly. I have an idea they had thought the councillors were handing out free peat to some rich artist friend of theirs and that they resented the whole project. But they see we are truly poor, not to say destitute, and live in a hovel very like their own, no doubt, and they turn into good fellows.

"Where you want it?" Grunting under their hods, which are piled high with squares of peat. I direct them to a corner of the shed. The load will take up nearly half the space, but I plan to move a few squares into the house every night to stack by the hearth and keep dry.

They have the carts unloaded in the time it takes me to go up the street and buy a beaker of ale. I pour it out into three roemers and hand them out, the men now cheerfully toasting me. "This'll last all winter," I say, gloating over the dark frowsty piles, waist-high and looking rather like stacks of aged compost.

The word for the piles was *beschimmeld*, which meant merely "musty." But Peter had caught the diarist's jolly mood.

"Another load in the fall," growls the leader, the grimiest of all, with a great black smear across his bald head and another on the front of his smock where the belly sticks out as though long gone in pregnancy.

They leave with hearty waves, trundling their carts behind them. She is out of bed and waiting, arms folded.

"You gave them beer?"

"Ale," I reply, saluting her with uplifted beaker.

"When we haven't money to buy a sausage?"

"Of course we do. Go back to bed."

"You are making me sick, Hals. I can't leave you two minutes with a stuiver in your hand. Can't you ever learn?"

"They do me a favor, I'm going to do them a favor."

"For heaven's sake, they get paid perfectly well. You think you're rich, you can tip a workman?"

"I can tip whom I like," I say, reaching for my hat and scarf. "And now I am off to my club."

She mumbles something, sulking. It is strange. I used to be the one who sulked and she the one who roared and ranted. We seem to be getting more interchangeable than ever.

Just before I close the door on her I lean back into the room and tell her to keep warm. "It's cold out," I inform her. "Put some peat on the fire and stay close."

She has no answer to that. She knows I humiliated myself at the Town Hall to get that peat and she owes me a thank-you.

January 18. It is set. I have it on paper. It is an actual fact: They are paying me six hundred. More than two years of pension. I bought some wine and a chicken and we had a feast in front of the fire while the wind howled outside. She broiled it in a pan and put together a wonderful sauce of wine and chicken gravy and a bit of cream, and with some of our very old and wrinkled potatoes, boiled and mashed, we had everything we could wish for. I lit up my old meerschaum, the one Olycan gave me when I painted him, with some fresh Avocaat, my one indulgence, the price goes up because of the perique, I think, and I considered the shapes in my new picture. I will need a spot of color somewhere.

January 19. Full day of work. The brains of the group is a lawyer named Everswijn, who affects a dark long mustache and looks at you over it with hooded eyes. A big bent nose. So calm you might think he was a little stupid, but he is not. He gently baits de Jong, the minister.

"We are having the Good Book in the picture?" he says in his soft but clear voice.

De Jong, whose nose is suspiciously red today (the cold, I

presume), draws himself up in a way that makes you understand he frequently draws himself up. "Of course. It is a symbol of our function."

Everswijn: Our function? Do we have a function?

De Jong: Why . . . guidance, my friend. What do you think?

Everswijn: You mean our charges here? We are here to guide them?

De Jong (withering glance): Bring them to Jesus, if we may. Bring them to the light.

Everswijn: Because they are sinners. . . .

De Jong: Exactly, my friend.

Short pause. Everswijn a master of pauses. Then he says in that same quiet voice, "But I thought they were here because they're poor."

"Yes, well."

"Then the poor are the worse sinners? Worse than us?"

De Jong coughs behind his hand. "Of course," kaff kaff, "of course we are all sinners," and coughs at length.

At this point I take mercy on him. "Dr. de Jong," I say innocently, "do you by any chance have a Bible with a lighter cover? That black is going to be lost here, I'm afraid."

We desperately need color. Everswijn glances my way and, with deathly solemn faces, we silently laugh together. I am going to give him a chessboard.

Afterward Deinoot hung around and stopped by the canvas as I was cleaning up.

"How is it?" he says shyly.

"A good group," I say.

"Not like the soldiers, I guess. We are drab men."

"Oh, I don't know. Those soldiers, you can't get them to sit still."

"Don't let my twitch bother you," he says in a light tone.

"No, of course not, sir. I take everyone's best face."

But I will put in the damaged eye. That's who he is.

January 21. It is going to be too dark. I wish we had the ruffs of old. I told Walles to wear the fanciest cuffs he has. He laughed.

"You have found out my vice," he said.

"What's that?" said I, preoccupied.

"Why, my vanity. My clothes."

He wears gloves at the sittings.

January 22. Stayed in bed today. I could not straighten my leg. The cold seeps through the walls in spite of the fire, seeps through the blankets, seeps through the skin. She is bustling about with poultices. Lucky we are not both down at the same time. They were to give me an advance today, but she won't let me out of the house. The wind howls.

January 24. Still stiff but I walked to the almshouse on my two canes. Westerloo much concerned.

"Is it rheumatism?" he asked. I have decided he has quite a kind face. "You should be in bed."

"No no," I said, "just my old knee. I twisted it a long time ago and it acts up in this weather."

All through the morning I had the uneasy feeling that they were watching me with a particular look that I know: This man belongs in the almshouse. This man belongs to us. So I made a point of roaring a lot and telling stories. I had them laughing to hear about the St. George's bunch and the others.

"I'd rather do you folks than soldiers any day," I said. "At least you sit still."

And you don't drink, I might have added. I could have used a geneva or two by dinnertime, and when I finally put down the palette and dismissed them for lunch (they are docile as schoolboys when they pose, they act slightly awed at themselves as though they were taking part in some historic event, not to say a sacrament), I nodded at old Smoot and we went off together to the kitchen.

We took a couple of plates and found the cook and chatted her up while she loaded us with smoked pork and potatoes and gravy. We were getting the same thing as the directors, except bigger portions, and she told us to come back for an apple tart. Then Smoot winked and jerked his head at me and I followed him through a pantry to a little storage room that he has fixed up with a couch and table. He sat down on the couch and patted it for me to sit beside him. And from under the table he drew a locked seaman's trunk, a small one, its leather sides battered and scratched and stained. He pulled a large key from his pocket and turned it in the ornate copper lock. And with a grin drew forth a huge stone jug of aged geneva.

"Not permitted," he whispered. "I would get thrown out."

"It looks like heaven," I said.

He produced two mugs from the chest. "This is my office, and no one is allowed in here. I'm safe, long as I act right."

The fact is, he acts a little drunk at all times, so how would they know? We chuckled like a pair of old cronies and tipped up our mugs. Oh it was good. You don't want it cold, not the aged stuff.

I flexed my leg. It was better already.

"You must have a supplier," I said.

He winked. "We are poor here. No one has any money. But you'd be surprised."

I suppose he meant people have relatives who send them things.

"It's not so bad," he said, eyeing me. "Better than being out there in the cold."

I shook my head. Never. Never. It crossed my mind that he might have been instructed to feel me out. Decided not.

"I knew some of those birds in the St. George," he said. "Went to school with Jacob Olycan. He wouldn't know me now."

"One thing I can tell you," I said, "you'll never see him in here."

He laughed.

He used to be a counter down at the docks. Spent his days tabulating barrels of fish. He worked in the south market, which would explain why I had never run into him before. You would think I would know every soul in this town by now, but they get past you. These board members, I have seen them around. They are half my age. Everyone is half my age.

When I was done, about midafternoon (when the light went), Westerloo took me aside and handed me a sealed packet.

"The contract," he murmured, "and a bit to start on."

"Thank you," I said, vaguely annoyed at this secrecy, which made me feel like a servant getting a tip. Why couldn't he say, We are giving you an advance of fifty guilders. Which is what it was.

Then he sidled around to draw me farther from the others. "Did Pieter give you a good dinner?" With the genial smile of one who would feel entitled to call Smoot by his first name.

"Oh yes," I said, smirking cravenly and hoping he didn't catch my breath.

"And your knee. It's better."

"Comes and goes," I said, flexing it, oiled in geneva. "It's fine now."

"Good, good. We will see you next Monday, then. Walles has to be in Leiden tomorrow."

I bought some geneva with the fifty. Just a quarter-bottle. For the pain, I told her. She actually smiled. I gave her the rest.

January 28. Short sitting today. Snow clouds, very dark. The sky was black. We are to have a blizzard. As I was leaving, Westerloo came to me with a package wrapped in oilskin.

"I think we will not try to meet tomorrow," he said. "A storm is coming and I do not want you wandering about there with your knee. Here is something from the kitchen."

"I beg your pardon."

He pressed it into my hands. "It is a roaster. It is cooked."

"You are giving me food?"

He grinned. "We have to keep our artist in fine form, here. You did not get your dinner today, so this is —"

"Dinner? I don't understand."

"You are to get your dinner when you work here, my dear Hals. Part of the agreement."

"Thank you, sir, but I—"

"Let us say it is our tradition. A custom of the house. All right?"

He was backing away from the look on my face.

"Sir. I am not in the habit—"

At this moment de Jong came up behind me and patted my back. "Of course, of course, a custom of the house. No one goes hungry here."

And now Everswijn turned to face our little tableau, took it all in at a glance, and smiled his half smile. "Well I'm hungry," he announced loudly, "and why can I not get something from the kitchen?"

Sputterings and mutterings. Finally Westerloo said grandly, "And so you can, Mattheus. So can everyone who is hungry."

De Jong put on his Moses face and boomed, "Yaas, yaas, We Give To All Those Who—"

"Wonderful, wonderful." Westerloo cut him off. "Let's all go to the kitchen."

Everswijn looked directly at me and we exchanged our grave laughter.

I took the chicken and carried it home under my arm. It was still very warm.

"What is this?" she said with a suspicious scowl.

"A fine roasting chicken," I said. "Compliments of the directors."

"What?"

I began to unwrap it on the table. I could see a pot of stew over the fire.

"From the almshouse?"

"Certainly. It's a tradition."

She folded her arms. "You're bringing food from the almshouse? They are giving you handouts?"

"Nonsense. Everyone gets this. It's the custom."

"Hals, this is charity. I will not have it."

"Nonsense. The directors are having it too. They were lined up to get their free chicken when I left."

"I don't believe it."

"True. True. Come on, it's getting cold."

It smelled marvelous. Steam rose from its crisp gleaming brown flanks. It had been stuffed with Java rice, all spicy and dark and leaking from between the lacings.

"I promise you," I said, "that this is not charity. This is a mere chicken and I declare I am going to eat it."

I gave her my best courtier's bow. "And I invite you to join me. And I will pour you a cup of our good wine which might be French. Even though it is a red — "

"Hals," she said.

"And tomorrow I will present the almshouse with a donation of five guilders."

Her head reared back. She stared at me.

"That," she muttered, seating herself neatly on the bench and tucking her skirts under, "will not be necessary."

January 31. Sick again. Still snowing. She couldn't open the door and the boy next door had to dig it out.

February 2. Just made it to the Town Hall yesterday to get my so-called pension. I am sure they don't know about the work for the almshouse or they would never give me the full amount. On the way back I fell in the street and was helped by a young woman. Everyone is stronger than I. I am back in bed. We are swimming in guilders.

February 4. It has gone to my chest again. There is a sharp pain under the ribs if I breathe deeply, and it is agony to cough. She is worried and keeps looking in on me (to see if I am dead yet, no doubt). She put a mustard plaster on me yesterday, but I told her the only cure is more geneva. I had a crazy impulse for a smoke today and actually took a puff on my pipe. It set me to coughing and tasted terrible, as I knew it would. She was furious.

"You are doing your best to kill yourself," she said. "Even a monkey would know enough not to smoke in your condition."

"A monkey couldn't afford Avocaat," I said.

"Neither can you," she snapped. She has me there.

I thought about the monkey sitting hunched on his branch and contentedly sucking away on a good meerschaum. I envied him. I spend the days reading or staring at the ceiling thinking about the picture. They are wondering if I will be able to finish.

February 5. I knew it. They sent Smoot to inquire about me today. I haven't worked for a week. I said I would try to be over in a day or two, but he insisted I wait at least until next Monday. No hurry, he said. The longer it takes, the more important it must be.

I worry nevertheless. If this one goes so hard, maybe they will want someone else for the second picture. Plenty of painters in town who can do it. We had a skirt from some ox ribs she bought with our new wealth. We are eating meat almost every night, which sends me to the outhouse four times a day. I tell her not to work so hard at building me up. I will catch my death trudging out to the privy in all weathers. I hate to use the pot.

February 7. She was sad today. It has been a blustery cold day, everything so clear, wiped clean by the wind, and it reminded her of the day we heard about Anthonie. Years ago. I found her crying quietly by the fire.

"He was such a boy, Hals. He was only a child. Not even a letter. He just disappeared off the earth."

That is the worst. When you don't know how they died. We had notice from the captain of the *Walrus* that he had died in Tonkin. No way to write back and find out the details. We did get his back pay from the East India people, but they had no more information.

I always see him standing in the door in his heavy coat, his bag at his feet. The big collar raised against the cold. The breathless grin, he always seemed breathless with excitement. "I'm off, Fa."

I kissed him and felt the dark curly hair on the back of his head. I never saw him again. I envied him those warm places halfway around the world, the brown women, smiling and naked, the great palms whose enormous leaves rattle in the breeze, the soft air that smells of lilac and oranges. Once I saw a beautiful black man from Africa, not brown but truly black, his skin shining almost blue.

February 11. Back to work today. She didn't want me to go. My chest no longer gives me the sharp pain, but my breath comes short, and I am tired, a deadly weariness, it worries me. When I got home at dusk I went straight to the bed and lay flat on it on my back with my hands crossed on my breast like a knight's effigy. My whole self sighed in pleasure. Just to lie down a minute. After supper I was yearning for bed again. It is frightening.

"I am tired," I said.

"You are eighty-two years old," she said in her accusing way.

I wish my knee would stop complaining and be satisfied with what I can do for it. My back has been aching fiercely when I stand too long. It stiffens until I am half-crippled. I think I get it from her. She has had a back for years, as we know so well. I give her poultices while she lies on her stomach and then she gives me some on my leg. We are a dandy pair.

The work is coming. I am putting Deinoot somewhat into shadow. Poor man, he looks half-drunk with his deformed eyelid sagging down, also, he insists on wearing his hat skewed the way all the young cocks wear them. The Spanish influence: They think it looks dashing, but on him it only looks idiotic.

February 12. Met Dame Schouten today, the head regentess. An aged lady, intelligent, accustomed to command, the kind born to money who have never been crossed in all their days. A tyrant, I think, in her own family.

"Ah, Mijnheer Hals," she says briskly, unsmiling, as I come into the hall. "You are to do our portrait."

"So I'm told," I say.

"Oh? Isn't it definite?"

"I had the impression we would do the regents first and then see."

She draws herself up. There is fairness in her eyes, a power of deliberation, a sense of justice. But so cold. "I will speak to Westerloo," she announces. "Of course you will do it. We will want you to do it," amending as she realizes her words sound too peremptory.

"I was hoping," I say. "Would be nice to have both groups as a pair."

"When do you finish here?"

"Perhaps a month," I say. "Sooner if I can get them together more often."

She ignores my light tone and shoots an iron glance at me. "We shall give you no such trouble. We shall be completely at your disposal."

I bow. These people do bring out my polite streak. "I'm sure," I say, trying not to see the unpleasant vision of Dame Schouten making certain her fellow regentesses are where she wants them, on schedule. "Will you have it in this hall?"

"Oh no, in the women's hall," she replies briskly. "The light is better there."

Oh. Thank you so much. I wouldn't know about such things.

We shake hands, or rather she lays her long, thin, cold fingers in mine for an instant. I look at her hand—so fragile, almost translucent. For the first time I am aware of her physical frailty. Nothing but bones and veined yellow skin. That cool intelligence, those wise old eyes, that tremendous, unconquerable will doomed to reside inside such a delicate envelope. Westerloo is to let her know when I am done here.

February 17. There is a new pastor. Very young and conscious of it in this large parish. He tries to make a grand sermon on a scale with the cathedral. My mind wandered. He would do better to stick to specifics. There is a Massa in one of the windows. I cannot read the first name. It is not Isaac. He is gone twenty years.

A young man, plump with good living and full of plans. Even the old ones are gone, the ones I thought would never die. Old Leenders. Suyderhoef. The tobacco woman. I am alone, a prisoner in this place. Three of the children dead already. My brother. Only herself, snoring her dear cat snore now in the other room, a part of me. It goes on. My journey.

I was so gloomy today that she broke out the brandy Harmen gave us, and we talked out the evening in front of the fire remembering the houses we have lived in. I had forgotten two of them. There are whole years that I can no longer remember.

February 18. Another Monday, and it will be all I can do to walk to the almshouse. We are having a thaw, but the wind is off the coast and wet and heavy, and my leg wants to stay in bed. I am waiting for the wind to drop. Have decided to pamper myself as Westerloo is always insisting. The leg, the chest, the head, the stomach, I am a compendium of medical phenomena, a dictionary of pain.

I arrived rather late. Walles was there waiting for me, all of them a bit abrupt—so much for my pampering myself—and he had on all his cuffs and gloves and paraphernalia. And he pointed down at his leg. Knee britches, blinding scarlet!

"You wanted color," he drawled. "How's this?"

I had to laugh. Maybe it will work. But one only.

I have decided there is humor in his face after all.

February 19. Quite jolly today. Westerloo went to dinner at the senior Coymanses last night and they were teasing him. "Did you get a big donation?" "Did you offer him a room?" And so on. At the end he got so exasperated that he was shouting.

"We had English pheasant!" he cried. "Shot by Milord Rainsford and brought over for the occasion!"

They howled. Only a milord! And what was the pheasant's rank?

The man finally realized they were having him on and smiled a wan smile. How I wish I could get this into a picture.

February 20. A freeze. She is very sick. I took a beef shoulder to Biesboer's to be cooked.

February 21. Both of us in bed, wheezing. My teeth pain me and I cannot take cold foods. I was up long enough to cook us some potatoes. I am thinking of that roast ox.

February 22. By some magic they found out. A lanky lout appeared at the door around noon, knocking with both fists, or so it sounded. "Mr. Smoot sent me." Carrot hair sticking straight up from his bony head. I was afraid he was bringing a bounty-basket, but Smoot had more sense than that. I sent him out right away to Biesboer's bakery and gave him a couple of guilders. Now Mrs. Biesboer will know we are sick and will come around, which is very nice except that she will stay all afternoon. I also told him to buy a meat pie. It was snowing again when he got back. Snow all over the skirt of his coat. He had slipped on the ice, and the pie was dented a bit, but the roast was still warm. The boy's name is Hendrik. I gave him a few stuivers and he grinned and loped off. He will tell Smoot that we are wealthy. Maybe not a bad idea.

The fact is we haven't had so much money in hand since the big days. I turn it all over to her so I won't be tempted. I was born to be rich.

Susanna has been over twice in the past week. Usually she keeps her distance, since marrying that idiot. She offers to cook and even to stay a day or two if she can bring the little ones. I have had enough of babies.

I do hate to call on the children. She is at me all the time. "Why don't you call Harmen? He's right across town. Or Frans? Or Addie? Addie could come in and cook for us."

"Not wise," I said. "Addie has her own problems."

"If she knew, she'd be here in a minute."

"What would she do that we can't do for ourselves?"

"Go fetch the roast, for one thing." She gave me her "why am I talking to this imbecile" look. She doesn't understand that once they got to worrying about us they would start thinking about getting the city to help. They have no choice; not one of them has any money.

Besides, like most children they are a hard lot when it comes to aged parents. The cruelty of good sense.

"We could send for Sara," I said.

"Are you mad?" she snapped.

If Sara was here, she would fight them all to the death before she'd agree to send us to the almshouse. I am sure of it. My Sara.

We said no more about it. Sometimes there is nothing I can say to that woman. We spit and snarl and accuse each other of the same things. We forget which faults belong to whom. She says I make too much noise in the night, when in fact she is the one who clumps around and knocks over the pitchers. It is too boring.

━━━━━━━━◄O►━━━━━━━━

When Peter got back to his apartment he checked a few more facts. Even the three cartloads of peat were listed in the catalog. And the changing fashions in beards and ruffs. And Daniel Deinoot with his damaged face. Peter put away the books with deliberate care. It was 5:30.

Someone knocked. It must be Scott, forgot his keys again.

But when Peter opened the door a curious figure pushed him back and followed him into the room. The person was hardly over five feet tall, stumpy, dressed in a trench coat with the collar up and a dirty baseball cap. He had long thick black hair with a few strands of white. The hair was chopped neatly off below the ears.

It was the face that got Peter. There was no face, only a twisted suggestion of features, a Francis Bacon painting.

Then he realized the figure was wearing a stocking over his face. The gun he held before him was a long-barreled target pistol.

"The books. Gimme the books."

299

Peter froze. The voice was a scratchy low growl, almost a whisper.

The gun barrel jerked up and down.

"Now!"

"Wh—what books?"

"The diaries."

Peter thought he might faint. Who could know this? Where had he heard the voice?

"N—not me. No. I don't have them. I gave them—"

The pistol barrel jabbed at his ribs.

"I mean now! You got 'em. Gimme them."

"What you think you can—"

"Your name Van Overloop?"

"Yeah, but—"

"Quit lookin' at me!"

Peter was squinting at the mashed features, trying to make out what they must look like. He couldn't believe he was being held up by a person half his size. He felt no fear, only an academic caution before the pistol. Except for that, it would be so easy just to reach out and swat the person down.

"Come on, kid. It ain't worth it. Gimme."

Peter backed up to the table, hands in the air. Why did the man hesitate when he said *ain't*? This was like some terrible movie. The gun looked beautifully oiled and efficient. It was definitely real.

When they reached the table the intruder brushed aside the pile of papers and quickly uncovered the worn old volumes. He snatched them up and stuffed them into the wide pocket of his coat.

As he backed through the door he growled, "You call the desk before I get outta here—" Hesitated, glanced around, the whites of his eyes garish behind the mesh, saw the phone. Stepped over to it and yanked the cord from the wall.

"Just stay put there, kid," he whispered. And backed out of the room and was gone.

Peter ran to the door after a couple of seconds but saw nobody in the corridor.

He sat down, breathless.

He would have to call Silverstein.

He should call the police.

Running to the elevator, he rushed over to the desk clerk and reported the holdup. Had the man seen anyone in the lobby a few minutes ago?

Nope, nobody.

Was there a guy in a baseball cap through here just now?

Nope.

The police were not excited. Everyone Peter knew, practically, had been mugged at least once in the last year or two. Amy had been held up with a jackknife right in the elevator of her Fifth Avenue apartment building.

An officer took the report, gave him a serial number for his insurance, and left rather apologetically, saying there probably wasn't much chance they would find the guy. Peter had told him the diaries were the ones written up in the papers, but the guy had not been impressed. Peter thought he should check with Silverstein before telling anyone how valuable the diaries might be.

Much too late, Peter remembered that he had a phone in his own bedroom. He went back up and called Silverstein. His heart slammed against his ribs as he waited to speak. My God, would he be held responsible? The Hals diaries in his hands and they get stolen? They could be worth millions. It had happened so fast.

"Peter!" Silverstein's voice broke. "I was just calling you. I just got robbed!"

"What? So did I!"

"Little guy in a stocking mask?"

"Little guy in a stocking mask."

"He got both of yours?"

"Yup. Did he get yours? I thought they were at the lab."

"Just got 'em back this morning."

"I'm coming over," Peter said.

He sat in the gallery's back room with Silverstein and a friend, a city detective named Korngold whom the dealer had summoned. The holdup there had happened just two hours earlier. The guy had drifted in with some customers and had gone straight to the rear room, apparently shielding his face en route so that nobody noticed he was masked. He ordered Silverstein into the washroom after taking the two books, still lying on the desk, having just been delivered.

"He knew they were gonna be here," Korngold muttered. "Who woulda told him that?"

"The people at Columbia. Professor Smith's team."

Korngold made a note.

"And how did he know I had the other two?" Peter asked.

"Well, he knew there were four volumes and he already had two," said the detective. "You sure this was the same guy?"

Oh yes. Peter and Silverstein exchanged a nod. Very short, they said. Long black hair with some white. Very gruff voice, pitched oddly low but almost a whisper. Winced when he said *ain't*.

The three men stared at each other.

"Wait a minute," Peter said.

They looked at him.

"How do we know it was a guy? That voice was kind of high."

Then he remembered where he had heard it. He gaped at Silverstein.

Silverstein gaped at him.

In unison they pointed at each other.

In unison they shouted:

"Mrs. Barnett!"

Silverstein slapped his forehead. "She would know where the books were! I told her!"

"But why? She owns them. What's the deal?"

"She wants to sell them before the word gets around they're fakes."

Korngold looked from one face to the other like a tennis spectator.

"Mrs. Barnett is five feet two," the dealer told him. "She wears her hair in a pageboy bob and it is thick and black with white streaks. And if she could get those books out of the country she could make a fast deal with some speculator, someone eager enough not to wait for the official word."

Silverstein slapped his hands together and chuckled. "Hey, that's my kind of woman. That is some kind of woman."

"So what do you want to do now?" Korngold said.

"I don't know. We see if it surfaces somewhere. I would expect it would be Europe or possibly Japan. Hell, it could be anywhere. It could be California. Chances are, whoever buys it will get in contact with me or Smith."

"Some woman, all right," Peter muttered. "Scared the pants off me."

"For a minute there, yeah," Silverstein said. Then they both laughed again, but feebly.

On the way home Peter could think only of the fact that he had never finished the diary. Only a few pages to go. If only he had read just a little faster. He had never been so depressed. Then he asked himself why he was so depressed when he knew it couldn't be authentic. And when he thought about that, he became even more depressed.

When he got in, Laura was on the phone. "Can you come over?" She sounded breathless. "I've been trying to reach you. Can you get here right away?"

"What is it? George?"

"I threw him out. It's my place, you know. But he won't go."

Oh great. The guy stood practically a head taller than Peter and had muscles.

"What am I supposed to do?"

"He's coming here. Can you be here? I really need someone to be here."

He said okay. He did not feel stalwart. He wished he was the sort of person who would own a gun. He took a cab downtown. When was he going to get some control over his life? He wore a blue cord jacket and red rep tie. They went nicely with the new white pants.

Laura was waiting at the top of the stairs. She looked pale and worried, but she brightened when she saw him. With her black hair falling sleekly to her shoulders and her large eyes, she had never looked so beautiful. She couldn't stop talking.

"Oh Peter, I'm so glad you could come, I really appreciate it, I'm just frantic with George. He's turned into a total shit. He is trying to claim the apartment because we split the rent but it's my apartment, I found it and I was living here when he came along, and now he refuses to let go of it."

"What does he want? Did you throw him out?"

"I said I'm not going with him anymore. I said I wanted him out of here, and he did, he did move out. He took his stuff and everything and went to stay with his brother in Brooklyn Heights. But now he says he has an interest in the place and I owe him for his half of the rent."

She ushered him inside, where Leopold curvetted against

his ankle. "And last week he changed the lock on me! Can you imagine that? He says he paid a month's rent in advance, the whole thing, and that gives him the rights to the apartment."

"Well that can't be right. He wants to pay your rent for you, fine. Whose name is it in?"

"Mine. Mine and my former roommate's. She was just here, I was paying for it myself when I brought George into it."

"Jesus, he changed the lock? My God. What did you do?"

She snorted. "I went to the super. George wasn't here. See, he goes to work an hour later than I do and gets back even later, so he got in and had the lock changed just to screw me up. What I did, I called another locksmith, and the super knows—see, George doesn't know the super and I do, I'm a friend of his, we talk about stuff and everything—and he came right over and put another lock in."

"But he wasn't staying here."

"No. He was in Brooklyn. But he calls me up that night. I said, Look, we can do this every day, you can change the lock in the morning and I can change it at night, but it's not going to solve anything."

Good old George, Peter thought. He had disliked the guy from the first minute.

"So he agreed to a truce on the locks but he says he will see a lawyer about getting compensation unless I let him come back. I said, George, no way. No way."

Her lips made a perfect bow, the lower lip quite full, the upper one neatly defined by the subtly curving line of her mouth. She wore no lipstick, which was nice. Once she touched the edge of his jacket to emphasize something she was saying. Her black hair shone.

"He said he was coming over tonight. I think he wants to get back with me, which is why I wanted you here."

"You mean like I'm your new guy?"

She darted a look at him. She smiled. "Well that isn't what I meant exactly, but—"

"Jeez. You think he's gonna beat me up?"

"No. I hope not. I don't think so."

"So do I."

He straightened his spine and felt that he could go down in a blaze of fists for her.

"When do you expect him?"

"Any minute. I don't think he'll stay long, he has to go back to Brooklyn."

"Can I take you out afterward?"

"Oh, you don't—"

"I know I don't. I want to." He touched her hair where it swayed away from her cheek. "Will you allow me to take you out to dinner?"

Peter saw his history book on the table by the door. He stood around with the cats as she checked the refrigerator for what drinks she could offer him. They decided on white wine. When they retired to the sofa, Dave leapt on Leopold and bit him on the back, then on the rear ankle, and chased him furiously across the room. She said they only fought when she was around. He told her he never had pets in Cicero. He said Lee slept on his bed sometimes. Then they didn't talk for a while because they were remembering that he had lived in this loft not so long ago.

The intercom buzzer announced George. Laura went to greet him at the door when he arrived, somewhat breathless from climbing stairs. The second he passed over the threshold he spotted Peter.

"What are you doing here?" he asked in a clear, loud voice.

Peter was going to explain himself. Then he was going to say, I'm taking Laura out. Instead he took a leisurely breath and glared back at the peevish face lowering above him. For the first time in his life he sensed the power of silence.

"Who wants to know?" he said at last.

George turned to Laura. "Who is this guy?"

"What's it to you, George?"

"This is the house-sitter guy. What's he doing here?"

Peter stepped in front of Laura. He was trying to think what he should say next, but the gesture worked better than anything. George was distinctly taken aback.

"I'm taking her out to dinner, George. That all right with you?"

George attempted to ignore this pushy rival and give Laura the stare but couldn't see around the interloper without craning.

"Would you mind," he said, "I'm trying to talk to Laura."

"You'll have to talk to Peter too," she snapped.

George stepped back and took in the scene, the two of them facing him with determination in their eyes and glasses in their hands. He still hadn't gotten six feet inside the room.

"I'm talking to you, Laura. Either I get my share back or I sue."

Peter, his heart pounding, took another step forward.

"You shared in the rent, you shared in the apartment. You got what you paid for. You got nothing else coming. You know that perfectly well, George."

George turned on him. "Who the fuck are you anyway?"

"You want to talk law, you were trespassing when you came in to change the lock. Not to mention extremely chickenshit."

"Lissen—"

He was pointing. Peter hated being pointed at.

"Hey. Knock it off with the threatening gestures, will ya George? The lady doesn't want to see you. Let it go. It's over."

The finger wavered, aimed at Laura, dropped. Peter

suddenly realized an important fact: George had never actually had to get into a fight all his life because he was so big.

And here was this person standing directly in front of him with fists clenched, about to start swinging. So literal-minded.

Peter had to stop himself from smiling. He had always laughed at those movies, the James Bonds, the Steven Seagals, not to mention Peter Sellers, where somebody has this stupendous plan to blow up the world and some fabulous science-fiction machine to do it with, and every time, without fail, the whole plot comes down to a fistfight on the edge of a cliff. So much for technology. He kept his face a stone mask.

"You tell me, then," George said to Laura.

"George, I told you a week ago. We have nothing more to say to each other. Now let it go. I'll pay you back the advance, whatever you paid."

He glared at her, then at Peter, then at her again. Shook his head. Sneered. Renewed the glare.

Then executed a military about-face and opened the door.

"You know where to reach me," he snarled. And was gone.

Peter and Laura exchanged grins. They toasted each other with the white wine.

"Did you have a good day at the office?" he said. He hoped they didn't have to talk about George anymore.

"Good day!" she said, "Mr. Meyerowitz made me the assistant designer! I get to make all the decisions on what fabrics and how much and how many buttons and all that stuff. You know what that means? It's so interesting, Peter. Did you know that in some companies they roll up the template?"

"I beg your pardon?" They were sitting close together on the sofa. He loved to hear her talk.

"You ever wonder why with cheaper clothes the sizes always seem a little smaller? Well, they draw the patterns of all the parts on this great big huge sheet of paper, maybe thirty feet long and ten feet wide. What they do, they ball it all up like a giant snowball, crumple it up as tightly as it will go, and then smooth it all out so it's flat again, but with millions of little wrinkles, so the sheet turns out to be three or four inches shorter than it was. You multiply four inches times a thousand layers of fabric, you're saving considerable money. But all the parts come out just a tiny bit smaller."

"But you don't do that."

"Oh no. Not Lovely Lady. We are definitely upscale at Lovely Lady."

He adored her righteous sniff. He started to toast her but found he was out of wine. So he kissed her instead. It turned into a long kiss and they didn't get to the restaurant until nearly nine. They agreed that sex was better if you didn't talk about it before.

That night Peter slept over, and the next morning he went back uptown to fetch his belongings. He was just checking his notes—the names of the almshouse directors were listed in a monograph on the major group paintings, including one Daniel Deinoot, who had a damaged face—when Silverstein rang.

He was laughing. "Mrs. Barnett was an English major at Columbia," he said. "Smith looked her up. You know what her middle name was? Her mother's maiden name?"

"Tell me."

"Van Steen. Is that Dutch or is that Dutch?"

"Are you telling me that Mrs. Barnett wrote that diary?"

"What a thought, huh? What do you think?"

Peter didn't answer. He didn't care whether she hated to say *ain't*. She couldn't have written that diary. He would not allow the thought.

"Peter? You there? Hey, my big news is that I found out a collector in Switzerland called the Hals Museum in

Haarlem. I know who he is. He specializes in fakes. He owns a bunch of van Meegerens, you know, the guy who did all those Vermeers."

"You think he bought the diary?"

"Wouldn't say. They never do, you know. The stuff just disappears into their libraries and is never heard of again. But I have a surprise for you."

Peter was tired of surprises. He wanted to get out of this place and back down to Laura's.

"What's your surprise?" he said.

"I have a copy."

"Copy? Of what?"

"Of the diary. The whole thing! I Xeroxed it when I first got it."

"You have a—"

Silverstein whinnied in glee. "I couldn't tell you before. I was scared to tell anyone. But I did it! I'm having it messengered over there right now."

"You mean you made a—"

"Oh don't worry, I checked it out first. I tested it on a damaged page and it didn't hurt the surface at all. So I ran it all through. How about that?"

He still couldn't believe it.

"The whole thing?"

"That's right! It's all there—in perfect condition. I'm trusting you with it, Peter. For God's sake, don't get robbed again."

Peter waited in the lobby until the messenger showed up with the thick package. Then he rushed downtown with all his belongings.

By the second day Peter felt he had lived there forever. They were sitting together companionably, he at the table, she close by in a stuffed chair reading. Laura had made dinner

310

from frozen stuffed rigatoni. They had been taking turns making dinner, but Peter had done all the shopping. He had moved into the big bed the first night.

"I can't stand it that this isn't actually Hals," he said, looking up from his work. "I can't believe it is some modern person. This guy is so wise, so old and wise. He seems to have lived his life already before. He knows everything."

"Except the tulips," she murmured. He had told her all about the diaries.

"Yeah, but look what he does then. He has to change his whole way of life and move into rented rooms, and it doesn't seem to throw him. And here he is now"—Peter patted the papers before him—"and he's eighty-two years old and practically destitute, and he's painting what has got to be the masterpiece of his life. Here he is, dependent on the city fathers for everything, for the stuff to heat the house, and they want him to paint a nice complimentary portrait with the wrinkles smoothed out."

He waved his hand in the air. "So what does he do? He paints their pictures just the way they are, no puffery, no cosmetics, just the way they actually look, with their warts and bleary eyes and red noses. You can recognize those people. He did the women directors the same year, and they're the same, they're real people up there with their characters written on their faces. Eighty-two. My God. And it's the best work he ever did."

Laura smiled and gently shook her head. "You're in love with that old man," she said.

"And they're telling me that this was written by some car dealer's wife on Long Island?"

Laura suddenly sat up as though goosed. "You know what you should do?"

"What's that?"

"You should do your doctorate on Hals, on the diary."

Peter pushed back from the table. He let the papers drop from his hands.

"Jeez," he whispered.

He had all but forgotten de Hooch.

"You could get a grant, I bet. Your guy at Columbia would help."

It was so obvious. It was like snapping on a light.

He thought of Smith and his entire department turning over every leaf and stone to track down the diary's provenance. And he, Peter Van Overloop, was holding the only copy of the thing right here on this table.

"Jeez. I could. You know it?"

Suddenly Peter knew what he was going to do.

He would have to track down all the sources in the catalog for starters and then plow through the mountain of Hals material built up by scholars over the centuries. He would check those Haarlem town records—even if he had to get someone to send him to Holland, maybe Silverstein, maybe even Tony. He would trace the background of the paintings that had been found with the diary, the background of that forgotten nineteenth-century dealer, the history of Barnett's farm. He would interview everyone he could find.

Including Mrs. Barnett, of course, who was now telling the papers that she didn't speak a word of Dutch, that she certainly would never forge a diary, knew nothing about it but believed it to be authentic. And who was insisting that she had no idea how the diary got into the hands of a Swiss collector. And who refused to confirm reports that the man had paid over $100,000 for the books. In any case, she was moving to the Virgin Islands.

He would have to check out the snowfalls and rainy days mentioned in the diary against the Haarlem almanacs, if he could find ones for the seventeenth century. He would have to go over the local details with a microscope. Was there indeed a stone bench by the Zijlstraat bridge? It could take years.

The thought delighted him. He might spend the rest of his life parsing this diary and searching for the hoaxer, this person, this not-Hals diarist, whom he was coming to know so well. It could never take too long.

He was so excited that he had to stride around the room six times before settling down with his Xeroxes again. As he walked, Laura's eyes followed him, an expectant smile on her face.

———————————◄O►———————————

February 25. Back to work today. They were looking for me. I had a slice of Edam and a rusk for breakfast. I am not eating, my stomach cramps up in the morning. I make no bones about the two canes, would never get there without them. A carriage would be nice. All day a murderous headache.

Except, of course, when I am working. Why I look forward to it. It is work but I can hardly wait to get set there again in my place on the stool, staring at the familiar battlefield, the chessboard, my world, my secret world. I forget everything, my fingers grow nimble again. I can even stand before the canvas for hours without noticing my back. Today it was Walles's eyes, which must seem intelligent but not too much, caring but not too much. I have him looking beyond the viewer, off to the side a little, to suggest his remoteness. I spent a long time, ten minutes, an hour, I have no idea, pushing a tiny dot of black along the edge of his pupil. Sometimes the paint rushes ahead of you on its own, inevitable as a wave rolling onto the beach, but other times it resists and you have to nudge it, harry it, force it to go where you want, precisely to the right place, working on such a tiny scale, so intimate with the canvas that you can feel its individual ribs under your brush, moving the little dot so delicately that you forget to breathe.

And then to rest, to finish off the hair with a few lovely great sweeps and some elegant twisting touches to make the stray ends where they lie on his bib. And then to step back and see it all once again, the whole picture, the balance of it, the rightness of the book and the ridiculous red knee and the hands and Everswijn's hat, and then to dive in yet another time, nose to the canvas, palette held so close to the chest it stains my smock, as I start my attack on the other eye.

When I finish it is like coming out of a dream. Like waking up in a strange room and gradually picking up the threads of my life. Oh, and here they all are, here is de Jong, and Deinoot, and here smiling at me is Walles himself, and his eyes are bright and don't look in the least the way I had been painting them. I must seem dazed, for they always offer me a drink right away. And I take a step away from the easel, and my leg reminds me that it is still with me, oh thank you my faithful leg, and my back pain suddenly wants to be remembered too, forcing me to straighten and stretch, hands on kidneys.

February 26. Sick in the night, bowels opened. Dizzy headache. I am never right. The old must learn patience, but for what? Make do, make do, it will never get better. She refused to let me go and I am in bed with cheese and apples to bind me.

February 27. Still dizzy, it frightens me, faint on my feet but I went anyway. I have to. I get another installment next week. It was all right when I was back at the canvas. More highlights for Everswijn. A white edge and a touch on the nose. His eyes, so deep in shadow but must get his keenness. Reworked the left eye until lunchtime. He had to leave. Kept expecting him to rub the eye. I thought madly for a moment it must surely be sore after all that niggling work I had done on the pupil.

On the way home I had to stop at Piet's just to sit. They gave me a small geneva. For nothing. I don't know them anymore, Piet is dead forty years and his grandson must be an old man, I wouldn't recognize him, but they seem to know me. I could barely stand up my knee had locked itself in a bent position in just the time I was sitting.

February 28. Stayed home again. Another tract from Maire. He can't expect me to pay, surely. I will go this afternoon. I must do the other eye, it doesn't match. I woke up in the night and saw it in my mind. I must get back there. Must hurry, too late we learn that we must hurry. Fix de Jong's nose, too big on top. What would happen if I didn't finish it and de Jong went down in history with the wrong nose?

◄○►

That was it. No finishing flourish. The diary just stopped. Hals had two more years to live, and the regentesses' portrait still ahead of him.

But as Peter gazed at the last page his eye fell on one line: "Another tract from Maire. He can't expect me to pay, surely."

Tract? What tract? Did he mean a book of some sort? Maire was sending him tracts on approval. Why? Who was Maire?

Tensely, Peter turned to the catalog and rummaged in it for some minutes. In the index: Maire, Jan. He flipped quickly to the right page.

There it was: Jan Maire, a bookseller in Leiden who published Descartes's *Discourse on Method* in 1637.

A bookseller who apparently was in the habit of sending books to Hals. A friend, a man who owned several Hals paintings, because they were listed in his estate when he died, just two weeks after the death of Hals himself. A man who undoubtedly knew Schrevelius well, a friend of Descartes too, a man who corresponded with French scholars, a man who could logically be expected to stock notebooks from Paris.

He almost shouted. The French paper!

Maire could travel to Paris and pick up merchandise anytime. He could easily stock expensive French notebooks. Hals, wonderful impulsive improvident Hals, who bought paintings at auctions when he didn't have a guilder in his pocket, Hals was just the sort of person who might buy an elegant notebook for his diary. And another, and another, having them sent to him from Leiden when he couldn't get there himself. Tearing out pages now and then for other uses but assuring himself that he could always get another volume as soon as he sold the next picture.

Peter stared at the Xerox page before him, the final page.

That voice, that sardonic, wise old voice. It really could be Hals. Had to be.

It's really you, he thought. I knew it, I always knew it. I was sure of it.

And he laughed aloud because as he pressed both hands down on the pages of the Xeroxed diary he could feel the old man right there next to him, a large disreputable presence in a stained smock, weaving and wobbling there on his two canes, and the old man was laughing too.